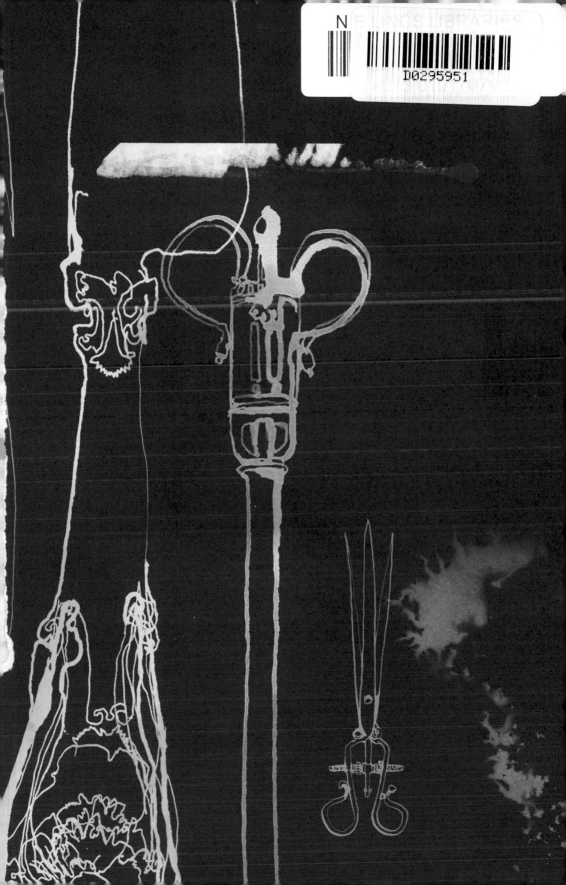

The TALE of
RAW HEAD
& BLOODY
BONES

The TALE of RAW HEAD & BLOODY BONES

JACK WOLF

CHATTO & WINDUS

LONDON

Published by Chatto & Windus 2013

2 4 6 8 10 9 7 5 3 1

Copyright © Jack Wolf 2013

Jack Wolf has asserted his right under the Copyright, Designs
and Patents Act 1988 to be identified as the author of this work

First published in Great Britain in 2013 by
Chatto & Windus
Random House, 20 Vauxhall Bridge Road,
London SW1V 2SA
www.vintage-books.co.uk

Addresses for companies within The Random House Group Limited can be found at:
www.randomhouse.co.uk/offices.htm

The Random House Group Limited Reg. No. 954009

A CIP catalogue record for this book
is available from the British Library

ISBN 9780701186876

The Random House Group Limited supports The Forest Stewardship Council (FSC®),
the leading international forest certification organisation. Our books carrying the FSC
label are printed on FSC® certified paper. FSC is the only forest certification scheme
endorsed by the leading environmental organisations, including Greenpeace.
Our paper procurement policy can be found at www.randomhouse.co.uk/environment

Typeset in Dante MT by Palimpsest Book Production Limited,
Falkirk, Stirlingshire
Printed and bound in Great Britain by
CPI Group (UK) Ltd, Croydon CR0 4YY

FOR TANIS AND LUCIEN

CHAPTER ONE

One Morning in the Autumn of seventeen forty-one, when I was not yet eleven Yeares of Age, still round in Figure and innocent in Mind, Nathaniel Ravenscroft took me a-walking by the River. I supposed that this small River, the Coller, must have emerged from beneath the chalk Hills somewhere to the South; and as I had once been told that it did not, as other local Rivers, tribute the Isis at Oxford, I imagined that it must somewhere have an equivalent Place at which it sank again beneath them, to flow silent and unseen below the White Horse.

Shirelands Hall, my Father's House, stands a fair Mile north of the Coller, on the main Road between Faringdon and Highworth.

It is a Country House of Palladian Design, built largely of Sandstone and Marble about the Time of the first Protectorate; and being the largest House for several Miles it was usually first Point of Call for wandering Beggars and Tradesmen as they travelled thro' the County on their Way around Oxford. To travel by Carriage to the nearby Village of Collerton, as I had been obliged every Sundaye in my short Life to do, required that the Coachman follow this main Road eastwards for some short Distance before turning the Horses on to Collerton Lane, which after a Mile and an Half brought the Carriage straight up to the Doorway of Collerton Church. If one then continued along the Lane, eventually one would arrive at the Lamb Inn, where my Parents had celebrated my Christening and that of my Sister, Jane; and finally the River, which tho' it had given Collerton its Name maintained an aloof Distance betwixt it and the Human Settlement.

If, however, upon quitting Shirelands' Drive, one turned one's Horses to the West, and continued toward Highworth, one would come upon a Crossroads marked with a Way-Stone, and a coaching Inn under the Sign of the Bull. Proceed West, and one would find oneself at Highworth; turn North, and the tedious winding Track led thro' Hamlets and Farmsteads in the vague Direction of Lechlade. But turn Left, and South, and the Road travelled on to Shrivenham past a small Number of grand Houses, which had been built beside the Coller to enjoy the fine Views of the antient Chalk-cut Monument upon the Hill provided by the River's gently lowering Slopes.

My Father's Estate, which consisted of a number of large un-inclosed Haymeadows and arable Fields, began at the Inn Crossroads and stretched as far as the eastern parish Boundary of Collerton, including also a short Stretch of the Coller itself, whereupon I greatly enjoyed to fish. The Living of Collerton Rectory, which lay well within this Compass, fell naturally therefore under my Family's Disposal. Its present Incumbent, whom my Grandfather had installed in both Position and House upon the Death of the previous Rector twenty Yeares before, was a fat and torrid tempered Cleric by the Name of Ravenscroft, about whom I had nothing Good to say or think except that he was Nathaniel's Father; at which Fact I admired wondrous much.

Nathaniel, Nathaniel Ravenscroft, who was two Yeares older than I, was my dearest Friend and closest Companion. In truth, I must admit, attaining this Distinction would not have been difficult for him had he possesst but one Quarter of his Charm; for I was a shy and sullen Child, cursed, I had heard my Father say, when I had been believed well out of Earshot, with a melancholic Disposition that I had surely inherited from my Sephardic Mother. This Reference was a Revelation to me, for in the six Yeares since her Death I had never heard anyone speak of my Mother, and I remembered little more of her than her Voice. His Words stirred a Curiosity in me to know more, but I did not dare to ask.

My Lack of Desire to make Friends with Boys of mine own Age and Station was not, however, intirely due to my Disposition. Verily, I knew, even at that tender Age, and without overhearing anyone, that I had inherited more from my Mother than her Humour. I was a dark Child, brown skinned and black eyed as a Spaniard, with unmistakable upon my Countenance all those distinguishing Features supposed to be indicative of Jewry; and even tho' I had been raised a Christian, with no more Knowledge of Talmud and Torah than I had of the internal Workings of the Sunne, I received no Mercy from those who had been born unmistakably English, and I had long ago learned that it was better for mine Health if I avoided their Society.

But Nathaniel was a true Sanguine, in every Sense. Long of Limb, even at thirteen, and athletick of Build, he towered laughingly over mine Head, and with merry Jibes and chearfull Jests made me to feel ashamed of my round Belly, and my clumsy Movements. Nathaniel's Hair, unlike my black Mop, was the finest and fairest I had ever seen upon a living Youth, white-gold in Colour and each Strand as soft to the Touch as a downy Feather. His Eyes, which, his Father insisted, were a marshy grey, always appeared to me in the most dazzling and verdant Shade of green.

I loved Nathaniel Ravenscroft marvellous much, and looked up to him as one might an older Brother; and perhaps it was on Account of this Love I bore him, and naught else, neither Fear for mine own Sanity nor Punishment, that I did not ever speak to any Body concerning his strange Habits. Of these Nathaniel had many; but the worst, which he had disclosed to me when I was six, and which caused me much Disgust and Dismay, was his perpetual Delight in snatching blue Tits from the Hedges, and consuming them direct upon the Spot. This inevitably took Place in identical Fashion. Nathaniel and I would be walking, or riding, and engaged in Conversation or idly playing Games, when he would spy a Flutter of Blue in the Briar. At once he would fall stiff and still, and so would I, dreading the Scene I was about to witness, yet unable to look askance; then out would snap his Hand, fast as a striking Snake, and the small Bird would disappear in a Flurry of pathetic Twittering and Blood. Then Nathaniel would turn to me, and smile the happy and innocent Smile of a Babe that hath eaten a Sweetmeat; whilst I would watch the tiny Feathers tumbling from his Mouth, delicate as many coloured Snowflakes. His eye Teeth were surprizing long, and white, and deadly sharp as Poniards.

I would recoil from Nathaniel then in sudden Fear; for always

4

it seemed to me that no Human Creature could behave in such a Way; and sometimes I would flee; but ever he, long shanked and agile, would catch me, and, smiling, demand to know what was the Trouble. I could never tell him.

Unlike My Self, who had but the one Sister, Jane, two Yeares my Senior, Nathaniel was the oldest Child of a large and still increasing Brood of Youngsters, all of whom in some Degree resembled the Rector, whether by a somewhat portly Build or in the Cast of their Features. None possesst any Shine akin to his Fairness, and none was as dark as I; all were, Nathaniel told me, intirely mediocre, and unworthy of our Interest, our Contempt or our Approbation.

"They all," he told me confidently, "will meet grisly Ends in the clutching Claws of Raw-Head-and-Bloody-Bones, for they tell petty Lies, and make up malicious Tales; and everyone knows how he lieth in Wait for wicked Children, crouching in the Dark atop his Pile of Bones and jibber-jabbering."

I did not allow My Self to pay much Attention to Nathaniel's Words, for I was, in some childish Part of me, mortally afraid of Raw Head, who, my Nurse had told me when I had been about four, was lurking silent at the Bottom of the River Coller, waiting to leap out and drag me to my Death. Whether Raw Head was real Creature, or Phantasm, I was not intirely sure, but it made little difference; it, or he, was an Horrour: an half known, formless Dread that poisoned the Night and kept blameless Infants from their Dreams. Nathaniel, who shewed no Fear, and claimed to know the Goblin right well, made it Sport to teaze those of us who were not so brave. One autumn Evening, when I was six, he crept up behind me whilst I lay on my Belly watching Minnows thro' my Reflection, and leaning over my Shoulder, created of us both a veritable Monster. Crying out: "Two Heads, two Faces, and two

Persons, as the Almighty hath three!" he convinced me that I had really perceived Raw-Head-and-Bloody-Bones. I did not sleep for many Nights.

On this September Morning, in my twelfth Yeare, we had put Raw Head quite out of our Minds and spent several Houres at our favourite fishing Spot upon the Coller. We had wandered westwards thro' the uncut Corn and well grazed Pastures till we had come upon a Loop in the River, about an half Mile from the Shrivenham Road. There stood here a short Row of half ruined Cottages, which had not been let for several Yeares as they had proved subject to Flooding, and my Father had eventually grown tired of their Repair and had moved all their Tenants to higher Ground. The Earth here was soft and often boggy, and when the swollen River ran fast and lethal, as it always did in Winter, it would become quite treacherous. Todaye, however, it was dry and hard, and the Waters looked as placid as a Millpond.

We set up our Rods, and sate, and waited, and entertained ourselves until the Sunne was long past its Highest; and then Nathaniel's Stomach beginning to call him homewards, we packed up our Equipments, and our few Fish, and returned thro' the yellowing Fields to Shirelands Hall.

I had been of the Expectation that we would ask the Hall Kitchen to fill our Bellies for us, but as we drew near to the House, Nathaniel all on a Sudden turned about, and said: "I have a better Idea, Tris. What sayst we visit my Father's apple Orchard?"

This Suggestion made mine Heart to skip a Beat, for the Rectory Orchard was strict forbidden both to Nathaniel and to My Self. Nathaniel hugely disliked this Restriction, as, indeed, he disliked any authoritative Limitation placed upon his Freedom, and he did his Best to disregard it. I knew that if we were to visit the Orchard, we ran an high Risk of being discovered, having our Spoils confiscated, and our Ears sorely harangued; but I found My Self immediately nodding in Assent.

We ran fast to the kitchen Step, deposited our Fish, and then once more we were running away from Shirelands, this Time along the Driveway that would take us thro' the iron Gates on to the Faringdon Road.

Shirelands' Driveway was flanked by an Avenue of ash Trees, and the Ground beneath our Feet was littered with their Leaves, the first that Yeare to have fallen. Nathaniel stoppt at the Foot of the Tallest, for I was somewhat out of Breath from our sudden Exertion, and struggling to keep Pace with him, who sprinted like a Greyhound.

Nathaniel laughed, and put his Hand upon my Shoulder. "Alas! You are poorly named, Tristan Hart; not nearly as fleet footed as your name-Sake."

"I cannot help that," I mumbled, ashamed.

"Fie, Tris, I do but teaze you," Nathaniel said, not unkindly. "Sit down here, until your Breath come back to you."

I sate me down upon the mossy Roots, gratefull for the Rest, and watched Nathaniel prowl betwixt the Trees like a great, golden Cat.

If I were like you, I thought, how fine and easy my Life must surely be.

Nathaniel gave an impatient Sigh, which I suppose I should not have noticed, and taking out his pocket Knife, set about carving his Initials into the the great Trunk at my Back.

A strange Thought came to me: Doth not the Tree feel it?

I dismisst this Notion instantly, for 'twas Nonsense. I was well aware that there was no Possibility of a mere Tree feeling anything at all, least of all Pain, as an Human might; but then, snapping at the Heels of its Dismissal came another: Might not it be possible? Might not it be real?

I got quickly to my Feet, and asked Nathaniel at once if I might borrow his Knife. He was happy to lend it, and so, having the Blade in mine Hand, I turned about and forcibly inscribed into the surprizing soft Bark of the Tree mine own Initials. *T. H.* Tristan Hart.

If the Tree screamed, I did not hear it.

"Look thro'," Nathaniel said, pointing upward. "Mistletoe, upon an ash Tree."

I squinted both mine Eyes and peered upwards, but I could distinguish no Difference between one leafy Mass and another. "What is special in that?" I said, feeling somewhat resentfull of his sharp Sight.

"It is a Rarity," Nathaniel said. "Mistletoe grows easily upon the Apple, and the Oak; but it is scarce found on the Ash, and is most magickal when it doth so."

"I did not know that," I said.

"You do not know anything. It is possible; it is real. Let's go. My Father's Apples are ripe for the Picking. Canst not hear them calling? Pluck us, they cry! Eat!"

I smiled, and returned Nathaniel his Knife. Then we passt out thro' Shirelands' open Gates and made our Way along the Road toward Collerton.

The Rectory stood on the north Side of the Village, before one reached the Church, and so from Shirelands Hall it was a long Walk. By the Time Nathaniel and I came into the Village, my Stomach was beginning to complain of its Neglect, and I had begun to feel a little dizzy. Nathaniel, however, seemed to have compleat forgot his Hunger, for he gave no Indication of it, and had made no more

Mention of our eating the Apples we were out to steal. I hoped this did not mean that he had changed his Mind and was leading me, without Explanation, somewhere else intirely; Nathaniel's Character was changeable in the Extream, and his Desires also.

We reached the Rectory and made our Way, without shewing ourselves to the Inhabitants within, to the Rector's treasured cider Trees behind. The orchard Gate being locked, as was quite usual, Nathaniel assisted me to scramble over the dry, crumbling Wall into the glowing Eden that lay inclosed therein. Once I was down, he scurried over the Wall himself with a marten-like Agility and Speed that made me to ponder why the Rector had ever troubled to have locked his Gate, for open or shut, it provided no Defense.

The apple Orchard, in the late afternoon Sunneshine, seemed to mine Eyes a veritable Oasis of sweet Bounties and Delights. The Aire was warm, and slightly humid, and the Perfume of ripening Fruit hung upon it as light as a Breath. Bees buzzed happily about mine Ears; a song Thrush whistled. And on every Tree, in every Cranny and Corner of the Orchard, hung the most delicious Apples of every Hue from the brightest yellow to the deepest crimson. My Mouth watered.

I hastened over to the most heavily laden of the Trees and began to rip the red-gold Apples from the Boughs; more, I was certain, than I would eat; but it did not matter. I sate down upon the Greensward, and fell to with a great Relish. Nathaniel laughed aloud, and told me that I must be a very Pig to have made such a crude Mess of my Meal. This Censure stung me at my Quick, as Nathaniel, surely, had known it must. From mine earliest Infancy I had disliked and feared Pigs.

"If you are sick tonight," Nathaniel said, "don't blame me, tho' you will never hear the last of it from Mrs H.; or from your Father."

I said: "My Father cares naught." But I began to eat more slowly.

I do not now think it was true that my Father cared nothing for my Welfare, or even, for that Matter, my Behaviour. Certainly, whenever I was caught, as I frequently was, about some Misdemeanour, his Reaction was not that of an usual Parent, for it was to refrain from both Punishment and Guidance by ignoring the Instance altogether. This curious Blindness of his was, I know now, a Source of Friction between him and our Neighbours, who took the more Christian Approach and did not spare the Rod, but again, as a Child, I was quite unaware of it. All I knew was that when Nathaniel and I would play a Trick, however cruel, upon some unsuspecting Soule, I would not be punished and Nathaniel would not be caught. Nathaniel Ravenscroft had the Ability, in Addition to his other Peculiarities, of being able to vanish utterly into thin Aire at the first Whisper of Trouble. He had never, to my certain Knowledge, taken any Blame for any Wickedness in which we had been discovered; and altho' this Circumstance appeared hugely unjust, it did have its Advantages. Nathaniel could get clean away with Mischief that no other Boy would dare dream of, and afterwards he would share the Spoils with me, whether they were his Sisters' Secrets or his Father's Cider.

Nathaniel, intirely unconcerned by my ruffled Sentiments, laughed aloud, and scrambled up the Trunk of the tallest apple Tree with the same efficient Ease that had taken him up and over the orchard Wall. He perched himself merrily in the upper Branches, and plucking himself an Apple, said: "I shall act as our Lookout, Tris. If I see someone approaching, I shall caw, thus": he made a chattering Noise identical in Pitch and Intensity to that of a Magpie. "An you hear it, you must straightway hide."

This Strategy of Nathaniel's was not in itself a bad one, for he must have had a good View of the Pathway from his Perch; but having no Fear for himself of being caught, he was not the most reliable of Sentries. Perhaps he gave the warning Signal too late, or perhaps he had already given it and I, intent upon filling my Belly, had not noticed; but all in one Second I became aware of the Rat-tat-tattling of a Pie, and the Rattling of a Key in the iron Lock of the orchard Gate; and before I had Wit or Time to hide My Self it opened wide, and there stood the Rector.

To mine own Detriment and Defeat—for if I had but remained silent and still he might, perhaps, not have seen me, and I might have been able to slip unobserved out of the Gate—I gave a guilty Start, and let from my Lips a small Cry of Surprize.

The Rector Ravenscroft, for his Part, was also somewhat astonished; but his Recovery was rapid, and his Retribution swift. With a Bellow of Rage, he bore down on me like a fat, cassocked Epitome of Death. His thick fingered Hand, sweating from the Shock of his Passion or his sudden bodily Exertion, clamped itself upon the Back of my Neck.

"So!" he shouted. "Tristan Hart! Caught in the Act, yet again, by God!"

He hauled me to my Feet. Half eaten Apples tumbled from my Lap. The Rector stiffened at the Sight.

"You have the Devil in you, Tristan Hart!" he roared. "He is in your Blood, your very Blood, and you have your Foot firm and fast upon the Road to Hell! I tell you, Boy, if your Father won't take it upon himself to beat him out of you, I shall! Never let it be said that I let anyone's Soule go to the Devil without battling to save him!"

Without any more ado, he thrust me roughly up against the nearest Tree, and with his walking Cane proceeded to inflict upon my tender young Body as brutal and prolonged a Thrashing as I have ever witnessed; and if I had not been fully cloathed I have no Doubt but that the resultant Injuries would have been severe. You may be certain that I screamed, and cried, and begged for Mercy, and fought, and struggled hard to make good mine Escape; but all to no Effect. When it was finally over I collapsed exhausted on the velvet Ground, my Ribs and Spine bruised black, in such an Intensity of Pain and Shock that I could neither stand nor weep.

As I have said, my Father, the Squire, had never beaten me, nor suffered me to be beaten at the Hand of any of our Servants; so altho' by this Age of eleven Yeares I had endured from them many a Scolding, I had never once been hit; and as my Body cried out in Pain, so my Mind staggered under the Shock of what had happened, so suddenly, so unexpectedly, to me.

I did not know what had befallen Nathaniel. I supposed that he was yet in the apple Tree, but as I had no Way of finding out without discovering his Presence to his Father I kept quiet, and did not resist as the Rector dragged me once again to my Feet and hauled me from his Orchard. I was terrified now lest of Course he should thrash me again, but to my Surprize he called instead for his Chaise, and forced me inside.

"I will have Words with your Father," he said. "For there is a Wickedness bred in you, Boy, and it must be curbed, by whatever Means he chooseth, else you grow up vicious as the Devil. Too long have you been left unchecked, too long have you been left to his Devices."

The Whip cracked over the Pony's Back. The Animal sprang forward, into a lively Trot, and the Chaise rumbled out of the Rectory Grounds, and along Collerton Lane towards Shirelands Hall, and my looming Disgrace.

CHAPTER TWO

So I became, for the next four Yeares of my Life, a Scholar. The Theft of the Rector's Apples from his Orchard was the last Straw for that choleric Cleric, and in his Determination to preserve my Soule, not to mention the peacefull Enjoyment of his own Property, he inflicted upon my Father so bitter a Sermon regarding mine evil Nature that my Father's Reserve finally cracked, and he muttered somewhat upon the Topic of Dispatching me to School. The Rector Ravenscroft seized on this Notion, and insisted that my Father write the relevant Letters then and there. My Father, however, regaining some of his Dignity, baulked at this Demand, coming as it did from the very Divine of whom he had been Benefactor; and, complaining that he had neither Time nor Inclination to set about the Business, politely requested that the Rector either take up mine Education himself, or find me a suitable Tutor. The Rector, for his Part, was most vexed by this new and unexpected Development, and refused at once to have me in his school Room; but to my Displeasure, he found me a Tutor; and within Dayes I had been sentenced and confined. A school Room was set up for me on the ground Floor of the House, hard by my Father's Library so that he might, theoretically at least, have an Ear to my Progress, and I was kept busy about my Books between the Houres of seven and five upon every Daye of the Week excepting, naturally, the Sabbath. I complained most bitterly at this, but as mine only Sympathiser was my Father's aged housekeeper, Mrs Henderson—fondly called Mrs H.—a Woman who, since the Departure of the Last of my Nurses, had fulfilled something of the maternal Part towards me, my Disquiet went unremarked.

My school Room, which had been a sitting Room not much used before, was dark, dampe and musty with tall, curtained Windows. The only Comfort was the Fire, which was lit every Daye in Winter, to preserve the Books. Often I stared out across the rain-swept or sunne-filled Shirelands Grounds towards the High Chalk, and wished with mine whole Heart that I had yet Liberty to walk across the flower dotted Turf, to listen to the Buzzards scream, and feel the rough Winds play about mine Ears. Other Times, I thought that if I could have left the Place, alone, I would have crept soft to the River's Edge and slipt.

I sorely missed Nathaniel, and wept much for him at first; but we saw each other still across Church, and were permitted to write. From his, infrequent, Letters I discovered that he, too, was deeply unhappy, and longing to depart his Father's Society. It was the

Rector's Desire, to which Nathaniel was vehemently opposed, that he should take Orders, and follow him into the Church. Even I could see that this fatherly Determination was misguided: I could no more imagine Nathaniel wearing a Cassock than I could My Self playing the Syrinx. Nathaniel considered himself already a Man in Nature, if not in Law, and he saw no Reason to obey his Father.

By the Summer of forty-four I was still in my Mind very much a Boy, but I had grown and altered much. Gone, almost forgotten, was the small, rounded Puppy I had been. Now I was a gangling, bony Youth; tall and angular with large Hands and long, narrow Fingers. It would have been difficult for the Rector Ravenscroft now to have said that my Soule was bound to the Devil, for I was Word perfect in all my Religious Observances. But what the Rector did not suspect was that my Soule belonged to a rational God.

I could no more give Credence to the terrifying Mystery of Scripture and Pulpit than I could have turned Water into Wine. Mine was a God of knowable Purpose, a God whose Principles might be discovered, tested, and found comprehensible by Human Reason. The World was as an open Bible; the Challenge was in learning how to read it.

I went to the Philosophers; to Descartes, to Harvey, to Baglivi, to Hook. I began to comprehend how the intire World was built according to the Principles of Number, Weight, and Measure, and to see clearly how these applied to the Operation of the Human Body. Whatever the Condition of the Soule within, the Human Body was a Machine, susceptible of Damage, Illness and Decay – but also of Repair.

These Thinkers became my Comfort, in those dark Houres after Church, when my Senses reeled. When my Father dies and Shirelands Hall is mine, I thought, I will construct a great Laboratory in the eastern Wing, where I shall pass every one of my waking Houres in Experimentation. No mere Surgeon, I will become a Giant of Natural Philosophy, teazing apart the intimate Bonds of the Flesh to discover the Workings of the Machine underneath. I will be the Prophet of a new World, where Logick and Reason will Rule where once Superstition held all Sway. So sweet a Taste, I said to My Self, hath the Electuary of Reason, more effective than any Theriac. Knowledge could heal all Ills. It would be my Mind's Solvent, my Soule's Salvation. I should study all the Processes of Life, from the most insignificant to the most profound. I would measure and circumscribe Pain itself.

I told no one of mine Ambition. None would have understood.

In the early Autumn of forty-five, when I was approaching the Age of fifteen, it was decided that I should have yet another Tutor. By this Age, I had been under the Tutelage of perhaps six of these Masters, and each Episode had ended in the same Way. "His Wits are too sharp," each had said to my Father; "Latin and Euclid are too easy for him; with Respect, Mr Hart, you must pay for a learned Scholar from Oxford or London to undertake your Son's Instruction." And on each Occasion my Father had sighed, and another poor Curate or struggling Student had been engaged.

This Time, however, he took on a Protestant Scotsman by the Name of Robert Simmins, who had been several Yeares an Officer in the Army before taking up the Position of Master at St Paul's School—of which Place he had recently, and hurriedly it seemed, been acquitted. I suspected that some Scandal lay at the Bottom of this, which had almost certainly to do with Drink, but I never found it out. Colonel Simmins' Prejudice against me, which became plain to me very early in our Association, was founded, I now conceive, in nothing more than that intellectual Laziness of a certain

Breed of ordinary Man, which fancies to discern a Threat in every-thing and everyone considered clever; and which, rather than striving to comprehend it, habitually contemns. He was not, verily, a bad Man, and his own Faults naught but common, venial Weaknesses for which he should perhaps be envied rather than despised. However, at the impatient Age of fifteen, despise him I did, and I could not perceive how I could learn aught usefull from a Tutor whose primary Aim in mine Education was to cure me of Cleverness.

This Tutor had a Son of his own going by the Name of Isaac, who was several Yeares my junior; and to mine Astonishment and Disgust it was decided that this Son should be allowed to receive Education alongside me, like a Flea riding upon an Hound. He was eleven Yeares of Age, and he turned out to be a light built, girlish little Scrap with shaggy brown Hair, large dark brown Eyes, and Eyebrows of surprizing thickness and excitability. I disliked him immediately on Account of his Father, but it quickly became apparent that Simmins did not return mine Antipathy, but rather liked me very much; and I found that he was perfectly willing to act the Part of Servant and Scapegoat both within the school Room and without it. If the Father set me a tedious and pointless Sum, the Son would solve it; if I was supposed to be working hard upon a Translation of Tacitus, when I would far rather read Ovid, he would cover up mine Inattention by drawing the Tutor's Anger to some Wrongdoing of his own; moreover, he carried my Books for me, shone my Shoes, and was perfectly happy to assist me to dress. This servile Devotion, which did indeed inspire much reluctant Affection within my selfish Breast, began to seem all the more remarkable when I learned something of Simmins' Parentage, for his Mother had been the only Niece of a minor Baronet, and his

Station could have been something akin to mine had his Father been rich. But upon such Infelicities the World doth spin.

On Saturdaye, the fourth Daye of December, seventeen forty-five, Charles the Pretender, who had been Months causing Trouble in the North, captured Derby. These Tidings, which reached first Collerton, and then Shirelands later that Evening, filled our Household with Dread; and tho' Mrs H. instructed the Servants to hide both this Anxiety, and, more significantly, its Cause, from us, she was not successful. Opinion among them held that it could be only a few Houres before Charles presst South to London, and rustick as Shirelands' Location was, if he decided to take Oxford first, he would come dangerously near. The Spectre of War terrified me more horribly than the Fable of Raw-Head-and-Bloody-Bones had ever done; I found it impossible that Night to sleep.

At half-past four in the Morn I gave up the Assay, and left my bed Chamber to creep silent thro' the slumbering House to that of little Isaac Simmins, who would, I conceived, listen to my Worries with an attentive and sympathetic Ear, despite the Earliness of the Houre. I knocked more than once upon Simmins' Door, but he, who plainly was not suffering the Agonies I was, did not answer. I tried the Handle, and when to my Surprize I found the Door unlocked, I slippt quietly within and went to stand at Simmins' Bedside.

Isaac Simmins was indeed quite fast asleep. His Mouth was open, and his white Nightcap, which was too large for his young Head, was pulled down so low that it covered Eyes, Ears, and much of his Face, like a gallows Hood.

"Simmins," I whispered. "Isaac."

He did not move. I reached out, and gently pulled back the Cloth from his Face. It had initially been mine Intent, in doing so, to wake him, but in the Event I had not the Stomach to spoil so pretty and tender a Picture as that presented by the Sleeper. I stood back, and regarded Simmins with an almost proprietary Pride, as if we had been in Rome, and I an Emperor gazing fondly on his favourite Slave.

A disturbing Notion quickened then within my Mind, its Seed surely consisting in that horrible Anxiety which had forced me to rise out of my Bed. Suppose, I thought, a Stranger had crept into Simmins' Chamber instead of My Self; one of Charles Stuart's Rebels, a Spy, a Murderer; and suppose that it was he, not I, who stood here, looking silently and grimly down upon the Boy's defenseless Form. Would not he bend forwards, as I imagined My Self doing now, and close one Hand fast over Simmins' Mouth, thus, and his other hard upon his Throat, and press down remorselessly until the Boy's small Candle was snuffed out, and there was no Power on this Earth, scientific or otherwise, that could rekindle it?

The Notion terrified me, both in its Essence and in the Fact that it had been mine Imagination that gave it Birth. I backed violently away from Simmins, upon whose Body, really, I had not laid even the lightest Fingertip, and fled swift from his Chamber to hide behind the locked Door of mine own, where I cowered abed the Remainder of the Night in a trembling Sweat, my Senses all agog for any Whisper that might herald the Enemy's Advance, and the Horrour of my Phantasy becoming real.

By Mondaye Morning, after I had passt that Night, then one Daye and then another Night in this fearfully agitated State, mine Head was aching, and my Vision appeared darkly clouded, as if for me the Sunne had never risen, but hovered the whole Morn just below the Horizon. I struggled to concentrate in my Lessons, and the Time crawled.

Colonel Simmins began the Morning with a Focus upon the multiplication Table, in which I, usually, was fully fluent. Todaye, however, I struggled, and this, of Course, brought his Wrath down upon mine Head.

"Have you no Mind?" he demanded angrily. "To study todaye? Mayhap your Wits are not as sharp as you would have us believe. Dunderhead! Begin the Table over!"

I did so, and failed again to compleat the Task.

"Your Pride, Master Hart, verily hath come before a Fall," my Tutor remarked, with considerable Satisfaction.

"Egad!" I protested, stung. "How can I be expected to concentrate with Threat of War upon me?"

Colonel Simmins' Lip curled. "You have been forbidden, with good Reason, from listening to Servants' Gossip," he said. He had a Chill in his Voice that made me all at once to shudder, tho' I had no Idea why it should. My Tutor and I had not seen Eye-to-Eye about anything since the sorry Houre upon which we had met, and it was not unusual for him to address me coldly. "Speak impertinently of such vile Nonsense again, and I shall thrash you, Boy, and soundly."

After that, he set both his Son and My Self about the close Translation of a very long Passage from Suetonius on the Twelve Caesars, which he said must serve to recollect my wandering Wits, and forbade me say aught else, on any Topic, for the Remainder of the Daye.

So we sate in Silence until five o' the Clock, at which Point a curious Expression stole over the Visage of the Tutor, and without Explanation he departed from the school Room. I flung down my Quill and hurried to the narrow Window, where I peered out into the Black.

"Wh-at are you d-oing, Master Hart?" Simmins inquired of me timidly, after a Moment or more during which I neither moved nor spoke.

"I am looking for the Scots," I said.

"But—" Simmins ventured, in a Tone of mild Remonstration. "The Pretender's Army is M-iles away, Sir, and if my Father c-atches you away from your S-eat, he will be furious."

"Dost think," I said, turning about to stare at him, "your Father's Anger frightens me? The Scots are close, and you are a Fool if you don't believe they will be here Tonight. When they come, Simmins, their Displeasure will make your Father's a mere Sneeze by Comparison. As shall mine, an you question me again."

Simmins hung his Head. "'Sdeath, Isaac," I said, with a Sigh. "You are still a Puppy. Come here, I shall pat you on your Head."

Simmins left his Chair and came towards me, Head bowed, and knelt at my Feet. I smiled, remembering, for the nonce without any sinister Implication, the pretty Picture he had presented to me two Nights before, and I put mine Hand atop his shaggy Crown, ruffling his Hair. "Sweet as a sugar Plum," I said. "'Tis to be hoped the Rebels spare you."

I had said this joking, tho' cruelly; but as the Words left my Lips they seemed to fill the Aire like a Curse. My Terrour rushed back. Would the Scots spare Simmins? Would they spare me? Would the Intruder stand beside my Bed, and put his smothering Palm over my Mouth? I kept mine Hand on Simmins' Head, and turned mine Attention quickly back to the shrouded Dark beyond the window Pane. The Enemy was close; I could feel his encroaching Circle like a Noose about my Neck, drawing ever tighter. The Tutor had been a military Man, I thought. Surely, he must know the Foe was present? Surely, he did not underestimate the Danger?

A faint Sound echoed across the Distance: a low Drumming. Drumming, Drumming.

Suddenly, I felt Simmins spring away; the school room Door opened, and Simmins' Father, mine erstwhile Tutor, stumbled into the Room, followed close at Hand by the Stench of Port Wine. At Sight of me, standing seemingly unoccupied beside the undraped Window, my Translation of Suetonius abandoned and mine open ink Pot drying out, he let out an infuriated Roar that put me in Mind of the Rector, and lurched forwards. "Get to your Work, Boy!"

I dodged out of the Way of his flailing Arm, and sate down in my Place as quick as Light, protesting that I had only been about the shortest of Pauses. The Tutor, glowering and sweating profusely underneath his heavy serge frock Coat, strode across the school Room to where I was sitting. Placing his meaty Hands full-square upon my Translation, he leaned forwards across the Desk and pushed his Face so close to mine own that I could see the tiny red Capillaries throbbing in his Eyeballs.

"You, Mr Hart, are a Disgrace," he spat. "A lazy, shiftless Wastrel of a Boy! How long have you been about this Suetonius? Young Isaac here—a mere Child of Eleven—he hath finished it! I doubt you have even read as far as Caligula! There will be no Supper for you tonight! You will stay seated, and you will work!"

The Drumming became suddenly much louder. I started, and upon an Instinct turned once more toward the approaching Danger, as doth a Coney when it heareth Hounds.

"What?" cried my Tutor. "Do you shrug, Sir?"

Seizing my Shoulders, he forced me roughly about, so that I was forced to face him.

"No," I protested. "'Tis—"

The Drumming became deafening; I marvelled that Colonel

Simmins did not appear to hear it. Then the Notion struck me that perhaps he could; perhaps that was why he was shouting, why little Flecks of Spittle were collecting on his Chin, and why his Adam's Apple was straining against his thick white linen Stock. He was struggling to make himself heard above the Drumming.

"They are here!" I shouted.

"What, Sir?" Could not he hear me?

"The Scots!"

The Tutor appeared, for a Moment, quite confounded. Then a peculiar Expression, in mine Estimation sly, crosst his Face. Narrowing his Eyes, he said: "There are no Rebels here, Mr Hart."

This Assertion, which as far as I could tell was outright Lie, and the contemptuous Manner in which it was spoke, frightened me in my very Bowels. I suddenly perceived a very good Reason why Colonel Robert Simmins, Scotsman that he was, might not appear to care about, nay, even to hear the Drumming, which was now so forceful that the Walls about me vibrated upon every Beat. What Proof had I—indeed, what Proof had any of us that he was, verily, loyal to our King George? My Father, as far as I was aware, had taken him on after only the most cursory Inquiry into his History. He must be, I thought, an Enemy; a Spy in the Employ of Charles Stuart; or something much, much worse, and I dreaded what that could be.

Why had he been gone from the Room? Had he unlocked the Gate?

The Tutor returned to his Desk, and as I watched, terrified and appalled, he took out a birchen Cane. His Lip twitched. He took two Steps toward me. "Stand up, Mr Hart."

I did not move.

"Stand up!"

And then, all on a Sudden, to mine utter and undivided

Astonishment, as Colonel Simmins took one farther Step in my Direction, he shrank to a miniature Size, like a Man seen thro' the wrong End of a Telescope. His Voice sounded like the Squealing of a Rat. I remembered Nathaniel Ravenscroft summoning barn Owls at Sunneset, on the Backs of his Hands. The Ice in my Bowels turned to Water.

Before I knew it I was on my Feet, leaping across the Room, and I caught the white Switch in mine open Hand, wresting it easily from his Grip. "No!" I cried.

The Drumming beat about mine Ears, more furious than ever.

I gave the Birch an exploratory Swish thro' the Aire. I smiled. An Owl's Wingbeat. Somehow, by my sudden Leap, I had rid me of all Traces of the Terrour that hitherto had frozen me in my Place. The Cane whistled once more, in a Figure of Eight; Infinity before mine Eyes. The Tutor was a ridiculous Homunculus; a Gnome.

Witchcraft! I thought. 'Tis Scottish Witchcraft! I hissed at the Idea, like a Countryman banishing Evil.

To mine Amazement, at my Making of this Sound, the Gnome began to edge away, backing slowly across the Floor, as if it were afraid. "What, little Spy!" I cried. "So, art frightened of me, now! I will give you a fine Message to take to your Pretender!" I advanced upon it, the Cane high in mine Hand.

All at once, little Simmins leapt up from his Chair and interposed himself between My Self and the small, jabbering Creature, which seemed, in mine Estimation, to be heading for the Doorway.

"Mr H-art, calm d-own," he said, putting his small Hands softly upon my Cheeks and turning mine Head, so that I was induced to look at him. "Please calm d-own, S-ir. They will send me away from you."

"Pretty Simmins," I said. "I will not let him hurt you."

Mine Attention had been diverted from the Gnome for no longer than a Second, yet when I looked back I saw to my Surprize that it had grown again to man-Size. This pleased me, for there had been a small Part of me that had thought it unfair to have whippt so meagre and defenseless a Sprite, no Matter what Crime it had committed. I had now no Qualm; I steppt past little Simmins, and thrusting the Tutor face-first into the heavy Door, brought down the Switch upon his Back. A Grunt broke from his Lips; his clumsy Fingers struggled with the Latch.

I whippt him hard again, and then a third Time; but then something, perhaps Pity, stayed mine Hand. I steppt back, lowering mine Arm. The Tutor scrabbled at the Door a Minute longer, but it appeared to be stuck. I did not move. Finally, he turned slowly about, and eyed me with an affrighted Craftiness, like a threatened Rat.

"The Birch," he finally demanded. His Eyes danced over my Shoulder, searching for Escape. I stared at him.

"No," I said. And I shrugged.

"You," the Tutor squeaked, "are in Trouble, Boy; give me the Birch."

I leapt forward half a Pace, brandishing mine Hand as if to take him at his Word, really only to see what he might do; at once the Tutor gave a Yelp, and cowered, his Arms covering his Head and his Expression terrified. Pity had stayed mine Hand; Contempt now enraged it. "Faugh!" I spat. "You deserve none of my Compassion, Rat! Gnome! Spy!"

Dropping the Cane, I leapt forward and seized him by the Throat, forcing him rough against the plastered Wall of the school Room. "Brute," I said. "Shalt profit from thine own Teaching."

I drew back my Fist and punched him in the Mouth, once, twice, I know not how many Times. Sweet Calm descended on me. I did not stop. I did not want to stop. The Drums, in mine Ears, rolled on and on.

Many Weeks after this, long after Charles Stuart—who never, in Reality, came any farther South than Derby—had retreated, it was explained to me, slowly and carefully, that this violent Episode had been the Result of my being on a Sudden taken ill. With what Disease, I was My Self uncertain; although my Father's Physician, who was possesst of a mediaeval Mind, had diagnosed that I was suffering from a Surfeit of the Choleric and Melancholic Humours. He prescribed a Treatment of compleat Rest, frequent Bleeding, and a very careful Diet, by which means the Balance of the Fluxes was to be restored. I was required moreover to shun anything that would stimulate the production of the yellow Bile and the black, and also to ensure that the Phlegm did not become too pre-eminent.

When Mrs H. and the under-Footman had pulled me off, the Tutor's Eyes had been purple and his Nose bleeding badly. He had subsequently departed, with a golden Reference and considerably more than his full Wage; and my Father having now lost both Patience with and Confidence in the Notion that I could success-fully be tutored, he was not replaced. The Freedom that I had thus now regained suited me perfectly and, I am sure, kept the Ratio of mine Humours in appropriate Order. For a little while I missed young Isaac Simmins, who had been more of a Comfort to me than I had admitted to My Self, but this soon passed. The Drumming, which, it seemed, had been some Manner of

Hallucination within mine own Head, quickly faded. By New Yeare, which fell, then, at the Latter End of March, I was quite well; by May I was back in Church and, by July, to my immense Surprize, a welcome Visitor at the Rectory; so perhaps it was inevitable that by that August of seventeen forty-six I was, once again, roaming the Countryside with Nathaniel Ravenscroft.

CHAPTER THREE

Nathaniel, who had contacted me for the first Time in many Months on the first Daye of June, was still blessed with the Sanguinity I lacked. Still silver haired, green eyed, still wiry as a Birch, he seemed to me almost unchanged. I was now some Inches taller than he, however, which pleased me immensely.

For several Weeks after this reinstitution of our Friendship we were not allowed to wander abroad without the Chaperonage of one of the Hall or Rectory Servants, in case I grew unwell. Before long, however, this Requirement was deemed unnecessary, and it being generally assumed that we would not now disgrace ourselves by committing any of the Felonies to which we had been inclined as Boys—altho' as I have previously explained, Nathaniel had never taken any of the Blame for our Misdeeds, up to and including our Raid upon the Orchard, and all had fallen upon mine Head—by the first Saturdaye of August he and I were free to return to our original Habit. Our first unaccompanied Sortie took us vaguely in the Direction of Collerton. We walked on Foot along stony, rutted Lanes between tall Hedges purple with Elderberries, thro' Coppices latticed with ripening Hazelnuts. Late Swallows wheeled and Swifts shrieked in the Blue above us. We were heading nowhere, changing our Direction as the cloud-Shaddowes directed. Nathaniel delighted in such Mutability.

Now that we were alone, I revealed to Nathaniel the Details of my Collapse, as they appeared to me to have been. Nathaniel had known, naturally, that I had been ill, as had all the Neighbourhood; but my Father, acting under the Advice of mine Aunt, had let it be known that I was suffering from mere Exhaustion, and had hushed up all Mention of mine Assault upon the Tutor.

"You perceived him as what?" Nathaniel said.

"A Gnome," I answered.

"A Gnome. How did he appear, this Gnome?"

"Like the Tutor, but tiny. Highly entertaining."

"Verily, you were mistaken," Nathaniel said, idly ripping a Spray of Elderberries from the Hedge. "Because a Gnome is not at all amusing. Nor doth he resemble a shrunken Tutor. No, no, dear Tristan, the ordinary, every-daye, commonplace English Gnome is a tiny brown Creature with a Visage like a pickled Walnut, who, like all Faeries, hath very sharp Teeth. And an exceeding foul Temper."

"You have described the Tutor," I said, laughing.

"I have no love for Gnomes," Nathaniel said. "I have had to waste far too many valuable Houres of a ridiculously short Life in finding things that they have mischievously moved. Whenever I catch a Gnome I dispatch it straight—whoosh!—up the Chimney."

"Wherefore?"

"It takes the little Buggers Houres to find their Way out. Fire is a barrier to them, you see. They are Beings of Earth."

"Cannot they climb to the Top?"

"There was a Man," Nathaniel said, "some fifty Yeares ago, in a Village not too many Miles from here, who sustained a Kick in the Head from a Bullock. What was so surprizing was not that he survived—though that was admirable enough, 'twas an hefty Kick—it was the Fact that afterward he could not turn Left. Left, for him, had ceased to exist. When he reached for his Ale, it was with his Right Hand. He would only chew with the Teeth on the right Side of his Head. Left was an Impossibility, a nothing. Neither had he any Memory that he ever had possesst a Left, or any Conceit of Leftness."

"Truly," I said. "That is astonishing."

"Quite. And so 'tis with the Gnomes. They cannot perceive up. Therefore, they cannot climb it."

"Mrs H. is still terrified of Faeries," I remarked.

"Even so? Doth she still deposit little Saucers of sour Milk around the Kitchen?"

"That and worse," I said. "One Daye, one of the kitchen Cats brought in a dead Bat, and she flew into a Panick, saying that the Cat had murdered a Goblin Babe, and she would not rest until the Cat had been drowned for it. Now she always wears her Apron back to front, and traces little Lines of Salt upon all the Doorsteps."

Nathaniel Ravenscroft began to strip the Berries from their Stems with his Tongue. He smiled, and his Teeth drippt crimson from the Juice. "It doth not do to anger them," he said.

30

"Housekeepers?"

Nathaniel laughed. "Faeries, you Booby."

I punched Nathaniel playfully on the Arm. "I do not think," I said, "that you have said one Word you have truly meant for the past five Minutes. Otherwise I shall have to conclude that you share with Mrs H. a Belief in Mummery."

Nathaniel smiled. "In Truth," he said, "I do not know quite what I believe, often from one Moment to the next. I seem to hold only three Creeds with any Stability, and two of them are Uncertainties. I believe that the Earth travels around the Sunne, that the Stars are very far away, and that most People in the World are born into Misery and die unfulfilled less than a Mile away from where they were conceived. People are mere Clocks, marking tedious Time. But I sincerely doubt that I share any one of these Beliefs with Mrs Henderson."

Nathaniel vaulted over a low Stile between two Oaks into a wheat Field. I followed him. A few more Dayes of Sunneshine would see this Wheat cut down, but todaye it reached almost to the top of mine Head. I stood still for a Moment, amazed. I had forgotten how it felt to be thus surrounded. Nathaniel began to sing a rousing Verse of some country Ditty that set the Crows a-rattling in the Branches above.

Nathaniel's Voice was clear and sinuous. I was not certain, being no Musician myself, but I suspected that it might be Pitch perfect. I could easy imagine that Voice filling St Paul's, or the Abbey of Westminster. People might come to hear it over that of any of our celebrated Castrati. The Song, on the other Hand, was fit only for a Covent Garden Brothel.

Nathaniel waved at me to accompany him, so I joined in the Chorus, tentatively at first, but when I realised that he and I had

no Audience except each other and the Birds I became more confident, and soon I was belting out the Words as loudly as he:

"O Polly why so faint and pale? Why dost thou moan and cry?
Why do thine Eyes turn in thy Head, thy fair Breast heave and sigh?
With a Whack! Fol al a-diddle, al a-diddle o!"

It was at this Point that I distinguished, unmistakable above
Nathaniel's Voice and the Whistle of the Blackbird, the unrestrained
Laughter of several young country Females drifting on the light
Breeze from the nearby Road.

"Hush!" I cried out in a Panick. "There are Women near!" Then
I doubled up on the Spot as sudden Laughter caught me in the
Stomach like a Blow, mine Head at last dipping beneath those of
the dancing Wheat.

Nathaniel stoppt singing and grinned at me, his green Eyes
glittering in the filtered Sunnelight. "You," he said, when finally I
had regained Control of My Self, "have been leading an uncommon
sheltered Life if you think that Song is cockish. We need to get
you with a Wench. There are many delectable Beauties in the
Village, and 'tis but a Mile away. What say you?"

I was startled. When we had raided his Father's Orchard,
Nathaniel Ravenscroft and I had seemed the same Age, near enough.
Now, it suddenly seemed that he was Yeares ahead of me in Growth
and in Experience. I was not sure that I was ready to follow him.
I knew that there were several handsome Lasses in the Village; I
had spent Houres in Church, only last Sundaye, during the Rector's
interminable Sermon, contemplating them; but I did not want to
visit with any of them todaye, and certainly not, I realised with a
Shock, in Nathaniel's Company.

Perhaps Nathaniel understood. Perhaps merely he changed his Mind. Whichever Way, he linked his Arm thro' mine and we resumed our Wanderings, leaving the Village and its exciting Possibilities behind us. A Red Kite whistled above us as we walked, his Tail a perfect Arrowhead.

We walked on quietly together for perhaps a Quarter of a Mile, without noticing overmuch where we trod, until it occurred to me that we were gone in a Loop, and were now walking in the Direction of the Rectory. I pulled up short at this Realisation, and released mine Arm from Nathaniel's.

Altho' I was now a regular Visitor to Nathaniel's home, I did not enjoy the Place, as it was crammed with noisy Children. On my last Visit, three Dayes since, I had counted seventeen of the pestering Brats; the Rector's twelve and an additional five female Cousins, all under the Age of ten, who, Nathaniel told me, were spending some Weeks over the Summer while their Mother recovered from the Shock of being recently widdowed.

"Did you confront your Sister about those damned Flowers?" I asked.

"I did. She denies all Knowledge."

"Honestly?"

"It isn't Sophy's Stile to fill a Fellow's Pockets with Meadowsweet. Especially not Tristan Hart's."

"I don't know how you suffer them," I said. "Thank God, I have only Jane."

"I have perswaded them to leave me alone, unless I will it differently."

"How? Would I could do likewise!"

Nathaniel's Eyes glittered. "Time for another Song," he said. "This is a particular Favourite of my young Cousins." He laughed.

"Raw-Head-and-Bloody-Bones,
Steals naughty Children from their Homes,
Drags them to his grisly Den,
And they are never seen again."

"So!" I cried. "Is that it? You have terrified them into Silence by the mere Threat of a childish Monster?" I gave a violent Shudder, intirely against my Will, and then feeling most ridiculous, pretended that I had stumbled on a loose Stone, and crouched low in the Lane, rubbing mine Ankle. "It cannot last," I muttered.

Nathaniel narrowed his Eyes. "Ah, but Raw Head is no mere nursery Boggart," he said. "He hath other Games besides, for like all Faeries he may shift his Shape to any that pleaseth him. Listen, Tris; dost not know this?

"The two faced Knight rides o'er the Hill,
Green, green the Willows.
He bloweth his Horn, so Loud and Shrill.
Green the Willows, o.
Let me come in, Leonora, says he,
Green, green the Willows.
And your Maidenhead I will have of thee.
Green the Willows, o.
Fair Knight, wilt thou be True unto me?
Green, green the Willows.
True as Death, Leonora, 'tis your Time to die.
Green the Willows, o.
Your pretty Bones I will steal away,
Green, green the Willows.
Beneath my cold Bed they buried shall be.

Green the Willows, o.
False goblin Knight, do not Murder me,
Green, green the Willows.
Alone 'neath your cold Bed I should fear to lie.
Green the Willows, o.
She's taken his Dagger, so Long and Sharp,
Green, green the Willows.
And plunged it straight thro' his dark Heart.
Green the Willows, o."

"If you mean, do I not know that Song, indeed I do," I said, when he had finished. "'Tis well known, and verily, it hath naught to do with Raw Head or Bloody Bones. It is the *Ballad of the Goblin Knight and Fair Leonora.*"

"Surely, Tris, dost not believe that Raw Head would not enjoy taking Maidenheads, if the Maids have kept their Heads, stayed away from the River, and lived long enough to have missed becoming Breakfast?"

"Egad," I said impatiently. "Let Goblin Knight be Raw Head or what Monster you will." I was beginning now to feel a deep Unease, and keen to drop the Notion of Raw Head as quickly as could be. "However you have it, the Lady wins; she kills him."

"That, I grant you, is errant Nonsense. Faeries have no Hearts."

As we approached the Rectory we heard, for the second Time that Afternoon, girlish Voices on the Breeze, and on entering the Gardens we came across a Gaggle of Nathaniel's young female Relatives playing Oranges and Lemons in the Shaddowe of the hawthorn Hedge. I braced My Self, but soon perceiving Sophy not to be among them, began to relax somewhat. The Children, espying Nathaniel and My Self, immediately ceased their Play and scampered towards us over the Grass, which the Rector keeping a small Flock of Sheep upon the Lawn, was maintained very short.

I did not yet know the Names and Faces of Nathaniel's Cousins, and neither had I any Inclination to learn them; but despite my Sentiments in this Regard I quickly recognised one of the Party: a slightly built, fair haired little Maiden of perhaps eight or nine, who had proved such an Annoy upon my previous Visit, with her incessant Prattlings and rabbitty Leapings that I had lost all Patience and chided her so severely that she had burst into Tears. Nathaniel had found this most amusing, and had hoisted her aloft, as one might a Cat caught in the Dairy, and thrown her out, threatening to wring her Neck if she told Tale of either of us to any Body.

Remembering the Event, I felt a Prick of Shame, and took Care to smile instead of scowl at her, but I perceived the Damage to have been done; she hung back, and stared at me with a strangely wistful Expression upon her pale Face.

The remaining Cousins began to beg Nathaniel to play, to which Plea he, being of chearful Mind, readily assented; and so for ten Minutes or so the Garden echoed to happy Shrieks as he pretended to be a were-Wolf and chased them round the mulberry Trees. Their Sister did not join in, but walked away to sit beneath a weeping Willow that stood some fifty Feet away. Altho' she gave Appearance of watching the others, I had the unsettling Suspicion that her Attention was really fixt upon My Self; and I was deeply grateful when at last Nathaniel grew bored, and returned to my Side.

"Which Cousin is she?" I asked, inclining mine Head toward the watching Child.

"She? Katherine Montague. Why?"

"She has been studying me."

"Sly little Miss. Hoi! Kitty! Morris off before I pull out your Arms!"

The poor little Maid turned as red as an Apple, and gathering her Skirts, she leapt to her Feet and ran off in the Direction of the House, leading-Strings flying. Nathaniel laughed.

"She is like a string-Puppet, that one may twist and turn every Way; only pull too hard and her Joints pop; 'tis a freakish thing. Come, Tris, let us to the House, and eat."

Nathaniel and I left the Rectory at Dusk, and returned home by Moonlight. As I watched the changing Shapes in the semi-Darkness I thought about the farm Hand who had been kicked in the Head and suffered an Insult to his Perception. Damage to the Cranium had damaged the Mind. How could such Things be? I had no Answer.

My Thoughts raced to mine Ambitions. How, I thought, with sudden Anguish, was I to become a great Philosopher unless my Father agree to mine Attendance at a University where Medicine, and, more importantly, Anatomy, was studied? I would require practical Experience within both these Disciplines, or my Dreams were as Dust. I had no Idea how he would respond to such a Request. Surely, I thought bitterly, his Hippocratic Physician will counsel him against granting it.

We turned up a steep Pathway that led across the lower Fields to Shirelands Hall. Bats fluttered over our Heads. Nathaniel's Hat was off, and his silvery Hair shone brilliant in the Moonlight ahead of me. Then suddenly, half-way up the Slope, a white Owl swooped, sudden and swift, out of the Darkness and plummeted into the

Grass barely six Feet from where I trod. One faint, shrill Scream, then Stillness: another Mouse dead. The Bird remained where she had droppt, her razor Beak ripping apart the small Corpse beneath her Claw. I ceased all Movement, fascinated. The Owl threw up her Head and the Mouse disappeared in one quick Snap. Then she stretched out both Wings and rose.

"A fig for your Faeries!" I called to Nathaniel. "I have just witnessed a Wonder of ordinary Nature."

"Not so ordinary. I saw her, too."

Looking southward as we now were, Nathaniel and I could see across the Valley to its farther Side, with its antient Chalk-working. And just above that—or above where I presumed the White Horse to be, in the Darkness—we could both perceive a Cavalcade of tiny winking Lights. They appeared to be moving.

"Gypsies?" I wondered.

We stood and watched as the thin Train of Lights processed along the open Downland of the Ridge and began the near vertical Descent to the valley Floor.

"Damned if I'm going inside yet, then," said Nathaniel. "Do you come with me, Tristan?"

"There? Now? It must be many Miles."

"You have Horses, don't you?"

"Even so, it would take us at least three Houres to get there, and the same to return. We wouldn't be back before Dawn."

"What Matter? We can threaten Mrs H. to keep silent."

"What of your Father?"

"I shall tell him that I was with you."

That this Proposition was a bad Idea, I was certain. What I was to do concerning it was something of which I was less sure. I had always craved Nathaniel's Esteem, and moreover I was desperate to prove to him that in four Yeares I had not changed, and could be again the close Friend I had been previously. But I was tired. My Body was still soft from its Confinement, and I began to fear that if I rode with Nathaniel thro' the Night after walking with him thro' the Daye it would intirely fail me. My Limbs ached.

Nathaniel caught me by the Elbow and danced me up the Hill to Shirelands Hall. "Tristan, Man, you can't back out. They may be gone upon the Morrow."

We came upon Shirelands from the Front, although very quietly and some Distance leftward of the Driveway and the great front Door. I could tell as we approached that something unusual was happening within the House. Candles flickered in the Windows of both front and back drawing Rooms, and the red sandstone Entranceway basked in the yellow Glow of six tall Lanthorns placed in Pairs upon the wide Steps.

"Oh, my Father has Visitors," I said.

"Then we must be Beggars, and slip round the Rear."

Nathaniel span about and began to retrace his Steps towards the low Bushes that screened the Driveway from the Fields beyond. I turned to follow, only to be brought up short by a loud, sharp Call: "Master Hart!"

"Damn it," groaned Nathaniel. "Was she watching for you?"

My father's Housekeeper was hurrying towards us, crunching the unrolled Gravel underneath her sturdy Boots. I turned again, reluctantly, to face her.

Mrs H. was a Woman of advanced Yeares, somewhere in her sixth Decade. She was tall and scraggy and otherwise unremarkable except for the Apron that she wore, pinned back to front, over her grey serge Bodice and Skirt. She was holding forth a Candle, which she lifted before my Face, shielding the Flame from the night Breeze with her other Hand. She peered into mine Eyes.

"Master Tristan, you must come away inside. You are not yet well—and your Aunt Mrs Barnaby is here to visit your Father."

"Mistress Henderson, Good Evening," Nathaniel said. "Might I be permitted to wish you Luck in perswading Master Hart to such an unappealing Prospect as a Night spent with his melancholy Father and revolting Aunt."

Mrs H. raised her Candle high between herself and Nathaniel. She caught mine Arm. Her bony Fingers presst urgently into my Biceps.

"Unhand him, Woman!" Nathaniel said, backing quick away from the candle Flame. "Put that thing down! Do you mean to set Fire to mine Eyebrows?"

"Master Ravenscroft, I must ask you to go home," Mrs H. said. The candle Flame began to gutter, and grow small. "The young Master is required by his Father."

"My Requirement is greater," Nathaniel said. The candle went out.

I felt Mrs H.'s Hand begin to tighten. "And what of your Father?" she said. "Sitting there all the live-long Daye wondering where you are, whether you have not been robbed or murdered on the Road? What of him, Master Ravenscroft?"

"You crazy old Crone," Nathaniel said. "How darest speak to me like this? I shall complain to your Master of your Impertinence."

"Oh, let her be, Nat," I said. " I imagine that my Father hath told her to fetch me no matter what. She intends no Harm."

"None indeed," Mrs H. agreed. "I am sorry if I spoke out of turn. But Master Hart must come inside now and there be an End to it. 'Tis on the Squire's Orders."

Her Fingertips bit into mine Arm.

"It looks as if there is no Help for it," I said. "You can borrow my Chestnut, though, if you are still of a Mind to ride. The Groom will ready him for you. He's fast."

"Zounds," said Nathaniel, sighing deeply. "So be it then, Tristan, if you say so. 'Tis Pity."

"Master Ravenscroft, if you'll take my Advice, and no Impertinence meant, you'll go home," Mrs H. said, in a Voice that quavered slightly as she spoke.

Nathaniel looked at her strangely, like a Duellist assessing an Enemy. "I intend to, Mistress Henderson," he said. He made her a low, mocking Bow and winked at me. Then he melted away into the Darkness of the Hedge.

"He still doth that!" I exclaimed. "He used to pull that Trick all the time when we were Children."

Mrs H. plucked at mine Arm. "We must go inside, Master Tristan."

She headed across the gravel Drive and I followed. I was not displeased by her Interruption. She had saved me from the Embarrassment of explaining to Nathaniel mine Exhaustion and Unease, and provided me with the perfect Excuse for going home. Now that Nathaniel was gone, also, I was beginning to realise that I was very hungry. Mrs H.'s next Words, however, caused me much Disquiet.

"I wish you wouldn't spend so much Time with Master Ravenscroft, Sir," she said.

"I beg your Pardon, Mrs H.?"

"I'm sorry, Master Tristan, but 'tis the Truth. He's grown wild, Sir, dreadful wild these past two Yeares. And there's young Rebecca Clifton with that Babe they say is his, and they're saying the Child's not right—"

"Mrs H.!"

My Father's Housekeeper took a deep Breath. I caught hold of her Wrist. "Mrs H., you have always been like a Mother to me, but—" I paused, trying to determine the proper Way in which to correct her. "But I cannot permit you to repeat malicious Gossip. It is fit only for the servants' Hall. Indeed, 'tis not even fit to be repeated there. Master Ravenscroft is my dear Friend. You are never to speak of him again in such a Stile."

"Master Tristan—"

"No, I mean it, Mrs H. Never again."

We had reached the Steps. In the reddish Lamplight I could see her Expression. The Woman was deeply worried. " Very well," she said. "But please be careful of him, Sir."

I felt almost touched. "I am not a Fool," I said. "I know who my Friends are."

CHAPTER FOUR

Mrs H. chivvied me quickly to the dining Room, which was on the first Floor of the House, just off the great Hall, and served me herself from the cold Remains that had not yet been cleared away on Chance that I returned before Supper. I had already decided that I had no Intention of seeing mine Aunt, or my Father, but I was unsure how to avoid the Interview without overly upsetting Mrs H., on whose Goodwill, as Housekeeper, I was largely reliant.

"I must change my Cloathes," I said between Mouthfuls, becoming painfully conscious all on a Sudden of the chalky Soil that dusted my Frock and the Ruffles of my Sleeves. "I cannot be seen like this by Aunt Barnaby."

"Peace, young Sir; do not agitate yourself."

I finished my Platter and demanded a second. "I do not want to see my Father or mine Aunt tonight," I said. "I want to take a Bath and retire to my Bed."

Mrs H. stood up and crosst to the far Wall to ring the Bell. "'Tis your Father's express Wish, Master Tristan."

What can she do? I thought. She cannot drag me where I will not go. And my Father—what will he do? He's neither Tutor nor Rector. He may possess more Right than either, but I know for certain he will never try to whip me.

"I am going to Bed," I said to Mrs H., finishing my Meal. "I am exhausted and my Feet are sore. Have a Bath filled for me. Send my Regards to my Father and to mine Aunt Barnaby."

"Your Father will be disappointed, Sir!"

"Remind him of how ill I have been," I said, upon a sudden Inspiration.

Mrs H. sighed heavily; I sensed her Willpower falter, and finally fail. I narrowed mine Eyes, and surveyed her closely. Mention of mine Illness, it appeared, had won the Trick. I pondered this. Whatever Appellation it was given, whether Exhaustion or Melancholy or even—I hesitated—sheer Insanity, Mrs H. had been terrified by my Illness. She had been the one to sit by my Bedside for one whole Daye and Night, after a Bleeding had brought on a low Fever. She had gone with me when I had roamed thro' every Room of the House, seeking the Source of the dreadful, incessant Drumming that I, alone, could hear. She had brought me back to My Self. Looking into her Countenance, I saw writ upon it how much she feared losing me again. And suddenly, I understood this one, plain, uncontrovertible Fact: that Mrs H. would let me get away with anything, anything at all, if she believed that it would make

44

me sane; all I would have to do to influence her would be to threaten that I felt unwell again, or, if mere Threat should fail, to counterfeit Sickness.

I pushed back my Chair and rose to my Feet. The red marble Mantelpiece stood at mine Eye level. I was a young Man; I was strong, I was something over six Feet tall and, seemingly, I was quite mad. I smiled.

Thus was I that Evening relieved of the Unpleasantness of meeting with mine Aunt Barnaby. Mrs H. left me alone to bathe after Midnight and I retired to Bed around the Stroake of one. I slept until the next Middaye.

I woke to find a Letter on my Dressing Table.

My Deare Tristan,

You are a confounded Nincompoop to have stayed behind last Night, and you will regret it Evermore.

I have acquired a Drum! You do not want to know what I traded for it, but it was not yr Chestnut. He is eating Hay in his Stable and I thank you very Kindly for the Loan of him.

Your Friend

Nathaniel Ravenscroft

My Peace of Mind did not last. My Father was displeased by my Refusal to attend him—not a thing that troubled me much in itself itself—but it transpired that he had had a particular Reason for requesting my Presence. Mine Aunt Barnaby and my Father had decided that it would be desirable for James, her Son, to marry my Sister as soon as practicable after she reached the Age of one-and-twenty. Neither James nor Jane had any Objection to the Marriage; or if either did, they did not voice it.

Mine Aunt, whose Christian Name was Ann, was my Father's half Sister. A few Yeares older than he, she was a Widdowe and kept a grand House in Faringdon, with her own Carriage, and a Manservant in addition to an Housekeeper and several Maids. Mine Aunt liked to appear more magnificent than she really was. We were many Miles from London, yet she wore her Wigg tall and fashionably dresst, exceptionally high heeled Shoes, and the Skirt of her Dress extended by an Hoop so wide that she was forced to pass thro' every Doorway crabwise. Her Visage was thick with white Lead and usually decorated with a Number of Patches to obscure the worst Ravages of childhood small Pox. I could never contemplate her without some Stirrings of Disgust.

When I was a Child I used to flee from her Visitations to the Ha-ha and the High Field. If she caught me running, I would have to suffer a lengthy Chastisement for all my Sins, which she plainly considered it her Duty to discharge. One Afternoon, when I was seven and still in Mourning for my Mother, she made me stand still with my Back against the chill drawing Room Wall for three Houres, while she played Cards with my Sister and her own Son before the flaming Fire.

Somedaye, I thought, my Mother will come back, and you shall never come here; no, not even for one Houre.

James Barnaby, my Cousin, was seven Yeares older than I, and when I was a small Boy I had considered him, as I was encouraged by mine Elders to do, a serious, high minded young Man. As I grew older, I revised mine Opinion. I now judged Barnaby a canting Hypocrite of the worst Kind, dresst like a Clergyman from his Hat to his Shoes, with an open Prayer Book in one Hand and a shut Purse in the other. He spoke loftily of his Longing to take Orders and enter the Church, but I believed that he had no real Intent of ever turning pious Semblance to useful Truth. The Fact was that his Father had left him more than tolerably wealthy, and a small country Living would have provided little Increase to his Income whilst adding hugely to his Work – which at present consisted of nothing more taxing than censuring others as and when he wished.

I was annoyed that Barnaby was to marry Jane, but as I pondered, I finally had to admit that there seemed some Sense in the Match. My Sister had been a placid Child, generally kind, and hard to dislike—although I had tried. She had grown into a fashionable young Lady who took her Reputation very seriously. The general Cast of her Physiognomy resembled that of our Father; tho' her Skin would never achieve a fashionable Pallour, and she was become very fond of white Lead. Once her Judgement was fixt, it rarely changed, and her Opinion of Barnaby retained the favourable Impression it had taken in her Girlhood. On Barnaby's Part, although it piqued me much to recognise it, there appeared a genuine Esteem for Jane, which, I hoped, might in Time make him shed some of his unappealing Habits. They have Potential to make each other happy, I thought, if they but choose to fulfil it. I was surprized by how much this mattered to me.

So James Barnaby and mine Aunt became Frequent Visitors, but altho' I swallowed the Reason, I found the Reality of their near daily Presence impossible to stomach.

I recalled my Dream of constructing mine own Laboratory. I knew, naturally, that I could not yet devote any great Amount of

Space or Expense to this Adventure, for my Father was as fit as a Flea and I was many Yeares away from mine Inheritance. Nevertheless, I thought, with no Tutors to waste my Time, I might spend as many Houres as I wished about the noble Art of Scientific Inquiry into the Processes of Life. I had no intention of beginning my Study upon living Animals, for I felt certain that such Attempt would only end badly. I had, however, easy Access to dead ones, and I knew that a few Months devoted to the Tissues of Rats, Coneys, Foxes, and Crows would teach me more about the animal Form than a whole Lifetime of Reading.

I realised very quick that I could not fit even a small Laboratory within my Bedchamber, large as it was, and so, after much Consideration, I demanded the Key to my Mother's old sitting Room from Mrs H. This Chamber, in which I had spent many happy Houres in mine Infancy, was a peaceful Spot, directly above my Father's Library and well away from the Traffick of the House, and but one Staircase from my Bedchamber; and for a few Months after my Mother's Death, after my Father had the Room shuttered and the Door locked, I had sometimes crept out of my Bed and curled up in the Hallway against the old Wood.

To my Amazement, in View of the Insight I had experienced into her Character regarding me, Mrs H. refused even to consider it. Seeing that I had to let my sick Cat yowl, I threw My Self into a methodic Fit of Melancholy that lasted for a Sennight. This proved efficacious; Mrs H. agreed at least to ask my Father's Permission to give the Key into mine Hand. He refused.

I was very annoyed by this second, more significant, Denial. I began to ponder whether I aught to make direct Application to my Father for the Key, but the Infrequency and Coldness of our Dealings made me reluctant to speak to him upon anything at all.

I therefore decided to cultivate my Sister's Approval and Assistance. Jane had always been our Father's Favourite.

I dedicated August to Jane's Society and Comfort, and to my Delight, this Method too met with general Success. At the end of the Month I applied to her, as subtly as I could, to ask our Father for the Key to our Mother's Room for me.

"Dearest Sister," I said, "you know how our Father's Intractability in this Matter of his Grief causes unpleasant Comment among our Acquaintances. I think 'tis Time for him to shew some proper Sensitivity to your Position. It will not do, dear Jane, to have him appear at your Wedding like an antient Crow, casting a Shaddowe over all our Merriment."

Jane seemed convinced—and a little upset, though she tried not to shew it. "I believe," she said, "'twill be best if I ask our Aunt to speak on your Behalf—then it shall seem the Idea comes from her. He hath always been better inclined to listen to her than to me."

So Jane prevailed upon our Aunt, and that redoubtable Woman went to my Father with the Suggestion that he should at last give over his interminable Mourning and surrender my Mother's sitting Room to me. Jane and I followed in secret, and waited, Ears presst to our Father's library Door, for his Reaction.

"Young Master Hart," said mine Aunt, forcefully, "is grown into as respectful and as excellent a Son as anyone could wish; and that you don't see it, John, is your Folly. He hath put all his wicked Ways behind him—" (I blinked) "—and I am sure he is intirely deserving of his own Chambers."

My Father muttered something that I could not catch.

"Eugenia is dead!" Aunt Barnaby retorted. "Dead and gone to Heaven, God rest her Soule, these ten Yeares; and I can tell you,

Brother, she would never want to think that you would deny her Son and spoil her Daughter's Wedding for her Memory's Sake."

A second indistinguishable Response from my Father.

"How now?" shouted mine Aunt. "Not spoiled? I am surprized your Children can stand to be seen in Church with you at all, still in your Black whilst they are all in blue and grey. Enough is enough! Master Hart is out of Mourning, and so should you be! Let him have the Key. Call your Taylor and have him sew you something chearful in brown or burgundy!"

A muttered Answer, followed by a very long Pause.

"Well!" said mine Aunt at last. She sounded, to mine Ears at least, still surprized. "I am grateful to think that you are shewing a little Sense at last, John. The Room will need clearing out, and re-furnishing to a Gentleman's Taste. The Lady's Furniture that is there will do very well for Jane."

I smiled at Jane, delighted. She smiled back, and unexpectedly caught Hold of my right Hand in her own and lightly squeezed it. A long Second passed; then Noises within my Father's Study alerted both of us to Aunt Barnaby's Re-appearance. We scattered like affrighted Hares.

Mrs H. organised the Removal of my Mother's old Furniture and set a Team of Housemaids to Work cleaning the Residue of ten Yeares from the Woodwork and the Mantelpiece. I watched these Removals with an odd Detachment. My Mother was neither in the Chairs, nor in the Draperies.

Mine Aunt arranged the Purchase, from Oxford and London, of certain scientific Instruments, of which I had given her a List, and one or two Items of Furniture that could not be requisitioned from other Rooms in the House; and my Father, I believe, signed the Bills without Comment. The Servants moved these Furnishings into Place as they arrived, under my strict Supervision, and I personally then set about moving my Books, which I had been keeping upon several Shelves hard by my Bed, into their new Home.

On the twelfth Daye of September, seventeen forty-six, after what had felt to me six very long Weeks, I stood, my Key in Hand, finally alone at the Centre of mine own miniature Universe, and I laughed loud at the Irony; the very Woman I was desperate to avoid had brought about my Deliverance. Seeming, it seemed, was everything to mine Aunt Barnaby. Then I ran mine Hands across the fine polished Walnut of my writing Desk. I counted up the Books within its glass-fronted Case; my Treasures, locked behind Dozens of tiny diamond Panes. *Homer* and *Virgil, Caesar* and *Suetonius; Catullus, Ovid; Aristotle, Euclid, Pythagoras;* a *Bible; Spenser, Shakespeare, Marlowe, Donne; Aristotle* (What? out of Place!); *Copernicus, Galileo, Newton; Paracelsus, Hobbes, Hooke, Locke, Boyle, Harvey, Descartes, Vesalius, Cheselden.*

On the long dark oaken Table, before the south-facing Window, stood my Chymistry Instruments. Two short, round bellied Alembics, four fat Bottles and eight Flasks, three Thermometers, a white marble Pestle and Mortar, a small leather Bellows. A Microscope, brought all the way from London. A Board for Dissections, a Sett of Bowls. And my precious Medical Etui, containing Scalpels, Needles, a Curette and a Retractor, Scizzors, a Thumb Lancet, and a Bone Saw. Mine only Lack was Subjects for Experimentation.

I turned about, and ran as quick as I could to the Basement.

The Kitchen was busy, and the sweet Scent of baking Bread rose on the warm Aire like a Benediction. The Clamour quietened somewhat as I came a-bursting in, and the Cook, who was up to her Elbows in Dough, shot me an inquisitive Glare, and bid me tell her sharp what I was about.

"Vermin!" I answered. "I require a large dead Rat, or some other Animal of that Ilk, for Dissection. Have you any?"

"A Rat!" cried the Cook. "As I live and breathe! A Rat! In my Kitchen! No, Master Hart, there are no Rats! I would sooner lose my Place than work in any Kitchen that had Rats! Heaven forbid!"

"Egad, Woman, there is no Need for that Carry-on," I said. "What about a Mouse?"

Eventually, one of the Maids agreed to search the Traps, and so after about half an Houre I had secured my Specimen, and hurried with it to my Study to begin its Evisceration.

My Subject was an house-Mouse, round eared and grey furred. I laid it out carefully on the sheer Surface of my Desk, and examined it closely. I had never before looked so intently at the Body of any Animal, even one with which I was familiar, and I was at once surprized. An immediate Change seemed to have been wrought upon the Creature by my mere Observation. This Mouse was, I am sure, almost identical to every Mouse I had previously seen, scuttling beside the skirting Board or atop my highest book-Shelf, but it seemed to me as if its Mouseness had become more exact—its Skeleton more precise in its Proportions, its Eyes more truly black, its minute Teeth more specific in their Shape and Number. I realised of Course that the Mouse had not been altered in any Way by my Looking at it, but that the Change had been in my Perceptions. From this Moment, I perceived, with a marvelling Jolt, that all living things, whatever their Species, would appear to me as Wonders of Ordinary Nature.

I pinned the Mouse Belly up on my Dissecting Board, opened mine Etui and took out my sharpest Scalpel. Then I paused, for I was not at all sure how to continue. I wanted to explore the Body, but I also wanted to preserve the Skeleton as the first of what I intended to become a varied Collection. The Neck of the Creature having been crushed by the Trap, I pondered whether to conduct mine Investigation from the Chest downward, and open the Body at the Throat, but at last I gave up this Idea as too likely to damage the Ribcage, and instead my first Incision into animal Matter was made at the Anus.

Immediately, Blood spurted out, along with a small Quantity of faecal Material. Caught by Surprize, I looked around for a Rag, but had none, and in the Event was forced to mop up the Mess with my Sleeve, which Act I found so repulsive that I almost abandoned my Dissection then and there. My Curiosity, however, soon re-asserted itself, and I continued to cut more carefully, my Sleeve always at the ready in Case of a Recurrence. I worked on the little Corpse all Afternoon, taking detailed Notes as I progressed, and tho' I made something of a pig's Ear of the Dissection, I was pleased with it none the less, and attempted to clean the bloody Bones in a Cup filled with Vinegar.

To my great Astonishment, when I returned to this four Nights later, I discovered that the tiny Skeleton had turned as pliable as Glue. I could do nothing with the Bones in that State, so I disposed of them in a flower Bed. I repeated this unintentional Experiment on Purpose with different Kinds and Sizes of Bone, and always achieved a similar Result, but I never discovered precisely what it is about Vinegar and Bone that causeth the one to undergo so peculiar an Alteration in the Presence of the other.

From then on, I took Care to clean all skeletal Remains with a small Brush, and a Solution of white Salt in clear Water. I kept my finished Skeletons on Top of my Bookcase, until after a Twelvemonth the Collection grew too numerous, and I was forced to move it.

CHAPTER FIVE

April, 1750, had proved a dismal Month beset by steady Clouds and Showers of heavy Rain. But it had not been a freezing Dampe. The Thermometer upon the window-Sill of my Bedchamber told me daily that at last the Temperature had begun to rise; the long cruel Winter that had stoppt the Clocks and frozen the River had ended. Now the Effects of this new Mildness were becoming visible in the budding, twittering Hedgerows all around Shirelands Hall. In my Study, I had kept the Fire piled high and fiercely hot, and I had stood within my Walls and watched the Rain pour out across the Valley of the Horse.

My Laboratory had developed somewhat since its first

Establishment. My long Table sate yet before the south Window, but it was flanked now by two large wire fronted Cages, in which I kept my living Specimens until I could make Use of them. Each of these Cages being sub-divided, I had thereby Housing for forty small Animals, and consequently the Room had often the Smell of an Aviary or a game-Keeper's Hut. This Arrangement taking up the whole Length of that Wall, I had been forced to move my Desk into the Centre, for I had had more Bookcases and Cabinets built upon the other Walls from Floor to Ceiling, and there was not a spare Inch of Space anywhere. From behind Glass peered down the Skulls of Foxes, Otters, Badgers, and a Roebuck, and the mounted Skeletons of Cats and Mice danced along the Shelves in between Jars housing their pickled Viscera. For my Comfort when Reading, I had installed a small Sofa before the Fire, and I had spent a Deal of Time upon it over the preceding Months, wrappt in a Blanket.

I had turned nineteen in January, and I wanted to go up to the University in Oxford, but that was impossible. My Father, when presst, gave the poor Excuse of my still fragile Mind. This appeared unfair to me; in the three and an half Yeares since I had taken up Possession of my Laboratory, I had not fallen more than twice into the melancholy Sea. The Mania that had brought about my Deliverance from the last of my Tutors seemed an half forgotten Nightmare. Mine Unhappiness was compounded by the Fact that on Christmas Eve, Nathaniel, whilst visiting my Chambers and extreamly drunk, had told me that he was to attend the Theological College from September in Accordance with his Father's Wish that he take Orders. Seeing that I was put severely out of Sorts by these Newes, he had pleaded with me to return with him to the Rectory and restore our good Humour in Company with several of the local Maids—one of whom, he hinted, was particularly taken with me—but I had refused. I kept to My Self how much I would miss him.

At nine of the Clock, on the thirtieth Daye of April, I was painstakingly involved in the Dissection of a large gravid Rat when someone rapped unexpectedly upon my study Door. I startled wildly, and sliced intirely thro' one of the delicate Amnions, which I had intended to preserve intact, cutting off the Head and dextral fore-Limb of the Foetus in the Process.

"Damnation!" Clutching my Scalpel still in my Hand, I strode across to the Door, turned the Key and threw the Room open. "What the Hell is it?"

"Is that any Way to greet your oldest Friend?" Nathaniel said.

"Oh, 'tis you! I thought it had been the under-Footman."

"It would have been," Nathaniel said. "But I perswaded him otherwise. Do you know that your Hands are covered with Blood? And here I am come to steal you away to a Night's Revellry."

"Revellry? What? The Blood is from that Rat you sent me. A beautifull Specimen, Nat; but I am running out of pickling Vinegar."

"I do not take your Meaning."

"I can't preserve the Rat in toto; 'tis too big. So I have decided to excise the Uterus and embryo Pups only. And I was managing the Operation exceeding well, before your bloody loud Knock interrupted me. Come and see what you have made me do."

I crosst over to the long Table and placed my Scalpel carefully upon the thickly felted wooden Board, positioned at the mid-Point of a three-quarter Circle of tall wax Candles, where I had pinned the Rat. Nathaniel peered into the Corpse with a perplext Expression.

56

"Here, Nat, for God's sake," I said.

"Which is the Uterus?" Nathaniel asked.

"That." I presst the Organ lightly with my smallest Fingertip.

"I see it now, I think. Little Questions, peremptorily dismisst. If her Pregnancy had occurred to me I might not have offered her to you."

"'Tis but a Rat," I said. "And I must practise upon something. You know not what Human Suffering may yet be relieved because I have just spent three Houres on this Rat. Though I should have preferred it had been a Monkey."

"I did not have a Monkey. And as for alleviating human Suffering, I should say 'tis barely worth the Effort. If you were to ease a Man's Pain by a full Half, he would only curse you for failing to remove the Whole. Now you must wash your Hands and Face, for you have a broad Smear of Rat above your left Eyebrow; change your Attire and come with me. I have tonight called in a Favour of the Landlord of the Bull, and he hath agreed to let me have the upper Room for a private Ridotto."

This Information was so unexpected that I was forced to look away from my Work and stare at Nathaniel. For the first Time I took in the delicate Embroidery upon his green velvet Frock, the smart Cut of his silken Breeches. His natural Hair lay in perfect Rolls about his slender Neck, and he wore his new Hat. He was not carrying a Cane; instead, he wore a small, silver Sword upon his Hip. The ornate, complicated Hilt gleamed like wrought Sunnelight atop its finely tooled Scabbard. On his opposite Thigh, beneath the Folds of his Coat, he seemed to be carrying something that resembled an hunting Horn. Under his left Arm was tucked the small skin Drum he had traded from the Gypsies.

"What the Devil?" I said. "Did you say Ridotto or Court?" I began to be intrigued, despite mine Intention not to be. "The Landlord will not bill you for this? I imagine he is not well pleased."

"Indeed; he is a miserly old Fart. But he was somewhat relieved."

"How so?"

"Because he had placed himself in an invidious Position, my dear Tris; he had agreed to owe me a Favour without first stipulating what Form that Favour should take."

I frowned. "A Favour? Why should that worry him?"

"Because I could have asked him for anything, Tristan. Anything."

"He could still have refused, if 'twas unreasonable. What did you do to get the Cully in your Debt, anyway?"

"He would never have dared to refuse," Nathaniel said with a Laugh. "But what I did for him is a Secret betwixt us; 'twould be against the Rules for me to tell it."

"Then you are too damned secretive," I said. "And most of the Time speak Gibberish. Tell me, why should I attend this Assembly of yours when I could be dissecting my Rat?"

"Because Margaret Haynes will be there."

Margaret Haynes was the Innkeeper's oldest Daughter. Dark Haired, bright Eyed, and a considerable Beauty, she was the prime Envy of all our local Belles. She was also the Woman who had initiated me, two Months previously, into the Mystery of intimate Intercourse, and she had lately begun to drill me in the Procedure's Methods. "It ent enow," she had said, "that you knows how to fuck. Every Fool knows how to fuck. You needs to learn how to make my Cunny glow."

I did not imagine myself in love with Margaret; indeed, I knew that I was not. But I appreciated the Affection she shewed me when her Father was not nearby, and I did my best to reciprocate it as far as Propriety and mine own lack of Confidence would allow. I also knew that she was not in Love with me. I was a Gentleman's Son and a Greenhorn, and Margaret Haynes had too much Wit to dally for long with either.

When Nathaniel said that she would be in Attendance at his private Party, he did not, naturally, mean to imply that she would be present as a Guest. Margaret would be there in her Capacity of serving Wench, to ensure that the Wine and Merriment kept flowing.

"You both could slip away to a quiet Closet at some Point during the Evening's Festivities." Nathaniel said. "Margaret Haynes on May Eve, and almost under the very Nose of her demented Da, to boot."

It was a delightful Image; and yet, not intirely compelling. I did not know precisely why. But I did know, silently, within My Self, that as fond as I was of Margaret Haynes, there was something missing from our Intercourse; and I suspected just as silently that no matter how brightly I made her Cunny glow, I would not find it. I did not even understand what it was. It was a distant, unformed, nameless Thing.

Yet, I thought, what kind of Man would that make me, if I were truly to prefer the Idea of pickling twelve rat Foetuses to fucking Margaret Haynes?

"I shall change my Cloathes," I said.

The Bull was a Coaching Inn situated at the Crossroads two Miles westward of the Village, slightly less than that Distance from Shirelands. It was popular with our Tenants, and with People from the outlying Hamlets for whom two Miles' drunken Stagger home from the village Inn was not an acceptable Prospect. It was a dark, brooding Building constructed out of foreign Stone and black Oak sometime during the fourteenth Century. Beside the heavy Door swung a single brass Lanthorn, its low Candle casting a guttering Glow upon the Latch. Tiny leaded Windows squinted at the Road from the Bedchambers above the Tavern, while at the back lay the Kitchen, and above this, the larger Room Nathaniel had borrowed for the Evening. The Stables lay to the rear, beyond the flagged and slippery Yard.

I climbed down carefully from the Rector's Chaise, of which Nathaniel had also the Use for the Time, and tip-toed around the Shit and Puddles to the back Door. Nathaniel handed the Pony to the stable Lad and promised him an extra Coin if he saw to it that the Animal received a Rub down and a Feed of warm Oats.

"He hath a long Night's Work ahead of him later," Nathaniel said. "Let the poor Bugger rest well while he may." He stroaked the Pony's white Muzzle and the Creature pricked up its Ears, as if it could comprehend him.

Nathaniel released the Pony and leapt across the Yard with such sure Footsteps it seemed he were flying. "No," he said, taking mine Arm. "No sneaking in thro' the back Door for us tonight."

He led me around the Mud to the front Door of the Bull. The Clouds above us parted momentarily, and some weird Instinct impelled me to look around, tho' I could hear no Traffick. The Roads extending away on every Side of us seemed thick, black Ribbands betwixt the open Fields that glowed near grey in the weak Illumination of the Moon, which had just entered on its final Quarter. On the opposite Side of the Crossroads I could just distinguish the white Arch of the Way-Stone, yellowing faintly in the Lanthorn light, its Script invisible. I glanced back to Nathaniel. For one Second—and it cannot have been longer—his Eyes made a sharp, glittering Connexion with mine, and the intire World about us both fell as silent as Starlight. The Cold sparkled upon my Skin.

Nathaniel was a clock Spring, wound too tight; every Muscle in his beautifull Face screamed desperate Release. I thought I recognised his Expression. I thought it had, three Yeares ago, been mine. Thro' the Silence, I could hear the frantick Ticking of his Heartbeat, Seconds drumming past like fleeting Cavalry.

"The only Way out is to smash the Clock," I said.

"I know it," said Nathaniel.

Then there was Noise again; loud Carousing, and drunken Spirits from within the Tavern, the Fluting of an Owl from somewhere on the Road.

Nathaniel opened the heavy oaken Door, and the Moment drowned in a Surge of tallow-Light and Smoake and Racket. He turned and grinned at me, himself again, his Eyes afire with mocking Laughter.

"Come, Tristan," he said. "Let us make such an Entrance that these rustick Curs will never forget it, should they live an hundred Yeares."

Nathaniel steppt forwards over the door Sill into the Inn. I followed, bowing my Head low as I passt underneath the mediaeval Lintel. The Room within reeked of old Sweat, Dogges, dark Ale, and burning Coal. Pipe Smoake coarsened the Aire into a brown Funk that spiralled slowly towards the low Ceiling and clung there like Treacle. I coughed, and tried, hopelessly, to wave the Fog away from my Nostrils.

"Friends, Yokels, Countrymen," Nathaniel began, sweeping portentously into the Centre of the Room like James Quin, full of Gravity and Bombast. He stood still, poised expectantly for Silence between the Inglenook and the Bar.

To mine Amazement, he was given it. Every Face in the Tavern turned towards him, every Voice immediately hushed.

"I stand before you this Night," Nathaniel said, "not as a Gentleman, but as a Man, mortal and perpetual as ye. This Night, in the Eyes of God and Devil and Faerie Queen, we are all equal in Aspect and in Truth. This Night, the Veil thins, and Men and Spirits walk the Earth in Parity. Who shall dare to sunder that which is one? Who shall draw the Line betwixt the Angel and the Beast?"

Not a Soule moved. The intire lower Floor of the Bull Inn was staring at Nathaniel in Astonishment, Mouths dropping open. I struggled to maintain my Countenance.

"If none shall speak," Nathaniel said, "let there be Joy unto this House! Mr Haynes! A Tankard of his Choice for every Fellow here!"

The Locals understood that. "Egad, Nat," I said, suddenly alarmed.

Nathaniel put his Hand into his waistcoat Pocket and withdrew a small silken Purse tied with a golden Thread. He threw it casually to the serving Wench—who was not Margaret—whose Surprize was such that she fumbled the Catch and almost droppt it.

"Drink and be merry!" Nathaniel cried. "Tomorrow we may all be dead. And all I shall ask in Return is that if someone should ask: 'What of Nathaniel Ravenscroft?' you will speak well of me."

The young Betty stared at the silk Purse within her Hand, and with clumsy Fingers began to pick apart the golden Knot. I watched her Expression, as Greed succeeded unto Amazement. She looked up at Nathaniel, smiling, like a Kitten got among the Cream, and a low Chear rumbled round the Tavern.

I steppt up beside Nathaniel and looked at him in Disbelief. "What in Hell's Name are you doing, Nat?"

"Settling my Debts. Now there is none to whom I owe a thing."

The Hubbub had started up again, as with much Jollity, the Wench had fetched her small brown Jug, and was busily refilling the Tankards of all who asked her. Nathaniel took my Elbow again, and we presst thro' the friendly Mob towards the Door that led to the Kitchen, and the Stairs. "That Tosspot, over there," Nathaniel said, opening the Door, "believes that I impregnated his Daughter, whom I have never met. I know not who got the Wench with Pup but 'twas not me. Ha! There's an Irony! This Bully, hard by the Pillar, holds me responsible for the Deaths of several of his finest Cattle. That other Pissmaker with him insists that I can summon Thunderstorms."

"You jest," I said.

"I do not, Tris. The Mind of the English Peasant is a curious Thing."

"They are happy enough to quaff the Ale you buy them."

"As I said, curious. And not always very clever."

"What do they say about me?" I asked him.

We mounted the Stairs.

The upper Chamber at the Bull was not often used for anything but the Sessions of the local Assize Court. The Inn was too distant from our local Towns to host publick Assemblys, and the Stile of the Room was almost as rustick as the lower. The Walls were white with lime Plaster, but that was the only substantial Difference. When Nathaniel opened this final Door, however, I was at once bathed, not in tallow-Light, but in the clean Brilliance of many waxen Tapers. The Scents of Hyacinthus and Daffodil melded with the sweet Perfume of apple Smoake and some other, sharper Fragrance I could not recognise. The narrow cup Boards along three Sides of the low Room had come alive with Flowers. Crimson Tulips, yellow Daffodills and golden Irises billowed from blue porcelain Planters, which sate at each End of an intertwining Banner of Blackthorn, Apple, and budding May that arched over the Table, where rested the Punchbowl and the Glasses. There were more Petals, too, blooming about the Chimney-piece and the Hearth, where a large apple Log was blazing. Above the whole carried the clear Voice of a Girl, her Singing pure and wistful as a mistle Thrush.

I steppt forwards in Wonderment, looking around the Room.

"Don't ask," Nathaniel said.

The Room's Benches were already crowded with Nathaniel's Friends. Many of these were utter Strangers to me – Nathaniel had as many Acquaintances as there were Coneys on the Downs. I noticed, without Surprize, that not one Person here seemed to be above the Age of five-and-twenty. Nat's Admirers, I thought. Every young Man of our Station wanted to be Nathaniel Ravenscroft. When he changed the Colour of his Coat, so did the Neighbourhood. The Women, or at least the ones I recognised, were the young Wives and Sisters of these Wags; some of them unmarried, and some out, I was sure, without Permission or an appropriate Chaperone. I could never have commanded such a Crowd.

Next to the Fireplace stood a small Group of Musicians, and I quickly realised that the Girl whose Singing I could hear was the Foremost of these. They were not Locals, nor were they from Faringdon or anywhere I would have known. They were Gypsies.

"This is too much—where did you find them?" I said.

"On the Ridge Way."

"And they have agreed to play for you?—Oh, but you have traded something for their Services, have not you? Not the Pony?"

Nathaniel laughed. "These good Folk are here of nothing but the Love they bear to me. I have claimed Kinship with them these three Yeares, and more."

"But by Hell, Nat," I said. "They will never do something for nothing."

"Kinship, Tris."

"You are Kin more to me than to any bloody Gypsy." I was suddenly angry, but unable to understand wherefore.

"You are more my Brother than my Brother," Nathaniel said, looking straight into mine Eyes. "But you cannot play the Fiddle or the Flute. Put your Anxieties to Bed, Tristan; no Harm will come to either of us here. Look, there is your Margaret, dresst as pretty as you please and glancing over in our Direction. She adores you; 'tis a Fact."

"She trifles with me, merely."

"Then she does only as you do. 'Tis May Eve, Tris; go to."

Nathaniel was not to be resisted, so I did, despite my Misgivings, go to. Nathaniel joined marvellous Play with the Musicians upon his Drum and their Strings, although when he was not so engaged he found the Time to enchant every one of his Guests with his rare Manners and exceptional good Looks. I reached into my sociable Etui and extracted Charm. I was polite, witty, amusing. I drank more than my fair Share of Punch and made meaningless Conversation with Nathaniel's Hangers-on. I danced *Greenwood* and *Chirping of the Lark* with several of the Wives and Sisters, including those who had not been invited to stand up with anybody else. Margaret dragged me off to a vacant Chamber at about half-past Midnight and did her best to wear me out before kicking me back to the Assembly at a quarter to two.

I was shamefacedly aware of the Figure I must cut—my Shirt

disturbed, my Breeches unlaced—but to my Shock I quickly understood that I was not the only Gentleman in the upper Room in such a State. The Gypsy Musicians had ceased their Playing. The wax Candles, having been allowed, in the Absence of Margaret, to burn down, had grown dim; and in some Corners of the Room, Darkness prevailed intirely. Within its Penumbrae, I could discern vague Human Shapes, writhing about upon one another like Serpents.

I had never visited a Bagnio, but the Scene before me was such as to put me compleatly in Mind of one.

"'Tis a Debauch," I said aloud, in Wonderment and exquisite Horrour. Then I thought: Where is Nathaniel?—and before I could stop My Self, for I knew that Nathaniel would certainly be busy in the darkest Corner with the prettiest Girl—I shouted: "Nat!"

Several Seconds later—it may have been a full half Minute—Nathaniel materialised out of nothing at my Side.

"What Devilry is this, Nat?" I demanded. "'Tis an Orgy."

"Indeed, 'tis not," Nathaniel said.

"Should I disbelieve the Evidence of mine own Eyes?"

"Look around you once again."

I did so; and as my Vision became accustomed to the warm Dimness I began to perceive more properly those Figures that had seemed twisted and uncertain. One Couple, whose lower Limbs I had seemed to see entwined in strenuous Congress up against the farthest Wall, stood innocently together in plain Conversation. A second, who had appeared to be likewise engaged upon one of the low Benches beside the Table, sat now quietly listening to the Opinions of a third, whose Presence I had not noticed at all.

"I thought I saw them fucking," I said.

Nathaniel stared at me.

"I think I had ought go home, Nat," I said.

"Then I shall accompany you," Nathaniel said. "And we shall take our Revells with us. The Party here is ending, anyway. I have given enough of My Self to these poor Ingrates for one Evening. We shall raid your Father's wine Cellar and watch the Sunne rise from the Steps of Shirelands Hall."

"Gladly," I replied. "Where are your Gypsies? Are they gone ahead to wait upon the Road and rob us as we pass?"

"No, Tristan. You are too suspicious. The Brothers are gone to the Stables and the Sister is here. Do you not see her?"

Nathaniel indicated the Seat nearest to the dying Fire, and suddenly, almost it seemed because he had shewn me where to look, the Girl appeared.

I had not seen her clearly before. I had only heard her Song. Distracted by the general Excitement of the Assembly, I had taken a fleeting Impression of some Body small and dark, and not particularly handsome. Now that I had the Chance to examine her more closely, I could tell that she was, in Truth, very beautifull. Her Hair was in its every Strand as black as mine, but it shone in the coal Light like the Sky shortly after Dusk, reflecting Shades of deepest indigo. Upon her Ears, which were pointed, almost like a Cat's, she wore seven golden Hoops, that clashed and glittered as she turned her slender Neck and looked upon me. Her Skin was as white as Indian Ivory. I caught a flash of blackthorn Eyes framed by long, heavy Lashes. For a Second she gazed right at me. Her Lips were Blood bright as they parted; I could see her Teeth, perfect white, sharp as Nathaniel's.

About her Shoulders, she had pinned a black woollen Shawl fringed with scarlet and gold. Her Gown was the Colour of Chalk, and embroidered with an intricate Tracery of Leaves and Flowers.

"What is her Name, Nathaniel?" I asked.

"You must ask her yourself. I am not at Liberty to give it. I shall offer you a Word in Warning, tho'; do not give her yours."

"As if I were in the Habit of telling my Name to Gypsy Sluts," I said, although I could not in all Honesty guess what Nathaniel was trying to imply. "But she is uncommon handsome."

"She would be happy to return to Shirelands with us."

"Egad, yes," I said instantly, without thinking. "Oh, but what of her Brothers, Nat? They will never permit it."

"She is the Rule by which they abide. An she decide to do a Thing, they will never oppose it."

The Gypsy turned her Face to me again. Surely, I thought, she is by far the prettiest Girl in the whole of Berkshire, let alone the Assembly. I wondered if Nathaniel had previously been sitting with her upon the fireside Seat. A small Spark of Envy flickered in my Bowels. I looked into her black Eyes and the Spark began to flame. I remembered the clear blue Arc of her Song, stretching sinuously over the mortal Gabble of the Crowd. One pure Note, viscerally thrilling, as painfull as it was beautifull.

"Yes, Nat," I said. "We will take her home."

Nathaniel had the pony-Chaise brought from the Yard, and while he drove the Gypsy sate upon my Lap. I understood now from the easy Familiarity of their Discourse that they were more than Kin. Indeed, I could not doubt but that the Gypsy Girl was Nathaniel's Mistress, and that their Arrangement must be of considerable Duration and Standing. That they had been murmuring together in the Hadean Darkness of the upper Room was now more than Conjecture; I was certain of it. Every Expression upon the Countenance of one was reflected upon the other; every movement echoed. Yet if the Thing they shared was Love, it was Love of a

Species previously unknown to me, for the Gypsy made it clear by minute Gestures that the present Target of her Affections was not Nathaniel, but My Self; and Nathaniel shewed as plainly in his own Looks that he both knew and approved of her Design. He was neither jealous nor possessive, nor would he seek to curb her wild Behaviour, Mistress or Lover or Whore or whatever she was.

I placed my Hands upon her Ribcage to steady her as the Chaise lurched and jolted thro' the darkling Night. For a Time I could detect no Heartbeat, then, finally, I thought I found it, the rhythmic Thud of vital Force. I closed mine Eyes and pictured the convulsing Organ beneath the sixth and seventh Ribs, drumming, drumming.

Nathaniel was not jealous, no; but I was.

I began to understand that I wanted to possess this untameable Thing; to control and subdue her, bend her fully to my Will, my Desire, my Rule. I felt the Palms of mine Hands begin to sweat.

The Thought came on me, unbidden: How would it feel to break her? To hurt her, to force her to cry out.

"Monstrous," I said, aloud.

The Gypsy Girl laughed at something Nathaniel was saying, and clappt her Hands. I held on to her more tightly.

A Phrenzy of vile Images beset mine Imagination, tumbling one upon another. I looked upon the Gypsy Girl, and she was naked and bound upon a vertically rotating Wheel; her Arms and Legs were spread into four Points of a Star, and her Head became the fifth. Her pure Skin was bloody from an hundred whip-Cuts. The Phantasm changed: I beheld her pinned open on mine own dissecting Board, her inner Parts brightly shining. Now she was no more than her own poor Self at mine Hands, weeping and screaming to me, in God's Name, to cease.

I will hurt her, I thought.

"Stop the Chaise," I shouted. "We must put her off!"

"Are you mad? Damned if I shall—we are almost at the Hall."

I want to hurt her, I thought.

CHAPTER SIX

When we reached Shirelands everything was quiet. With great Caution that it should remain so, Nathaniel and I unhitched the Pony and stabled him in an empty Box. Then Nathaniel took mine Hand upon one Arm and the Gypsy's on the other, and we made our Way with much nauseous Yearning upon my Part and suppresst Laughter on hers into the kitchen Pantry, where Nathaniel began to search for the Keys to the wine Cellar. "Don't blame me," he said, emerging with a Bottle of port Wine in each Hand. "This is all we have; the old Witch keeps the cursed Keys about her. No Matter. Do you see if you can find some Tankards for us—unless you will drink from the Bottle."

"Egad, no," I answered, crossing the Kitchen in a Hurry and returning with three pewter Vessels from the Servants' Shelf. "I am no Savage."

Nathaniel filled all three to the Brim and we retreated to the Garden. The Sky was beginning slowly to brighten above the yew-Hedge to the East; Dawn must not be more than an Houre away. Soon the first Birds would start, the chill Aire soften, and the Girl run back to her People. We sate upon the wooden arbour Seat, our Coats wrappt tight about us, and I began to allow My Self a little Hope that all would end up well. Then the Gypsy complained that she had emptied her Cup; Nathaniel agreed that his was dry, too, and before I could prevent it he was up and heading toward the Pantry in search of another Bottle.

"Nat, stay!" I shouted, scrambling to my Feet. "For the Lord's Sake, stay!"

Nathaniel laughed. "Don't be a Gelding!"

So I was left alone with her under an indigo Sky, empty even of its waning Moon. She turned and spoke, for the first Time, to me: "What's your Name?"

Do not give her your Name, Nathaniel had told me. So I said: "Caligula."

"Caligula," she repeated. "That is not your Name."

"'Tis the Name you may call me by."

"I see you have been well warned," she answered, laughing. "You may call me, in your own Turn, Viviane."

"Viviane."

"Walk with me, Caligula," Viviane said, rising to her Feet. "Shew me what lies beyond these prickly Hedges of yours. Shew me which Way lies the Horse."

"That would be a bad Idea," I said.

"Are you afraid of me?" Viviane asked.

"No." But I am terrified of My Self.

The Lust to hurt her—to hurt Viviane—was growing stronger with every Second that passed. Moreover, learning her Name had only increased the Ache in mine Hands and in my Loins to such a dreadful Intensity that I could not foresee how I was to deny it. Pure Evil, the Tutor had said. Devilish, said the Rector.

"Shew me," Viviane said. "Or are you, after all, a Mouse?" She began to walk towards the Ha-ha.

"There are only Fields and Woods," I said, struggling not to follow her. "We do not even have a Lake."

Viviane steppt thro' the rickety wooden Gate that led into the Ha ha. Beyond her sate the low Stile into the High Field where Nathaniel and I had once watched strange Lights travelling upon the Ridge. "Come," she said, and put her Foot upon the lowest Step. She paused, her slender Form a deep Shaddowe against the pre-Dawn violet of the eastern Sky. "Will you come?" she repeated, and she held out her right Hand, as one might to a reluctant and unhappy Child.

I passed thro' the Gate and stood beneath the Hawthorns in the Blackness of the Ditch, close by her. Seated as she now was upon the topmost Step of the Stile, her Mouth was upon a Level with mine own, and I could taste her Breath. I began to hear, as if from far away, the old, familiar Drumming. Could it truly be, as I had been told, within mine own Head? It was the Drumming of Viviane's Heart, of Nathaniel's Snare; the Drumming of an Army marching south. It was the Sound of Hoofbeats underneath the Surface of the Earth.

Closer, now, and loud, so loud it deadened every Thought save this: I must subjugate this Woman, this Viviane.

I reached forward and seized her Hand by its slim Wrist, then dragged her roughly from the Stile. She gave a Cry of Surprize. I caught her before she could hit the Earth and spun her round so that her Back was turned toward me. I felt the small Bones of the Carpus shift within her Hand as I twisted it between her Scapulae. It must have hurt; Viviane shrieked.

A dark Joy flooded thro' me. Everything made Sense. Here, at this Extremity of Passion beyond Delight and Fear, Release was possible. I forced Viviane onto her Knees and placed my free Hand upon the Vertebrae of her Neck, pressing her Face down to the Path. The Drumming continued, but softly, softly. As I controlled her, so I was not afraid of it.

Was this it—this, this Pain, the Mystery that had been absent from mine Intercourse with Margaret Haynes?

Yet as I began to feel that I might attain some Catharsis, a sudden Horrour at what I was, at what this Lust, this evil Need must surely make of me, caused my Senses to spin and mine Hands to grow weak. As suddenly as I had taken Hold, I released my Grip from Viviane. She lost her Balance and tumbled forwards upon the Stones. I sate back upon mine Heels. In Truth, I did not know what to do next. The evil Passion had exhausted itself.

The Drumming rolled on; low, incessant, victorious.

Viviane sate up, sucking her injured Hand, and punched me hard in the Mouth with the other, so that my Lip began to bleed.

"You dare to harm me?" she hissed. "Me, who would have lain with you without Force? Me?"

"I am sorry," I whispered.

"Not enough. You will pay for it, Caligula."

"Is that a Gypsy's Curse?" I said.

Viviane rose to her Feet. She climbed the Stile, and I could see

her clear Shape for a Moment against the blue Glow of the eastern
Sky. Then she turned her Back on me, and her Body seemed to
undergo a Metamorphosis, shrinking small; silent Pinions sprouted
in place of her Hands, silken soft Feathers her white Gown.

Owl she became, White Owl; she spread her Wings and soared
away from me, over the High Field towards the South.

I did not see that, I thought. It is impossible.

Nausea at the Act I had lately performed began to seep inside
me. I struggled to my Feet and staggered over to the Stile, searching
frantickly with mine Eyes in all Directions for the Gypsy Girl, who
I knew must be there, somewhere. "Where is she?"

Impossible, impossible; and yet I had seen her change, seen her
as clearly as I saw mine own Fingers atop the wooden Bar of the
Stile. More clearly, certainly, than I had seen those dark contorted
Bodies in the upper Room. More clearly than I had seen Nathaniel,
wound so tight he must spring free or break, in that Moment before
we had entered the Bull. Should I disbelieve the Evidence of mine
own Eyes? No. But yes; for if I did not, then I had witnessed the
Impossible, and I must be a mad Man. But, if this was not real, if
Viviane had not transformed into an Owl, and flown from me,
then where was she? The Dawn was rising and the Light was grey
and cold, the Sky in the East the deep blue of a Sapphire streaked
with violet and crimson. Surely sufficient Light to perceive her,
running thro' the High Field, her black Cloak a dark Star? There
was no Sign, no Trace upon the dewy Grass or in the quiet Aire.

How can she fly, I thought, with a dislocated Wing?

"Viviane!" I shouted. "Viviane!"

I felt the Shock, the Countryside recoiling. My Voice was an
Intrusion; too harsh, too Human in this Stillness. I steppt back from
its Echo.

A cock Pheasant cried out in the Valley; up in the hawthorn Trees a Chaffinch began to trill. May Morning, and a beautifull one; yet in every Chirp and upon every budding Stem I could perceive only a terrible Accusation.

"I don't believe in Curses!" I cried.

No Answer. Nothing.

As I stood there, it came to me that Nathaniel must presently be returning with the Wine, and that I had no Idea what I should say to him to explain that Viviane was gone. I feared that telling the whole Truth might cause him to turn from me with the same Repugnance that had infected the Notes of the Chaffinch. And if I were to tell him that I had seen her become an Owl, then even he must surely doubt my Sanity. Who would not?

I had, it appeared, one Choice. I must discover Nathaniel and tell him that Viviane had run away across the High Field and I was not able to perswade her to come back again. I would tell him truly that we had fought—I would not tell him why.

In Truth, that Question: Why?—was something I could not fathom for My Self. Why had I hurt the Gypsy Girl? It had not been thro' Hate, nor even Dislike.

When I laid mine Hands on her, I thought, I became truly alive.

I hastily quitted the Ha-ha, retracing my Steps over the Lawn, to the arbour Seat, from which Location I beheld Nathaniel returning empty handed from the Kitchens, seeming from his Hat to his Shoes as if he had been cast in Silver.

"Tristan Hart, what hath happened?" he said, approaching me. "Blood on your Face for the second time tonight, and this Time 'tis your own."

"Viviane is gone. We had a Disagreement," I said.

"Aha. She can box better than a doe Hare when the Mood is upon her."

"She ran into the Field. Do you know where she hath gone?"

"To her Kin. I shall follow her, and see her safe Arrival."

"How do you intend to find her? I can see no Sign."

"I have better Eyes than you, and she better Ears than both of us. I shall call her from the Road and she will come to me."

I rose hurriedly to my Feet. "Your Father's Chaise is in the Stable; your Pony, too. I will help you make ready."

"No need. I require but the Pony, and he will be quick bridled. Someone will come for the Chaise tomorrow, I suppose."

"Are you not going home?"

Nathaniel turned to me, and caught hold of the Biceps of mine Arms. "I am going home," he said. I was struck once more by the strange Notion of something long suppresst, being on the Point at last of flying free.

"'Tis Pity you did not please her," Nathaniel said. "I had hoped to bring you with us."

"Do not teaze me, Nat." I said.

To mine Amazement, Nathaniel steppt forwards and embraced me heartily. "I love you, Tristan," he said. "I will miss you. If ever you have Need of me, send Word by Owl, or Cat, or Hare, and I shall answer you mine own Self, if 'tis possible for me to do so."

I began to think that Nathaniel must be extreamly drunk. The Conceit gave me Confidence. Perhaps he would not find Viviane; perhaps even if he did, she would be every Bit as foxed as he was, and would not recall what had taken place between us. Perhaps I was, My Self, more drunk than I had thought, and it was that, only that, which had caused me to act so abominably, and witness an impossible Transformation from a Woman to a white Owl.

"Nat," I said, disentangling My Self. "Go home. You are as piddled as a Newt. I shall visit you within a Daye or two. You are not going up to Oxford until September, and when you do we will not need the Wildlife to carry Letters."

"I am not piddled," Nathaniel said. "But you are. Get you to Bed, Tris. Go, go. I shall see you soon enough."

Nathaniel smiled, a dazzling, glittering Smile of such Anticipation and Delight his Eyes changed from jade to emerald. As if he were bound upon some great and wild Adventure, I thought. Then he bowed, in his customary mocking Fashion, and began to run with great Alacrity towards the Stable Blocks; and I lost Sight of him.

I did not go to bed. The Drumming in mine Ears, and the Agitation of my Thoughts, had put Sleep out of the Question, and I dared not rest for Fear of witnessing again that dreadful Incident with Viviane. And all the Time the Drums grew louder, till I wondered that I could still hear mine own Thoughts. It mattered naught now whether they were within or without mine Head. I began to hypothesise that even if they were indeed within, Phantoms of mine own Delusion or Creation, then there nevertheless must be another Human Spirit on the Planet who could hear them, somewhere.

I considered for a Moment returning to my Study and concluding the Dissection of my Rat, but I was afraid that I might be too drunk properly to compleat the Procedure. I had Wish to remove neither another foetal Appendage nor any one of mine own Fingers if mine Hand should slip. I thought that I had better search thro' my Library for some Material that I might find soothing in my present State; but then I realised that there was nothing on my Shelves that could bring about that Effect.

The Remembrance fell upon me of how, when it had been my Mother's sitting Room, and she yet alive, I had crept in sometimes to hear her singing in both her own old Castilian Tongue and in the Dutch as she embroidered Flowers upon my Father's Waistcoats before the Fire, or painted them from Life before the south Window.

"Blanca sos, blanca vistes,
Blanca la tu Figura.
Blancas flores caen di ti,
De la tu hermozura"
White art thou, white thou seemst,
White is thy Figure;
White Flowers tumble from thy Beauty.

White Owl.

I wheeled abruptly, directing my Feet away from the House. I was heading back toward the Inn, altho' I was barely conscious of that. I needed People, Movement, Light. This I knew instinctively, without Reason, as a Swallow knoweth to fly the Country when the Harvest is all done. Life—only Life—would banish from my Head the tormenting Sounds and Images of the Night. I ran along the Road, ignoring the Mud that gradually covered my Shoes and Stockings, striving to maintain my Balance thro' the Ruts. I ran until my Lungs felt hard afire. I was fleet away from Shirelands towards Humanity; toward the plain Simplicity of Margaret Haynes with her open Affections and her open Legs.

I reached the Inn of the Bull before the Cocks had finished crowing. The Sunne had risen. May Daye poured across the brown Earth, and every Daiseye turned east to receive it. Soon the village

Children, and those of the Estate, would begin their yearly March across the uninclosed Fields from House to House, until they arrived at Shirelands Hall; where Mrs H. would bind together sharp Sprays of blackberry Stems and whirl them furiously round her Head to chase the wicked Goblins out. Then she, on behalf of everyone, would offer Honey and a Bowl of Curds to the kind Gentry, and beg their generous Assistance for another Half a Yeare. When I, once, had asked her wherefore she did this, Mrs H. had explained that May Daye and All Soules' were special Times when the Veil between Worlds grew thin; when the Faeries, and those unfortunate Bodies whom they had stolen away, could cross or return into this one, to do Good or Ill to those who called upon them. I did not mock this Superstition, but it always perplext me that she refused to go the whole Hog on May Morning and ask the Gentry for a full Twelvemonth. It would have seemed to me better Economy.

So here I was, bent double, breathless beneath the Sign of the Bull in the golden morning Light. The Inn was already stirring. Windows were thrown open above, and from one descended the rough Sound of a Woman coughing. I hurriedly leapt away from the Wall lest the Coughing be followed by the Contents of the chamber Pot, but nothing happened. Plainly, the Bull's Daughters were Betties of the nicer sort.

I was determined to find Margaret, so in the Hope that she was already risen, I headed to the back Door where I had waited only the previous Evening with Nathaniel. The Yard was alive with Activity, but there was no Sign of her. The Bull's only Manservant, a swarthy Bully who went by the Appellation of Joseph Cox, was carrying two Buckets of Swill to the Swine, accompanied by the young Wench from last Night, who looked set to raid the hen Houses. A second Daughter was sweeping the Flags. Perhaps Margaret was yet abed.

I steppt into the Doorway and tried the Latch. It was not locked; the Door swung inwards with an uneasy Creak. I crosst the Threshold and looked about me. To my left was the Door leading to the Tavern; to my right, its Twin, which gave way into the Kitchen; ahead of me, the steep Staircase. I hastily, silently too, I hoped, mounted the Stairs.

I felt My Self to be in a better State since mine Arrival at the Bull. The Sunnelight had cheared me, and the Exertion of the Run had caused mine own Heart to outpace the thundering of Viviane's within mine Head; I allowed My Self to think that I could intirely silence it—if only I could be with Margaret.

At the Summit of the Stairs I was confronted by a great many Doors. I opened the Nearest. It was the Doorway to the upper Room. Instantly all the Sounds and Scents of the Evening before burst in upon me. The Singing of the Gypsy Girl; Nathaniel's Playing; May-Eve Revellers fucking. I lost my Balance, thrust out an Arm to steady My Self against the Wall. Dizziness overwhelmed me; the vertiginous Sickness of a Man upon the Edge of a Precipice.

Where was Margaret? I had no Idea. I had never visited her Bedchamber, never even thought about where she might sleep.

I was grippt by a Panick. I remembered the White Owl flying above the Valley of the Horse.

"Margaret!" I cried.

Then it appeared to me that she must be still within the Room that we had used for our nocturnal Activities. I strode to the Door and attempted to open it. The Room was locked. I beat upon the heavy Wood with my Fist. "Margaret!" I shouted again. I could not understand her Refusal to let me in. I could not shield My Self from the conceit that perhaps I had hurt her as I had hurt Viviane.

The Drumming of my Fist merged with the Drumming in mine

Ears until it was beyond my Power to tell the one from the other. I thought that I had left Margaret unharmed; but my Senses were in such Disarray I could not be certain. The fact of my Recollection was no Proof of the Event's Veracity. I was certain of nothing except that she must be within that Room.

Mine Agitation increasing with every Second in which I received no Reply, I ceased hammering upon the Door, steppt back and kicked it. The dark Oak shuddered, but did not give Way. I re-gathered mine Energies, and attacked it again, this Time with my full Force. There came the Sound of splintering Wood as the Latch within tore from its Fixings, and the Door fell open. I leapt into the Chamber.

"Margaret!"

The Room was dim, lit by one Candle burning by the Bed, the Shutters not yet opened. Upon the Bed a female Form cowered against the Pillows in an Attitude of Terrour, Blankets and Counterpane pulled tight up to her Chin, her Mouth a silent O.

I attempted to come to a stop, but mine own Momentum carried me onwards and I crashed into the Post at the foot of the Bed. I lost my Balance and snatched at the bed Curtain to steady My Self, but slippt over, landing on mine Arse and bringing the Curtain down on top of me. Disentangling My Self, I scrambled to my Feet. The Woman in the Bed had overcome her first Shock. She was sitting upright and as I turned to face her she screamed at the top of her Voice.

I perceived at once that she was not Margaret. I had not the faintest Notion who she was. I could see that she was of middling Age, somewhat fat, and wearing atop her Head a night-Cap of rose Linen. "Shut up!" I told her. "I want Margaret, not you. Where is she?"

Right then I became dimly aware of the Shouting of many Voices somewhere to my Rear, and heavy Footsteps pounding up the Stairs. An half-Second later, a rough Hand caught violent hold of my Shoulder and swung me hard about. I almost lost my Footing for the second Time, but regained my Balance and looked upon the Face of mine Assailant.

It was Joseph Cox; inn Servant, pig-Man. He was come at a Run straight from the Stye, and the sour Stench of Pig rose from him in a vicious Cloud. I steppt backwards, away from him, with an involuntary Shudder. It was not merely the Smell. As I looked upon the Visage of Joseph Cox, I felt mine Entrails twist, as if it were that I looked upon the Face of Evil.

"What have you done with Margaret?" I demanded.

The Occupant of the Bedchamber screamed again, this Time more in Rage, I thought, than in genuine Fear. She got up, and from her Perch amid the Pillows began to hurl the Contents of her Bedside in my Direction. She was a poor Shot; more of these Missiles hit her supposed Rescuer than me, altho' she did succeed in clipping mine Ear with an Hairbrush.

"What's Margaret to you?" Cox said, his Lip curling. "Get out of the Lady's Room, now, Sir, before there's any Unpleasantness."

There was much in the Manner of his saying "Sir" that I did not like.

"Insolent Brute," I said.

"Call me what 'ee likes," he said. "I do know what you are."

My Stomach clenched in Horrour. I advanced swiftly upon Joe Cox, raising my Fist. "And what is that?"

But as I strode forward to strike, a second Person steppt out from behind Cox and raised towards my Face the trumpet Muzzle of an antient Blunderbuss. "Now, Master Hart, Sir, you'd best calm down. We ent wantin' no Trouble, any of us, are we?"

Looking beyond the Muzzle of the Gunne, I recognised the florid Figure of Haynes the Landlord, clad in a red damask night-Gown and Turban, his Feet slip-shod, his hands quivering upon the Butt of his Weapon. He looked afraid; his Eyes upon the point of leaping from his Head. This perplext me; I was surely more frightened than he, and he was, after all, the one holding the Blunderbuss.

"I am only come," I cried, "to learn how it goeth with Margaret and whether she is well."

"He keeps a-raving," exclaimed the Occupant of the Room. "About a Margaret, and I don't know any Margaret. 'Tis a mad Man he is, escaped from the Bedlam."

"Did I not tell you to shut up?" I shouted.

"Master Hart," came a Woman's Voice from the Stairs. "Master Hart, I'm here, and I don't know what the Row is about."

"Margaret!" I cried, starting forwards—only to be prevented by the Landlord Haynes thrusting his thunder Gunne once more at my Person. "Margaret, are you well?"

"I am well, Master Hart." A short Pause. Then: "How are you?"

"Ill," I said. "Very ill."

"Oh, dear," said Margaret Haynes. "I am sorry to hear that, Sir."

"'Tis these damnable Drums," I told her. "They will not stop. And they cause me to think terrible things. Am I evil, Margaret Haynes?"

"No, Sir. I doubt you is any worser'n any other Sinner."

The Landlord manoeuvred himself and his Blunderbuss to stand behind me, and the Doggesbody Cox behind him, so that the Way was cleared for me to depart from the Room. This I did peaceably enough, now that I was assured of Margaret's safety. Haynes at once dispatched Joe Cox to alert mine Household as to my Whereabouts. I permitted him to steer me down the Stairs and into the Tavern, where he presst me to understand that we were to sit quiet together to await the pig-Man's Return.

From outside in the Yard, the Sound of Voices seeped thro' the small Window.

"How daft dost think I am, Joe Cox, to ha' bin goin' with a Gentleman? You thinks I wants to end up motherin' a Bastard like Rebecca Clifton? I ent bin with no Gentlemen an I'll thank you to take your ugly Nose out of where it've got no Right to be."

"Idn' un being a Gentleman that do vex I," growled the other. "'Tis him bein' a dirty half-bred Jew. Do it go all the Way down, the Stain o' Tawny?"

"Go to Hell."

"You do want a proper Englishman," said Joseph Cox. "The Likes of I."

"Fuck off," said Margaret Haynes. She returned within, slamming the yard Door after her.

Joe Cox, in the Yard, began to whistle. I thought: There goeth a Man this World would be better without.

I leapt to my Feet, thinking that I must find Cox and deal with him. I did not want the Villain anywhere in the Vicinity of my Home. I had a terrible Conviction that he would bring Harm to my Family—perhaps to Jane. But I was too slow; by the Time I had reached the yard Door and pulled it open, the Landlord Haynes had caught mine Arm to bring me back, and the pig-Man had departed. I had not Power to chase him. Horrified Despair overwhelmed me, and I collapsed upon my Knees. I could not get up again, and knelt, Heart pounding, Legs all a-tremble, whilst the Drums rolled on and on.

I was unwell on this Occasion for four Weeks. Altho' everyone insisted that the infernal Drums that tormented me beat compleatly within the Confines of mine own Head, this Conceit made the Din no easier to bear, and oft-times it drove me to Screaming. Finally, however, they faded as they had done before, and I was left with only their Memory.

I did not see Margaret again; she went into Service in Oxford before I was able to apologise for the Confusion I had caused. I hoped that she had been able to convince her Father that there had been naught between us.

At the same time that she told me of Margaret's Departure, Mrs H. took Pains to acquaint me with the Extent of her Father's Forbearance towards me, which I had not at the Time thought great. The Landlord Haynes had silenced the Lady whose Repose I had disrupted by waiving her Bill, and scotched any Desire she might have had to call the Constable by pointing out that my Father paid the Constable's Wages. He believed that mine irrational Conduct had been the Result of strong Wine and youthful Spirits, and put a Stop upon the Mouths of those inclined to impute it to a more serious Cause. Only the broken Latch had he asked my Father to make good, by standing the Expense of its Repair; which was a fair Request, since he had lost full eighteen Pence already on the Lady.

Mrs H. cautioned me that Haynes' Restraint was wholly due to the Interest he maintained in being on friendly Terms with my Father. "Who is a good Squire, and not someone Mr Haynes'd want un-neighbourly. You are in your Father's Debt, Master Tristan; if you had been anyone else, he would never have shewn such fellow Feeling. You are lucky to have been born to such Parentage."

Aye, I thought, and 'tis as like that Haynes has a Mind to his future Interest with me, when I shall be the Squire. But I said nothing.

I received no Newes from Nathaniel, and when I demanded of Mrs H. and my Father why this should be so, received no intelligible Answer. I could not believe that Nat did not want to see me, tho' secretly I feared it. Instead, I concluded that our Fathers had joined in a Conspiracy to keep us separate, and for this Injury I berated my Father at every Opportunity. He stayed silent.

CHAPTER SEVEN

The cold Spring matured into a warm and humid Summer. I had
been obliged more than once to throw off my Frock and perform
mine Experiments in my shirt Sleeves with the open Windows
draped, rather than endure the harsh Sunne thro' my study Window.
I had stoppt this, however, after the Goose I was working upon
escaped.

Since May Daye I had scarcely left the Hall. I told no one why,
for my Cause was not a rational one. Yet every Time I set one Foot
without the Close, it seemed as if on every Branch and Blade of
quivering Grass was scribed my Mittimus. Transgressor, bend thy
Neck before the Axe. I had begun to fear the hunting Owl.

I nevertheless wanted very much to go up and join Nathaniel who, I had concluded, must have gone already to University. It appeared to me that once I was beyond the Valley of the Horse I should be beyond the Reach of whatever Terrour it was that menaced me. But my Father remained adamant: I should not go; and nothing I could say would move him. I approached mine Aunt, but she was not my Friend in this as she had been in my previous Scheme, as she could see no Virtue in a Gentleman's attending a University at all. I had, she said, no Need to enter the Church or the Law, and as such a college Education would be worthless. I should better spend mine Energy in improving my Shot.

I sulked, I pleaded, I argued; my Father refused, he retreated, he gave up speaking to me altogether. By July, Relations between us had reached such a Nadir that neither of us would stand to be in Company with the other, and Jane was forced to sup alone in the dining Room whilst we took our separate Meals upon Trays at odd Houres of the Daye and Night. Jane wept, and wished that she was already married. I understood her Sentiment; Shirelands had become almost as much a Bridewell for her as it had for me.

Left to My Self, I read, and I re-read, Descartes and Locke. And although it made me sick to do it, I repeated, over and again within mine Imagination, the Events of May Eve. Was it my Mind that was corrupted, or my Soule? I had ceased believing that the two were identical. If there could be discovered some Mechanism within the Brain that was responsible for the Creation of Images; if there could be another that translated Passion into Desire, then perhaps I was neither irrevocably evil nor insane. Like all bodily things, such Processes must be vulnerable to Injury and Disease. The Disorder could be overcome; it would be no more than a broken Wrist, or bloody Fluxes; or the inability to turn Left.

I feared, without admitting it, the Possibility that I was intirely wrong.

My Father had not recognised my Existence for two Weeks, so it was with considerable Astonishment and no less Disgust that I received thro' Mrs H. his Summons to attend him forthwith in his Library.

"I shall not," I told her. I was studying Locke's *Essay* and I had no desire to break off. "I have much Reading to do. There is, by the by, a great Amount of Dust upon this Skeleton Case; you must have stern Words with Martha about it."

"Master Tristan, the Squire says there is to be no shall-nots. He says there is a Gentleman he'd like for you to meet and who is pressing keen to be introduced to you."

"He said so? Egad, 'tis rare for a talking Ass to use so many Words. Tell my Father that if the Gentleman wish to see me he must attend me in my Study, as I have no Desire to intrude into his."

"Master Tristan, please."

"No," I said. I altered my Voice, pitching it in scornful Imitation of my Father's toneless Mutter. "'Tis my final Word. I am adamant. Importune me no longer."

"'Tis your filial Duty, Sir," said Mrs H.

"It could have been," I answered her, "if he had ever fulfilled the paternal Part towards me. In Truth, I know not whose Son I am, for he hath never given me much Cause to believe that I am his."

"Young Sir," retorted Mrs H. severely, "you go too far. Your Father is a good Man."

"Oh, I know how you doat on him."

"Sir!"

"Look at me!" I shouted, standing up, and slamming down the Book. "Am I a Child, to be summoned and chastised? Tell my Father to hang himself!"

This Ejaculation on my Part was met by a sharp Intake of Breath from Mrs H. "I shall tell him," she said, "that he is the unfortuate Sire to the most unworthy Son, who will not come down even when it would be to his Benefit, who sulks and complains and cries the most terrible things against a Father who hath never done aught by him but Good. I shall tell him—"

I realised then that I had, for once, gone too far; with Mrs H. at least. I could not risk damaging mine Interest with her. I did not doubt that if we were to fall out, I should require her Assistance with something immediately after, and regret the Altercation. Damn, I thought. This means that I shall have to see my Father.

"Oh, I am sorry!" I cried, vaulting over the Back of my Sopha and putting both Arms about her scrawny Shoulders. "I am truly the most ungrateful Wretch, and I should not have spoken so. You know the Cause of it, his cruel Intractability, Mrs H."

Mrs H., who had started violently when I had leapt across the Sopha, slowly relaxed and with an heavy Sigh patted me upon the Back, as if I had been an Infant. "Come now, Master Tristan," she said. "That's enow. Your Father is awaiting."

I argued no longer, altho' I had no greater a Desire to see my Father now than I had before, and permitted Mrs H. to accompany me down-Stairs to his Door.

In four Yeares, I had visited within my Father's Library only once, which had been upon the Occasion of his telling me that Jane was betrothed to James Barnaby. I repeat that he was telling me; for this must have been the Case despite the Fact that three Quarters of his Remarks were addresst to a Space several Inches above my left Ear, and the Remainder to the window Sill. Once he had done, he had immediately returned to his Papers as if I was no longer present, and I had stood for some Minutes in a bewildered Silence before Mrs H. had led me out again. I feared the Prospect of a similar Interview todaye.

I need not have worried; when Mrs H. opened the library Door the Scene that met mine Eyes was, by my Father's Standards, a chearful one. My Father, clad yet in his customary Black, which all mine Aunt's Encouragements had failed to get him to give up, sate in an Armchair before the empty Grate smoking pipe Tobacco. The Windows were open, the dark Curtains pulled back, and in the strong Sunnelight a hundred thousand dust Motes seemed as if to dance upon the swift Notes of a Wren, cascading from the ivied Wall outside. Beside the Window stood a well-built Man of perhaps my Father's Age, clad in a plain grey Waistcoat and Breeches, and leaning his considerable Weight upon a sturdy walking Stick that could easily have doubled as a small Cudgel. He was not unpleasant of Countenance, despite his having an uncommonly long Nose with a severe Bend in it. Mine Eyes opened wide as I apprehended his Height, which was within an Inch or so of mine own.

"Mr Fielding," said my Father, waving his Pipe in my general Direction. "My Son."

"Well, now," said Mr Fielding, turning to me and beckoning me forwards. "Step into the Light, Boy, and let me take a good Look at you. Egad, Sir; he is the Picture of his Mother. And like her in other Ways, I understand?" This Last addresst to me; but as I had not the faintest Idea what he was talking about, I frowned, and shrugged one Shoulder.

"You don't know?" he exclaimed. "Why, she was a true Intellectual, your Mother; the cleverest Woman I have ever met."

At this Intelligence I surely appeared even more perplext. My Father had given me no Hint that my Mother, excepting in her Jewish Heritage, was anything but commonplace; and as to the Notion that I resembled her closely enough to be her Picture, it was not one with which I was at all comfortable.

"Oh, Good Lord," Mr Fielding said to my Father. "Have you raised the Boy in a Cave?" Turning back to me, he continued: "So, Tristan, your Father tells me that you insist upon going up to a University, and will not take his Word that it is no necessary Part of a Gentleman's Education. What have you to say upon that Subject?"

I shut up my Mouth, as it had fallen open. Mustering my Thoughts, which had been scattered as effectively by Mr Fielding's Speech as by the four Winds, I attempted a Reply. "Well, Sir, I—that is—I wish to continue my Studies, Sir."

"From what your Father gives me to understand, Study for you at any University would be quite pointless. There is little they can teach you that you do not already know. 'Tis not my belief that our Universities spawn Men of Genius any more than our publick Schools spawn Gentlemen. Tell me, what is your Reading at the Present?"

I answered that I was studying Locke upon the Understanding.

"And what Thought have you upon said Tractate?"

"Upon all of it?"

"Perhaps only that Portion you are reading presently."

I regarded Mr Fielding with some Surprize and not a little Suspicion. I was neither accustomed to such a Stile of Interrogation, nor to such Questions. I wondered what his Interest in mine Answers could be. "In Truth," I began, "I am disappointed. Mr Locke hath nothing useful to import upon the Problem of whether Sensation is located within the Body or the Soule. He seems happy to give it up as divine Mystery. But this is a Cavill of mine own; I have a great Interest in that Question and was hoping to find a thorough Refutation of M. Descartes' Assertion that Sensation is intirely mental." My Enthusiasm for the Topic beginning to overcome my Diffidence, I drew a Breath, and continued, much more quickly: "None the less, Mr Locke's Delineation of sensitive Knowledge is compelling and his Argument that the Mind perceive naught but its own Ideas hath perswaded me compleatly. I am quite certain that he is right; and right, too, in his Argument, *contra* Descartes, that the Mind's Ideas are not innate, but drawn from Experience. I think, Sir, that if God had truly caused our Ideas to be innate, as Descartes says, then they would never err; yet is it not possible for a Man to perceive Monsters in half-Light?" I stoppt abruptly, in Fear lest my Words threaten to reveal too much of My Self.

Mr Fielding was staring at me. He seemed startled. "How old are you, Tristan?" he asked.

"Nineteen, Sir."

"So," said Mr Fielding, shaking his Head. He looked quizzically upon my Father. "Are we still of one Opinion, John?"

My Father knocked his Pipe into the empty Fireplace. "Yes."

"I have suggested," Mr Fielding said, "and your Father has agreed, that it would be to your Advantage to return with me to London, should you wish it. Your Stay would not be protracted—a Yeare or two at most—and little would be expected of you beyond Gentlemanly Behaviour. You would have as much Time as you required to pursue your Studies, and I should be happy to introduce you to an Acquaintance of mine who is prominent in the Scientific Circle. That is my Proposal, Master Hart; now, what is your View of it?"

I was forced to be silent for a full half-Minute. Eventually, when the Shock of Mr Fielding's Offer had receded sufficient for me to speak, I stammered: "And he—my Father—hath he verily consented to this? Have you, Sir?"

My Father grunted in Affirmation at the Grate.

"Then, Yes!" I cried. "Yes, Sir, and gladly! When do we leave?"

"Tomorrow Morn, young Man; so you had better see about your Belongings. I have only Space in my Carriage for two Trunks, and before you fill them both with Books, I have a Library, which you are welcome to peruse. You will need Cloathes. Tell your Housekeeper to pack for you; she seems the practical Sort."

"Thank you, Mr Fielding," I said, finally recollecting my Manners. Then I thanked my Father also, altho' I did not imagine that he cared one Way or the other. He did not raise his Glance from the Chimney-piece, and waved me away. I made a Bow to Mr Fielding, then departed from the Room.

I was so excited by this new Development that I ran the whole Distance up the Stairs back to my Study; then, recalling that it was Cloathing I required and not Reading, the farther Flight to my Bedroom, bellowing all the Time for Mrs H. to attend me. I made so much Row that I awoke Jane from her afternoon Nap, and she presently began to holler for the Housekeeper to come and tell her what was happening. Mrs H. came puffing and blowing up the Stairs in a State of great Agitation at having to answer two competing Claims at once. I seized upon her first, being so much more forward than Jane, who was, I imagined, still undresst, and pulled her into my Chamber.

"You must pack for me, Mrs H.," I said. "I am to London tomorrow, with Mr Fielding, and I must have Cloathes. Pack me nothing that hath Blood upon it. Mine embroidered Frock—and my fine Wigg,

95

and my silvered Cane. And anything you think fit for a Stay of a Yeare or more—tho' I shall surely see a Taylor—and quick, quick!"

"What is this, Sir?" Mrs H. wheezed, breathless from her hasty Climb and apparently as confused as I had been not twenty Minutes since.

"I go to London," I repeated. "Tomorrow."

"Tomorrow?"

"Yes, yes!"

At this Juncture, Jane, who had been continually calling all the while, gave up and came out into the Landing to discover for herself what was the Matter. She appeared within my Doorway, her Gown dishabille, her Expression vexed.

"What is wrong, Brother?" she demanded. I told her what I had twice told Mrs H. Thankfully, Jane was somewhat swifter on the Uptake. "You are leaving?" she exclaimed, dismayed. "And so suddenly? Oh, Tristan!"

"What?" I said. "You cannot be surprized. You know how desperate I have been to go."

"But you will leave me all alone," she said.

"You must visit more often with our Aunt," I answered. "Then you will not have Time to ponder how alone you are. It will be Ridottos all the Way. Step aside, I must run down and inquire of Mr F. whether there is Room for any of mine Instruments. He spoke of having a Library, but that alone will not suffice."

"But I shall miss you, Tristan," Jane said.

"Oh, stow your Snivelling," I said. "'Tis Green-sickness afflicts you, not my Going. Now either assist me with my Preparations or go back to Bed."

My Sister's Eyes grew wide as Saucers. "There is no need to insult me," she said, after a Moment, her Lip trembling. "When I am—I was saddened by your Leaving. Now I think that I shall not miss you at all. The House will be an happier Place with you gone from it."

"Good," I said. "Now get out of my Way."

Jane spun pettishly upon her Heel and flounced back into her Bedroom, doubtless to indulge herself in another Fit of Weeping or some other Tantrum. At that Moment, I could not have given a Fig.

I ran downstairs once more toward my Father's Library. As I grew closer, however, it occurred to me that perhaps I could learn something if I employed some Stealth, as I could hear Mr Fielding's Voice clearly resounding from behind the Door. I therefore muffled my Steps as best I could, and, standing stock-still, put mine Ear up to the Wood.

"Well, John," Mr Fielding said. "I take your Point, and you may rest assured that I shall take no Chances. He seems what they call high strung, but he is remarkably clever; and the Subject of his Discourse, John, suggested to me a Degree of Insight into the Derangement of his Senses that is utterly beyond the Capability of any Lunatick. I suspect that some other Cause may yet be found. We both know how difficult it can be for Persons of so sensible a Disposition to cope with the blunt Brutality of everydaye Life."

"'Tis worse," my Father answered—and I strained to hear him, for he spake so low—"than mere Sensibility. If only 'twere so—but there is a Mania that descends upon him. He becomes delusional, phrenzied, violent. He broke thro' a barred Door—"

"You have told me," Mr Fielding interrupted. "And I shall be careful, John. But you did write me for mine Assistance; now you must allow me to offer it."

"If his Mother had lived," I heard my Father mutter after a Pause,

"things would never have come to this. I suppose you think something similar between Times, Henry?"

"I do. There is not a Daye that I do not think of Charlotte. But
it doth no Man good to dwell upon that which he hath lost. She
is in Heaven; I pray we shall meet again hereafter."

"I have not that Consolation," my Father said.

"I do declare," said Mr Fielding, "that for all your stubborn
Adherence to it, Free-Thinking hath caused more Misery to you
than all the Doctrine you could shake a Stick at."

"A Man cannot be preached into Belief, for all the Comfort Belief
may give him," my Father said.

I was astonished. My Father, a Free-thinker?

My Father, the beloved—at least, according to Mrs H.—country
Squire, who for all his Eccentricities seemed no rarer than Mud, a
Follower of Toland and Woolston?

Egad, I thought in Admiration. 'Tis small Wonder, then, if I am
mad, sprung thus all unknowing from a Free-thinker and a—but I
could not let My Self think the Word "Jewess", and so I pulled my
Thought to an abrupt Surcease.

I did not know what I was now to do. If I was to knock, their
marvellous Conversation must end; worse, they might suspect that
I had heard it; but I knew that I could not continue with mine Ear
against the Door for very much longer. My Request, I decided,
would have to wait. I straightened my Spine and on tiptoes I crept
silently away to mine own Study, to digest in Privacy the strange
Meal of which I had just partaken. I had an uneasy feeling in the
Pit of my Stomach.

My Father, a Free-thinker. A Deist, or an Atheist; and it pained
me suddenly that I did not fully comprehend the Difference between
the two. I had never read any of the Free-thinkers' Works.

I made my Way to a low Sopha I had positioned in front of my Fireplace, and sate down upon it.

"I have not that Consolation," my Father had said, and he had been talking about my Mother. He had loved her, then. Another Surprize.

Yet, truly, I thought, it ought not have been. Why else the Depth of his Mourning, that seemed ceaseless? My Father had loved my Mother, and when she had died he had lost her so utterly that a Part of himself had died also. What had I thought? That his Refusal to wear any Colour, or to take a second Wife, was mere Stubbornness? No, if he was indeed a Free-thinker, believing in no God, no Forgiveness, no Resurrection, he could have no Consolation, for he could not expect her in Heaven, nor awaiting the last Trump on Judgement Daye. His World was one of black Despair and everlasting Grief.

An horrible Thought came to me: How can a Man who hath no Faith be truly good? I held my left Hand up before mine Eyes, and struggled to bestill the Trembling that had come upon it, but I might as well have tried to calm the shivering Grass.

CHAPTER EIGHT

On the Morrow, the fifteenth Daye of July, I left Shirelands in Company with Mr Fielding, and we travelled post-haste across Country to London, arriving at his Bow Street House a mere thirty-six Houres after our Departure.

We crosst a Landscape Sunneshine-bright with Wheat, and verily pleasing to the Eye, with Villages and Cottages spread out upon it as decorative Shapes upon a Pie-crust. Here and there on our first Daye of Travel we would pass an Hostelry, its Sign hanging above its Door and chearful Parson outside smoking on his Pipe; but we did not stop until very late, at a small roadside Inn whose Landlord I do not remember, for I fell straight into my borrowed Bed and slept solid for five Houres, after which Time Mr Fielding roused me, and we resumed our Journey.

I was most curious about Mr Fielding, whom I had now discovered to be none other than the celebrated—or rather, notorious—Author of *Tom Jones, A Foundling*. I found it astonishing that such a Personage should be known to my Father, and even more so that he should have known my Mother; but I was too shy to ask him about these Matters. Instead, I concentrated my Questioning upon Mr Fielding himself, and wherefore he had made the seeming odd Change of Profession from Novellist to Westminster Magistrate.

"When I wrote my Literary Works," Mr Fielding replied, "I wrote of things as they appear, not as they might be if we lived in a perfect World; I hoped perhaps to stir some Modicum of Human Compassion in my Readers' Breasts for those less fortunate, and possibly less virtuous, than themselves; but all my Achievement has been to make a convincing Fiction out of mine Impressions. My Tales have no Substance beyond their Pages. I have realised that 'tis far better to attempt to make a Difference beyond my Quill. So, Sir, I have downed it for the nonce—as far as Novels are concerned, at least.

"This Country," he continued, over the Rumble of the Carriage, "is presently undergoing a Period of great Consequence to its History, tho' most People know't not and could not care less if they did. The Whole of Europe is being tried and tested; worn out Philosophies, and the legal Edifices that sit upon them, are crumbling; the Discoveries and Decisions we make now will determine whether in two Centuries our Descendants are living under Civilisation or Barbarism. The Nation which we now create will form the Backbone of that future one—and I would ensure it—and to this End you may be sure that I use all my Influence—that they should habit in a World that is governed by fair and coherent Laws, in which Rich and Poor alike have no Fear to walk the Highways lest they be attacked in broad Dayelight. Indeed, that is a World I should fain live in My Self! I do my very best to ensure not only that our Laws are respected and upheld, but that they are just; for unjust Laws lend Legitimacy to future Tyrannies. As Magistrate, Tristan, I do not merely convict, I judge; and 'tis to be hoped I do so fairly."

I thought Mr Fielding's Ambition exceeding grand, as for the Life of me I could not apprehend how the Law, which by my Reckoning was more Fetter than Leash, could lead a culpable Nation out of Darkness and Ignorance, when Centuries of Religion had not managed it. Science, I thought, was far better suited to that Task, and had a stronger Chance of Success. But I kept my Peace.

Several Houres later, tired out and hungry after the Travel, I sate beside the Window in Mr Fielding's drawing Room, and listened to the City's Noises. Dogges barked, Children wailed, Wives argued, Horses neighed, Carts rumbled, Bells rang. I wondered for a Moment how I should stand to be immersed in all this Din and Filth, but before I could begin to be alarmed I heard Footsteps and a rattling Sound behind me. I turned to see the Lady of the House, to whom I had been but briefly introduced, entering the Room with a tea Tray in her Hands. Mrs Fielding smiled, put the Tray down upon a small Table, and began to stir the Tea with a long-handled silver Spoon. "Good Evening to you, Mr 'Art," she said, dropping her H upon the Floor and trampling on it. "'Ow do you like your Tea?"

Somewhat taken aback, but compleatly fascinated, I left the Window and took up a Seat opposite Mrs Fielding. I was aware that I was staring and I tried to recollect my Manners, but when she let the Spoon fall with a Clatter on the Tray and began to pour out the Tea, I could not help My Self.

Mrs Fielding did not seem to mind; unabashed, she presst into mine Hands a hot steaming Cup of sweet Tea, almost white with Milk. "There you go, Sir," she said. "Get that down you and you'll soon feel right as Rain." She smiled. She had a round, warm, pleasant Face that reminded me a little of Margaret. I thought she must be young; eight-and-twenty, perhaps. I smiled in return and took a tentative Sip from my Cup. The Tea tasted of Milk and Sugar and very little else.

"I'm sorry if 'tis weak," Mrs Fielding said. "But they are old Leaves. I would see about acquiring some Fresh, but we are practising Economy."

"Aha," I said.

Presumably in the Interest of Economy, Mrs Fielding did not take Tea herself, but instead sate with me whilst I drank, making light Conversation out of the Contents of the Pantry and the Price of Starch. When I had finished, she got to her Feet and had just lifted the Tray to take it back to the Kitchen when Mr Fielding appeared in the Doorway.

"Mary!" he cried, his Tone that of the most intense Anguish. "Put it down, Woman, for God's Sake!"

Mrs Fielding quickly replaced the tea Tray on the Tabletop, and rang the Bell for the parlour Maid. Then, she looked to be at something of a Loss, and after making a quick half-Curtsey to me, she left the Room.

Mr Fielding sighed, and came across to the Table, where he peered down at the tea things with an Expression not unlike that with which a convicted Man may look upon the Noose. "I must apologise for my Wife," he said. "She forgets her Place sometimes."

"I like her immensely," I said.

Mr Fielding looked at me somewhat strangely. "Do you?" he said.

"Well, so did I—so do I. She is a good Woman, despite . . ." his Voice trailed off. Then he cleared his Throat. "'Tis no Secret," he said, "but you may not know it: Mary is my second Wife; she was my first Wife's Maid."

"I see." I said, slowly.

"Do you, indeed? Do not you presume to smile at me, young Man. I am not proud of my Actions, but I did what my Conscience— and Justice—required of me."

"Yes, Sir," I said.

"Don't you 'Yes Sir, No Sir' at me, either, Tristan Hart. If you have something to say, then you must say it."

Brought thus unexpectedly to Scratch, I struggled to find the right Words with which to answer him. "I think, Sir," I said, carefully, "that Mrs Fielding is not a Wife of whom you need feel ashamed. Altho' I was somewhat startled by her Manner at first, she seems goodhearted, and kind."

Mr Fielding looked at me with the same penetrating Gaze he had turned upon my Father. "That," he told me, "was well said, and honestly, too, by your Countenance. There are many Men who would not—who could not—have answered thus. You will meet with some of them."

I realised by this that Mr Fielding's Marriage was considered by polite Society to be a great Scandal. Yet, to me, the Idea, tho' startling, did not seem improper, but rather the Opposite. It was surely intirely right that a Man should marry the Woman he had otherwise ruined; what Difference that she was of lower Station? Then I thought how unlike it had been that I should ever have married Margaret, especially if I had got her with Child. Should I have ruined her? I had never given it any Thought. Moreover, I realised that it was past Chance that I should have agreed with Mr

Fielding's Action toward Mary if I had not met and liked her before I had known it. I should have thought her naught but a conniving Whore, and him an old Fool.

The Houre being late, I shortly afterwards retired to Bed, and gave the Question no more Thought. It became apparent, though, in the Dayes that followed, that the Issue was a live one; scarce twenty-four Houres could be suffered to pass without the Sound of Mr Fielding's Voice groaning: "Mary, no!" at some small Lapse of Propriety upon her Part. Mary bore it well; she was indeed a goodhearted Woman and retained a surprizing Affection for her Husband despite his prickly Temper and evident Embarrassment. She was quite sensible of how her Station had been altered by her Marriage, but she was a practical Soule who disliked waiting for someone else to perform any Task she could compleat herself. Her Husband, for all his Disapproval, took full Advantage of this. Mr Fielding suffered greatly with the Gout, and altho' his Wits were as sharp as ever, the Pain made him absent minded. This Forgetfulness, combined with a Degree of Impetuosity that had not been curbed by Experience, led to many of his Affairs becoming shrouded in a Web of Confusion, which his Wife did her best to disentangle. In short, altho' he did not know it, he was as dependent upon Mary as my Father was upon Mrs H., and had she begun to act the Lady, he would have been utterly confounded.

The Habit, I must admit, was contagious; and deplorable as it is to offer to treat the Lady of the House as if she were its Maid, within seven Dayes I found My Self about it. It was simply easier to call on Mary Fielding's Help in practical Matters than to summon any of the household Servants. Nevertheless, I felt more than a little uncomfortable; and altho' Mary did not object, I sought to put a Check on my Demands and do as well as possible for My

Self. The Results of this Experiment were not encouraging; after mine Attempt to light the dining room Fire led Mrs Fielding to inquire loudly whether all Gentlemen were born Incompetents, I gave it up, and allowed things to continue as they were.

I had barely become accustomed to the Routine of the House, and it to me, when it was disrupted again, by the Advent of Mr Fielding's Brother.

Mr John Fielding had begun his Career in the Navy, and so could not be accused of congenital practical Incompetence. He was, however, compleatly blind, and commonly wore upon his Brow a black Ribband to signify his Condition to others. He was Resident in the Strand, where he was Proprietor of the Universal Register Office. However, he was commonly to be found in Bow Street, purportedly to assist his Brother in the carrying out of his Duties as Westminister Magistrate. This seemed strange to me. "How," I asked Mary, "can a blind Man tell whether the Accused hath a look of Guilt about him, or of Innocence?" Mary looked upon me pityingly, and continued polishing her Spoons.

Mr John Fielding, she explained, was blessed not only with an Intellect that was in every way the Equal of his Brother's, but also with a Power of Memory that Mary had never seen bettered. In addition to this, his Senses of Hearing, Touch, and Smell were so brilliantly acute that he was more aware of his Surroundings than many who retained their Sight. He was not easily fooled, and he did not suffer Fools gladly. In the Street, she said, he strode forth as if he expected all others to fall out of his Path, and to her ceaseless Amazement, they did.

My first Meeting with John Fielding took place upon the Afternoon of the first Daye of August, mere Houres after his own Arrival in Bow Street. Like his Brother, he had asked to meet me;

unlike him, he had the Advantage of being preceded by his Reputation. I answered his Summons with Alacrity.

Mr Fielding was waiting for me in the dining Room. He was a tall Man, quite young, but heavy of Build and deliberate in his Movements. He was seated at the Table, which as usual was bestrewn with his Brother's literary and legal Papers, with a wine Glass in his right Hand, and a pair of Mr Dolland's Spectacles, which he had just removed from his Nose, in his left. He did not look up, but gestured with his Spectacles towards a Chair upon the other Side of the Table and said: "Sit down, Sir."

I obeyed.

Mr John Fielding held the Spectacles up for me to inspect. "Black Lenses," he said. He placed them down upon the Table. "They are of no practical Use. Did you wonder?"

"I did, Sir."

"You thought: What Use are eye-Glasses to a blind Man? Make yourself comfortable; pour yourself a Glass of Claret."

"Thank you, Mr Fielding."

"So," John Fielding said, slowly. "You are Tristan Hart."

"I am, Sir." I was beginning to feel distinctly ill at Ease.

"When Henry told me that he had invited you to stay, I thought he must have gone stark mad. I told him as much. His Position, as Magistrate, is extreamly taxing. He has a Wife and young Children whom he barely sees, and he is not well. I told him that he could not additionally be responsible for the Education of so troubled a young Man as you appear to be."

"I have caused no Inconvenience!" I cried, suddenly afraid that the Path along which this Interview was leading was one which would return me to Berkshire.

"Yes; Henry also told me that. You have made a fair Impression upon my Brother, Mr Hart. So we have reached an Agreement. From now on your Interest must lie with me. If you require anything, then it is to me you must apply; likewise, should you commit any Misdemeanour whilst you are here, it will be to me that you will answer for it."

"Yes, Sir," I said. My Relief was such that it would have been audible to one even without John Fielding's Powers of Perception. His Expression softened, and his Manner with it.

"Forgive me, Tristan," he said. "I have no Desire to affright or oppress you. I have never had any Children of mine own. But I shall do my best by you *in loco parentis*. As long as you keep by the Rules of this Household, and of common Decency, I anticipate that we shall find our Association amicable." He took a deep Draught of Wine. Had he not been blind, I would have sworn on Oath that he was regarding me with a Stare every bit as piercing as his Brother's.

John Fielding, whether he desired it or not, had succeeded so perfectly in putting up my Guard that I dared not to approach him in any Matter whatsoever. For the whole Length of August and September I remained the most careful of house Guests. I made no Demands and sought to disturb the Rhythm of the Fielding House as little as possible. Rising every Daye at seven, I broke my Fast with the Family and then I spent Houres alone, exploring Mr Fielding's Library, where I remained, for the large Part, until Dinner. He was plainly a wider Reader than I; upon his Shelves I found Works of Theology and Law which I had never before seen; even the Writings of those Free-thinkers who had seduced mine own Father. However, the Intimations that Mr Fielding had given of my Preferment within the Scientific Circle remained unfulfilled, and although I did not think them forgotten on Purpose, it annoyed me that they had been forgot at all. On our Journey to London, he had suggested that it would be a desirable thing for me to visit the Anatomist William Hunter, whose Dissections and so forth were highly spoken of. I had been greatly excited by this Possibility; nothing, it seemed, would better further mine Education than the Opportunity of Study under this noted Man; but after that once no more Mention had been made of it. If I had been still permitted to tap Mr Fielding on the Issue I imagined that he would have corrected his Oversight at once; but I was now to deal directly with his Brother, and I would sooner have been thrown headlong into a bear Pit. I cursed My Self for not pressing the Matter when I had the Chance.

I had been frustrated in my dearest Wish, and as I could perceive no present Means of furthering it, I quickly became angry and rebellious. Having read my Way thro' the Library, I began the Habit of taking regular afternoon Walks thro' Covent Garden, in Company with the High Constable for Holborn, Mr Saunders Welch. Mr Welch had been, before he had been called to his present Profession, a Grocer, tho' I could not easily imagine him as such. He was a Titan of a Man; twice as wide as he was tall, and blessed, I was told, with a right Hook that could have floored a stallion Mule. His Manner was quiet, his Mode of Speech compelling, his Judgement, as far as I could ascertain, without Prejudice. I supposed that he had been assigned to me partly for my Protection and partly in Case I should do as my Father had warned and become violent. Much as I respected Mr Welch, I deeply resented this.

CHAPTER NINE

Mine Interest in the Covent Garden lay, of course, within its Brothels: those painted Ladies who inclined their Heads toward me as I passed, and sometimes blew me Kisses. If I could not be about the Business of Dissection, I thought, I should at least perform one Experiment. I would attempt Coition with one of these sweet Whores, and determine whether I could derive any Pleasure from the Act. If I could, then perhaps I could restore my Soule to the Innocence of its Time with Margaret. Perhaps I could perswade My Self that mere animal Intimacy could be enough.

Ever since that Night when I had put mine accursed Hands on Viviane, I had almost ceased to experience carnal Lust in the usual

Manner. I could not become aroused by the Thoughts of a Woman's Body, nor even of the Act itself; all that would suffice me was Pain; that foul Image of her Suffering that horrified and yet compelled me. More than once, longing for Release, I had attempted to turn the Desire inwards upon My Self; I had taken up my Cane and beat My Self as hard as I could stand across mine Arms and Thighs, but this achieved nothing. Bodily, I flinched from Pain; I hated it, as much as ever I had done; and yet some Flaw, some Insult, some Disease within my Passions caused me the Need to inflict it.

Mrs Haywood's was one of the most famous of the Houses of Pleasure operating out of Covent Garden at that Time. The Building itself was imposing, with a colonnaded Grecian Frontage and carved Stonework that bathed in the pink Light from the many Lamps that burned within its Windows. Upon the Doorstep stood Mrs Haywood's Bully, a heftily built Blackamoor who went by the Name of Daniel Bright. I liked him, altho' he terrified most People; for all his frightening Appearance, I could discern in him an Intelligence superior to that found among the common Herd of Men. He was roughly half the Width of Saunders Welch, but several Inches taller; I had made no Estimation of the Power of his Punch. It was Bright's Task to ensure that nothing disturbed the Peace and Tranquillity of the Establishment's Patrons as they arrived and left. He was much disliked by Footpads and by Beggars, and was not very much more popular with the Constables. Bailiffs, universally, hated him.

Mrs Haywood herself aspired to Elegance. She had been the Mistress of a prominent Peer of the Realm some Yeares before, and in Consequence saw no Reason why she should not stile herself a Person of Fashion of the first Water. Somewhere in her forties, tho' 'twas hard to tell her Age with any Surety, she wore burgundy

Silks, and a tall Wigg of dark chestnut Colouration that was composed almost intirely of Human Hair. Her Complexion, by contrast, was compleat Whitelead. She was taller than most Women, even without the Wigg, and cut an admirable Figure. I was not certain whether I liked her or not. She had a measuring Look when she regarded me, which I mistrusted, as if she thought that she should understand me better than I did. Saunders Welch, for his Part, liked her. He said she kept a tight Ship and gave little Trouble to the Law, altho' he feared her to be deep in Debt.

Nevertheless, when I decided to proceed with mine Experiment, it was Mrs Haywood's Brothel that I chose for my Laboratory. Mr Welch, who privately, I thought, considered me a Nuisance, was more than happy to leave me within the Portico under the Eye of Daniel Bright, and so I passed within, mine own King for the first Time in many Months.

I sate My Self upon a side Chair and waited for Mrs Haywood, who, it had been explained to me, would attend as soon as she was able. To pass the Time, I looked around the Hall. The classical Theme of the Outside had been continued and extended here, as if to perswade the Visitor that he had left his own Century and entered Rome. At each Corner stood a Statue of Venus, illuminated by a tall Candelabrum. The Floor was covered by a tiled Pattern of red and white Diamonds, about a central Mosaic depicting the Rape of the Sabine Women. Not any Rome, then, but Rome at its Height, the Rome of Octavius and Virgil, beautifull, sensual, potent. The Image did not arouse me. I crosst my Fingers and hoped.

I had not been waiting longer than three Minutes when Mrs Haywood emerged from a Chamber to my left and came forwards to catch both mine Hands in hers and buss me warmly upon the Cheek. I was so startled that I winced.

"You are very welcome, Sir," she said. "Pray accompany me into my sitting Room, where we may talk in Comfort."

I permitted her to lead me thro' the Door into the Chamber beyond. The Light in here was low, despite that it was yet Daye. The Shutters were closed, the Curtains drawn, and red Coals smoaked in the ornate Fireplace. Two Roman-stiled Lamps stood in here, also; these were lit, and an intimate golden Circle spread about them. Near the Centre of this were positioned three hard backed Chairs and a small Table. Mrs Haywood did not remark on these, but led me to a long Sopha lying just without the Compass of the Light, and bade me sit beside her.

"Now, my dear Sir," she said. "We shall get to know each Other a little, and then, if you are of such a Mind, I shall introduce you to some of my charming Girls and you may have your Choice of them."

I understood that I ought to speak, but my Voice had deserted me. I merely nodded. Mrs Haywood smiled and presst mine Hand in a Manner that she must have meant to be reassuring. "You are quite safe here, Mr Hart," she said. "My Business is with Pleasure, not with Law. Within these Walls you will find that you are free to pursue whatever Desire you incline toward. I like my Visitors to feel that they are utterly at home." She tilted her Head, graciously, and smiled again.

"Indeed," I said. "I have, I trust, no Desires that are unnatural." I stoppt suddenly, then began anew. "I seek only a natural, healthy, country Girl—mine Appetites are intirely—healthy." I stoppt again. I seemed determined to damn My Self, and ruin mine Experiment, with every Word that I let out of my Mouth.

"I have a full dozen such pretty Girls in my Care," said Mrs Haywood. "None of them are Virgins, of course, but you need not mind that. You are lodging at Mr Fielding's House, are you not?"

"I have Money with me," I said.

"There is no need to think about that yet; I know you will be good for the Sum. Do you wish to proceed?"

"What?" I said. "Oh—yes."

Mrs Haywood clappt her Hands, and a very young Maidservant entered from another Room beyond bearing a silver Tray, upon which was a single crystal Glass three Quarters full and a small Plate of sugar Flowers. She was followed by three Girls of varying Proportions, all most winningly attired in country Caps and Dresses of light coloured Calico. They seated themselves upon the three hard backed Chairs, and without a Word or a Glance in my Direction took out their Workbaskets and began to Stitch.

I lifted the crystal Glass from the Maid's Tray, and had half drained it before I had realised what I was doing.

Mrs Haywood, plainly sensing mine Anxiety, placed her cool Hand softly upon my heated Cheek, and with that same measuring Look that she had turned on me before, said: "Are you certain that this is really what you want, Mr Hart?"

"They are pretty Girls," I said.

"Indeed, they are. And not one of them will disappoint." She got to her Feet and crosst the Room to where the Girls were sitting, and placed her Hand upon the back of the nearest, who had blonde Hair in Curls under her little Cap, and Breasts that seemed upon the Point of bursting from her tight Bodice. "This is Juliette," she said. "She possesses great Skill with her Mouth."

Juliette looked up, ran her Tongue round her Teeth, and smiled; the vacant, calculated Smile of a Woman who cares nothing, neither one Way nor the other. I tried to imagine My Self lying with her, and found the mere Act of Imagination beyond me. This pretty, natural young Whore had nothing, was nothing, that I could desire.

Perhaps, I thought, Margaret hath spoiled me, even before I laid mine Eye upon Viviane. She had, at least, wanted me, if only for a Time. The Recollection flashed upon me of our first Moment of Intimacy.

"Get on wi' it then," Margaret had said; and then, sitting up again as I franticklly had pondered how I was supposed to do that: "Oh, Mr Hart, you ent got the leastest Clue, 'ave you? Never mind. Come here, my Darling."

Mrs Haywood narrowed her Eyes, and regarded me again. Then, without Warning, she clappt her Hands. "Leave us," she said. The three Girls rose at once, as silently and obediently as they had come in, and departed.

"Why have you done that?" I cried.

"Mr Hart," Mrs Haywood said, settling herself once more beside me on the Sopha. "I have no Wish to waste my Girls' Time, or yours, or, least of all, mine own. Let us speak plainly. Is it your own Sex that you desire?"

"What! No! No. Would that—I wish—"

"You wish what? You may speak freely, Sir: indeed, you must. There is no one here who would judge you."

Some small Alteration in her Voice, or in her Eyes, I knew not what, gave me the Courage to believe her. I cleared my Throat and took a deep Breath.

"I wish that it were Boys," I said. I spoke slowly. "It is not. There is a Demon within me, Mrs Haywood. I have Desires, Longings, that no Man should have. Dreadful Longings."

"Do you crave the Lash?"

"What?"

"How now, Sir," she said. "You are not the only Gentleman to have such exotick Tastes. Why, I have among my Patrons an highly respected Member of the Privy Council who comes every Tuesdaye for a Whipping."

"It is not that!" I exclaimed. "I have tried it— it doth nothing. The Evil is within mine Hands, and in my Head, and my—" Yet again I came to an abrupt Halt. This Time, however, it was not thro' Fear of what I should say. As I spoke, mine Imagination was running wild upon an hundred things, too terrible to voice, and my Lusts had at once arisen, like a Volcano.

Mrs Haywood looked over my State, stood up, and took mine Hand again. "My Dear," she said, with surprizing Friendliness. "I would very much like you to meet Pauline."

Taking a Candle in her Hand, despite the Daye, Mrs Haywood led me thro' the House and several Pad-locked Doors, which she took Care to seal again after our Passage, till we came to a low attick Bedroom furnished intirely in burgundy Satin and dark Iron. A low Fire burned within the Grate, with a Sopha before it, just as in my Laboratory, and the Room was comfortably warm. Supine upon the Bed was a young Woman, wearing only a night-Shift, her Ankles and her Wrists secured by thick Shackles, such as I had seen upon Prisoners, to the bed Posts. I caught my Breath.

"Pauline," said Mrs Haywood softly, approaching the Bed. "Pauline, my Dear, you have a Visitor."

Pauline—but I did not believe that to be her true Name—opened her Eyes, and looked upon Mrs Haywood with such a Gaze as Lovers use, between themselves, when they are alone. She was neither particularly young, nor pretty; being quite scrawny, with a hardened Face; and yet there was a Quality about her, of Grace, perhaps, that I had never before seen in a Woman and could never have imagined in a Whore.

Mrs Haywood turned to me and held out her Hand for me to grasp. It was well that she did. I was beginning to feel as tho' I might fall down. God help me, I thought. Nat's Orgy was nothing compared to this. Then she waved her other Hand, and to my farther Surprize, from the darkest Corner of the Room shuffled an old Whore, dresst intirely in shabby Black, and carrying a laced Pocket, which, with a wordless and clumsy Curtsey, she handed to Mrs Haywood before returning to an Armchair, in which, I realised, she had been seated.

Mrs Haywood unlaced the Pocket and withdrew the Keys to Pauline's Shackles. The Locks opened without Sound, without Resistance. Finally, the Woman was free. I wanted to watch her stretch her sore Limbs, to apply Salve to the raw Skin where her Shackles had chafed; she did neither. She knelt before us on the Bed, her Eyes cast down.

"Turn around," Mrs Haywood said. "And lift up your Gown."

Pauline obeyed at once. Mrs Haywood raised the Candle close by her Hindquarters, so that I might see more clearly.

"Great God!" I said.

The Woman's Buttocks and Thighs were criss-crosst by a great Number of savage Weals, some red, some black, some fading to dull yellow, some mere Scars. Some, I perceived, had been formed by the Action of a Whip; still others bore the smooth, sharp Outline of the Birch, deathly white Flesh upraised about a single scarlet Thread, where the soft Skin had been rippt open by the Blow. She had lifted the night-Dress only to her Waist, but I could discern the Traces of still more Welts, still more Cuts, extending upwards over the soft Tissue of her Ribs towards her Scapulae.

I was horrified, and yet; and yet—a dark Wonder began to shiver and to rise within me, black as the Wave that once had consumed me; glorious and terrible as Joy.

Half unthinking, I stretched forwards mine other Arm, and at a Nod from Mrs Haywood, I carefully caressed the devastated Flesh. The Ridges of scar Tissue were surprizing hard against my Fingertips, but between them, Pauline's Skin was delicate as Spidersilk.

"Oh," I said. "She is beautifull."

Desire began to pulse within me. Desire to hurt; Desire, Desire.

"You may whip her, or fuck her, as you please," Mrs Haywood said.

Desire, both like and unlike that which had driven me to attack Viviane, drummed hard thro'out my Body. It beat fierce and fast within mine Hands, within my Loins, a Passion overwhelming, irresistible, and yet seeming now as if it were mine own, a Part of me. I suddenly understood that not only could I do whatever I liked to this Pauline, but that she would not struggle, or curse, but would accept, without Resentment or Disgust, every Mortification I should lay upon her Flesh. The Realisation caused mine Head to reel, and my Body to sway a little as I stood. I remembered how I had forced Viviane to her Knees and thus forced back the Drumming. I recalled the cruel Delight I had taken in her Pain as I had twisted her Arm, and she had screamed aloud; the Power, ultimate as it had then seemed, in that Instant; transfiguring every Atom of my Body, of my Mind, of my frightened Soule.

Was it Wickedness? Perhaps.

Pauline shuddered under my Caress, and the candle Flame flickered.

"Shall you whip her?" Mrs Haywood asked.

"No," I said. "Not yet." The Truth was that I did not know how. I feared lest I should misjudge my Blow and infict some lasting Injury upon her Kidneys, or her Spine.

"Very well." Mrs Haywood smiled, and releasing mine Hand from her Grasp, she departed the Room, pulling the Door shut behind her. The old Whore coughed in her Corner.

Was it Wickedness? I could not tell. I did not care. Horrour and Lust had merged in me to cast a Shaddowe over my Will. I knew that I should not have fought it, even if I could have.

"Take off your Gown," I instructed Pauline. My Voice sounded thick and greedy in mine Ears. With the same obedient Grace she had shewn Mrs Haywood, Pauline complied, and I at last beheld her in her Nakedness.

The fresh Skin of her Back was latticed with a Plethora of Lashes, red and black and white. I stroked mine Hand along the undulating Depression of her Spine, feeling the Expansion and Contraction of her Ribcage as she breathed, the crimson Rhythm of her Heartbeat.

Swiftly, but with shaking Hands, I unlaced my Breeches. I could hear mine own Breath, raw and fast within the warm Stillness. I placed mine Hand upon the Base of her Cranium and pushed her forwards, Face down upon the Bed in front of me. I hesitated for an Instant, then the red Shaddowe fell once more across mine Heart, and I reached between her Thighs and pulled them open to reveal the pale Slit of her Cunt, hairless and smooth as Glass. With the Fingers of my free Hand I spread apart both Pairs of Lips, then climbed upon the Bed behind her. I entered her as forcibly, as intirely, as I dared; then the whole World turned to Scarlet.

Minutes later, I collapsed, with mine Heart hammering within me and every Muscle in my Body turned to Water. I withdrew, lay down beside her on the silken Sheets, and for the first Time, properly looked into her Face.

Pauline's Face was flushed, her thin Lips swollen. My Reason slowly coming back to me, I reflected that it was strangely gratifying to think that I might have somehow given her Pleasure, despite that she was but a Whore and I had not thought of it once. Then I thought of mine Experiment and could not decide whether it had proved Failure or Success. I had lain with a Woman, I had experienced Pleasure, but under such Circumstances that I could hardly imagine mine Innocence to have been regained. I thought of Margaret, and of how she should have chided if I had left her so precipitantly after a mere Minute. But there was, in Truth, no Comparison. Margaret would never have suffered the Indignities of Lash and Shackle that had both debased and elevated this Pauline.

I caught my near Hand within Pauline's Hair and dragged her down to lie beside me. "What is your Name?" I asked her. "Your real Name, not the one that Mrs Haywood hath given you."

She blinked, surprized. "Polly Smith," she said, at last. Her Accent was that of my native Berkshire.

"Mine is Mr Hart," I told her. "We will meet again, I think. If 'meet' can be said to be the proper Word."

Polly Smith smiled, and averted her Gaze.

"Doth my Countenance offend you?" I asked.

Polly looked puzzled. "No, Sir," she said.

"Then why look you away?"

In Answer, Polly turned her Eyes towards me, and meeting mine without the least Trace of Shame, she said. "You better hit me."

"Wherefore?"

"No one wants to buy a Pig in a Poke," Polly said. "You 'aven't made me bawl."

I stared at her in Admiration, and no little Disbelief. Her Expression was intirely serious, without Sophistry or Deceit. But I did not want to hurt her. That Passion had been pacified in me when I had fucked her, and I could not at Will re-agitate it. Yet, if I did not hurt her, why was I here, and not with pretty Juliette?

"What will you do?" I asked her. "When your Backside is as tough as Leather, and no Man will even look at you? When Mrs Haywood hath no longer any Use for you, and you can be of no Use to yourself?"

She smiled. "Mrs Haywood will always have a Use for me," she said. "The Thing is whether I 'ave any Use for you."

I drew back my free Hand and struck her hard across the Face.

CHAPTER TEN

To the open Amusement of Saunders Welch, I became a frequent Visitor to Mrs Haywood's Establishment. He might have been somewhat less diverted had he been at all aware of the Nature of the Activity in which I was participating. Mr Welch had strong Views, as did both Brothers Fielding, on Violence between Men and Women. But the Innocent who had feared that he was devilish had gone; his Place taken by a Fiend who feared I knew not what.

I still enjoyed, occasionally, to fuck, but these Times were becoming rarer. The Act itself delighted me no more now than it had ever done, but sometimes it was necessary for me to surrender to the red Mist and throw Polly, or one of the other experienced Whores, to the Floor, or pin her down upon a Bed. Mrs Haywood did not offer me her pretty young Girls any more.

Under Mrs Haywood's Tutelage, and the expressionless Visage of the old Whore, I dedicated Houres to the Acquisition and Perfection of my Form with the Lash, the Cat, the Scourge, and the Birch Rod. I diligently practised the fine Art of binding Ankles, Wrists, and Knees in such Ways as to induce the most exquisite Agonies, without dangerously limiting the Flow of Blood; which, as Harvey had proved before me, doth indeed pass betwixt the Heart and the Extremities at a tremendous Rate. I became adept at provoking Screams of the truest Pitch and Intensity; bright Rainbows of refracted Anguish that lit up the Room. The purest Shrieks often would be enough to bring me compleat Satisfaction.

Sometimes, when I was still at the Start of this Education, I imagined My Self in my Laboratory, and the Whore before me my Subject, as I had imagined Viviane; but these Phantasms really disturbed me more than they delighted, and after a short while I gave up their Pretense.

Outside the Brothel, I became more confident. I sang, I skippt, I whistled. I carried Trays for Mary and even kissed her upon the Cheek when her Husband and Brother-in-Law were nowhere near. Life was become a Joy to me instead of a Chore. I even began to forget mine apparent Madness. No longer did I study Descartes and Locke with the Desperation of a condamned Man. I suffered no Delusion, no Phrenzy, no Melancholia. If I had, verily, been mad once, I thought, I never need be so again. Perhaps I never had been. Perhaps the Disorders my Senses had suffered indeed had sprung from some other Cause. Perhaps I had eaten something rotten.

Perhaps I had been exceptionally drunk. Perhaps there had been in the Aire some Drugge.

Fascinating, the Possibility that the non-natural things could effect such an Alteration upon my Perceptions.

This Mutation in my Spirits, and the Change it wrought upon mine whole Demeanour, made an unlooked-for Impression upon John Fielding, who before had considered me to be both troubled and troublesome. Upon St Lucie's Daye, he called me into his Presence to deliver a Rebuke upon my Conduct. The after-dinner Room was still, and apart from that given by the lively Fire, without Light. I stood, mute and resentful, before the Chimney-piece, my Face more than half in Shaddowe.

"'Twere preferable," he said, sitting back in his Chair and staring unnervingly in my very Direction thro' his darkened Glasses, "that you devote less of your Time, and your Father's Fortune, to Whoring."

"'Tis not excessive," I protested.

Mr Fielding laughed, the first Time I had ever heard him to do so. It was not an unkind Laugh, and it carried about it some small Intimations of Regret. "And that were ever the Defense!" he said. "But it will not wash out in your Case, Tristan. Mr Welch has told me; you call upon Mrs Haywood three Dayes out of every seven, and nine in this past Fortnight. Your Whoring is excessive; and, I suspect, obsessive also."

I felt my Colour rise within my Cheeks. It was not for Mr Fielding to judge the Quality of my Whoring, I thought, nor for Saunders Welch to bear Witness to him upon it. But I said nothing.

"It is clear to me that you are restless and bored," Mr Fielding went on. "Exactly as I should expect from a young Man of your Wit and Intelligence who hath no useful Occupation to pursue.

Therefore, my Brother and I have made Arrangements for you to begin your Studies in Anatomy with Dr William Hunter."

"I thought it to have been forgot," I stammered.

"Not so," Mr Fielding said. "My Brother and I came to the Conclusion that it were better if you were not faced with too much Expectation immediate upon your Arrival. Now you are settled, it is best that you proceed upon your Education."

I stared at Mr Fielding, and I was glad, deeply glad, that he could not see my Face, for I had no Control of it. If it had but occurred to the Brothers Fielding to inform me at the first of their Decision— but it had not and so here I stood; my Mind, for sure, as clean and sharp as a Lancet, but mine Hands as cruel as a Cut, and my Soule so steept in Vice it might as well been given straight up to the Devil. And all this come about because I feared to have been forgot! How was I now to go to Dr Hunter and study Dissection and Medicine; how could I stand within his Rooms and state that I wished to study Pain in order to prevent it? How could I, in short, convince him of a Creed in which I did not now believe? I could not. And yet, if I were to say that I had changed my Mind and no longer felt deserving of the Prize I had dedicated mine whole Life to achieving, I should be conceding not only my Soule, but a clear Victory.

No, no! I shook My Self, recalled to Mind those Justifications I had taken Comfort from when Doubts about mine Habit had before assailed me. It was true, I told My Self, that mine were not common Tastes, but my Vice was minor in Comparison to many. I did not desire Children, or Beasts. Moreover, it was not necessarily true that I was intirely evil. How could I be evil when the bright Sunne stroaked me, the Rains kissed me, and the Beauty of Creation arched over me in the blue Bowl of the winter Sky? How could I be evil when I took such Care that the Screams that pealed about mine Ears were followed always by the Chimes of sweet Relief when Pain came to an End? How could I be evil when I felt so happy?

The Rector had been wrong. The Tutor had been wrong. I had been wrong.

Whatever the Cause and Nature of my Need, it did not unfit me for the Study of Anatomy or the furtherance of the Human Condition. It was mine; mine was therefore its Comprehension, mine its Control. It dictated nothing. It would make no Difference.

"I shall be glad," I said, "to begin Work with Dr Hunter as soon as may be."

"You have until the twentieth of January to prepare yourself. And you had better explain to Mrs Haywood that she will not be seeing you so often in the Future. I am sure that this Intelligence will leave her quite bereft, but she will recover."

I could not determine whether it would seem impudent if I were to laugh, so I remained silent. Mr Fielding sighed, and leaned back in his Chair. Then, to my Surprize, he removed his Wigg, ran his Fingers across the Stubble that covered his Head, and scratched his Scalp.

"Damned things, Wiggs," he said. "Ridiculously expensive, in constant Need of Maintenance, and as full of Lice as this wretched City. Why do we wear them?"

I was not certain whether his Question was rhetorical, but I ventured upon an Answer. "Habit," I said. "And the Fashion, Sir."

"Fashion! Ha! Naught but a Means to delude and torment innocent Men and Women. What Virtue hath Fashion, truly?"

I looked down at My Self. My grey silk Frock, which I had purchased from my Taylor only two Dayes since, gleamed in the

Firelight with the perfect Sheen of newly polished Pewter. I had delighted in the Knowledge that its Shade was matched exactly by that of my Shoes, and that the silver Buttons of the Frock had been cast with the same Imprint as the Buckles thereof. I looked up.

"None, Sir, I suppose—excepting perhaps an aesthetic one."

"Do you believe that Virtue and Beauty are, therefore, equivalent?"

"Perhaps," I said.

"And yet the most thorough Corruption may lurk within the fairest of Breasts. In Medicine, Sir, as you will see; and in Law, and certainly too within the Human Soule."

"But what of non Human things?" I protested. "I was thinking of the Beauty of a clear Sky, or of a Seabird in Flight against a Cloud, or a musical Note, perfect in its Execution. Are these things not good?"

"Of the three," John Fielding said. "Only the third hath any Good I can appreciate. But continue, Tristan."

"If they have any Good," I said, "'tis surely by respect of some Virtue that inhere within them; and this Virtue, plainly, is Beauty."

"Then you have suggested that Beauty is a Virtue, but not that Virtue is Beauty."

"Is not Virtue beautifull, Sir?"

"Truly, it is; because Beauty inheres within it, as it inheres within a clear Sky or a Note of perfect Musick. But you must not confuse a Quality inherent in a thing with the thing itself."

I was silent for a Minute as I reconsidered my Position. It had become of personal Importance to me that I should emerge victorious from this Spat, and this Desire momentarily overpowered mine Adherence to the Rules of philosophical Engagement. "I did not state that the two things are equivalent," I said. "I merely answered: 'Perhaps'. But for the Purpose of our Question regarding Fashion it doth not matter whether Beauty be a Virtue or a Quality within it. Beauty necessarily inheres within Fashion; 'tis as much Fashion's Purpose as is Signification of Rank or Fortune. If it were not, Persons of Fashion would perforce appear as dull as Ducks. So Fashion hath the Quality of Beauty, if not necessarily the Virtue." I paused. "But you, Sir, have not proved that Virtue doth not inhere within Beauty. If a clear Note be good, 'tis not Beauty alone that can make it so, but Goodness."

Mr Fielding laughed. "Therefore, Beauty and Virtue may not be intirely identical, but it is the Devil's Job to separate them. I salute you, Sir; but I still shall not put on that insufferable Wigg."

I did not know whether I had won, or whether he had chosen to let me think it so. But at that Moment I began to perceive how it could be possible for me to germinate a real and honest Liking for Mr John Fielding. I permitted My Self the Risk of a small Snicker.

I wrote at once with these exciting Newes to Nathaniel, and also to Jane. To Jane, in addition, I apologised for my brutish Behaviour on my last Night at Shirelands Hall. I told her that I was plagued by the deepest Remorse, which was true, and that I was missing her, which was not. To Nathaniel I wrote the Opposite. I was missing him dreadfully, and whenever I considered the Circumstances of our Severance I felt a Nail drive thro' mine whole Heart. But I could not apologise for the thing that I had done.

I received on Christmas Eve a Reply from Jane, who in a most forgiving Tone that made me feel my Shame all the more keenly,

told me that mine Apologies were unnecessary. My Father had
at last resumed taking his Meals out of his Study, and Life
continued at Shirelands more or less as it had always done.
Christmas was to be a quiet Affair, and I should be glad that I
was in London, despite the Season. Mine Aunt sent her Regards,
and so did James Barnaby.

"*It will gladden yr Heart to know, Brother,* (Jane wrote) *that a Dayte
has finally been Fixt upon for my Weddynge. We are to be Marryed from
Shirelands, in St Peter's Church, next Yeare upon the Eighth of June. Mr
B. has taken up the Lease of Withy Grange, which is barely five Miles
Distant from Shirelands, and which shall suit us very Well. He is determined that it be readye for June, and is about some fashionable Improvements
to the View which must be Compleated before we can move in. We are to
have fine Lawns and a Grecian Valley, such as Mr Broun hath made at
Stowe.*

She continued in this Vein for an intire Page, but I had lost
Interest, and skippt ahead to the Ending.

*Rector R. and Family are Well, and have askd me to Conveye to you their
best Wishes. They are Presently quite Crampt as they have*

(here I was forced to turn the Letter)

*their Montague Cousins staying with them againe. Their Mother is Ill
and the eldest Boy gone into the Nayvye so there is no one to look after
them except—*

(I turned the Letter)

an Unmarried Uncle. I send you my Deepest Love, deare Tristan, and I praye to see you soon, upon my Weddynge if not before. I am rn out of Spc, d^r B^r. But I rem y^r hum. and lov^g S^r, Jane Hart."

If the Rector's Family are well, I thought, then why no Newes of Nathaniel?

"Doth it not seem strange to you," I complained to Mary Fielding, who was presently come into the Room, "that my Sister says nothing of my Friend, whom I had expressly asked after?"

I held out the Letter for her to peruse. Mary took the Sheet from me and read it, carefully, and every Word aloud. I left her in the drawing room Doorway and kicked mine Heels beside the Window, watching an antient Pedlar and his Dogg make an erratick, circuitous Progress thro' the busy Street. Mrs Fielding finished, refolded the Letter, and held it out to me. "I don't know, Mr 'Art," she said. "If your Sister hath naught to do with your Friend, mayhap she hath no Newes of him to repeat."

I took the Missive back and regarded Mary more closely than I had done before. "You look troubled, Mrs Fielding," I said.

Mary sighed. "I am, Sir," she said. She seemed then upon the Point of saying more, but stoppt, and wrung her Hands. I put mine Hand upon her Shoulder.

"Mrs Fielding," I said. "What is the Matter?"

Mary Fielding pulled herself together, shaking mine Hand away and giving Vent to a small Laugh, high and thin, that had no Mirth in it. "'Tis of no Consequence to you." She paused for a Moment, then went on: "Altho' how Liza is to get those blood Spatters from your Shirts I don't know. If you must visit the Cockpits, Sir, I would that you'd stand farther from the Ring. Not that there'll be any 'ope of getting them out now, not with you going off to study with Dr 'Unter." She gave a shudder. "'E is a great Doctor, Mr

Fielding says, and a kind Man, with lovely Manners, and a charming Accent. I'll tell Liza to try Vinegar."

"Mary!"

"What, Sir?"

"What is wrong?"

"Oh, Mr 'Art," she said. "I'm feared I have done something very stupid."

Then she explained about the Gypsy. There were many of them about, she said, all over the Country, by the Sound of it; and she knew it was dangerous to have aught to do with them. But this one had been an old Woman; harmless, Mary thought; so very old her Eyes were like black Prunes in her Head, which had been brown and wrinkled as a Conker. She had come to the back Door selling Holly and Mistletoe; and Mary did so love fresh Greenery indoors at Christmas-time, she would have as much of it as possible; so she had—foolish Mary!—invited her in, and they had talked long over Tea. And then, only then, had Mary Fielding noticed the Baby on the Gypsy's Back.

"The prettiest little thing I ever did see," Mary said. "I can't understand how it was I didn't see it at the first, for once I had I couldn't look at anything else, so dear it was. So then she asked me to look after it, for but an Houre or two—"

All this, she said, had taken place at nine in the Morning, and it was now well past four.

"If you believe that she hath abandoned it, then it must go into the Foundling Hospital," I said.

"Oh!" Mary wailed. "And won't Mr Fielding be angry! A Foundling, left in this 'ouse! But—but would you come and see it, Mr 'Art? I thought, with your Knowledge of Anatomy you might—"

"What?"

"Please come and see, Sir; I darest not talk too loud on it."

Thoroughly perplext, altho' greatly amused by the Irony of a Foundling being left in Henry Fielding's House (altho' not, as in his infamous novel, in his bed), I let Mary lead me to the Kitchen, where a plain willow Basket sate at safe Distance from the Fire, which was crackling chearfully. The Kitchen smelled deliciously of Sausage-meat and Spices, despite the Fact that we were only to eat Sundaye's Leftovers tonight. Mrs Fielding, acting on my behalf, had won the Argument over which Stuffing to order for the Morrow's Turkey, and I caught the distinctive salty Whiff of Oysters mixt with the sharp Tang of Lemon. My Mouth began to water.

"I warn you, Mrs Fielding, I have no Experience of Children," I said. "And little Liking for them, either. I shall doubtless make it squall."

The Infant did indeed begin to stir at the Sound of my Voice, and kicking forth its Feet and flailing its Hands it set the Basket quite into Motion. But it did not weep. Instead, an high pitched, wheezing Cry came from it, halfway betwixt a musical Note and an Hiss.

"There there, my pretty Poppet," Mrs Fielding said, and she lifted the small wriggling thing, still wrappt in its woollen Blanket, from its Bed. "Oh, I don't know how to hold you, I'm sure. There—" changing the Babe's Position somehow—"That's better. Mr 'Art, please take a Look. I don't know what to think."

At first, I thought the Child perfectly common. It had a pretty enough Face, with large round grey Eyes that stared out at me with the unsettling Intensity typical of Children. It looked very young; a dozen Weeks at most; probably it was younger. I had no Measure by which to judge the Maturity of Babies. Then the Child yawned, and I caught a glimpse of a Row of white Teeth, lining its rosy Gums like miniature Needles.

Did I see that? I thought. I could not be intirely sure. I steppt closer and peered into the Infant's Face.

"That isn't all, Sir," said Mary Fielding. She began with the utmost Care to unwrap the Blanket, soothing and petting the Baby as she did so. "I thought to change her Clout; it had been a long while, and I thought she must be foulcd. I don't like that People leave them." The Blanket now open, she cradled the naked Infant in the Crook of her Arm. "Is she a 'Uman, Mr 'Art?"

The Baby was female, but that was the least noteworthy thing about it. Intirely along both Sides of the Torso, beginning halfway down the Forearm and extending to the Ankle, there stretched a wide Membrane of translucent living Tissue, pink with Blood. Immediately, I thought of Mrs H., of Nathaniel, and of Goblin Babes.

"Egad!" I said. "'Tis a young Bat!"

As if in Agreement with mine Assessment, the Baby began to wave its Hands; its Wings, for so I had already decided to stile them, causing a Turbulence in the Aire that set Mrs Fielding's Cap-strings all a-dancing.

"Is it Magick, Sir?" said Mary Fielding in a tremulous Voice.

"Aye," I said. "And Mary Toft gave birth to Rabbits. Mr Fielding would be angry indeed if he were to hear you say that. The Child is but deformed—spectacularly so."

"She is a 'Uman Child, then?"

"It is without Question a Human Child. Not a Bat, and not a Changeling." I indicated to Mary that she should lay the Child upon the Table, that I might examine it more closely. Mary called to Liza to make Room upon the Tabletop, which was covered otherwise with Breadcrumbs and Milk and other things that I assumed to have something to do with Christmas Dinner, then she laid down the Baby, still in its Blanket. I gently took hold of the Infant's right Arm and stretched it out, and did the same thing to the left. Both Limbs moved, I thought, normally. I repeated the Exercise with both Legs, and again found that the membranous Wings did not seem to interfere with the Action of the Parts. "Well, it will not be crippled," I said. With growing Excitement, for, I thought, I should greatly like to shew Dr Hunter this Marvell, I ran my Fingers lightly along the Tissue of the left Wing. It was as soft and pliable as Velvet. "How extraordinary," I said. I thought: How beautifull.

Fearing that the little thing take cold, I tried to fold the Blanket once again about it, but failed, and steppt back. Mrs Fielding shot me a withering Look, and with an Ease that was astonishing to me she swaddled the flapping Baby and replaced it delicately within its Basket.

"I am surprized," I said, "that the Gyspy hath left it. They earn much Money out of such Freaks at Fairs, and the Like."

"Shall I tell Liza to take 'er to the 'ospital, Mr 'Art?"

"No," I said. "I should very much like to keep it until I have shewn Dr Hunter. He may have another Suggestion. I must confess My Self reluctant to see it go; I had never imagined that a Deformity of this Nature was possible."

Mary Fielding's Shoulders sagged. "I don't suppose," she said, "that the old Woman will come back for her, will she?"

I looked again into Mary's anxious Face and came to a Decision. "If she doth not," I said, "then you need not trouble the Hospital. I shall procure a Wet Nurse in the Town to raise it at mine own Expense. It is the oddest Creature I have ever seen, and I am quite enchanted by it."

At this Declaration, about which I was in compleat earnest, Mary's Expression changed intirely; she began to laugh. "Mr 'Art," she said. "I credit you are getting as 'are-brained as Mr Fielding. He would have all the Sorrow in the World undo itself and fade away because he willed it so. You cannot support a Child, Sir; you are not yet twenty. I shall speak with Mr Fielding and he shall decide what is to be done. I know I should have told him already, but I had not the Courage."

At this Point the kitchen Clock chimed the Houre of five, and as this was nigh upon Time for Dinner, Mrs Fielding and her Servants chivvied me back up-Stairs. I returned to the drawing Room to await the Bell and ponder once again upon Jane's Letter, and the Absence of Nathaniel from it. Then I fell to considering the little Bat and what was to become of it. I feared for its Future should it enter the Foundling Hospital. Even supposing it survived— which was not likely—who would want a Maid with Wings? It would in all Probability end up in some Establishment akin to Mrs Haywood's, at the Mercy of some Monster like to Me. I disliked that Notion utterly.

Christmas Eve Dinner was not a grand Affair by any Means, as Festivities were planned for the Morrow; but evidently Mary did not feel it was sufficiently dull to enliven it with her Newes of the Foundling. We sate beneath the Holly in the dining Room, the ash Logs in the Fire burning high and fierce, and ate cold Beef. Mr Fielding complained loudly about his Gout, and then embarked upon a bitter Monologue contemning the open-palmed Practices of his Predecessor in the Magistracy, who had, he said, encouraged every Pimp in the Neighbourhood to think that he could buy the Law. I privately questioned whether Mr Fielding's relentless Integrity did not sometimes cause more Trouble than it deserved.

I would not normally have betrayed any Confidence of Mary's, but because I wholeheartedly believed that she would tell her Husband, when she met with the proper Moment to do so, and because I felt My Self to be involved in the Matter, I sought an Audience with John Fielding in the drawing Room after Dinner to ask his Advice upon it.

Mr Fielding was so taken aback that he almost let fall his Spectacles. The red Firelight danced within the darkened Lenses. "But it is not your Child, Tristan," he said.

"I know that, Sir."

"Then, why?"

"It is so unusual," I said.

"Tristan, tell me," said Mr Fielding, rubbing his Forehead upon his Fist. "Do you intend to keep a Menagerie of unusual Creatures, or to run a Side-show at a Fair?"

"Of course not," I said. "'Tis a Human Child. And naturally I have no Interest in parading it before a gawping Publick. 'Tis bad enough that Visitors are allowed in the Bedlam, and Bridewell."

"Yet you, yourself, wish only to admire at it."

"No," I said. Mr Fielding was in Fact more than half right; but not wholly, for I had another Sentiment besides, to which I could not put a Name. It made me want to carry off the pretty Freak and shelter it, far away from the ignorant Curiosity and well-meant Concern of those who would ask, like Mary: "Is she a 'Uman, Mr 'Art?"

I waited all Evening for the Sound of Henry Fielding's upraised Voice, which would mean that his Wife had told him of the Foundling, but it never came. Shortly before Midnight he retired in Pain and ill Humour to Bed, and Mary, telling him God knows what, slippt away again to the Kitchen. When I realised what she had done, I followed.

The Kitchen was still very warm, and the low tallow Candles gave it a friendly, welcoming Aspect. Mrs Fielding had dismisst Liza and the other Maids for the Night, and seemed, despite all common Sense, to be preparing to spend hers with the Baby before the Fire. She had unbound it from its Swaddling, and sate with it loose upon her Lap, attempting to Spoon-feed it Pananda from a blue China Bowl. She half leapt up in great Surprize as I approached, clutching the Infant to her as if she feared some fell Danger was fain to threaten it.

"Peace, Mrs Fielding," I said. "'Tis not your Husband, nor Mr John. 'Tis only Tristan."

I had previously planned that if I could not keep the Bat, I would at least draw its Likeness before it was taken away from me. I decided therefore to have Mary remain sitting with the Babe upon her Lap whilst I sketched, expecting in mine Ignorance that it would remain still whilst I began, and failed, and began over again, to capture its Quintessence upon Paper.

"Mr 'Art," said Mary desperately, after almost half an Houre of false Starts and muted Curses upon my Part, "I have a little Talent for Drawing. If you will but sit and hold her, I'll try to draw her for you."

So, we exchanged Places, and after some Confusion I discovered how to retain the Child in mine Arms without dropping or smothering it. This was, in truth, a Labour of Hercules, for the Babe would not be still for me any more easily than it would for Mrs Fielding, and I was extreamly glad when the Sketch was compleat and I could hand it back.

Mrs Fielding swaddled the Baby again in its Blanket, having somehow affixt a ragged Clout to its lower Extremity, and laid it back in the Basket. "I believe that I could learn the proper Manner of doing that," she said—to herself, I thought, rather than to me. "The Skin stretches so, it might be possible to fold it right away. Then she could mayhap wear ordinary Cloathes, when she is old enough."

"Mary." My previous Declaration hung unspoken in the Aire between us.

In that Moment I was convinced that I would keep my Bat. Mary would help me find a Nurse, and as regarding the Expense, had not John Fielding himself told me that I needed something else to squander my Fortune upon than Whoring?

For one long, silent Minute I believed it.

Then there came a loud, harsh Knock upon the Door that led from the Kitchen into the Street; and then another, till the solid Wood quaked with Drumming.

Mrs Fielding gasped and her Hand flew to her Breast; then she recollected herself, and straightened her Apron and her Cap before proceeding with great Dignity toward the Door. I stood close behind her. It was not like, I thought, that the Knockers were Robbers, but this was the Magistrate's House, and Mary his Wife; it did as well to be careful.

Mrs Fielding opened the Door and there stood the Gypsy.

I know not wherefore I was so surprized. I had, I think, so greatly desired that she should not return that I had perswaded My Self that she would not. Yet, here the leathery Creature stood, as gristly as a blackberry Bush. She winked up at us out of two glittering black Eyes and drew back her Lips in a Grin, revealing a set of broken Teeth, like Thorns. Her gnarled Hand grippt tight about a small lanthorn Staff, upon which I seemed to see, entwined, the carven Bodies of Toads and Adders. In the uncertain lanthorn Light they looked as if they had been alive. I shivered.

"I come for the Babe," she said. "I hope she hath given no Trouble."

"Oh!" Mrs Fielding cried, though whether with Relief or Disappointment I could not be sure. "No; no Trouble at all."

Mrs Fielding beckoned the Woman inside, and then fetched the Baby in its Swaddling from its Place near the Fire. "You will be careful that she don't take cold?" Mary said anxiously. "I shall fetch another Blanket, else the poor Mite will freeze."

"She won't freeze," the Woman said, taking the Baby with a low Laugh that sounded like the Echo of Branches breaking. "We know how to take care of our own, Mrs Fielding."

"What is the Child to you?" I demanded, as Mary ran up-Stairs to find a Blanket. "Is she a Grandchild, a Nurseling, or merely a Shilling in your Pocket?"

At this, and I saw it happen plain as Daye, the old Woman, who had ignored me heretofore, spun about and fixt me with a black Stare that turned into a mocking one when she perceived that I was not intimidated. "She is the Daughter of my Mistress," she answered "Who is a great Lady, a Queen among our People."

At these Words a sudden Chill ran though my Blood.

"What is the Lady's Name?" I asked, altho' my Tongue resisted me and my Voice was as pale as my Cheek.

"Merely visiting, weren't you, my Lovely; visiting; never staying. Tried to run away, didn't you; but Queen-Mother won't let pretty Baby go, no, no."

"Tell me!"

The old Woman cocked her Head upon one Side and smiled. "But you know her, Caligula. You may call her Viviane."

Then she was gone, and the kitchen Door slamming, and Mary Fielding running down the Stairs; and My Self on my Knees where I had fallen, for I had not the Power to stand.

That Night I lay a long while in a State of Misery. I had sustained a Shock, and altho' my Senses were not, seemingly, disordered or untrue, my Sensibilities were in utter Ruin.

The bitter Truth was that I could not verily remember whether I had ravished Viviane. I did not think I had. But I had also thought that I had seen her bodily transform into an Owl. How much Faith could I place in either Recollection? Moreover, the unwonted Visitation of the Child—if it were not—Great God!—my Child—was unintelligible to me.

At about three I rose, staggered down-Stairs and helped My Self to several Glasses of Mr Fielding's best Nantes. Feeling somewhat thereby encouraged, I returned to Bed and belatedly began the rational Calculation that would tell me whether it were possible the Child be mine, or not. Mathematics saved me. Even if it had been new born yesterdaye, which it was not, Viviane's Pup could not have been conceived beneath the Hawthorns on May Morning. January, I thought, was the probable date for its Conception, perhaps even earlier.

In January, I thought, Viviane must have shared her Favours more than once with Nathaniel Ravenscroft.

"But if 'twas Nat's," I said to My Self, "then why chose she to plague me with it, and not him?" Had she already shewn him the Babe, and he had denied it? Had she sent it to me, in Hopes that I might recognise it out of Guilt, or Fear?

There was, however, a Flaw in this Logick which I could not ignore, angry and half-fuddled as I was. If Viviane had wanted me to support her Bastard, why had she claimed it back from me at the precise Moment in which I had determined to do exactly that?

Had that been Viviane's Game? To send me a small Miracle, and snatch it back, and glory in my Disappointment? To teaze me with the false Supposition that it must be mine, and laugh to think me fallen upon my Knees in Horrour, even as I had forced her upon her own.

Had I raped Viviane? I thought that I had not. I did not know.

I needed Mrs Haywood's. I needed Polly. I needed my Lash.

CHAPTER ELEVEN

If she had intended that I should go mad, Viviane had failed. I did not lose my Wits, nor suffer the Disarray of my Senses that had followed upon my previous Encounter with her and her Kind. Instead, I beat back the Drumming with my Cane and with my Lash, and muffled my Fear beneath the Sound of someone else's Screaming.

In the Middle of January I began my Studies in the dissecting Rooms of Dr William Hunter, which were situated in a large House in the Little Piazza of Covent Garden. This Building served also as Lodging for a good many of Dr Hunter's other Students, some of whom, I discovered, had come from as far away as America. It was an elegant Address, set on several Floors above a vaulted and colon-naded walk-Way which, being paved, covered and open to the Publick was oft-times used by People of the better Sort in Pursuit of an houre's Exercise. This Quest proved often difficult; the Piazza was frequently so crowded as to make it nigh impossible to walk two abreast. Here congregated the City's Poor: squinting apple-Sellers carrying Trays of bruised Fruit that had been harvested last Autumn in Hackney Fields, hand-cart Hawkers, kitchen Maids running Errands for the Mistress or the Cook, Poulterers' Boys, cut-Purses, lame beggar Kids, poxed Whores, half-wild Dogges.

Dr Hunter's Lectures took place in a large, bright lit Theatre which in any other Household would have been the drawing Room. It was a cold, echoing, lofty ceilinged Chamber, with two large Fireplaces, neither of which gave out much Heat even when the Fires were high. In the very Centre of the Room stood three long Tables, similar to that one I had in mine own Study, and around these were positioned a Set of hard Benches upon which we Students sate, shivering and all agog to the Words of the esteemed Surgeon.

Dr Hunter himself was small, fastidious in his Dress and his Habits, and possesst of an ineffable Civility that never failed him. His Bearing was quiet and gentle, yet his Speeches, delivered in his mild Lanarkshire Accent, were given in a clear, calm Manner that was utterly compelling. For all his seeming Meekness, I should not have cared to cross him; I sensed that beneath his courtly Display lay all the Force of a contained Fire. "We Anatomists are combative People," he said to me a few Dayes after we had met—and I was thrown into such Transports by that inclusive "We" that I did not sleep the Night. "We all appreciate a good Scrap. And we do not like to lose."

I was familiar with the Battle to which he was referring, and in which he had no Intention of being bested. Both Dr Hunter and the Brothers Fielding, tho' of different Motives, were lobbying Parliament to pass a Murder Act proscribing those convicted of that Crime from Christian Burial. Mr Fielding professed Hopes, tho' they were slight, that so horrible a Punishment might reduce the Number of such unnatural Deaths within the City. Dr Hunter wished rather for a great Increase thereby in the supply of Cadavers, which was presently insufficient for both his own Practice and the Education of his Students. He was cross and apologetic that his current lecture Course, which usually he ran in the Parisian Manner, one Student to a Cadaver, was largely comprised of the Study of Engravings and anatomical Blocks. We should not, he said, be able to work upon fresh Corpses for some unknown Time, as he had fallen out, thro' no Fault of his own, with the Newgate Undertaker; and tho' he had sent several Letters to the Press beseeching the Publick to leave their Bodies for Dissection, his Supply had temporarily dried up.

"Next Yeare," he said, "once we have our Act inshrined in Law, it will be better. All shall be done in the legal Manner, and even for the Surgeons Hall there need be no more scrabbling to demonstrate Everything upon a single Corpse; all shall be shewn separately: Bones, Veins, Nerves, Digestion, Reproduction. But for now, Gentlemen, we must hope the Gaoler comes quick to his Senses, and struggle forwards in Company with Vesalius and a few Blocks of Wood."

I understood both Parts of Dr Hunter's Frustration, for the Thought of My Self as some Manner of scavenging Scrabbler was deeply unpleasant, and I could not help thinking of those Stories in which Men were murdered for Dissection. However, my Pleasure at finally achieving mine Aim of proper Instruction, and mine

Excitement at the Thought of working upon an Human Corpse at all, put such Discontentments from mine Head. The "Blocks of Wood", of which he had spoken with such Irritation, I discovered to be a Number of anatomical Preparations displaying the venous System and many other Structures, preserved upon a wooden Surface beneath a Varnish. These were to mine Eyes Objects of great Beauty, and I was happy to gaze upon them, despite their being twice removed from living Flesh. It was easy for me to perceive how each Structure was formed, and to imagine how it might function; upon the second Evening, whilst looking upon a Block of Breast Tissue, I seemed, for a Moment, to see it as if't had been vivified by the Motion of the Blood and bodily Fluids, full and perfect white as a Milkmaid's. Another Evening, he described to us the Condition of the developing Foetus within the Womb, and shewed some early Sketches he had commissioned of it, which he planned to publish as a Series of anatomical Engravings. I remembered those rat Pups I had dissected out of their Mother's Uterus, and Nathaniel's strange Suggestion that they were Questions which would never be answered. I could not prevent my Mind from wondering about the pregnant Women who had died.

One Evening, perhaps a Sennight after the Commencement of his Lectures—for I must confess that after a very few Dayes I ceased to have any Awareness of Time, and knew not whether 'twas Saturdaye or Mondaye—Dr Hunter presented his Audience with a Series of Engravings depicting the internal Structure of the Aortic Artery, and proceeded to discover the Shape and Progression, first recorded, he told us, by Paulus Aegineta, of an Aneurysm. I was not familiar with this Text, or, indeed, the Notion that an Artery may bow and swell beyond its Capacity, like a River bursting from its Banks. Yet the Idea grippt me; and as the great Surgeon continued in his Descriptions of this Condition, I began to ponder upon where else within the Body than the Thorax such Distortions might be found, and what Incapacity might result therefrom.

At eight o' the Clock, when the Lecture ended, I waited for the Room to clear, and then I approached Dr Hunter with the Result of my Deliberations, for I had formulated an interesting Hypothesis.

"Sir," I said. "In respect of the Question you ask us to consider regarding the possible Cause of a thoracic Aneurysm, I believe that it must be the tremendous Pressure of the Blood as it departs the Heart, which I know from mine own Experiments upon the Bodies of Animals to be very great; but I have a Query of mine own, upon which I would hear, if I may, Sir, your Opinion."

Dr Hunter, who was carefully putting his beautifull Etchings into a large Box, straightened up and gave me, at once, his full Attention. I flushed slightly, all at once conscious of My Self, standing in the extream Bright of the empty Theatre, which was lit by so many waxen Candles it appeared like Noon.

"Sir," I began, "if 'tis possible for an Artery to tear within the Chest, is it not equally like for it to do so elsewhere, if Circumstances cause the Pressure to be elevated? I was pondering whether, in Cases of sudden Apoplexy, the Cause is not the Rupturing of an arterial Vessel within the Cranium. It seems very likely to me that when a Man is in a Rage, his Jowls reddened and his Eyes bulging, the Pressure in his Skull must undergo dangerous Increase." I had been somewhat uncharitably remembering the Rector Ravenscroft.

Dr Hunter regarded me steadily. He seemed surprized, as if he had not been expecting any such Suggestion from me. My Stomach began to squirm. "It is an Hypothesis, merely," I said. My Voice piped small and reedy in the Vastness of the Chamber.

"Indeed," answered Dr Hunter. "And it is a good one. I take it, Mr Hart, that you have read Wepfer's *Apoplexia*?"

I was startled. "No, Sir; I have not heard of it."

"Then you should read it; for in it he describes the very Phenomenon you propose. Come, Sir, I shall give you the Loan of it."

Once he had finished packing up his Notes and Pictures, in which Endeavour he seemed quite happy to permit me to assist, Dr Hunter led me thro' the House to his impressive medical Library, and had an Assistant fetch from its high Shelf that Treatise upon Stroake, which he then personally presst into mine Hands. This done, he waved me off quick about my Business, for he had a private Patient to attend forthwith, and he had to change his Location, his Attire and his Manner. "'Twould not do," he said, "to terrify the poor Lady."

Over the following seven Weeks, Dr Hunter lent me many Books, and to mine immense Delight I eventually discovered My Self to be, if not his most preferred Student, among those select Few to whom he intimated that he might offer an Apprenticeship. I dedicated My Self to the Achievement of this Aim, which would necessitate my Presence at the Hospitals of St Bartholomew's, in Smithfield and St Thomas's, in Southwark, which were open to the Publick and even facilitated Treatment of Beggars.

I could not, however, apportion all my Time to formal Study, for I was outwith mine own Laboratory; and altho' Dr Hunter permitted his Students to use his Facilities for animal Dissection, there were a good many Students, and I had little Desire to fight off all other Takers merely to repeat mine Experiments upon lesser Species. Instead, I continued my Visits to Mrs Haywood's, and there I was able to observe many physical Prodigies that must otherwise have been beyond my Reach. I did not cause any significant Harm to Polly, altho' perhaps some of the Scars I left upon her Skin proved longer lasting than I had anticipated. However, I found in her a wondrous compliant Subject for Investigation, and 'twas thro' her Assistance, and no Dissection whatsoever, that I discovered, intirely for My Self, the Paths traversed by all the major Nerves in the Arms and the lower Legs. At every Squeak and Whimper, the internal Anatomy opened up before mine inner Vision, clear and sharp as an Engraving.

Thus the Pattern of my Life became established. I gravitated between lecture Room and Brothel, Library and Bedchamber, thinking of nothing but my Studies and my Gratification. Some Dayes I did not see the Sunne.

Shortly before New Yeare, I returned to Bow Street from the Brothel to meet with the exciting Newes that Dr Hunter had finally procured a Cadaver from Newgate, and that from the Mondaye we should work on it for three intire Evenings; longer, if the Corpse should last. I was delighted, and in mine Exuberance I lifted Mrs Fielding, who had delivered the Doctor's Message into mine Hand, clear off her Feet. Mary squawked in Outrage and thumped me hard upon the Shoulder.

"For Shame, Mr 'Art," she said, when I had put her down. "And me a married Woman! You, Sir, 'ave the Manners of a Clod!"

In Reply, I swept her a deep and courtly Bow, mine Hat tucked under mine Elbow, then dodged quickly out of the drawing Room before she could scold me any farther.

On the following Mondaye at precisely five o' Clock, I arrived at Dr Hunter's Chambers in a State of great Anticipation and Excitability. I could not begin to articulate the Thrill that had possesst me at the Thought of my first Dissection, my first Human Corpse; but my Fingers were a-trembling and mine Heart pounded in my Chest like an huge Gong.

I had never paid aught but the most minimal Attention to my fellow anatomy Students, so it came as somewhat of a Surprize to me to realise that mine Excitement was shared by the whole Colloquium; about mine Ears the Conversation clamoured. Mr Mills, who was a country Physician in his later thirties, had witnessed an Anatomy performed in Leiden some Yeares earlier, and finding it highly unsatisfactory, had ever since desired the Experience for himself. He had been so seriously displeased that Dr Hunter was not at present teaching in the Paris Manner that he had considered asking for his Sum to be returned, but had changed his Mind. I found My Self disliking him. Mr Glass, with whom he was in Conversation, was the Son of an Apothecary, and he planned, as I did, to become a Surgeon. He was a small Man, some Yeares older than My Self, and well suited his Name. His blue Frock was neat, but not fashionable; his Wigg brown; his Features regular, but not handsome; and his Demeanour quiet. When he spoke, it was in an even, thoughtful Tone that implied that he took great Care in forming his Opinions, and even greater Care in voicing them. He saw Dissection as a most important Step upon his Path, he said. No one, from what I could gather, had mine Experience of Animal Physiology.

Dr Hunter's Expression, as he led us to his lecture Room, was solemn. "Remember, Gentlemen," he said, "we are not Butchers. Respect and Care, and above all, Observation, are to be the Principles under which we shall operate. Anatomy is the Base, the Foundation, of our modern Medicine, and without it we should still be floundering in the Darknesses of Misapprehension and

Ignorance. Make careful and detailed Observations of all that you see; and if an Organ appears to you to be misshapen or diseased, call our Attention to it at once. Work with Diligence and Rectitude, and you will learn more in the next few Dayes than I could teach you otherwise in as many Months." He smiled. "And do not drop anything. I'll have none of Mr Hogarth's Quackery in here, Sirs!"

This provoked a general Laugh amongst those of the Company who were familiar with Hogarth's Opinions. I did not join in. Dr Hunter's Words had inspired me suddenly to fear that I should be the Student who disgraced him, and mortified My Self, by making a slap-dash Butchery of the Business. I had the horrifying Premonition that I should slop the Liver on my Foot and then slip Arse over Tip upon the bloody Floor. God grant not! I thought. No; in that Room, there will be no more diligent a Student than Tristan Hart.

Dr Hunter then led us all into his Theatre, into which the Last of the spring Sunnelight was streaming thro' the large, locked, Windows. The twin Fireplaces were empty. An unusual Odour clouded the unmoving Aire, colouring its Chill. Dust Motes danced upon slowly spiralling Vapours. Behind me, somebody coughed, and I saw Mr Mills put up an Handkerchief to his Nostrils. In the Centre of the Room, upon the largest of the black oaken Tables, and wrappt in a white muslin Sheet so that I could perceive naught but its Outline, lay an Human Corpse. Silence fell upon us all as we regarded it.

'Tis but a Rat, I had said once to Nathaniel Ravenscroft. Now I thought: That was a Man; until but a few Dayes ago he would have walked, and conversed, and had his own Thoughts. What is he, now? What, where? Hath his Soule departed to Heaven—or more like, to Hell—taking with it all he was, or would ever have been like to be? And if that is so, then what is this before me? Is it Something, or Nothing?

Dr Hunter proceeded swiftly to the Table and pulled back the Sheet. "Gather round, Gentlemen," he said.

The dead Man had a Face. Even if his Corpus was nothing now but a Complexity of Bones and Flesh, he had been—the Body had belonged to—a Man: in his forties, perhaps; his sparse Hair gone intirely grey, and too kindly of Countenance, it seemed to me, to have lived long a Rogue, tho' he had died one. I did not recall seeing him convicted.

I moved nearer. The Cadaver seemed at first Sight to have been fashioned out of Wax. The Skin was a pale yellowy grey, and glistened faintly in the strong Summelight. Then as I peered more closely I noticed a deep crimson Stain within the Tissues all along the right Side of the Body, where the Blood had settled after Death. How long, I wondered, had he lain dead in the Prison before anyone had found him? For the second Time I wondered what Crime had sent him thither. Poverty, I saw, had laid its Brand upon him, if Vice had not. His upper Chest and Ribs were poorly muscled, and almost devoid, I thought, of Fat; the Stomach Region also; whilst the Os Femoris and the Tibia bowed outwards as if he sate permanently astride an Horse. Surely, this Man grew up in St Giles, I thought. Had he been a petty Thief, a Pickpocket, an Whoremaster to Madam Geneva; or her increasingly desperate Lover?

The sweetish Smell, I realised suddenly, that had impresst me so strangely upon mine entering the Room, was emanating from the Cadaver. With nothing to preserve them, its soft Tissues already had begun the Processes of Decay. I had witnessed it before, in mine own Laboratory, when I had exhausted my Supplies both of Vinegar and of desiccating Salt. I understood at once wherefore we were to follow the traditional Method of Dissection, whereby the internal Organs should be excavated first, examined and then put aside. Galen's Way, beginning with the Skeletal Structure, may indeed have been more logickal; but pure Logick had here to give Way to Practicality. It would have been ridiculous to have left the Organs inside, whence their Corruption might have spread fast to the Remainder of the Corpse.

'Tis not a Man, I thought. 'Tis not Nothing; but it hath lost that Something by which it was ever more than mere Flesh, senseless and inert.

What lies here now is nothing but a broken Clock.

"Are we ready to begin Work, Gentlemen?" asked Dr Hunter.

I quickly removed my Frock and Waistcoat, and tucked my Ruffles right away inside my Sleeves. "Yes," I said.

I had hoped—tho' I had hardly dared admit the Hope—that Dr Hunter would permit me the Honour of making the initial Incision into the Corpse's Chest, but it was not to be. That Privilege went to Mr Glass, who accepted it with astounding Diffidence; altho', I grudgingly perceived, no want of Skill. A great Chear went up as his Scalpel pierced the Skin. I struggled to conceal my Jealousy.

Mr Glass cut from Shoulder to Shoulder, and downwards, then carefully peeled away the Flesh until it hung about both Sides of the Body like a Veil. He then paused, at Dr Hunter's Command, so that we might observe the Ribcage and Sternum directly below. The Ribs were woven together by a tight membranous Lace-work of Muscle. The Body being now opened to us all, Dr Hunter instructed that we begin by removing a Section of the Ribcage in order to easily reach the Organs contained within it. Later, we would excise the Bowel—"As if it were a Deer," said Mr Mills—and then proceed upon a slow Exploration of the abdominal Cavity.

I applied my Scalpel to the Tissue, and carefully I sliced the intire Length between the sixth and seventh Ribs, so that I was able easily to lift back first the one and then the other. Below them lay the purple Marvell that was the Heart. The Organ surprized me, for all that I had spent so many Houres drawing the Entrails of large Rats and Birds; for it appeared almost too large, too heavy to have been confined within so small a Space. Never in my Life, I thought, have I beheld such astonishing Proof of the Wisdom and Perfection of Our Lord's Creation! I could have happily fallen then and there upon my Knees, and offered up my Voice in Praise.

So it began; and for the next three Evenings I worked closely upon the Cadaver, and in between Dr Hunter's Sessions thought of nothing else. Truth had been laid out in front of me, and I was determined to learn all I could before the Door of Revelation should close again. Thus I discovered, for My Self, the true Structure of the Human Lung, and wondered at the beauteous Intricacy of the Arterial Pathways that conveyed bright Blood to all the Organs of the Body. No longer could any mere Block appear beautifull! I saw for My Self the undifferentiated Nature of the Liver, and appreciated at once how it could not be responsible for the Flow of Blood around the Venous System. I was re-making Discoveries over a Century late, but that did not signify. I was perceiving how precisely those Discoveries had been correct, confirming Harvey, disproving Galen, in the Length of Time it must have taken for the Heart I held within mine Hand to beat.

The Atmosphere within the closed Room did not improve, especially after the Removal of the Corpse's Stomach and Bowels, and by the third Night I was forced to work with a Wad of Muslin soaked in Hungary Water secured over my Nose and Mouth. Mine Eyes stung. Mr Mills decryed the Stink, and left before the Dissection was compleat, as did three Others; thus leaving the final Explorations of the Spinal, Ligamental and Skeletal Tissues to My Self, Mr Glass and Dr Hunter.

Now that there were present only three of us, I felt My Self better inclined to ask Questions of, and proffer mine own Ideas to Dr Hunter whilst we worked. He knew already mine Interest to learn everything I could of the Workings of the Nervous System, so when we had been an Houre about the intimate Investigation of the Skull and Brain, I asked whether Dr Hunter had any Opinion as to what became of the nervous Fibres, which were joined so clearly in the Spine, upon their Progression thither. "Do they then," I ventured, "become Part of the Brain itself? Yet the Brain is not intirely composed of Nervous Tissue."

"It would appear that it is," said Dr Hunter. "At least in Part."

"That would seem to imply," I said, "that Thought itself may run thro'out the Body, which is certainly improbable, if not, perhaps, impossible."

"How then," said Dr Hunter, "do you imagine that the Brain, the Seat of Intelligence, conveys its Orders to the Muscles? Newton, I believe, hath written upon it. What think you upon his Suggestion regarding animal Motion?"

"I do not know whether Newton is correct," I said, lifting my Curette from the internal Spine of the Os Frontis. "Mine Impulse would be to believe that he is, inasmuch as the Nerves carry the Commands of the Brain to the Muscles; but whether this be done by Aetheric Vibrations or by some other Mechanism, I cannot judge."

"Do you believe, Sir," said Mr Glass, raising his Attention briefly from the Orbitary Plate and fixing it upon me, "that the Soule doth nothing in maintaining the Vital Processes of the Body?"

"No, Sir," I said. "I cannot go so far; for then what true Difference would there be bewixt a living Body and a dead one?"

"Do you then admit the Possibility that every living Thing may have a Soule, of one Sort or another?"

"I do not know," I said, looking him in the Eye. "I know that I cannot equate Soule with Mind, as Descartes does. But to say that all Life hath a Soule would give Soules to the intire animal Kingdom."

Do Animals have Minds? I wondered suddenly. Doth Thought equate with Sensation? 'Tis the old Problem: Doth Sensation dwell within the Mind, or in the Body?

Mr Glass shrugged both his Shoulders. "Perhaps they have them," he said, and went back to his Study.

Dr Hunter laughed. "I perceive you are a good Aristotelian, Mr Glass! 'Tis well enough; perchance what this Profession needs is a few more Englishmen who recognise the Necessity of a Place for God in God's Creation. Man is not a Machine, Gentlemen!"

I joined in the Laughter, which was far from unkindly meant, altho' I still had achieved no useful Answer to my Query. Yet I began to ponder mine earlier Judgement that the Cadaver had been no more than a broken Clock; for if it were a Machine after Death, it had to have been one before it. I remembered again my Theory that mine own perceptual Difficulties had resulted from some physical Cause. The Machine of my Brain had become ill, and my Mind had suffered its Effects.

Perhaps the Question was not whether the Concept was right, or wrong, but to what Extent it was either. The Body may indeed be a Machine, I thought. But if it is, then 'tis a Machine of such Complexity and Subtilty that it ought not be described as one. Moreover, if the Word "Machine' cannot comprehend the Intirety of the Body, it fails even more dramatically to comprehend the compleat Being of a Man. There is a Soule, I do honestly believe; and when that vital Principle is lost, there is Death. Man is a conscious, animate Being; Life is more than mere clock-Work.

During the Houres we had spent working together, mine Opinion of Mr Glass had improved. Now I thought it odd that I had made no Attempt to converse with him during the many Weeks we had attended Dr Hunter's spoken Lectures. I had attached so little Significance to any of my Fellows that I did not know all their Names, let alone their Circumstances. But I was becoming curious about him.

Shortly after this Exchange, Dr Hunter decided that it was Time for us to cease, for we had over-run our allotted Time by an whole Houre. Looking down upon the Remains of the Cadaver—as a Man awakening from a Dream is suddenly faced with grim Reality—I realised that he was right. There was Nothing left.

The unexpectedness of the Cessation wrung me. 'Tis not enough! I thought. Instead of Satisfaction, I felt overwhelming Loss.

We scrubbed our Hands and Faces as clean as we could, and then Mr Glass and I departed from the Building to return to our respective Lodgings, change our Cloathes and prepare our Stomachs for Supper, as it was nearing nine o' the Clock. "Tho' I believe," said he, "that I shall eat nothing at all for the next Sennight; the Smell yet lingering in my Nostrils is so foul."

We walked together for some little Way along the dusty Street and then parted, on good Terms, Mr Glass having made the Suggestion that we should meet again outside the class-Room to compare our Opinions upon it.

"I shall be, come the Summer Months, about the Hospitals for

Instruction and for Experience," he added. "It would be in your Interest, perhaps, to do the same."

"Dr Hunter is of the same Mind," I said, desperately praying, as I said it, that 'twas true. "I hope to be his Apprentice; or perhaps more accurately, his Orderly."

Mr Fielding's House, when I reached it, was shut up, on the lower Floors at least, but not quiet; from outside I could detect the Sounds of irrepressible Life: Children laughing in the Passage, Mr Fielding shouting: "For God's Sake, Woman!" and Mary Fielding's Footsteps, defiantly practical, approaching the other Side of the front Door.

It was universally concurred that I should bathe before Supper, and send down my Cloathing to be laundered, so the Meal was permitted to be delayed and I retired to my Chamber. The steaming Water refreshed and eased me, as it lifted away all the Reek and Mess of the Daye's Endeavour. I lay back in the Tub and reflected long upon all I had learned. The first thing I realised, with Dismay, was the vast Amount of anatomical Knowledge I had still to accrue, before I could with Satisfaction stile My Self Surgeon. I must, I thought, perform many, many more human Dissections, to perfect mine Eye and the surety of mine Hand.

How was I to achieve this? Perhaps, I thought, hopefully, since Dr Hunter's Argument with the Newgate Gaoler was resolved, he would be able to return to his preferred teaching Method. I began to comprehend with greater Sympathy the Situation in which the famous Mr Harvey had found himself, when he had dissected the Corpses of his Father and his Sister. I shivered, tho' the Bath was warm. Imagine, I thought, if a Man could look upon the Bodies of those he loved, and covet their Bones. Must that not be a Monster?

Yet, Harvey, I had to believe, had not thought in such Manner at all. Perhaps his Family had offered, as Dr Hunter had hoped the Publick might, in some noble Spirit of Service to Philosophy. Or perhaps they had merely been partaking of the last Century's Fashion for Post Mortems.

I regarded my own Body, foreshortened to near six Feet beneath the Water, its olive Skin seeming lighter, for an illusory Instant, due to the reflecting Surface, and imagined for a long Moment what should become of it after my Death. It was unlikely that anyone would ever dissect it. That Horrour, once the Murder Bill was passed, would await only the Condamned. It ought to be so at least, I thought; 'tis an inhuman Fate to end up as Nothing on an Anatomist's Bench. Only those wicked Soules who have thrown away their Humanity already, thro' foul Murder or worse Villainy, should be the Anatomist's Prey. The poor Wretch who fell beneath my Knife todaye most like did not deserve it.

As I was now paying some Attention to my Body, I realised with Disgust that the coarse black Hairs that sprouted upon my Legs, Arms, and Chest had grown noticeably thicker since the last Occasion of my concerning My Self with them. Of course, I knew this had not happened over-Night; but lately I had been so deep involved with my Studies that I had not given any Thought to the Condition mine own wretched Body might be in. It frightened me to think that this Growth had taken Place without my Notice, tho' God alone knows what I could have done to slow it.

Lord help me, I thought. I look more the Foreigner with every passing Daye.

This Realisation shook me, and almost I leapt out of my Bath; but then I remembered that I had not yet washed mine Head or my Feet, and so I sank back down, and forced My Self to think of more pleasant things. I fell to considering where next on the medical Path my Foot should fall. In the Hospitals of Saints Thomas and Bartholomew, I would be faced with all Manner of Disease and Deformity. As Dr Hunter's Apprentice, if I should become it, I should, in all Probability, be allowed to practise my new surgical Skill upon living Human Beings. The Notion soothed me greatly.

I got out of the Bath, dried and dresst My Self, and hurried down to Supper.

CHAPTER TWELVE

At two o' Clock the following Afternoon, Dr Hunter invited both My Self and Mr John Fielding, whom he knew to be my London Guardian, to join him in Bedford's Coffee House for a Conversation regarding my Future. Mr John, however, was presently in court Session, dealing with an Abigail who was supposed to have stolen a Skein of Cloth from her Employer, and could not be disturbed on mine Account, so it fell to Mr Henry Fielding to accept Dr Hunter's Invitation, and accompany me thro' the foggy March Streets to the Piazza.

I was at once propelled into a State of prodigious Excitement. I knew that this Meeting, short as it would doubtless be, must exert over my Future such an Influence that every Hour—perhaps even of my very Life—was, by Comparison, as meaningless as Sleep. Leaving Mr Fielding standing in the dining Room, Mouth open and Letter in Hand, I ran up the Stairs to my Bedchamber and flung open my Closet. Dr Hunter's Injunction to his Students that we must, whenever on Business, attire ourselves appropriate to our Profession and its Responsibilities rang loud in mine Ears. I pulled my darkest blue Frock from amongst its Fellows and threw it upon my Bed. Not good enough. My Black, perhaps, with silver Waistcoat? But, I thought, with sudden Anguish, if I were to wear my Black, tho' 'tis more smart, I would look as if I were headed to a Funeral. I thrust mine Arm again into my Closet.

I knew that Dr Hunter liked me. But I did not know, with like Surety, that he genuinely perceived in me the Makings of a Surgeon, even despite his Intimations to that Effect. Mine hidden Dread, that really he did not, that he had merely taken me onto his Course as a Favour to Mr Fielding, surfaced like a drowned Corpse.

I remembered my Father telling me that I could not attend at a University because I was too frequently unwell. I recollected how, during the very first of his anatomy Classes, when I had sate before him in so enraptured a State that he could have averred the Sunne the very Moon and I would have agreed, Dr Hunter had embarked upon a detailed Description of the personal Qualities that he deemed necessary in a Surgeon.

"He must be," Dr Hunter had remarked—and in my Memory I could hear his Voice as plain as if the present Man had spoken in mine Ear—"of determined and dispassionate Character, steady of Hand and perceptive of Eye, swift of Wit and rational of Mind; for make no Mistake, Gentlemen, the Life of his Patient rests in his Care, and that Life is too precious a thing to entrust to a Quack or a Fool. A Surgeon must be, above all things, of *mens sana*; for despite the many Calumnies our Enemies lay at the Door of our Profession, we are not Monsters, or a Body of mad Men."

Fear punched my Gut. I fell down, breathless, on my Bed and wrappt mine Arms around my Stomach. Mine Hands shook with mine every Heartbeat. What if, I thought, I have revealed some Inconsistency, some Flaw that will, in Dr Hunter's Eyes, render me ineligible for Admittance to the medical Profession? Please God, I am a rational Man. Let him not have found me wanting.

After several Minutes during which I sate thus, painfully transfixt upon my Terrour, I heard the hall Clock chiming the quarter Houre, and realising that I had but a short while to attire and get me to Bedford's, I forced My Self to my Feet, and dresst carefully in blue brocaide Frock and Waistcoat, with buff Breeches.

Bedford's Coffee House was a favourite Haunt of the City's Men of Countenance and Wit. It was popular with both Brothers Fielding, who came hither to spend many Houres in lively Conversation and Debate. Henry Fielding had still many Friends in literary Circles, and he often made Complaint of their pressing him to return to his Fictions. I was not acquainted with Bedford's, partly because I had no Wish to pass my free Moments under the Eye of either Fielding, but also because I had not Time, in amongst all mine other Activities, to sit drinking Coffee and arguing Philosophy. Bedford's was no great Distance from Bow Street, but I was grateful to Mr Fielding when I found that he had sent for a Chairman; I had no Wish to arrive at so important an Interview with my white Stockings bespattered with city Mud.

The Clamour of the London Streets was muffled, as was usual during the cold Season, under a thick Cloud of greyish-yellow Fog, and so pushing open the coffee house Door, I was surprized by a

Wave of Noise that almost knocked me from my Feet. The crowded Place rang with Talk, Footsteps, and the loud Screeches of Chairs upon dirty Boards. The warm Aire had a Smell of coarse tobacco Smoake, mixt, naturally, with that stimulating Beverage the Patrons came to sample, which hung a-brewing over the low Fire in an huge coffee-Pot. A shabby book Shelf over the Mantel held Bottles, Cups, earthenware Pitchers, and long clay Pipes, and opposite it dangled a Parliamentary Ordinance against the Use of bad Language.

I held open the Door for Henry Fielding, and then followed him within. He appeared to know where he was going, so I trailed meekly in his Wake, avoiding as best I could the jostling Elbows and clumsy Feet of Strangers. We eventually arrived at a Niche in the farthest Corner of the Room and there sate down to wait for Dr Hunter.

"So, Tristan," said Mr Fielding, settling himself into an heavy carver Chair, his Back against the Wall. "Dr Hunter appears to be of Mind that you have taken to Anatomy like a Duck to Water. You have seized the Opportunity provided by your Talent and made the most of it."

I flushed hot at this Praise, and found mine Eyes drawn toward the Floor. "Indeed, Mr Fielding," I said, "I am under no Illusion as to who hath provided the Opportunity. 'Tis all due to you, yourself, that I have been able to study under Dr Hunter; had you not insisted upon my visiting in London, I should still have been vivisecting Squirrels in mine own Chambers with neither Tuition nor Assistance from anyone; and I sincerely doubt that I should ever have come near the Practice of real Physick. I owe you a great Deal, Sir."

"Thank you," Mr Fielding said. "But I must profess mine own Doubt as to whether you would not at some Stage have slippt your

Father's Net and made your own Way hither. Ah," he went on, seeing my startled Expression, "I do not speak ill of your Father, Tristan; he is a fine Man; but since your Mother died he has made himself a very Hermit, and he seems to think the same ought to be your Lot in Life." He sighed. "The World doth not cease for our Sorrows, tho' they seem enough to stop't."

I looked carefully into Mr Fielding's shaddowed Face wondering that he had made such unexpected Reference to my Father, and more importantly, my Mother. I remembered the Conversation we had held upon our Journey, and it struck me that mayhap Mr Fielding had sensed my Reluctance upon that Occasion to have questioned him about those Matters most delicately concerning My Self, and was now opening the Subject in case I should wish to pursue it.

A Free-thinker, and a Jewess? A Mystery, if not a very Wonder.

"Mr Fielding," I said, tentatively, for the Thought also occurred to me that I might be mistaken, and about to mire my Foot where Angels fear to tread. "Am I right in mine Impression that you knew my Father as a young Man, when he was first married to my Mother?"

Mr Fielding reached in his Greatcoat for his Pipe, withdrew it and tapped the Bowl in an explorative Manner. "I knew Mr Hart," he said, "before he was married to your Mother. And I knew your Mother too, after her first Husband died. I may have been responsible for your Parents' Introduction. I am not sure."

"My Mother was a Widdowe?" I exclaimed.

"She was, Sir. A young, a wealthy, and might I say, an handsome one. She was also, as you know, a Jewess, Spanish bred, Hollander born. Her first Husband was a Merchant, and a Scholar—until he was banished from his Synagogue and his Community."

"Had he become a Christian?" I asked.

"Not at all. He was a follower of Spinoza. He had become a Free-thinker or, as they insist on stiling themselves, a Deist—ah, I perceive you have heard of them—and he had foolishly asserted that there was no transcendent God. Your Mother, sharing his heretical Belief, was excommunicated with him, which was very hard on her, for she lost all her People. They immigrated to London from Amsterdam, and began their Lives anew in Spitalfield, I believe. A Yeare later he died, and left her compleatly alone; tho' I must say, if ever Woman were up to the Task of surviving in utter Exile, and honourably, it was she. She had a love of Literature, and she gave me great Encouragement whilst I was scribbling the first of my Plays " Mr Fielding smiled, and proceeded to fill his tobacco-Pipe, before continuing. "She would have been thoroughly disgusted by my magisterial Endeavour. She had little Patience with Laws, had Mrs Eugenia Hart."

I blinked. "So my Mother   " I stammered. "Was no Jewess at all?"

"Ah," Mr Fielding answered, "'tis not as simple as that, Tristan. She never to my Knowledge became a Christian, so under the Law of England she remained an Alien to her Death. As to that of Israel, I am not certain. But you and Miss Hart, I believe, have had the good Fortune to have been christened, and brought up in the English Church."

I stared, open mouthed, at Mr Fielding.

"As for your Father," Mr Fielding continued, "I knew him when he was your Age, fresh come into his Estate after your Grandfather had died, and green as Grass. I think he would have run thro' half his Fortune in the first six Months if't had not been that by then he had met your Mother, and she had, I suppose, a settling Effect;

tho' she did convert him to her unorthodox Way of Thinking about Religion. She was ten Yeares older than he, you understand, and she usually displayed uncommon good Sense."

I did not know what Remark I ought to make in Response to these Intelligences; the whole Notion was in my Mind so extraordinary that I should not have believed one Word had it not spilled from the Tongue of Henry Fielding, whose Gospel I trusted, upon some Matters, more confidently than that of Luke or John. I shut up my Mouth, and swallowed.

"Your Father, had he not lost his Fire when he lost your Mother, would have gone into Politicks," Mr Fielding said. "I believe he is still active, in a small Way, about several Causes dear to his Breast." Some Movement in the Crowd beyond mine Head catching his Eye, Mr Fielding looked up, and pausing in his Speech, held up his Hand in a welcoming Gesture. "I must desist now from my waffling," he said. "For here is Dr Hunter."

I turned sharply where I sate. All mine Apprehensions and Hopes, which mine Astonishment at Mr Fielding's Tale had temporarily obscured from View, rushed to oppress me again as I saw the slender russet and grey clad Figure of the Doctor some few Feet to my right, pausing momentarily to greet an Acquaintance, and then continuing in my Direction, beating a Path thro' the inattentive Crowd. He had a business-like Look. I felt certain he was come straight from a Patient.

"Sir," I said, as he drew close, and I attempted to rise; but Dr Hunter placed his Hand upon my Shoulder and applied thereon a gentle Pressure, thus forcing me to maintain my Seat.

"Mr Fielding," Dr Hunter said, removing his Hat and tucking it beneath his Elbow before executing a short Bow. "I had expected to be dealing with your Brother. A Pleasure, Sir."

"All mine, Dr Hunter, all mine," Mr Fielding replied, waving away the Preliminaries with good-humoured Impatience. "John is in Session at the Moment, and as he is bound by his Nature to deal with the Implementation of the Law with the detailed Attention that you yourself bestow upon the Sick, I believe he shall be there till supper-Time. I trust that you are well, Sir?"

"Very well, Mr Fielding." Dr Hunter pulled forward an high backed Chair and settled himself upon it, like a Robin perching upon a Twig. "How doth your Foot?"

"Poorly," Mr Fielding replied. "But 'tis of no Consequence. My Mission to bring forth a better World continues apace. How fares your coin Collection?"

"Indeed," Dr Hunter said, very quietly, Ignoring Mr Fielding's Reference to his hobby-Horse, "your Mission, as you call't, is Stuff and Nonsense, as I said to you only the other Night. Do what you will, Henry, your pet Police Force will not cure the lingering Malaise that afflicts our Civilisation; neither will my School of Anatomy. In seven Generations the Poor will still be with us, as will the Sick, and they will wear similar Faces. They will still commit Crime, and abuse their Wives, and drown their Miseries in Gin—or whatever shall be their Poison of Choice. I have more Concern for your Health than for theirs. Please, Henry, rest."

Feeling that I had intruded upon an Exchange not meant for mine Ears, I looked uncomfortably away.

"Alas," said Mr Fielding amiably. "We must continue to disagree upon that Point, Dr Hunter. Now, I believe you have a Suggestion to make concerning our young Mr Hart. Pray, spit it out."

Dr Hunter, who by his Nature placed almost as much Importance upon sustaining the Niceties of polite Intercourse with his Fellows as John Fielding did upon the righteous Application of the Law, seemed somewhat taken aback by Henry Fielding's sudden Directness, and the Vulgarity of his Term, and for an half-Second I watched his Features contort, as if he was undergoing an internal Struggle. My Stomach lurched. Mr Fielding's Lips twitched.

"Very well," answered Dr Hunter at last. "Mr Fielding, over the eight Weeks I have spent in Company with Tristan Hart, I have come to the Opinion that, despite his Youth, he is an exceptionally talented and diligent Student, whose natural Gifts must not be permitted to wither on the Vine. At the Conclusion of my current lecture Course I would like, therefore, to take him on as one of my Apprentices, to ensure that he is thoroughly schooled in the modern Science of Medicine. The young Man is aware of mine Interest in him, and he appears enthusiastic. If you and John, as his Guardians, have no Objection to my Proposal, then all that remains is to obtain Permission from Squire Hart."

Mine Heart, at these blessed Words, skippt a Beat. A bright Fountain of Relief and Excitement surged up my Spine, setting my Limbs a-tremble.

Dr Hunter had not guessed at mine Apprehension that he might reject me; he spoke as if the Matter was already all but concluded in my Favour, as if all that was left was to formalise our Connexion. Indeed, I realised suddenly, how could he, wherefore should he have guessed it? He had made it clear that I was one of his finest Students, and he would not have expected that I should have doubted him; why then, in Dr Hunter's Estimation, ought I ever to have feared that he would pass me over?

"So," said Mr Fielding. I turned mine Head. He smiled at me, as honestly and as openly delighted of Countenance as if he were one of the Country's simplest Men, instead of one of its most erudite, and said: "Good Tidings, indeed, by Jove. We must straightway write your Father, Tristan. He will be very proud of you, my young Friend; as, indeed, are we all."

Suddenly, I perceived, without Question, that Mr Fielding had told Dr Hunter nothing of mine Illness. A deep, unmixt Gratitude bloomed within my Breast, swelling and opening to the Sunnelight of this new Beginning like the largest and most sweet scented of Roses.

I looked from Mr Fielding to Dr Hunter, and back again. Their twinned Shaddowes danced upon the coffee house Wall in the flickering Candlelight, reminding me of Plato. Egad! I am lucky to have such Friends, I thought. I have the Interest of two of England's most remarkable Men, who tho' they might disagree upon Points of Argument, are not verily as unlike in their Purposes as they appear, even to each other. Both desire to comprehend the World as it is, rather than how Superstition and Ignorance might falsely perceive it; and both believe that in true Understanding lieth the Ability to rectify Corruption in the Bodies both of Man and State. And, I realised, with a Twinge of Shame, both are right. 'Tis not Science alone that may solve the great Questions of our Time; Law hath its Place, and Religion also. That Notion brought me up short, for I remembered all on a sudden my Father's Free-thinking, and my Mother's Heterodoxy; and how I knowing naught of either, had once pledged my Soule unto a rational God.

Our Business thus concluded, Mr Fielding and I departed the Bedford soon afterwards, to the evident Displeasure of the Proprietor, from whom we had had nothing except Room and Aire, returning by Chair to Bow Street. I had no Faith in mine own Ability to convince my Father of anything, so later that Afternoon Mr Fielding wrote explaining the Nature and potential Outcome of the Offer Dr Hunter had made, and strongly suggesting that I should be allowed to accept it. It was Mr Fielding's firmly expresst Belief that this Epistle would meet with a reasonable and favourable Response, so I put aside my Misgivings and made My Self to consider only the very positive Turn my Life had taken.

In this happy Frame of Mind I decided to write to Nathaniel, tho' I had no Idea whether or not I ought to expect a Reply; what Nat was doing, even whether he was still in Collerton or at Oxford, was now as deep a Mystery as the Eleusinian Rites.

My dear Nat (I wrote)

'Tis with Delight I must tell you that Dr Hunter has suggested I should be his Apprentice, and study under him the fine Points of Surgery and Physick. Mr Fielding is writing to my Father at this very Minute asking him for his Consent, which we do not doubt he will give. I am exceeding excited at the Thought that I shall soon be a Doctor.

Oh, Nat, everything that I could have desired has come to pass, except this: I have had neither Word nor Whisper from you since we parted in May, despite that I have written more than once. Are you even reading my Letters? Perhaps you are busy with your own Studies, but surely 'tis not too much to require that you scrawl a few Lines upon a Page, fold, and dispatch, for I would dearly love to hear your Newes, and your Reaction to mine. 'Tis hard to bear your Silence and Secrecy; you are my dearest Friend, and if ever I had a Brother, it was you.

I remain
Yours in Hope,
Tristan Hart

I sealed the Letter, addresst it, and put it upon the Fieldings' Table for the Post, but in mine Heart I had little Expectation of its ever reaching Nathaniel. In somewhat poorer Spirits now than I had been, I took My Self back up to my Chamber, and forced My Self to re-read Willis' *Cerebri anatome* until it was time to depart for Dr Hunter's.

CHAPTER THIRTEEN

Dr Hunter's Spring Lecture Course ran that Yeare until mid-April, and as the Newgate Gaoler, whose Palm, I think, had been generously greased, now proved more than ready to assist, we were fortunate enough to work upon a Variety of Cadavers of different Ages and Sexes before the Term was up. Towards the End of the Series, Dr Hunter began to introduce us to the Art of Surgery proper, and we spent many Evenings removing Growths and setting Splints; then before I knew it the Course was up, the Americans gone, and Mr Glass and I were adjusting our Minds to the many exhausting Houres we must now spend about St Thomas's and Barts, fetching, watching, assisting, and carrying out small

Procedures under the Supervision of the Surgeons we were following. Mr Glass, I discovered, was not to be Dr Hunter's Apprentice, but that of his Associate, one Dr Oliver, whom I knew from Repute to be a Physician of great Skill with an unfortunate Habit of telling the Truth to his Patients.

I had been only a Week about this hospital Duty, however, when I received Notice from Dr Hunter that I was to assist him the following Morning in his private Practice, as he was due to perform the Removal of a cancerous Tumour from the Breast of a Baroness, which was causing her much Pain and Terrour.

I was most excited at this Prospect, for it was the first Operation of a serious Nature in which I had been called upon to assist. I was determined to acquit My Self as efficiently as possible, and during the Houre before I left the House, I repeated the Procedure in mine Head as tho' I were to do it My Self. What, I wondered, must it be like to cut into a living Breast? I dresst all in black, by Reason of the Blood.

Dr Hunter was dresst extreamly smart, in silken Frock and a great Amount of Lace. He seemed in good Spirits, and as the Carriage hurried along Oxford Street, he conversed fluently with me upon the Particulars of the Case, and what he considered to be its likely Prognosis.

The Cancer, he said, was small, and his Belief was that it had not yet reached the Point of spreading, which more often than not ended the Life of its poor Sufferer. Lady B.—— was otherwise quite healthy; she had delivered four Children without any Difficulty whatsoever, and her Pulse usually was strong and regular; all Indications of a resilient Constitution. "The one thing that may impede her Recovery," he said, "is her Temperament; for she hath an unfortunate Tendency towards the Hysteric Fit, and often before hath feared herself about to die, quite contrary to all the Evidence. I have always been exceeding gentle and patient with her, in the Desire of reassuring her that her Fears were groundless; but since presently they are not, there is little Hope of Reassurance, whatever Kindnesses we offer her. Nevertheless, we must attempt it; an Operation of this Nature performed upon a compliant and trusting Subject hath, in mine Experience, twice the Potential for Success as the other Kind. So maintain a lively Countenance and friendly Conversation until that may be impossible. I shall perform the Extirpation of the Tumour as quickly as I can. Be sharp about the Irons and we should be finished in less than fifteen Minutes."

I nodded my Comprehension, altho' I knew these latter things already. The good Doctor was repeating Advice he had given to me many Times before, both during his own lecture Course and individually, and I guesst from this that privately he held a some-what darker Apprehension of the Lady's Case than he chose to reveal to me. Perhaps, I thought, he fears the Cancer be greater than he hath admitted. I knew he did not doubt his Skill, or even mine.

The B.——s' House, being in May Fair, was in an Area of the City I had not previously visited. It was a new and fashionable Locale populated largely by the better Sort of People, altho' there were also a Few who had secured thro' Trade sufficient Sum to pay the Lease demanded by the Grosvenors. Much of the District was still under Construction, which was a Pity, for 'twas impossible to see much of the Houses, their elegant Fronts being obscured behind Rack after Rack of rough Scaffolding. Occasionally the Carriage would pass a Row of Houses that had been compleated; and these were very grand indeed: uniform in outward Aspect and, I supposed, internal Design.

The Carriage slowed, and realising that we were arrived at the Address, I looked out of the Window to take Stock of the Appearance of the House, which I had been told was extreamly beautifull. In Truth, I thought, it was not so, altho' it was a fine big House, at the very Centre of a Row new finished out of pinkish Stone, which seemed to glimmer faintly thro' the late morning Mist. Perhaps, I thought, that very Newness is why I cannot call it beautifull.

Dr Hunter descended from the Carriage, and strode up the front Steps to the tall white Door. I followed quickly, and joined him just as he rapped once upon it with his silver-headed Cane. The Door opened directly. I thought that the Maid, her Ladyship's Abigail by her Dress, must have been awaiting our Arrival in the Atrium.

"Ah, Alice," Dr Hunter said, stepping over the Threshold. "How doth your Mistress? Is Dr Oliver here, and is all in Readiness?"

"Dr Oliver is above, Sir, with my Mistress," Alice replied, in a trembling Voice. "She is as well as could be expected, Sir."

"Good, good," said Dr Hunter, in a gentler Tone. "And the Room, Alice; is the Room prepared?"

"Yes," Alice said, and burst forth into Tears.

"Be at Ease, Lassie," Dr Hunter said, patting her Shoulder. "All will be well. Mr Hart and I shall find our own Way to the Salon. Go down to the Kitchens and remain there with the other Servants till her Ladyship rings for you."

Weeping, Alice went.

"Now," Dr Hunter said. "To Business."

We climbed thro' the unnerving silent House, Dr Hunter ahead, My Self following, as before. "Will his Lordship be present, also?" I asked.

Dr Hunter stoppt. "Lud, no," he said. "He hath been sent away, I do most dearly trust; there is naught worse than to have an Husband present at a Procedure such as this."

"Wherefore?" I said.

Dr Hunter regarded me steadily. "You will understand wherefore, Mr Hart, if ever you take a Wife," he said; and then turning abruptly from me, he resumed his swift Ascent of the wide, white Staircase.

Lady B.——'s Salon, where she was waiting for Dr Hunter, I discovered to be a large, airy sitting Room, fashionably furnished; and, which was to our Purpose, well lit, with a north facing Window. Her Ladyship herself was presently laid flat upon a silver brocaide Sopha, her left Arm resting theatrically across her Forehead, and her corsetless Bosom heaving with all Appearance of extream Distress. By her Side, awkwardly patting her Hand, knelt Dr Oliver. He stood up at once as Dr Hunter entered the Room, his coarse Physiognomy registering boundless Relief.

Lady B.—— lifted her Wrist from her Brow and stole a Look across the Salon. Her Eyes opened wide in seeming Horrour as she caught Sight of me. "Fie! Dr Hunter!" she cried. "What are you about, to bring a Jew in here! Is it not bad enough that Dr Oliver must witness mine Humiliation? Oh, Dr Hunter! Oh, Sir!"

I came to a shocked Halt in the Doorway. My Countenance must have registered my Distress, for Dr Hunter shot me a Look, to tell me to remain where I stood; then he crosst to her Ladyship's Side. Thro' her Sobs, which seemed to me somewhat exuberant, I heard his gentle Scottish Accents explaining to her that I was no Jew, and his own Pupil, and that she must somehow control her Passions, if he was to attempt the Operation.

I looked around the Room. Before the handsome Fireplace stood a lone Armchair, covered by a Number of old Sheets, and fearsome in its Emptiness. At its left Side, which was the farthest from the Fire, stood a long cup Board, atop which was piled an high Mound of Compresses, Bandages, Sponges, and Lint. Behind it, locked, for now, sate a small Chest, in which I knew were contained all the necessary Implements of Surgery.

Mine Heartbeat quickened. The Mercy Seat, I thought.

I was becoming most impatient to begin, and mine Attention returned to Lady B.—— whose Bawlings had seemingly ceased. Something about her Attitude perplext me. I could understand why she should be suffering, if indeed she was; but her Agonies seemed to mine experienced Ear intirely counterfeit, as if, in Truth, she was secretly delighted by her Predicament, and revelled in the Attention it brought her. This Woman, I thought, who oft makes Pretense that she is about to die, doth not comprehend the Severity of her present Sickness. She mistakes it for but another petty Alarum, that shall prove false, and be soothed by mere Words. But it is not such, and it shall not be so eased. The Room is ready and the Surgeons in Attendance, and the Cancer will not wait.

The Lady's apparent Quietude now gave to Dr Hunter the Opportunity of introducing me, and then of issuing the Instruction that I was to unpack and make ready the Contents of the Chest, whilst he and Dr Oliver prepared their Patient. I was gladdened to be given something to do. The Activity placated mine Annoyance at the Lady B.——'s Prevarications, and took me, moreover, out of her Sight. I removed my Frock, that it should not impede my Movement, and laid it to one Side before unlocking the Box and beginning to go about my Task.

The two Doctors now between them perswaded Lady B.— to quit her Sopha and to approach the Chair. She was not, I noted in passing, unpleasing in her Features, tho' she had called me Jew;

her Complexion was smooth and remarkably even despite her Weeping; pale, but not yet with the Pallour of Horrour. She was attired in a blue morning Gown, which reminded me, for one unaccountable Moment, of mine early Childhood. Dr Hunter, with some Difficulty, had her remove it. This left only her Shift and Petticoats, and tho' the Latter posed no Obstacle to the Doctor's Knife, the Former certainly did. It, too, was taken off, and then her Ladyship stood before us, strippt naked to the Waist and crimson with Humiliation. I let my Gaze hover about her Body. It was, by the common Measure, well formed; her Waist small, her Breasts heavy and round, free from any superficial Imperfection.

She was induced to sit; then Dr Oliver, over the Lady's Head, asked: "Shall she be strappt down, Sir?" Dr Hunter nodded, but Lady B.—— sprung straight up again, crying: "No! No! Please! No! Do not tie me! I beg you, do not tie me!"

Now, I thought, she is afraid. I can hear the Panick in her Voice. To mine Horrour, a Surge of dark Excitement travelled up my Spine. I set my Face into a Mask, and removed my cauterising Irons from the Chest.

Conciliatory as Dr Hunter's Manner had previously been towards her Ladyship, he shewed no Intention whatsoever of being swayed by her Wishes in this. Her Ladyship was to be restrained, he insisted, for her own Safety as much as that the Operation required it. She would find it impossible to sit still, for even knowing it to be necessary, what Creature would willingly submit to such a Mutilation? And what if she should faint, and fall?

Seeing her Physician unmoved, Lady B.—— began in full earnest to weep. Her Sobs had now a very different Timbre; quiet, low; the Protestations of Helplessness. I thanked my Stars, and Dr Hunter, that I had been sent behind the Chair, for my Loins sprang at once to full Attention at the Tone, and a pretty Picture I should have made had I been in Sight. Then Lady B.—— gave a despairing, high Wail, like to the Shrieking of a Frog. A thin Worm of Pity stirred within my Bowels. Weeping, she was put back into the Chair; weeping, she was tied.

The piteous Sight moved me thro'out mine intire Body. I wished I were the One to wield the Knife. A Storm of Excitation and the cruellest Desire raged within mine Hands, my Belly, my vicious, importunate Loins; yet mine Heart was wrung with Pity. Her Ladyship's Sufferings, I could discern, were now both real and extreamly great, whatever they had been before. The Reality of her Position had broken in, and the Pains in her Breast and her Arm were no longer perverse Sources of Comfort, but only of Terrour.

Those Pains, I thought, which I would so grievously worsen; and yet, by worsening, intirely take away; thro' harming, heal. The Notion was so beautifull that I could not speak, and mine own Eyes filled, to my greatest Astonishment, with Tears. I blinked.

Dr Oliver then placed a soft linen Band across her Ladyship's Eyes, and bade her shut up and be patient. In the loaded Stillness that descended Dr Hunter removed first his Coat, then his Waistcoat and the Ruffles of his Shirt, before signing to me to come around to the Front of the Chair in order to observe his and Dr Oliver's Deliberations. With some Caution, lest I betray My Self, I approached. He drew mine Attention to a solid Swelling within the outside Tissue of the left Breast, where the Skin was puckered and somewhat flushed. I droppt upon mine Haunches and peered closely at the infected Flesh. My Loins began, to my great Relief, to shrink. The Tumour seemed small, as Dr Hunter had suggested, but mine Instinct was that it lay in an unhappy Place, too near to the Opening of the Lymphatick Channel for my Liking. Indeed, I thought, 'tis past Time this Thing was got out; 'twill kill her frightening quick if it is not. The Knowledge coursed thro' mine Entrails with a sickening Chill. I pondered how deeply the Cancer had rooted within the Breast, and hoped that Dr Hunter's Assessment of its Proportions had been correct.

"Where would you make the Incision, Mr Hart?" Dr Hunter asked.

I understood that this Question was merely to test mine Apprehension of the Case rather than an eager Request for mine Advice. Nevertheless, I indicated silently the Places where I should decide to cut, and then looked to him to see his Reaction.

Dr Hunter nodded. "Intirely right," he said. "Dr Oliver, if you will hold the Organ, Sir, we must begin."

As the good Doctor's Blade bit into her Flesh, Lady B.—— screamed. At once, my Fire was back, as if 'twere never doused. Her Scream was a white Arrow, swift and light, a feathered Shaft vibrating with a stinging Hiss, and climbing, climbing, extatically high, one shining silver Note; but then, as it reached the Apex of its Flight it was suddenly gone. The Room rang with its Silence.

"She hath fainted," said Dr Oliver. "Good."

Good? I thought, with a cruel Spit of Anger. Good? My cheated Body howled Frustration. The aethereal Beauty of the Moment had dissolved into an ugly Lust that had neither Object nor Hope of Satiation. For the second Time, I could have wept.

As my vicious Desire dissipated, my medical Mind, which should always have been in the Ascendant, began more strongly to arouse. Oh, 'tis a Relief, I told My Self, that she is senseless; to me as much as 'tis to her. The Agony, of itself, can do her little Good, and to me 'tis a Distraction I would better do without. I directed mine

Attention closely upon the opened Breast. My Stomach tightened against a Stab of startling Fear. How can Dr Hunter properly assess her vital Condition, if she be not conscious? She may die, I thought.

The Tissue within the Breast was not Flesh, but Fat, and a white glandular Matter, richly supplied with Blood. I recalled the Doctor's Injunction to be quick with mine Irons, and I grippt them tightly, lest they slip. I would be as clever with mine Hand at the cauterising of the leaking Veins and showering Arteries as he was with the Scalpel itself. The Blood was hot upon my Fingers, salt-smelling, slippery, surprising plentiful.

Dr Hunter's Blade worked swiftly and with Precision. The Cancer was in a Lobe hard by the Pectoral Muscle, and it was necessary to cut away all the Glandular Tissue that surrounded it. Such was his Skill that within a very few Minutes, the gross red Body of the Cancer came free from the Flesh. It had the Appearance of a giant Louse, gorged fat with Blood, deeper and darker than the healthy Matter around it. Dr Hunter, keen as always to spare his Patient a Moment's Anguish, ordered Dr Oliver and My Self to begin the Closure and Bandaging of the Wound. But something prevented me.

"No, Sir," I said. I did not compleatly know wherefore. Her Ladyship had begun to revive. Perhaps, I thought, 'twas but the Hope she might be brought to scream again.

"What?" Dr Hunter said.

"You have not finished, Sir." As I spoke, the latent and clouded Suspicion, that had caused me to refuse, came suddenly into brilliant Clarity. Staring into the Body, I perceived, as if it were mapped out for me, the exact Strategy by which the Cancer sought to insinuate itself thro' the healthy Tissue, turning all morbid. I could see precisely where its Incursions began, and in what Direction they were headed. No Louse, but a parasitic Fungus, weaving its deadly Nexus within living Flesh. "There was too much Blood," I said. "From here—and here. The Arrangement of the Arteries in these two Spots is quite unlike to that of the Remainder of the Gland. The Flesh here is corrupt, Sir. I would swear to it."

Dr Hunter cast me an horrified Glance, but, seeing that I was not in any Doubt, he bent over the Lady's Breast to perform his own Inspection of the now cauterised Tissue. "I can see no Corruption," he said.

"Damme, Sir!" I said. "Can not you? The Cancer is growing, Sir."

"Quiet!" said Dr Hunter sharply. "She will hear you. Dr Oliver, your Opinion, please."

"I am, as you know, disinclined towards too much cutting," Dr Oliver said, slowly. "But I think in this Case 'twould be more harmful to excise too little, than too much."

The two Surgeons stared at each other, their Expressions grave. My Cheek grew cold. I could not believe that Dr Hunter would disagree now, after Dr Oliver had given me his Support. The Lady will die, I thought, if he doth not continue. She will die, and she must not. She must not! Time, and mine own Heart, seemed to stop. Then Dr Hunter nodded his Concurrence, and lifted his Scalpel again. Again the Steel sliced thro' the yielding Gland, again the red Blood leapt. The Doctor made no Sound, but from the Speed and Intensity with which he worked, I judged that he had found exactly what I had feared: the Tumour had sent forth two thick bloody Threads, which had burrowed thro' the Breast, towards the Lymph.

This Time, Dr Hunter did not hurry to close up the Wound, despite the Fact that Lady B.—— was now awake, and moaning softly. At his Invitation, Dr Oliver and I inspected the Place, our Eyes sharp to any Atom of infected Matter; but this Time neither of us could see anything amiss.

Dr Hunter gave a relieved Sigh, and having put his Instruments aside, he left the Room in order to wash and change back into his previous Finery. Dr Oliver and My Self were quite bespattered with the Lady's Blood, but that counted for nothing; it would be Dr Hunter she would look for when the linen Band was taken from her Eyes. I washed the Wound with Wine, then sutured it. Finally, I bandaged it as tightly as I could. Lady B.—— was pale as a Corpse, her Skin cold and her Breathing shallow. She said nothing as her Vision was at last unbound, and Dr Oliver and I assisted her to cross the Salon towards her adjoining Bedchamber.

Thank God, I thought, thank God that she is not my Wife.

Once her Ladyship was settled in her Bed, and the Bells rung for her Abigail and household Servants to clean up the Mess in her Salon, I made ready, on foot, to depart the Premises. Dr Hunter, restored to his courtly Dress, and looking almost as smart as if the Operation had never taken place, stayed, to reassure the Lady and her newly returned Husband of its likely Success. Dr Oliver left with me. He had been, he told me, about the House all Daye, and was now most desirous of fresh Aire and Exercise to clear the Blood and Screaming from his Head.

The Weather had brightened whilst we had been within the House. The last Traces of yesterdaye's heavy Fog lingered yet about the cold Corners where the Light did not reach, but the main Thorough-fare was now intirely clear, and thro' the covering Cloud above I could discern occasional Glimpses of the Sunne.

"I had the uncommon Pleasure, yesterdaye, of meeting with a young Man who claims an Aquaintanceship with you," Dr Oliver said, as we walked.

"Who, Sir?"

"One Lt. Isaac Simmins, of the 31st Foot."

"Simmins!" I said. "Little Simmins! Egad! I know not what Cause he should have to wish to claim any Connexion with me! He was my Tutor's Son and I treated him with precious little Kindness."

"He spoke fondly of you, in my Opinion. Perhaps you have more, and better, Friends than you know, Mr Hart."

"Indeed," I said. "I must have better Friends than I deserve. Where is Lt. Simmins staying? I shall write to him."

"I do not know the Address," Dr Oliver replied. "But I am sure you may smoake it easy enough. He was waiting upon an Associate of mine own, who hath, I believe, done him some Service I presume to be financial. Mine Associate hath no Child, and I believe your Friend to be the latest in a long Line of young Men whose Careers he hath seen fit to advance."

We had by now come to the Crossroads at the northern End of Covent Garden. Dr Oliver, whose Destination lay in the opposite Direction from mine, bade me Good Afternoon and turned to leave. He had gone no more than three Paces, however, when he stoppt and looked back. "That was a sound Judgement," he said. "You may well have saved the Lady's Life."

"Thank you, Sir," I said.

"Where do you go now? I should not go straight home, if I were you. I should visit one of these Houses and relieve that—Irritation. It amazes me that you were able to think at all, let alone so clearly."

With that, Dr Oliver touched his Hat, and scurried away thro' the Covent Garden Crowds. I stood in the Street, bestilled by Shock.

CHAPTER FOURTEEN

I continued to stand, mortified, mine Eyes fixt upon the Space into which Dr Oliver had disappeared. A cold Breath passed thro' me. Dr Oliver had seen it all. Dear God, I thought, and what did Dr Hunter see? Will he ever let me near to any of his Patients again? Yet Dr Oliver had also seen that I had perhaps saved the Lady's Life.

My Thoughts turned then to the Lady, and, despite my wishing they would not, to how she had called me Jew. I cursed my dark Countenance, and the Sephardic Heritage that had coloured it. If my Father, I thought, had but shewn the Sense to marry an Englishwoman, I should mayhap have been blessed with the bright

Skin and blue Eyes of Jacob, instead of the swarthy Complexion of Esau. Yet, even as I gave birth to the Thought, I disowned it. It was not in me truly to regret my Mother. None the less, I thought. It would have been a fine thing if I had favoured my Father's Family, instead of hers. I felt even my Mother would have admitted that.

The small Seed of Anger, which her Ladyship, by her Outburst, had sown, began to take Root within my Stomach. How dared she, I thought, insult me so? I had come to heal, not to humiliate her. Had I wished I could have dealt her such a Wound as she would never have recovered from. Had I not held the Irons?

At this Thought, a darkling Rage, a deep, slow Fury unlike anything I had before experienced, boiled up within my Stomach and mine Heart. I could not breathe. I stood aghast, as the Passion unopposed took first Possession of my Chest and then my Throat, squeezing all as if within the deadliest Compress. An ugly Roar, an Howl more potent than the Polyphemian Bawl swelled within mine Ears, within mine Head; a desolate, primitive Yowl of ragged Pain.

As if I had been an Automaton, I put mine Hands over mine Ears. I shook mine Head. The Howling continued. Mine Heart felt as if 'twere on the Point of bursting from my Ribs. As an Automaton, again, I began to walk toward Mrs Haywood's House, toward Polly Smith. Perhaps this was at Dr Oliver's Suggestion; perhaps, and more like, for his Remark had shrivelled any Concupiscence in me, it was merely the Prompting of fixt Habit. For Months, I had driven off the Drumming with my Lash. Mayhap, I could silence this raw Howl, bury this Rage within Polly's insulating Flesh.

As I walked, I recalled the silvery Cry Lady B.—— had given, and how it had died in mid Flight. My Desire began to stir, and this Time I did not resist it. I might succeed in coaxing such an aerial Scream from Polly; and it would be under mine own Hands and within my Power to maintain and to prolong. The Dread I had felt upon leaving Lady B.——; the aweful, speechless Fear that such Disease could ever afflict a Woman whom I loved, began to shrink. Mine Heart gave one great shuddering Leap within me; mine Hands began to itch. I quickened my Pace. My Lust cut thro' the Covent Garden Crowd and parted it, like Water.

Daniel Bright, under the Portico, bade me "Good Afternoon", and permitted me Entry despite my sombre and somewhat despoiled Attire. I was not expected, but I did not foresee that Circumstance occasioning Mrs Haywood any Difficulty.

The greatest Force of my Rage had begun to be soothed the Instant I had steppt toward the Brothel. Now, as I waited in the Roman Hallway, pacing to and fro across the Sabine Floor, I felt almost calm. After a few Minutes, Mrs Haywood's little Maid brought me mine accustomed Glass of red Wine, trembling on its Tray, and asked if she might take mine Hat and Greatcoat.

"I may have saved a Life todaye, Lily," I said, conscious of the blood Stains already upon my Person. I told her exactly how. She was quite pale by the Time I finished.

"Are you not going to congratulate me?" I said.

"Oh, yes, Sir," stammered Lily, dropping an half-Curtsey. "You are very clever, Sir."

"I know that," I said. "Tell me something else."

"What, Sir?" squeaked Lily, desperately. "What should I say?"

"Tell me that I am lucky."

At that Moment, to the plain Relief of Lily, the Door to the Stairwell at the far End of the Atrium clicked open, and Mrs Haywood appeared. She was clad in bright scarlet Silks, perhaps to make up for the dismal Weather, and sported upon her Head the grandest Wigg I had ever seen her wear. "Ah," I said, as Comprehension dawned. "How is the Privy Councillor?"

"Somewhat subdued," answered Mrs Haywood. She glided forward with her gloved Hand outstretched. I bent low over it. The mingled Scents of body Fluids and Hungary Water filled my Nostrils.

"My dear Mr Hart," said Mrs Haywood. "This is an unexpected Pleasure. What is it that you require?"

"I was hoping," I said, straightening up, "that I might have the Use of your Polly."

"When, Sir?"

"Now."

"'Tis impossible," Mrs Haywood said. "Pauline is sleeping, and will not be woken until tonight. I will not have her over-taxed."

"No, indeed," I said. I was greatly disappointed. "Polly—Pauline— is a Treasure. But what am I to do? I have in Truth, Madam, even now a very great and pressing Need, and I fear the Consequence if it cannot be met."

Mrs Haywood smiled. "If it were at all to your Taste," she said, narrowing her Eyes, "I should invite you to join the Privy Councillor and My Self in the great Chamber. He would not object."

I laughed. "I should be honoured," I said, returning the Jest. "But I would feel My Self to be too much *in statu pupillari* to enjoy the Experience."

"You flatter me too much, Sir, and you are too diffident of your own Accomplishments. You are no Novice."

"High Praise, Madam," I said, bowing. "But let us return to my Difficulty."

"Very well," said Mrs Haywood, becoming business-like. "You may spend the Afternoon with Antoinette, if that Prospect excites you. She is without a Suitor todaye, and she is far from inexperi-enced. Perhaps it is Time she learned how to please a different Taste. But you must take Care not to mark her."

Antoinette, christened Annie Moon by her Parents, was one of Mrs Haywood's pretty Girls. She was, however, well on into her twenties, and I had the Impression that she would not be much ruined by mine Approaches, if they were not overly ferocious. She had mouse brown Hair beneath her Cap, and Eyes that were beau-tifully blue, if woefully unintelligent. Her Forehead was high, and her Complexion compleatly fair, tho' I suspected this was not without Assistance. Her Breasts were full, and wobbled atop her Stays like rich Puddings. She had short Fingers, and soft fleshed, plump Wrists.

Under usual Circumstances, I would not have been aroused by the Prospect of using Annie. But my Circumstances were not usual, and my Desire was desperate. In the Absence of anyone better, Annie would have to do. I forced my Memory to flash back again to Lady B.—. If she had but remained conscious, I thought; for her Scream was perhaps the sweetest I have ever heard.

"I shall take Care," I said, "to leave Antoinette exactly as intact as I shall find her."

Mrs Haywood kissed me on the Cheek, and then, bidding me stay till I should be fetched, spun about in a red Hiss of Silk, and left the Atrium.

I was by now so cheared of mine earlier black Passion that it began to seem as if the Howling in mine Head had never been. The mere Decision to bury it had achieved that Design as efficiently as would its practical Enactment. I was astonished by this Fact, and intrigued. What wonderfull Faculty within mine Imagination had translated the Idea alone into the material Balm by which my bodily

Passions could be eased? Again, I thought, something hath closed the Gap betwixt Body and Thought.

"Mr Hart?"

Roused from my Reflexions, I lifted mine Head and beheld Annie standing in the far Doorway, which led to the Stairs. At the Sight of her, the Concupiscence of my Loins happily reawakened; the electric Fluid pooled at the base of my Spine.

I steppt smartly forward and took both her Hands in mine. A gentle Beginning, but already I was feeling for her Pulse.

She led me quietly up the Stairs to a back Bedroom, hastily prepared, in which all the common Regalia of the Harlot's Trade were in plain Sight; the Dildoes, the Brandy, the Laudanum. Upon a small Table at the Side of the Bed was a Roman Vase, filled, not with Flowers, but with many long, stiff Feathers, plucked originally from a Goose, but dyed into a Rainbow that shone out against the dark brown Curtain. Upon the Floor at the Base of the Bed was a small iron Chest. It was locked, but Mrs Haywood had, some Months ago, at my Request, furnished me with a Key.

I ordered Annie to strip intirely naked before me, whilst I watched. This she did, altho' initially she expresst Suspicion at the Presence of the Chest.

"Mrs Haywood didn't say nuffin' about that," she said.

I told her truthfully that it was not my Desire that she be whippt, and she then, quite chearfully, divested herself of her Garments. I pondered what, if anything, Mrs Haywood had told her, and for a Moment I thought that I ought to explain to her what mine Intention was. Previously, I had had no intimate Dealings with Annie, altho' she had been present once or twice in the early Dayes when, still compelled by the base Need to fuck, I had pinned down one of the other Women in her Presence.

Perhaps, I thought, that is what she imagines to be mine Intention now. Certainly, she hath Reason to assume it: I have never made Trial of any Woman here but Polly. But then I recalled that Annie was an experienced Whore, and that if Mrs Haywood had not told her, she ought to have guessed. Her Surprize is counterfeit, I told My Self. I smiled.

Seeing me smile, Annie wriggled her nude Form before my Face, and with an artful Expression doubtless intended to entice me, positioned herself atop the Bed with her fleshy Thighs spread to their farthest Extent, and her ample Breasts thrust upwards.

This fulfilled not half my Purpose, so, instructing her to remain thus poised, I withdrew my Key, which I kept always about my Person, and opened up the strong-Box. Alas, no hot Irons; but Instruments of Torture equally dear, and surely less equivocal. I quickly selected two Pairs of Shackles and a blindfold.

At the Sight of mine Appearance, Annie tried to quit the Bed, crying: "Liar!" and she put up a vigorous Resistance. But I was so much the stronger, that within very few Minutes I had her secured by her Ankles and her Wrists to the four Posts of the Bed, and the Blindfold tied across her Eyes. Then I took a deep Breath. I was ready to begin.

I shall take this slowly, I thought, hardening my Mind. I shall savour every Moment before quenching my Fire upon her at the very End.

I removed my Frock and my Waistcoat, and unlaced my Breeches. The black Hair of mine Arms was visible thro' the Lace of my Cuffs. I heard the Voice of Lady B.——, calling me Jew.

"Be quiet, you Bitch!" I snapped. Annie had begun to swear and cry. "There is worse to come than this," I said.

Mindful of Mrs Haywood's Prescription that I leave no Mark, I had already determined that the largest Portion of Annie's Torment should be mental. There was, I knew, a certain piteous Enchantment to be enjoyed in the Whimperings of Fear, as in those of Pain, altho' the Sound was subtilely different, and the Effects, generally, somewhat less dramatic. Additionally, as Annie had undresst, and engaged upon her little Pantomime, I had realised that I had neither Patience nor Desire to be attentive to her Condition, as I would have had to be if I had beat her. So I sate down upon the Bed at Annie's Side, and gently ran mine Hand over the Hollow of her Throat, the scarred, child-ruined Fat of her Belly.

"Dost honestly believe," I began, acting my Part, "that Mrs Haywood hath any genuine Regard for your Person, or, indeed, your Life? Poor, misguided Antoinette. Mrs Haywood hath told me that I may do anything I want with you, that you are quite dried up, and fit for nothing else. You are naught to her. But you can be very useful to me. For a long Time I have desired the Opportunity to perform a Vivisection upon an healthy Female, and you are to be the Specimen." I ran both my Hands again over the delicate Expanses of her Breasts, and the Image of the creamy glandular Tissue within opened up reflexively before my Mind's Eye. As I finished speaking, she became intirely still, and I judged that she was pondering whether I could be telling Truth or no; unless she simply did not apprehend the Meaning of the Word "Vivisection'. Against this latter Possibility, I put my Lips once more to her Ear, and explained precisely what it did mean, and the exquisite Agonies I imagined she would endure thereby.

"'Taint True," she said, tho I could hear the tiniest Gleam of Doubt in her Voice. "Mrs Haywood wouldn't. You daren't."

"Daren't? Wherefore should not I dare anything? Whoever would come after me? If you die, Mrs Haywood will help me to throw your Body in the Stink. You are not her precious Pauline. She hath decided to cut her Losses; you do not earn enough to pay for your Keep."

"I do!" Annie said. "I do!"

"If you have any Peace to make with God," I said, "'Twere better that you make it."

I then, for I was near upon the Point of attaining my Desire, took from the Vase upon the bedside Table, one of the long goose Feathers that had appeared so bright against the dark Hangings of the Bed. "Antoinette," I said softly. "I am going to cut you."

"No!" Annie cried, and she began to thrash and strain hard against her Bonds. Obscenities rose from her in a vicious Cloud. Yes, I thought. A wild, intoxicating Gush surged lightning fast from my Stomach to my Loins, and back again; so potent that I was nigh doubled over and thrown down upon my Knees. Panting hard, I turned the Feather in mine Hand and presst the hard Quill roughly into the soft Flesh of Annie's Breast.

Annie screamed.

It had not the extatic Beauty of Lady B.——'s anguished Shriek, but it was a fair Yell, sparkling and bright. I freed my virile Member from my Breeches, and poised My Self between Annie's Legs. But that first Scream was failing; I knew that I must induce another if I was to reach my Glory, so I dragged the Quill down, across the Breast, quite quick and in a slicing Motion. Once more she screamed; and as the high, volatile Sound filled the Alembic of the Chamber, my Mind vanished, the Feather tumbled from my Fingers, and I spilled mine heavenly Delight all over the plump Whiteness of her Thighs.

I did not intirely know how much Time had passt when I noticed that the Screaming had stoppt. I lifted my Body from Annie's, and saw, to mine Amazement, that she was limp and senseless. "Antoinette?" I ventured. Then I realised that, for the second Time that Daye, my Lady had lost Consciousness. I sate up. Annie's creamy Skin had taken on a greyish Pallour, and was clammy to my Touch. It appeared that she had fainted, truly fainted, thro' pure Fear.

"Damme! Damme!"

All my Desire for Annie, or for anyone else thro' her Proxy, was now extinguished. I swiftly removed her Blindfold and Shackles, bruising mine own Finger in mine Haste, and felt again to assess the Quality of her Pulse. Finding it regular, if somewhat shallow, I laid her upon her Side lest she should vomit, and covered her with the Counterpane before the Shock could chill her vital Organs. I hurriedly relaced my Breeches, and dresst.

Mine Attention then returned to Annie, who was beginning to regain her Senses. To mine unparalleled Relief I perceived that her Complexion had lost its deathly Aspect, and that a little Warmth was beginning to creep back into her Skin. I approached the small Table at the Bedside, and poured a Glass of Brandy from the Bottle thereon. Then I sate My Self upon the Bed. I stroaked Annie's Hair, and watched her Features closely as her Eyelids fluttered. She gave a tiny Whimper, then her blue Eyes flashed awake and she drew Breath to give me yet another Scream. I placed mine Hand over her Mouth.

"Hush, now," I said. "All is over. I shall not harm you. Nor have I; you are not cut."

I made her to sit up, and presst into her shivering Hands the Tumbler of Brandy. She recoiled from me and scrambled to the other Side of the Bed. "You Fuckster," she said. "You evil prick-docked Fuckster."

"As you wish," I said. "It is over, none the less." I got to my Feet. Annie's Words had reassured me that she was recovering rapidly from her Fright. Yet as I looked at her, her Face seemed, for one short, shifting Instant, to be not her own, but that of a Gypsy Girl, frightened and furious in the early dawn Light.

Evil, I thought. Evil, evil.

Guilt thudded thro' me like a Spear. I reached into my Pocket and withdrew my Purse. I took out three Shillings—all, presently, that it contained—and placed them upon the Table next to the candle Snuffer. "I lied," I said. "Mrs Haywood told me explicitly that you must not be marked. But we both know that will not last. Save what you can and pay off your Debts to her before you are too poxed and old for her to care what Condition anyone should leave you in."

I turned, and fled.

That night, I did not sleep. The peccant Medusa of the Cancer hung before me in mine Eye, its vicious Filaments spreading. I greatly feared that Dr Hunter had not cut all of it away. 'Twould be preferable, I thought, in such a Case, if the intire Breast were to be removed; there would be a far better Chance of excising the Whole. If one Morsel hath been retained, the Evil will revive; and she surely will not consent to a second Operation.

If I were evil, how could I credit my Diagnosis?

I vainly tried to distract My Self from mine Anxieties by letting my Mind run over the Incident at the Brothel. I knew that the Pain I had inflicted upon Annie had been minor, yet she had responded to it as if it had been the most extream Agony. I could only conclude that her Sensitivity to the physical Sensation had been intirely due to the Words and Ideas I had put into her Mind. These had, somehow, so heightened Annie's perceptual Experience of her Torture that she had verily perceived that I was cutting into her Flesh. Fear, and Pain, had become one Experience. As Dr Hunter had said: the State of Mind was paramount. I had been acting a Part, but Annie, clearly, had not. She had thought that the thing had been intirely real. The fearsome Idea of Pain—a purely mental thing—had so powerfully affected her Senses and her bodily Reactions that she had fainted away as cleanly as if I had genuinely made her the Subject of a Vivisection.

This Analysis gave no Comfort. It was slowly becoming horribly plain to me that I had done Annie Harm, real and most likely lasting, for all that it was not of a physical Nature. Moreover, I could not hide from the Knowledge that her Injury had not been accidental to my taking Pleasure or finding Relief. Bad enough, had it been so; but I had suspected at the first that she had not fully understood what was to happen, and because I was angry and impatient, I had let My Self believe that this did not matter. Perhaps, indeed, I had secretly preferred it thus. I had tortured her to play out the Phantasy of taking my Revenge upon that other Woman whose very Life had lain beneath mine Hands, and which for very Shame I should never have dreamed make manifest. It had not been accidental. I had wanted to break her.

Evil, evil.

Since the Incident with the infant Bat, it had become mine Habit, when I could not sleep, to steal down-Stairs in Search of a Panacea; so, at about three in the Morning, this I did. The House was silent and, I thought, abed. But upon opening the library Door, I discovered, to my Shock, that I was not alone. Mr Henry Fielding, who rarely left his Bed once he was got into it, had limped painfully down-Stairs and was sitting in a high backed Armchair, lawfully partaking of the very Nantes I had intended to pilfer. Seeing me stoppt short within the Doorway, he raised an Eyebrow and his Glass, and beckoned me to come forth.

"So," he said with a slow Chuckle. "Caught in the Act, Mr Hart. I take it that you were about to help yourself to my Brandy?"

Appalled, I stood motionless. "I apologise," I said, as my Face grew hot.

"I can always tell when Tristan Hart hath suffered a bad Night," Mr Fielding said. "For my Nantes will be half empty in the Morning, without fail."

I made an incoherent Sound, and wished that the Floor would chasm and swallow me; but naturally it did not, and I remained standing in the Doorway, my Cheeks blazing and my Sentiments dismayed.

Mr Fielding laughed. "Be easy," he said. "I shall not put you in the Bridewell, Robber tho' you be. Come and join me in a Glass."

Too horribly embarrassed to know whether I ought better to accept or to decline this kind Offer, I chose to accept it, and gratefully steppt up to the cup Board, where I poured My Self an half-Measure of Brandy.

"Do not you stint yourself, Tristan," Mr Fielding said. "You are not usually so abstemious. Double that and be damned."

"Mr Fielding," I said, taking him at his Word and sloshing a few more Ounces of the dark Liquid into my Glass. "I am sorry for my Conduct, and I do apologise, Sir; but I must object to being made fun of."

"Oho!" Mr Fielding exclaimed, sitting up in his Armchair. "Must you, indeed! Object, indeed! Well, well, young Man, I shall let pass your ill Humour in addition to your criminal one; if you will tell me what brings you down-Stairs in the Middle of as chill a Night as this?"

I picked up my candle Stub, which was more than half burned down, and my Drink, and seated My Self in an uncomfortable low Armchair facing Mr Fielding's. I had not thought the Night particularly cold; but now that he had drawn mine Attention to it, I noticed that a low Draught was gusting sporadically from the Hearth, whose Fire had long since died. I wrappt my night-Gown tightly about my Legs, and hoped that a rogue Breeze would not find its Way underneath the Hem.

I did not speak of Annie. "Corruption," I said. "In the fairest of Breasts."

"Explain your Meaning, and I may share your Sympathies."

"'Twas something Mr John once remarked," I said. "'Corruption may lurk within the Fairest of Breasts.' Todaye, I watched Dr Hunter do Battle with it; but I fear he may have left the Field too soon. I fear the Lady may be riddled with the Disease, and will die; and tho' I can do naught at all, I cannot sleep for Dread of it."

Mr Fielding regarded me with his piercing Stare for several Seconds. Then he cleared his Throat. "That," he said, "is no Surprize, surely?"

"Wherefore?" I asked him. "I have assisted in other Procedures without their occasioning me any Difficulty in sleeping."

"But Tristan," Mr Fielding said, quietly, "none of those Procedures was the one that could have saved your Mother."

Too astounded to respond, I stared at Mr Fielding.

"I have always believed," he went on, "that your Desire to study Medicine, and Surgery especially, hath its Roots in your Mother's Refusal to undergo it. A Boy with your Perspicacity, even at five, must have understood much of what was happening, even tho' his Father tried his best to shield him from it."

"I have no Memory," I stammered. "I recall my Mother, but nothing of her Death. One Daye I remember her being alive, the next, dead one whole Yeare. 'Tis usual, is it not, for small Children to remember little of their Lives before a certain Age?"

"It is." Mr Fielding was looking at me queerly. He took a Sip of his Brandy and I followed suit. The bitter-sweet Spirit burned my Throat. Tears came into mine Eyes; I coughed.

"My Father never speaks of her," I said.

"So I understand."

"He is not a bad Man," I said, tho' why I felt My Self suddenly compelled to defend my Father I had no Idea. "He hath tried to do his best by me, and by my Sister. But . . ." I struggled to find the correct Words. "But he hath so little Sensibility of our Feelings, one might sometimes imagine him to be intentionally cruel."

"Sometimes," said Mr Fielding, "that is how Grief works."

CHAPTER FIFTEEN

I did not learn whether Lady B.'s Cancer was, ultimately, cured or not. Certainly, it did not to my Knowledge recur during the Time I was to remain in London. But the whole Experience had rattled and disturbed me to an Extent greater than I was prepared to admit. Mr Fielding's Analysis of my Motives intrigued and frightened me in equal Measure. For the Remainder of April and the next Fortnight I could think of little else. Mine Instinct was to repudiate the Notion, even to ridicule it; but like—so I feared—the Cancer, I could not excise it. I buried My Self deep within my Work, but no matter how involved Mine Hands, how exhausted my Body, my Mind's relentless questioning would not abate.

I could perceive, altho' I did not want to, that if Mr Fielding were correct, his Argument would entail at least two bloody Threads of logical Extension and philosophic Inquiry, each of which led to a Conclusion as fearfull as it was remarkable.

If mine own Mother had died of the Disease, then my near Panick at the Notion of Lady B.——'s probable Death seemed almost comprehensible; excepting for the Fact that I had not known, and did not remember, anything of the Circumstances of my Mother's Death. If Mr Fielding's Analysis was right, then my whole Motive to become any sort of Doctor had its Origin in that infant Loss; but that was to suppose that I remembered an Event that I did not remember; that I was both ignorant and yet had full Cognition of at the same Time. How, I wondered, could such a Paradox possibly be true? 'Tis utterly impossible, I thought, that I could be unaware of an Awareness.

Yet the Conceit troubled me still. I knew from Experience that my Senses were not always to be trusted. Could the same thing be true of my Memory? I could not know. If I knew, I should be remembering what I did not, and the whole Wheel would spin again. What I did know, knew for certain, was that I had wanted to cause Pain to Lady B.——. I had desired to heal her, too; but I had wanted to hear her Scream, none the less. I had not known then—unless I had—that my Mother had died of the very Disease that I was trying to save the Lady from. But suppose, suppose some hidden Power in mine Imagination had transformed her, without even mine Awareness, into a Simulacrum of my Mother? The Implication then was that I wanted, or would have wanted, to hear—or to have heard—my Mother screaming also. That Thought, the Thought of her in Pain, terrified me to the Core. That Idea decanted a Chymistry of Horrour, innate and immediate; Fear and

Panick and Love and Anger mixt without Aire in a Crucible Flask, swirling and combining, never catching Fire.

And yet, and yet—if I had heard that Scream, my Mother might have lived.

The Idea that I might remember, and yet not remember, my Mother's Death; that I might desire to hurt her and yet recoil from the very Thought, was almost too horrible to contemplate. When I had witnessed Viviane's Transformation from Woman into Owl, I had blamed my physical Senses; when I had feared that I had ravished her, I had been able to blame them still, for I remembered only what my disordered Senses had shewn me. But this was of another Order of Madness. If my Memory, and mine Imagination, were as confused as this would seem to make them, then mine apparent Sanity was as illusory as the Shaddowes on the Wall in Bedford's Coffee-house.

And yet again—and here the second bloody Thread—I could not disswade My Self from pondering what it might mean if Mr Fielding were correct, and my Memory both was and was not; and I was not mad. Could it possibly be that all Men's Minds functioned thus? A Muddle of paradoxical Contradictions and seeming Impossibilities that somehow, almost magically, were true? Perhaps, I thought, there are Darknesses in the Mind where the Eye of Consciousness doth not penetrate. Where doth any ordinary Memory exist when it is not in Process of Recollection? It hath not ceased to be. Yet it is neither in Man's Awareness, nor is he aware of its Lack.

I could not foresee quite where this line of Questioning was like to lead me, nor did it even begin to address the Conundrum of how I, My Self, could possibly remember something I did not. But I could not abandon it. Mine Ideas spiralled like the darkening Sea. I felt sick and dizzy from the continued Motion.

At the End of the first Week of June, I returned home for my Sister's Nuptials. I was displeased, as this meant that I should have to take some Dayes off from the Hospital; but the Valley of the Horse was beautifull; its Woods in vibrant Leaf, chirring with the million Trills of Finches; its Fields sparkling with Butterflies. I had not feasted mine Eyes upon such a Glut of Greenery for so long, I soon felt My Self engorged beyond Satiety, and drew down the carriage Blinds.

Altho' I had left Shirelands in deep Dread of the Valley, which my Bones insisted had taken violent against me when I had accosted Viviane, returning home I experienced an odd Sensation of Reprieve, as if my Presence had not been noticed at all. Pondering this, it occurred to me that perhaps the *genius loci* must take time to recognise me, and I felt safe, if only for the nonce; for it did not occur to me once to presume my Mittimus exhausted.

The Carriage pulled up at the front Door of Shirelands Hall shortly before Noon on the second Daye of travelling. Jane must have been awaiting me, for no sooner had the Movement stoppt than I heard a quick feminine Tread upon the Gravel and her affectionate Voice impatiently calling my Name. The coach Door being opened by the Postillion, and the Step put down, I rapidly descended, grateful to stretch my constricted Limbs and Spine. My Shoes had scarcely touched the Ground when my Sister flung herself upon me.

"Dear Tristan!" she said. "It is so good to have you home!" She steered me straight into the House, chattering like a Yellowhammer. We took Tea within the turquoise Cool of the front drawing Room, the Shades half drawn. The Tea tasted like Tea.

Very little had changed at Shirelands Hall whilst I had been absent from it. My Father remained the same unapproachable

Recluse, altho' he had consented, after many harsh Scoldings from mine Aunt Barnaby, to exchange his Black for Grey upon the Daye of Jane's Wedding. Jane viewed this small Concession as a great Triumph, as she believed that once he had taken off his Mourning, he would not rush to put it on again. I thought that was unlikely, but I did not say so.

Apart from this, Jane's Nuptials, and Removal to Withy Grange, took up the whole of her Attention. I quietly perceived that she was much more delighted at the Prospect of becoming Mistress in her own House than she appeared to be at that of marrying Barnaby. I was not unamused by this.

"Over Christmas," she said, "I shall aim to entertain as much as possible. We shall hold a Ball on Boxing Daye, and all our Friends shall stay until February, if they will."

"Ah! You will hold Court."

Jane tilted up her Nose in Disgust at my poor Sarcasm. "I have had enough," she said, "of silent Meals."

"Of course you have," I said, regretting my Jibe. "I trust you shall have many Hundreds of happier ones."

Jane forgave me at once, it being beyond her Nature to hold any Grudge. She presst me to visit the Grange as soon as I was able, and to stay for at least a Month. I did not tell her how intolerable I should find such a Circumstance. To be an whole Month in Company with James Barnaby!

Eventually, when I could do so in a subtile Manner, I asked after the Ravenscrofts, meaning by this, Nathaniel.

"Oh," my Sister said, rolling her Eyes. "They are all very well, especially now that they have lost all the Montagues, apart from Kate the Cursed."

"Kate the What?"

"Oh, no! La! I did not mean to call her that! Kate the Cursed is Sophy's Nickname for their Cousin, Katherine. It is not kind or charitable of Sophy, but the Girl is, by all Accounts, quite dreadful. She is only twelve and already the most shameless Flirt I have ever heard of. Not only that, she is given to violent Passions and Outbursts of Temper. Sophy said that she was hit by her upon the Ear, and it began to bleed."

"What Cousin is this?" I asked. "I remember none having such a Temperament."

"You would not. She used to be rather sweet. She is staying at the Rectory now because her Mother cannot control her any longer. Can you imagine? I do pray she will not be at my Wedding. She could ruin it."

"No twelve yeare old Shrew will ruin your Wedding, Jane," I said. "I shall take it upon My Self to lock her in a Closet, or throw her in the River, if she looks set to begin a Scene."

I spoke in Jest, but for an Instant, Jane looked worried. "Tristan, please don't," she said.

The eighth Daye of June dawned the clear blue of a Sparrow's Egg, flecked with tiny Clouds of white and grey. The Aire was still, and a slight Chill lingered in the blossoming Elder and long, flowering Grass.

I had little to do before leaving for Church, so shortly after eight I took My Self away into the Gardens, to compleat some Observations upon a Sett of anatomical Drawings I had procured from Dr Hunter. I had just finished mine Annotations upon the Ligaments of the Symphysis Pubis when Mrs H. came hurrying across the Lawn to tell me that the Coach had been ready for some

Time, and that if I did not come quickly my Sister would be made late for her wedding.

I supposed that Jane looked very fetching in her Garland and her wedding Dress, which was of blue Silk, and had been made especially for the Occasion. But I could not tear mine Eyes away from my Father, who appeared to them as somebody I scarcely recognised. I had never seen my Father out of Black. Yet there he stood, a striking handsome Figure in dove grey Frock and Breeches, clutching an ebon Cane, the immaculate white Ringlets of his Wigg reaching below his Shoulders. The Ravenscrofts are right, I thought. He is but eight-and-forty. He should marry again.

My Father assisted Jane into the Coach and I climbed after. Jane was exuberantly lively, at first, on the Way to Church, and confabulated endlessly about the Weather, the wedding Breakfast and the House at Withy Grange. Finally, I was forced to follow my Father's Example and stare out of the Window in an Attempt to shut her up; but she merely continued to herself.

The Carriage was forced to slow as it entered the Village. I heard the excited Babble of country Voices in the Road, every one eager for a Sight of Jane in her wedding Gown and my Father out of his Mourning. Poor Jane, I thought. She would have done far better to have suffered him keep his Black.

St Peter's Church stood in the Centre of the Village, atop a small grassy Knolle. It was a crumbling Edifice dating from sometime during the Hundred Yeares War; brimming aloft with Gargoyles and below with Tombs of mine Ancestors. I could never approach it without a peculiar queasy Sensation stirring in my Gut, as if I had been underneath the Eyes of the multifarious Dead. Todaye, tho', the Church's grey Walls glowed in the summer Light. The

Bells were sounding brightly and with great Chear, and even the Graveyard's Rooks stalked with a sprightly Step.

The Coach stoppt at the church Gate. I dismounted smartly and hoppt out of the Way as first my Father and then Jane descended. The large Crowd of Locals who had gathered on the Spot parted before me like the Red Sea, and then stood at a respectful Distance to admire the wondrous Spectacle that was my Family.

A Flower had worked itself loose from Jane's bridal Wreath during the Journey, and she was now near to an Hysteric on Account of it, despite the Fact that no Deficiency was apparent in the Garland. Having tried once to explain this, and been violently rebuffed, I decided that the safest thing to do was to depart at once into the Church and take my Place whilst Jane composed herself. I supposed, too, that my Father should have some private Words for her at this Moment, tho' what Comfort he could give to her evaded me.

I left them, therefore, at the Gate, and passed thro' into the aged Building. Entering the musty Nave, I made my Way as quietly as possible to the family Pew, from where I surveyed the assembled Company.

The Barnabys had brought all their Relations; or at least, as many of them as could be got to fit within St Peter's Church. Across the Aisle, mine Aunt sate up beside James Barnaby, talking animatedly. He, for his part, seemed as unruffled as if he were about to listen in upon a boring Piece of chamber Musick. If he upsets my Sister, I thought, I shall break every Bone in his Body. The Resolution pleased me.

Behind me in the Rows sate the Rector's Wife; and Sophia, now grown very handsome, in dark blue Silks with a curled Wigg. She smiled at me. Next came the Remainder of the Ravenscrofts, now swelled to fourteen; and another whom I guessed must be Kate the Cursed.

I had expected, from what Jane had told me, that she should be dark, but Kate had Bianca's Colouring. She was well grown for twelve, if twelve she was, and sate as tall as Sophy, altho' she was considerably more slender. Her Gaze was fixt in an intense Scrutiny of the Back of the Pew in front of her, and her Expression, I thought, could have curdled Milk. A Pity, as she would otherwise have been a rare Beauty. The Sadness of her Aspect did not seem to fit with Jane's Description of her as a shameless Flirt. If anything, she appeared to me as one withdrawn, walled up inside a private Purgatory beyond the reach of Man, and disinclined to break out.

In mine Interest, I had looked at her a little too long; Katherine felt my Gaze upon her and lifted her Head to stare back at me out of clear grey Eyes as startling as the Moon.

At once her Countenance was transfigured, as if the Light had altered both without and within it. Her Eyes widened, and her Lips parted slightly in Surprize. Then she began to smile; not as a Flirt would do, but wistfully, as if she was not even aware that she was smiling; coloured, and turned her Face away.

You, I thought.

At that Moment Jane entered the Church with our Father, and a mended Garland, and the Service began. I whirled about, disguising my Confusion under the Pretext that I had droppt my prayer-Book. St John himself could not have been more stunned. Every Nerve in mine whole Flesh had caught afire.

She is but twelve, I told My Self as Jane and Barnaby linked Hands before the Altar. She is too young, and too nice to be interesting to me, by any Means whatever.

"Marriage," intoned the Rector Ravenscroft to Barnaby and Jane, "is not an Estate to be entered into lightly, for the Gratification of carnal Lusts; but a sacred Covenant, akin to that betwixt God and Mankind."

How rapid would her Heart beat 'neath mine Hand?

I stared forwards, but I did not perceive whatever it was that stood in front of me. Instead, I seemed to see Katherine Montague's Features, chisseled in high Relief upon the Stone: her light grey Eyes, that slanted very slightly upwards at the Corners; thickly lashed, and a little more prominent than they should have been, but only by enough that their Beauty was increased thereby; her high Cheekbones; her delicate Jaw, which ended in a Chin a mere Fraction too sharp; her small, uneven Teeth. I wondered at her translucent ivory Skin, her pale Lips, all without a Touch of Whitelead; and at that Aire of unbreachable Sadness thro' which I had somehow penetrated, tho' without Intention, tho' without Desire.

I know her, I thought.

What doth she sound like when she shrieks aloud? Surely it must be clear and fine, the Whistling of a Curlew in the cold Light shortly after Dawn. I want to take her down, and wrap her in mine Arms, and soothe the Agonies away.

The Service finally drawing to a close, I was at last able to turn around, but to my Disappointment neither Mrs Ravenscroft nor Katherine was there, and I beheld only Sophia. I concluded that the other two had left the Church sometime during an Hymn, and I began to imagine that Jane's Fears had come home to roost regarding Kate.

I could control her, I thought. And then: Control her! I? Damned if I could! I cannot even control mine own Thoughts. In Church, too. The sooner I am gone from Berkshire the better.

The Crowd by now having thinned, I was at last at Liberty to leave my Pew without Embarrassment. I straightened my Body, and, I hoped, my Mind, and followed some of Barnaby's countless Relations into the warm morning Sunnelight. The fresh Aire heartened me, but only for a Moment. Mrs Ravenscroft and Katherine Montague stood amidst the Gravestones on the Sward that sloped down to the open Meadow, surrounded by ruminating Sheep. Katherine looked me up and down. A slight Smile, subtily different in its Nature and Suggestion from her prior Expression, played about the Corners of her Lips. She turned her Head, cutting me intirely; then glanced back slyly, to see what I had thought and what I would do next about the Business.

Having more Sense than to walk straight past my Sister in her Houre of Triumph, I first kissed Jane, and wished her an happy Marriage. I then congratulated Barnaby. Mine Advice to him, I decided, should be given later, and not right in front of his joyful Bride. Nevertheless, I embraced him in a more than brotherly Hugg that cost him some Pains to get out of, and I am sure left him with a Soreness in his Neck, which had been always ridiculously stiff. Then I proceeded thro' the Graves towards Mrs Ravenscroft, and Katherine Montague.

Katherine was cloathed in a primrose-yellow Gown, over a small Hoop. Her little Feet, in silken Shoes, made shallow Depressions in the mossy Bank upon which she stood, in the dappled Shade of a white willow Tree. My Gaze travelled slowly upwards over the bright Silk of her Skirts to settle upon her Waist, which had been made so tiny by the Tightness of her laced Stays that I could have near encompassed it in mine Hands. A delicate Handkerchief of white Muslin embraced her slim Shoulders, and met in a careless Knot upon her Breast. June Sunnelight, filtering thro' the thin

Leaves of the Willow, licked the exposed Skin of her Throat; wherever it touched, the pale Ivory gleamed phosphorescent.

I proffered my "Good Morning" to Mrs Ravenscroft, who responded with the usual Civility.

Katherine said: "Mr Hart," and droppt an half-Curtsey with such breathtaking Insolence as seemed fit to turn my Condescension in coming to talk with her upon its Head.

Mrs Ravenscroft looked aghast. "I am sorry," she said. "She hath not been well brought up, I am afraid. Her Mother is a Widdowe of few Means, and they do not see enough of good Society. We are hoping to make an Impression upon her here, but our Effort doth not seem to be working."

Katherine staightened up, and looking direct into mine Eyes with an Expression of such sweet Defiance it near stoppt mine Heart, held forth her naked Hand as if for me to kiss. I took it. Her Skin was softer than Velvet, and strangely familiar to my Fingertips. The Phalangeal Ligaments tensed briefly beneath the Ball of my Thumb; delicate finger-Bones contracting, then extending lightly to press into the cupped Palm of mine Hand. I slid my Thumb slowly to the Knuckle Joint between her first and second Fingers, and applied my Fingertips to the rear Surface of the proximal Phalanx. The velvety Skin extended, and the small Bones shifted apart beneath my Touch. I released the Pressure and felt them retract into their proper Place, with a small Click.

Katherine looked down—tho' not out of Shyness, and mine Attention followed hers to where our two Hands were joined together within a Cataract of liquid Sunnelight.

"How dark your Skin is next to mine," said Katherine. She looked up at me, and smiled.

This Statement brought me back to My Self. I quickly released her Hand and, stepping back, executed the terse Bow I should have given her at the first.

"Mrs Ravenscroft; Miss Montague." I prepared to depart. I could not, in all truth, have sustained the Conversation for very much longer. Mine Imagination was beginning to gallop ahead upon its usual phrenzied Track. This would not do; I had to rein it in.

"Sir," called Katherine Montague.

I turned at once. "Yes?"

"Shall we see you at the Breakfast?"

"Of course. Good Morning."

I returned to the Path and sought out my Father, who was waiting beside mine Aunt Barnaby, appearing as greatly out of Countenance as I felt. I told My Self that as long as I could keep away from Katherine Montague and restrain my vile Mind, I should have nothing to fear. But for the second Time, too, I wished that I were back in London. Polly Smith's Body would have satisfied this Flame in Minutes.

The wedding Breakfast was to be held after long standing Tradition at the village Tavern, altho' mine Aunt had argued in Favour of holding it at Shirelands so that we need not be overlooked. My Sister—now Mrs Barnaby—and her Bridegroom departed for the Feast in Barnaby's Curricle. I followed on directly, with mine Aunt and Father, in our own Coach.

"Well," said Aunt Barnaby in a Tone of intense Contentment, spreading her Skirts across the intire Seat. "That's Jane well married; now we have but to settle Master Hart."

Her Words startled me. Not knowing whether to think her serious, and be subject to an Alarum, or not, I laughed.

"Tristan," said my Father, his Gaze never moving from the Road outside, "is not yet one-and-twenty."

"Tush, Brother," retorted mine Aunt. "You were wed at scarcely more than that. That you had your Fortune already, I'll grant you; but any Fool can see that Master Hart is already more a Man of the World than ever you were."

"Then he shall need no Help from you," my Father muttered.

"Brother, there are Pitfalls in such a City as London, into which even a clever young Man of Substance and Fashion may fall. And I am sure that Mr Henry Fielding sets no good Example upon that Score. Is he not married to his Housekeeper?"

I perceived then that mine Aunt was utterly in earnest. I could too easily anticipate what was to follow—a lengthy Lecture upon the dreadful Consequences of being tempted into Marriage by some virtuous young Wench—or even not so virtuous—who had nothing but her Face to recommend her.

Egad, I thought. If mine Aunt knew anything at all of me, surely even she would seek to protect the Wenches from me, rather than me from the Wenches.

I lifted up my Cane and rapped thrice upon the Roof of the Coach, which drew to an Halt at once. "Set me down here; I will walk," I called.

Mine Aunt gave Vent to a small Noise of Irritation. "Sir," she said, "you will be late in sitting down to Breakfast."

"There need be no Delay on mine Account; I am of little Importance," I said, vaulting down onto the Greensward. My Father, I thought, almost laughed, but I could not be certain.

The Coach then moving on without me, I stood still as a Statue on the Roadside, listening to the sweet repeated Whistle of a song Thrush in the thorny Hedge, and reflecting with Delight upon mine unplanned Escape from Supervison. I attended closely to the Thrush for a Moment, with a little Suspicion; but in its clear Note there was no Hint of Accusation. I thought then that perhaps I might locate a quiet Spot and continue my Remarks upon Dr Hunter's Drawings, returning to join the wedding Party after all the Crush was over; but then I realised that Jane would not thank me for this. I bent my Steps instead toward the Tavern, which was barely a quarter-Mile from where I had alighted. I took care to walk exceeding slowly, watching the Bees amid the Clover.

I walked so slow, in fact, that I had not gone far beyond the Cottages and the Forge when I was overtaken by the Ravenscrofts, walking two abreast in a Cavalcade. Sophia was in the Head of the Column with her Mother; she flashed me a charming Smile, and turning to Mrs Ravenscroft, begged to be allowed to walk with me instead.

I had no Stomach for that, fair as Sophy was, and I pleaded that I should only prove a sorry Tortoise to her Hare. I need not have worried, however, for Mrs Ravenscroft, perchance thinking upon a similar Principle to that which had excited mine Aunt, took Sophy sharply by the Elbow and led her away, saying to her only that haply we should meet up at the Tavern.

Am I beyond Sophy's Expectations? I thought. I had never once considered her like that, but still the Notion startled me. I had grown accustomed, in my long Association with Nathaniel, to think of the Ravenscrofts as mine Equals, and in many Ways this must have been true; but not in the Case of Marriage. Marriage required Money, and Money the Ravenscrofts did not have. Yet I should have been delighted, I thought, if Nathaniel, instead of Barnaby, had married Jane.

Mrs Ravenscroft may well have felt that if she had to choose between the Preservation of her Daughter's Reputation and that of her Niece, then her Loyalties must lie with her Daughter, and the Niece be damned to take her Chance. At any Rate, it fell out that last in the Column walked Katherine Montague, alone; and when she lifted up her smiting grey Eyes and stared hard at me, I could not resist falling in beside her.

For some Moments neither one of us spoke. Then I decided that this might be mine Opportunity to find out what the Devil had happened to Nathaniel, so I cleared my Throat and said, in as Carefree a Manner as I could affect: "Miss Montague, have you heard anything of your eldest Cousin?"

"Of—Nathaniel Ravenscroft? No. That is, nothing new. No."

She seemed flustered by my Question. She had spoken the name—Nathaniel—almost with Trepidation. I turned mine Head and regarded her closely. All the Colour—and she had little to begin with—had drained from her Cheeks. As if I had shewn her a Ghost, I thought. Oh, surely, something hath happened involving Nat. Something that neither his Family nor mine desires me to know. A small Alarum began to sound behind mine Heart.

"I trust Nathaniel is well," I said.

"As far as I know, he is well." She bit her Lip.

"You miss him?" I said.

"No," she answered. "I do not miss him at all."

"I see," I said, altho' in Truth I saw nothing but the Quivering of her lower Lip, which I precipitantly desired to kiss. This astonished me. I had kissed no Woman on the Lips since Margaret Haynes. Katherine Montague, beside me, was so slight, I could have apprehended her compleatly in mine Arms. I could shelter her, in Winter, within the Fronts of my Greatcoat.

"Was Nathaniel unkind to you?" I asked.

"No. Yes. Yes! He teazed me."

"He teazed me, too," I said, remembering the Events of that May Eve. 'Gelding', Nathaniel had called me.

"Did you hate him?" said Katherine.

"No; no," I said. "I love him. He is my dearest Friend."

Katherine said: "Oh," and fell silent.

We walked along together, slowly, and attempted no more Conversation. I was no nearer to learning the Answer to my Question, which annoyed me, but I did not press her. She seemed to have slippt back into her earlier fathomless Blackness. Yet she had not gone quite alone, for I could sense the Darkness, circling around us, like a Vortex in a quiet seeming Pool. And perhaps because of that, because her Silence, which was meant to shut out the intire World, included me, I knew that if anyone were to tell me what had happened to Nathaniel, it would be Katherine Montague.

We were almost at the Tavern when Katherine halted, looked up into mine Eyes and said: "Do you want to kiss me? You may, if you like. I should not mind it."

I stoppt dead, as one struck by a blue Thunderbolt out of a cloudless Heaven. Mine immediate Thought was that I had misheard her. "What?"

"You may kiss me," Katherine repeated. "Don't you like me?"

The Beginning of the Ravenscroft Column had entered the Tavern, and the Remainder was rapidly disappearing. Katherine and I, making up the Tail, stood by now a long Way behind; a good thing, for it meant that no one but My Self had heard her. I stared at her in open Amazement for a full ten Seconds, unable to marshall any Reply whatsoever. I did want to kiss her; and surely she could see the Desire etched upon my Physiognomy; but I had no Intention at all of acting upon it. For the first Time since our eye-Beams had twisted in St Peter's Church, her Expression was unsure.

"I do," I said. "I like you extreamly well; but you must not make such an Offer to me; or, God forbid! to anybody else. I shall put it down to your Inexperience—but, Miss Montague! What appears to me in the Light of Innocence must strike another as Forwardness. You will do yourself Harm by such Conduct."

"Wherefore should I care?" she said. "As if I have anything to look forward to. I shall not marry well, like Miss Hart; I shall die nursing Mama."

"By Christ!" I exclaimed. "Do not speak so of yourself." I hesitated, then decided to throw Discretion to the Devil and plunged onwards. "You are the most beautifull Girl that I have ever met, and you are but twelve. Your lack of Fortune need not blight your every Chance."

"Fortune hates me. I am not beautifull, and I am not twelve. I am a Fortnight past fourteen. Who told you I was twelve?"

"My Sister."

"She will have got it from Sophy. That lying Bitch! She hath nothing in her Heart but Spite and Jealousy."

This took my Breath away. "Miss Montague," I said, after some few Seconds during which I did not know whether to laugh or to disapprove. "You must not call Miss Ravenscroft a Bitch."

Katherine tossed her Head, and her white Throat glistened in the Sunnelight. "Should I not? It doth not make her any worse, or any more the Liar if I say plainly what she is. And she is a Bitch. What else hath she said to your Sister about me?"

I turned towards her. "That you are a disgraceful Flirt, which would seem no Lie; and that you boxed her Ear."

"Well, I did that; she was being horrid to me and deserved all that she got. But the Rest is a Lie, and a filthy one."

My Gaze fixt itself upon the Pulsation of the Aortic Artery within her Throat, swelling and twitching beneath her Skin, as her Life spun thro' it. "So say you? After the Offer you made just now to me?"

"That was because you were you. And as to your 'God forbids', Mr Hart, God forbid you think I'd offer Kisses to any Jacky or Tom. But I shall never offer again if you wish it so."

"Never? There may come a Time and Place for such Offers. Here and now, Miss Montague, I do wish it so; for your Interest must depend upon the Illusion of Propriety, if not the Reality."

She steppt up exceeding close to me, her little Teeth bared as in a Growl, and her grey Eyes sizzling with some Emotion I could not quite apprehend, altho' I felt its Force, and took an involuntary half-Pace backwards to escape it. The top of her blonde Head, in its white Cap, came barely past my Chest. Mine Hands began to ache.

"Propriety?" she said. "You use that Word to me, when I can see Thoughts of the improperest Kind writ all over your Face."

I had to bend my Neck to look at her; she stood so close to me our Bodies almost touched. "Most improper," I said. "The Superlative is formed thus: improper, more improper, most."

"Best improperest," hissed Katherine Montague.

I would have kissed her then; but before I could catch her, she suddenly reeled away from under mine Hands, and left me standing in the open Roadway, mine Heart pounding like a Blacksmith's Hammer and my Loins aroused to such a pretty Pitch I did not dare follow her into the Tavern. Instead, I waited, uncomfortable, upon the Verge beneath the Hedge, until mine Appearance should return to something approaching respectable. From the middle Branches by my Shoulder came the undistinguished twittering of a Dunnock. I listened closely; but again, there was no Need; and it occurred to me that mayhap the Birds within the Village were as friendly to me as were those within the Gardens of Shirelands. They are mine, I thought. Not Viviane's. The Notion encouraged me immensely. I was no longer intirely alone.

But what to do, I thought, about Miss Montague? I felt certain that she should have somewhat to say to me about Nathaniel; and, besides, there now remained the unfinished Matter of that Kiss. It is imperative, I thought, that I speak with her alone. Before the Thought was but half-finished I saw plainly how it was to be brought about. My Father, according to Tradition, was bound to invite the Rector and Mrs Ravenscroft to dine with us this Evening at Shirelands Hall. I would, for Politeness' Sake, extend the Invitation to Sophia, as evidently she was Out; and, once this had been accepted, insist in the Name of Charity that Miss Montague attend also, since she had been in such Want of good Society.

The Dunnock in the Holly ceased his Song and put his Wings to Flight, wisping past mine Head in a shy Flutter. The Aire breathed sweet upon my Face, and Daiseyes shone beneath my Feet. Upon the top Branch of a Rowan across the Lane, a Robin filled his small Breast and began an Aria.

CHAPTER SIXTEEN

So my Sister was married, and the cake Crumbs had been showered over her Head, and she had driven away at last with her new Barnaby to Withy Grange. I offered mine Invitation to Sophia and to Katherine Montague, and mine Aunt said loudly how Sophy had always been to me like a second Sister. She did not seem to think it necessary to warn me away from Katherine Montague. I wondered at this. Surely, Miss Montague was exactly the kind of Girl mine Aunt should have feared the most, being young and beautifull with no Dowry whatsoever; but then I realised that Jane must have misinformed her also regarding Katherine's Age. A Twelve-yeare-old could pose no Threat at all.

I decided to focus mine Attentions over Dinner very firmly upon Sophia. By this Method, I hoped to set mine Aunt and Mrs Ravenscroft about the Ears, and thereby distract all three Women from my true Objective.

I was not, anyway, intending anything beyond the claiming of one small Kiss and some Intelligence. I had no Desire to marry anyone.

I returned to Shirelands in my Father's Coach. He did not speak thro'out the Journey. This was perfect to my Purpose, for I took full Advantage of the Silence by retrieving from my Coat those Drawings from whose Study I had previously been disturbed, and did not notice the Distance in the least. Mine Aunt, for her Part, had announced that she should join us later; her motherly Devotion to her Son was such that she could not bear to leave him and his new Bride alone even on their Wedding Daye. How I pitied Jane! But she had made her Bed, and now would have to lie in it, however crowded.

We arrived at Shirelands at about two o' Clock in the Afternoon, and I at once took My Self up-Stairs to my Study where I remained till it was near on dinner Time.

I was very much afraid on entering the front drawing Room, where we were all assembled, for altho' I saw the Rector and mine Aunt I did not immediately see Katherine. Then I perceived that she had been coerced by Sophia to join her in Play upon the Harpsichord in the Back. After briefly offering my Politenesses to the Rector and his Wife, I proceeded thither, to observe.

Sophia played well, and it was apparent that she knew it. She could, moreover, be in little Doubt of the Fact that the golden evening Light streaming thro' the western Window displayed her handsome Features to their best extent. She was now dresst up in flaming red Silk, that was stood on end with Lace. Her Figure possesst the womanly Curves of a Titian, her Complexion was fresh, and her Profile very elegant; but she did not attract me and I thought it impossible that she ever would. Sophia was too ordinary; too base; and she seemed so much the more so when I compared her to the scowling Sylph who sate alongside, turning the Pages of her Musick with a thin-fingered Hand. Katherine also had changed her Dress for the Evening, and was now attired in a Gown of pale blue-grey, with white Facings.

"You play enchantingly, Madam," I said, when Sophia came to a natural Break. "'Twould do mine Heart good to hear you all Night." Sophia preened. Katherine glowered. "Miss Montague," I said. "Shall we not hear you play? Or should you rather sing?"

"I am no Songbird," Katherine said. "And I play badly."

"Fie, Sir! You must not make her, 'twould be most unkind!" Sophia twittered. "She is better employed as she is."

"In that case," I said, "you must play on; and sing, too, if you will."

I knew that Sophia was no Singer—a Truth which always had appeared somewhat strange to me, as Nathaniel's Voice could have made the Devil swoon—but tonight I was determined to be seen to give her the fullest Encouragement. So she began, and I sate on a Sopha nearby and affected Rapture; and Katherine threw me furious Looks, and turned the Musick over far too fast. Before long, tho', my Father's Butler came in to tell us that Dinner was served, and so the Pace of mine Entertainment met with a brief Caesura.

Tonight's Dinner at Shirelands was a significant Event, to be marked by the high Seriousness of its Demeanour and the superior Quality of its Food. Mrs H. had ordered several Courses of Quails and other small Fowles Malaret, followed not only by the Beef Alamode upon which my Father insisted almost every Daye, but a roasted Sirloin, with various Sauces. These were followed in their Turn by a delightful Array of iced Creams sculpted into the Shapes of Flowers, red Berries, Bees, and pretty Mice, and then a Syllabub flavoured with the best Nantes Brandy. When I was able, I made light Conversation with Sophia and observed from the Corner of mine Eye that mine Approaches were not passing un-noticed before her Mother and mine Aunt. This gave me Hope that mine Aunt at least would shortly seek to break me off. I stole a sly Look towards Katherine, who was seated next to me at Table, tho' some Distance away. To my Surprize, I apprehended at once that she had in her Hand one of our silver table-Forks, and was busy secreting it about her Person. I gave no Indication that I had seen her, and carried forward with my pointless Seduction of Sophy. Yet I wondered hugely at the Strangeness of it.

After Dinner we withdrew again all together. After some more Conversation, Mine Aunt called for an Hand of Quadrille, and when I made no Move to join her, called Sophia to sit beside her. The Ravenscrofts were summoned next, and I was left standing in an imagined Dudgeon with only my Father and Miss Montague for Company. This was all as I had intended, so I began to cross the Room towards Miss Montague, who had sate down at the Harpsichord with a Scowl as dark as Thunder.

Then my Father did an unexpected thing. Seating himself before the Fire, he took out his pocket-Book and opened it; but before beginning to read any of it, he looked direct at me, and made as if to speak. Before I had even begun to register my Surprize, however, he lowered his Gaze and began the Perusal of his precious Pages.

"Sir?" I ventured. He did not lift his Head.

There was a loud Crash at the far End of the drawing Room. The Ladies all cried out in Fright; my Father almost droppt his Book, and I came close to jumping from my Skin. Any Thoughts I may have entertained of disturbing my Father were driven quite out of mine Head. Miss Montague had taken violent Hold of the Lid and slammed it down onto the Keys.

"Oh!" cried mine Aunt and hers, with one Voice.

Katherine stared at me, her Teeth bared with the same Ferocity she had shewn me before; yet her Eyes looked wild as a Hare about to leap. Then leap she did, tearing thro' the drawing Room in a brilliant Storm of blue-grey Silk.

"Oh!" cried Sophia, a little late. "Whatever is wrong now?"

I nodded to the Rector, who was already half upon his Feet, and headed with Alacrity towards the Exit. "I shall discover the Matter," I said. Inclining mine Head to the three Ladies, I quitted the Room.

Still slightly trembling from the Shock, I stood still with my Back against the Door. There was no Sign without of Miss Montague's whereabouts, but that was nothing. I had Time to find her, Time a-plenty; and so many of Shirelands' Rooms were locked when not in use, there were few within which she could hide. I drew in a deep Breath. I had rather to thank her than to be annoyed, I thought. How to get Katherine Montague on her own had been the Evening's greatest Hurdle. I had not imagined that she would so presciently demolish it by running off into an House she had never before visited; but I was beginning to understand that where Katherine was concerned it was unwise to rely upon mere common Expectation. Still, I thought, where, truly, would she go? Not below Stairs, nor into any unknown Chamber. Perhaps outside; but first

I should try the only other Room I knew her to be acquainted with.

My Spine began to sparkle with Anticipation. Smiling quietly to My Self, I proceeded up-Stairs again, to the dining Room. I did not knock.

Katherine Montague, thinking herself alone, in the cleared and empty Room, stood before the high Mantel, where the Light was greatest. As I crosst the Threshold, she startled, every bit as roughly as I had done when she had crashed the Lid; and mine Attention was at once drawn to her Hand, in which she held the stolen silver Fork.

Her Intention, plainly, had not been to have replaced it. She had rolled back the Sleeve of her blue Gown, and when I had broken in had been upon the Point of piercing the fragile Epidermis on the inside of her Elbow with its Tines. Instantly, she tried to hide it; then, realising that already I had seen too much, she hurried over to the Table, threw down the brutal Implement upon its polished Surface, pulled down her Sleeve, and attempted to push past me into the dark Stairway.

This was her Mistake; or perhaps her Genius. I would not be pushed aside, and feeling that the intimate Nature of the Scene I had just witnessed, in addition to our earlier Flirtations, more than qualified me to act, I caught tight hold of her upper Arm and held her fast.

"Why?" I asked.

"You would not understand."

"Look me in mine Eyes," I said. "And tell me then I would not understand."

"Unhand my Arm, Mr Hart!"

"No."

She began violently to struggle, and applied her other Hand to my Fingers, which wrappt about her Biceps; but she had not a Fraction of my Strength and the Endeavour was beyond her. She began to twirl and writhe under mine Hand, wriggling within my Grasp like a lively Eel. Immediately, my Loins responded. She set her Teeth and a sharp Hiss escaped her; not of Fear, nor Rage, but of Determination. I do not know what Instinct prompted me, whether that of Monster or of Lover; but I executed upon her the sudden high Twist of the Arm that I had used on Viviane, and perfected upon Polly Smith. That should have been the End of it, but Katherine Montague, instead of crying out in Pain, began to laugh.

"You think that you can hurt me?" she said. "Like that?"

"Can I not?"

"Release me," she said. "And I shall shew you."

I let go my Grip, and steppt back, intrigued. Had she then desired it, she could have attempted to leave the Room and I would not have prevented it; but she turned toward me instead, and with the coquettish Smile she had bestowed upon me in the Graveyard, she revealed to me the wicker Pliability of all her upper Joints. Her Wrists she contorted backwards far beyond the Point at which any ordinary Person must have experienced Agony; likewise her Fingers and her Thumbs. Her Arms she could twist about until her Elbows appeared backwards upon her Body. This last Demonstration was too much for my Fascination to withstand. Bidding her remain so poised, I ran mine Hands along her upper Arms until I reached her Shoulders, where the Ball of the Os Humeri was so over-extended within its Socket as to be nigh upon the Point of Dislocation.

"This doth not pain you?" I exclaimed, incredulous.

"No, Mr Hart. It doth not."

"Wonderfull," I said.

I did not take mine Hands away, and as she returned her Arms to a more natural Alignment I became acutely sensible of the Rotation of the Humeri beneath my Palms. My Lust for her began to quicken anew; but close upon it came a sorry Sensation of Helplessness. If I cannot easily cause her to scream, I thought, how can I satisfy my Desire, or hers? Then I shook My Self, for the Problem was scarcely moot. Miss Montague was not a Woman with whom things were ever like to come to such a Pitch.

I still did not remove mine Hands. Katherine turned her Face toward me, and once more I experienced that devastating Longing to kiss her. In the flickering Light, I seemed to see again the Face of someone whom I had known long. I lifted my Fingers from her Shoulder, and gently traced the delicate Outline of her Inferior Maxilla from Ear to Chin. The velvet Skin rippled beneath my Touch. Her soft Lips parted slightly.

If I kissed her, I thought, I should be putting things onto such a Footing between us as to make my Life, and perhaps hers, very difficult. I drew back. But the Capacity did not exist in me to quit her intirely. Also, I reminded My Self, by Way of an Excuse, I had still yet to talk with her about Nathaniel, which was not something I could do amongst those who designed to keep him secret.

"Miss Montague," I said. "Earlier, with the Fork."

Her Expression darkened, but I did not let her pull away. "I needed to see the Blood," she said at last.

"Why?"

"Because I did. Because you made a Fool of yourself gawping after Sophy like some country Idiot, and ignored me."

"If I did," I said, "there was nothing in it. I have no Interest whatever in Sophia Ravenscroft."

"Truly? Then you have been doubly cruel, to her as well as me; altho' she deserves it."

"When you go back to the Rectory," I said, "what will you do? Will you steal another Fork?"

"I should not need to steal anything," she answered with a contemptuous Toss of her Head, by which I gathered that she probably had a Razor hidden underneath her Pillow.

Her Vice was almost the Mirrour of mine own, altho' I felt certain that she as yet derived no carnal Pleasure from it. Nevertheless, she found what I found, in the dark Heart of the Thing, the Pain: Relief.

"If you will come with me," I said, "I have within my Study the proper Equipment for Blood-letting." I spoke quickly, and in a low Tone. The hot Colour rose within my Face.

Then I saw that for the first Time since I had met her, I had Katherine Montague at a clear Disadvantage. My Reaction had so compleatly astonished her that her Mouth droppt open. Her small uneven Teeth glistened with Spittle in the vapid yellow Light, and the round Swell of her Tongue presst speechless against them. Then, with an apparent Effort, she swallowed, and sucked in a Breath.

"Dost do it, too?" she demanded.

"No," I answered. "'Tis not what I do. But you must believe me when I assure you, on my very Life, that I understand why you do it."

Katherine drew back at that, and looked at me with her Eyes narrowed, as if she were perceiving me anew. I could see that she did not comprehend the Whole of my Meaning, which was a good thing, I thought; but I could not intirely pretend away my Disappointment, and some of it must have shewn in mine Expression. Katherine put her delicate Hands to my Face. I did not flinch as she explored my Cheeks with curious Fingertips.

"I am studying Anatomy under William Hunter," I told her. "I shall be more skilled than any country Surgeon within a Yeare or two."

She put her Fingers softly to my Lips. "And then?"

"Then I shall devote My Self to the Study of Pain."

"Why?"

"I used to think," I said, "that I should discover a Means to take it away. Now I know not why; except that it is beautifull."

"Pain is beautifull?"

I could not resist: I kissed her Fingertip. "Yes," I said. "And terrible, and vile, and cruel. But beautifull, despiting all of that."

"In the Moment," she whispered. "The Moment when I see the Blood, I feel almost as if I were flying."

Her Gaze locked itself into mine. Again that Fear of what should follow; and then the Understanding, sent from Heaven or from Hell, that she and I were quite beyond such mundane Considerations as Reputation or Rank. We were Monsters, both of us; or perhaps fallen Angels, for I could not look upon her Countenance and see anything but the perfect and pure Creation of Almighty God.

I placed mine Hand beneath her sharp Chin, and tilted her Face upwards. Then before I could lose Courage, or my Reason change my Mind, I bent forward and presst my Lips to hers. Her Mouth was small, and her Lips as gentle as willow Catkins.

For an Instant, I was terrified lest I bruise her; then she twisted her Fingers in the loose Hairs upon the Nape of my Neck, and pulled me closer with a Force that took my Breath away. Mine

Heart began to pound and my Desires to rise like Demons out of the encompassing Dark. I did not mind them. I lowered mine other Hand to the Curve of her Back, where her sixth Rib joined with her Spine, and wished her out of her tight Stays. I held her; I kissed her; I cradled the Base of her Cranium upon my Fingertips.

I do not know how long we remained thus. Time had ceased to matter. But eventually we broke apart, and I realised that she had secured her other Hand high upon my Chest, over mine Heart. "How it drums," she murmured.

I went to put mine Arms about her again, but she was pushing me away, holding out before me her exposed Forearm. "Do it," she demanded. "Take away all the Ugliness, all the Filth."

I took her Hand in mine and led her to my Study.

The Aire within the Room was cool, as I had ordered no Fire to be lit; it was dark, and, since presently the Cages in which I had housed my living Subjects were empty, unusually silent. I carried my Candle to the long Table and lit the Tapers. At once my Laboratory came to life.

Katherine hovered within the open Doorway and looked around with the Expression of one admiring at an aweful Wonder. "What is it all?" she said.

I went back to shut the Door, and taking up her Hand again, I led her into my *Sanctum sanctorum*, and explained carefully the Purposes to which I put all mine Equipment. This took some considerable Time; Katherine had never seen a good many of the Objects that I took for granted: she had never set Eyes upon an Alembic, or imagined any Use for white Salt other than in the Kitchen. I shewed her, with Pride, my large Collection of articulated Skeletons, and described the Stages of the Process that had manifested those Results. She shrank back from the Human Skull I had brought down from London, and placed proud upon mine Escritoire. I could not understand why this should have upset her. I explained that it was that of a foreign Thief who had been executed in his native Country eighteen Yeares ago, and that I had received it in order that I might closely examine the Pattern of fused Bones in the upper Cranium. I did not tell her that I had a Child's Skull also in my Possession, for Comparison, which was too delicate to risk travelling. I had left it behind in London.

She inquired next about my Cages, and I could tell that she liked mine Answer as little as she had liked my Convict's Skull; but she said nothing, and I felt no pressing Need to defend my Practice. I bade her instead to lie down upon the Sopha whilst I retrieved my Lancet and bleeding-Bowl from the cup Board next to my specimen Case, where I stored mine Equipment. I was not certain, after so many Minutes, that she would still willingly permit me this Liberty, but she did as I asked. The Thought struck me that she was now in such a vulnerable Position that it would be very easy for me to take another, and for an Instant mine Attention was so diverted that I nigh cut My Self upon mine own Blade. There was no real Question of that, however, and I banished the Image, along with several dozen others, to the Corner of my Mind. Carrying mine Equipment, and a lighted Taper, I approached the Sopha. Kneeling beside Katherine, I carefully positioned her Elbow atop the grooved Depression in the Bowl's Rim. She gave a low Sigh, and closed her Eyes. I lifted the Taper and searched her inner Arm for an appropriate Vein. This Task proved to be less straightforward than I had anticipated, for the Skin had become quite scarred; it took me some Moments to locate a Place. Then I made one small, quick Cut, and wine-dark Blood streamed out over the pale Epidermis to pool in the white Porcelain below.

As she felt the Touch of my Blade, Katherine opened wide her Eyes, and stared hard at her own Arm with a fearfull Longing. As the Blood flowed across her Skin, she let out a tranquil Whimper, half Pain, half Happiness, and smiled. Her grey Eyes had become Tear-filled. I placed mine Hand upon her Head, and stroaked her gossamer Hair.

I did not bleed her long, for there was no medical Need and I dared not to risk it. After perhaps half a Minute I sealed up the little Wound, and put away my Tools; altho' at her Request I left the Bowl where she could continue to see it.

Katherine seemed now so quiescent I was almost anxious lest she be unwell. Her Expression, however, had so delightful a Look that I decided that this could not be the Case. She was, I realised, at Peace, brought to a State not unlike to that of someone whose Screams I had stoppt; altho' I had never witnessed quite such Extasie upon the face of Polly Smith, or any other Woman, for that matter.

I thought then that I must kiss her again, and so I did. Her Lips felt cool and still upon mine own. Then I sate on the Floor beside her until such Time as she felt ready to sit up, and pull down her Sleeve, and shew me Signs of being herself once more.

"Thank you," she whispered.

"For the Kiss?"

"Dunce. You know for what."

"Tell me how it began," I asked her.

"I was very ill," she said. "Last Yeare. And the Surgeon seemed to come Daye upon Daye. I nearly died. But after I was well again I found that I still needed to do it."

I leaned close in beside her, and took both her Hands betwixt mine own. Her Breath was nectar sweet upon my Face. "Now," I said, "'tis Time for you to stop. I fear greatly you will injure yourself; you have no Way of knowing where properly to cut, or how deep, or of how much Blood to let. Tonight, you attempted the Operation with a dining-Fork."

Her face fell. "I can't," she said.

"You will. There are other Methods of purging the Soule; and I am highly accomplished at most of them."

"I expect you are," she said, looking slowly again around my Study. "Bloody Bones, that's what you are; that's what you are, Mr Hart: Bloody Bones beneath the Bed, to scare the Children off to Sleep."

"I am no Raw-Head-and-Bloody-Bones!" I exclaimed.

"That is true; you are no Raw Head; I say you are Bloody Bones; the Fiend who collects the marrow-Bones of the Dead, and prizes them more dearly than the Living."

"Hold forth your Hand," I told her.

"Why?"

I seized firm Hold of her slender Wrist, and twisted her Hand so that her open Fingers lay uncurled before me. Then before she had a Chance to pull away I rapped her Palm with mine own Hand, as hard as I could suffer it My Self. Katherine squeaked and tried instinctively to close her Fingers and to free her Hand, but I did not allow this, and I struck her again in the same Manner six or seven Times more. Mine own Palm was by now too sore for me to continue, but she had taken my Point as well as my Chastisement. Her Eyes were wide as much in Shock as in Pain, but I could discern behind her Tears a marvelling Excitement that made mine Heart race.

"I repeat," I said. "This Blood-letting, by yourself, Madam, shall cease; and likewise those Behaviours that may do Harm to your Person or to your Honour. Do we have—" I swallowed, then continued anyway: "an Understanding?"

Katherine stared at me as if I had said something she could not intirely apprehend. "What do you mean?" she stammered.

I looked closely into her Eyes, wondering at the Question; and it occurred to me that I My Self was not compleatly certain of my Meaning. "I mean," I said slowly, "that you will come to me, and ask me for mine Assistance."

Katherine sat quite upright upon the Sopha, and examined my Face. "Do you say this in good Faith?" she demanded at last. "Or do you try to test me, or to trick me?"

"I am not that Sort of Monster," I said.

"Then I will try," she said. "But we must correspond, or I shall run mad."

"Your Mother would mislike our doing that," I said.

"My Mama," said Katherine savagely, "hath paid not one Whit of Attention to aught I have said or done since I was eight Yeares old. She will not care that I receive any Letter."

"Then I shall write," I said. "But you must not expect my Letters to be frequent, or long. I shall be at Mr Fielding's House, in London, and have much Study to do."

"Study!" she exclaimed, rolling her Eyes. "I know better anyway than to expect much from a Man's Letter. Do not worry, Bloody Bones. I shall be content with the little I shall get."

"Brat," I said. "Then I shall write setting you Lessons; that Temper of yours must be curbed. You will come to dread my Correspondence."

"Never! But an you do, 'twill anyway disguise us from Sophy, who would not think twice of opening my Mail. And I shall write— but you shall see; I shall surprize you."

Leaning forwards, I kissed her gently upon the golden Crown of her Head.

Jacob to Rachel.

CHAPTER SEVENTEEN

In the early Morning of the third Daye after Jane's Wedding, I was awakened by a strange Sound stealing into my Chamber thro' the opened Window: the loud, shrill Note of an hunting-Horn. I sate at once bolt upright in my Bed, as if it had been an Alarum, and listened hard lest the Blast be repeated; but I heard nothing but the Twittering of the morning Birds and the Chatter of a Magpie from beyond the high Hedge. I must have been dreaming. It was not the hunting Season, and unlikely too, I thought, that the Fanfare should have been blown by some Wag in Jest. I laid My Self down again, altho' mine Heart was racing with the wild Speed of a pursued Deer.

I could not easily fall back to Sleep, and so I rose, dresst, and betook My Self to my Study to read awhile before breakfast Time. The Sound of the Horn had caused me to ponder once more on Nathaniel.

Over Breakfast, I received into mine Hand a pressing Invitation from my Sister to call upon Withy Grange that very Afternoon. She seemed concerned that if I did not come, I should return to London without seeing her again, or visiting her brave and beauteous new Estate; and that I would not be in Berkshire again before Christmas. Feeling that Jane was in all Probability quite right in this Estimation, I quit my Studies for the nonce, and headed out to the Stables. It had been Months since I had ridden my Chestnut, and I was anxious to see whether he had been improved or spoiled in mine Absence. If spoiled, I thought, I should have stern Words with the head Groom, for he was not a Horse with which I would have been willing to part. He was an handsome Animal, and elegant in his Paces. He went, however, like a Swallow. I was doubly glad of this, for altho' it did mine Heart joy to wander betwixt the Colours of the Meadows and thro' the lively Woods, I could not help but be mindful of Viviane, and of the fact that the Valley of the Horse was her Domain. I did not believe that it were safe for me to be without mine own Lands for too long. After about three Miles, the Road grew stony, so I chose to abandon it and traced instead the winding Ribband of the River, which would take me at a Gallop all the Way to Withy Grange.

The House appeared all of a sudden as I rounded a Bend, atop a long grassy Slope that led down towards the Water. I perceived at once the open Prospect about which Jane had spoken with Enthusiasm; a full half-Mile of unbroken Green extending in a steady Declivity to the very Edge of the River, which here, she said, ran thick with Trout. Only one Obstacle stood between the River and the Grange: a tangled Stand of Willows and other Trees, extending an hundred Feet or more hard by the rushy Bank; the last Survivors, perhaps, of those old Withies that had given the Place its Name. Jane had told me much of Barnaby's planned Improvements, which being in the modern Stile, required the Laying of bland Lawns where once there had been complex formal Gardens, and the Substitution by its tame Reflection of wild, unfettered Nature. I supposed that these must be the Willows he intended to uproot, so that the View from the drawing Room should not be interrupted.

Seeing the Stand now, I felt a sudden Anger at what appeared a brutal Act upon Barnaby's Part. Verily, there is no Need, I thought, to ruin an whole Grove of Willows, that mayhap stood there before the House was built, purely for Barnaby to have a fashionably unobstructed View. It is senseless; moreover, 'tis petty; and that bodes ill for Jane.

I reined in mine Horse, and stood still for a Moment by the quiet Water. About mine Ears wavered the noiseless Wings of Butterflies, and the low Murmuring of Bees. From his hidden Nest within the Reeds, a Warbler burst his Breast in tumbling Song. I drew in a long, slow, deep Breath, drinking in the summer Aire as if it were sweet Wine, and closed mine Eyes. The golden morning Sunne was honey warm upon my Face.

The Warbler by the Stream was almost friendly; tho' how he would sing to me when he had got Intelligence of who I was, I did not like to guess. I dug mine Heels into my Chestnut's Flanks and cantered toward the willow Trees. I remembered how I had seen Katherine in the Churchyard, the Sunnelight dappling her pale Features thro' the flickering Leaves.

The Wood was more extensive than I had first thought, and as I approached it I saw that it was comprised of several hundred Trees. Near the Water, as I had expected, the Willows were most numerous, reaching out over the Stream with white Fingers, but away from the River grew Hawthorns in a tight Covert. I cantered along the Edge of the Woodland for some Distance before turning my Chestnut to begin the long Ascent toward the Grange. It was then, to mine Astonishment, that I saw Katherine Montague.

She was running down the Slope, in my Direction, very fast. The pale Calico of her Skirts billowed about her like a wind tosst Cloud, and her white linen Cap had all but slippt from her Head. I stoppt mine Horse and without any second Thought jumped down upon the Sward. "Is it you?" I called, uncertain whether my Senses were playing upon me the cruellest Trick.

"Yes!" she cried, tho' she was breathless with Running. "Yes!"

I looped the Horse's Reins over mine Arm and hurried up the Slope to meet her. I half expected, or half hoped, that she would throw herself into mine Arms, for which I should have had to punish her, but when we were about five Yards apart, she drew to a polite Halt. Her Ribcage heaved with the Effort of her Exertion; her Eyes sparkled with its vivid Satisfaction. Her Hair, now loosened from its Constraints, shook in wild golden Ringlets about her delicate Neck. Yet again I cursed the long View from Withy Grange, which meant that we were even now most likely overlooked; had it not been so I should have carried her off then and there beneath the Willows.

"I saw you coming from the House," she gasped. "I ran—all the Way."

"You looked as if you were flying," I said.

"I felt as if I were! I thought I should fall, but something held me up. I am under Instruction never to run lest some Bone come out of place, but I do not care!"

I positioned my Chestnut between My Self and the House, and held out mine Hand to Katherine. "Come here," I said. "I must satisfy My Self that you really exist. Whatever are you doing here?"

Katherine steppt up beside me and I took her small Hands in mine. She was warm and solid, living and real, and she smelled lightly of Sweat and fresh mown Grasses.

"Jane—Mrs Barnaby—sent Sophy an Invitation, and I guessed—I hoped—so I made her bring me too."

"Stand still until you have caught your Breath," I said. "So, 'tis a Mixture of Luck and Design. I shall not ask what vile Means you employed upon Miss Ravenscroft, as they have brought you to me; whom I expected least, and am happiest to see."

"Oh," she answered lightly, "I did nothing unkind or even unseemly. I told Sophy that I wished to thank Mrs Barnaby for allowing me to attend her Wedding, and Aunt Ravenscroft thought this shewed such Promise that she told Sophy she must agree."

"Is your Aunt here too, then?"

"No, no; 'tis only me and Sophy."

"Sophy and My Self," I said.

"I think not!" Katherine said. "I am certain Mrs B. is match-making; but she will make nothing there, if I have aught to do about the Business."

"Nor I," I said. I kissed her Hands and then, reluctantly, released her. "My Sister will be watching, from the House."

We turned back towards the long Ascent, and resumed our long, slow Climb out of the Valley.

As we walked, I remembered Nathaniel again. I stoppt, not wanting my Words to be overheard by anyone upon the front Lawn of the House, altho' it was unlikely that my Voice should carry so far. "Will you tell me," I said, "what hath happened to Nathaniel? I am sure that something is very wrong, but no one will speak of him."

Katherine ceased walking, and her Features momentarily fell into Shaddowe. She droppt her Gaze to the daiseyed Green beneath her Feet, and then, turning her Back upon the Grange, she looked up and stared out over the Valley. "Nathaniel—" Again that Hesitation on his Name. "Hath run away," she said.

"What? Impossible!"

"Not impossible. His Father is telling he hath gone into the Army."

"Nathaniel would never do that," I said. "What, gone? Intirely gone? He hath sent no Word?"

"None."

"Egad!" I cried. "When was this? Why would nobody tell me?"

"I don't know. My Uncle says that he disappeared, last Yeare, in May."

"But I was with him on May Morning! I—" My Voice failed me. Suddenly, Nathaniel's extraordinary Manner and Actions at the Bull, and at our Parting, made compleat Sense. He had planned to leave that Night; and he had not run away to join the Army, but his beloved Gypsies. "Oh, Lord," I said, slowly. "Now I conceive it. He wanted me to go with him, but I—" Again, I stoppt. Suppose I had lain down with Viviane, as both she and Nathaniel had desired; would I have followed them, Over the Hills and Far Away, as the Song hath it? I might. Truly, I might.

"What Attempt do they make to find him?" I asked.

Katherine did not appear to know. "My Uncle is so angry," she said, "that I think they make none. He wanted Nathaniel to go into the Church."

"Aye, so he did." I began to laugh, altho' I felt like weeping. "Canst imagine it? Nat, in Churchman's Weeds?"

Katherine produced a feeble Simulacrum of a Smile, but her Eyes were hollow.

"'Tis anyway certain," I said, taking her Arm thro' mine own in an Effort at Comfort, and bending yet again toward Withy Grange, "that Nat will return sometime when we do not expect him. Have no Fears for your Cousin, Katherine; I know him exceeding well, and he doth not readily fall into Trouble."

"No," she said. "That is true. He was always the one to bring Trouble upon others."

Thus linked, we continued climbing the Valley. Altho' I had sought to pacify Katherine, mine Head was now full, and mine Heart also, with fearfull Thoughts and Sentiments generated by this new Intelligence. Plainly, I had been the last Person to have seen Nathaniel Ravenscroft. Excepting possibly the stable-Boy—and Viviane.

A Thought broke in upon me, horrible in its Array: Perhaps Nathaniel is dead. Perhaps the Gypsies murdered him. Perhaps, even as I was racing back along the Road towards the Bull, Viviane's Brothers were slitting Nathaniel's white Throat in some green Meadow hard by.

I pushed the Thought away, for altho' it frightened me greatly, I could perceive that it was neither wholly rational nor likely. Whatever Revenge Viviane sought against me, she would never have taken it out upon Nathaniel. Never once in his Life had he suffered any Punishment for his own Misdemeanours, let alone mine. The Course of things had altogether run the other Way.

No, no, I thought. Nathaniel and Viviane are together, wherever they are. They were perhaps—I caught my Breath—even in London last Christmas-tide.

Was it Nathaniel who sent me my Bat? By Owl, or Cat, or Hare, he said. Is not a Bat a wild Creature, too?

Katherine Montague, at my Side, caught unexpectedly a tight Hold of mine Hand, and her thin Fingers twined about mine own. "Mr Hart?"

I feared lest I had spoke aloud. I paused mid-Step, and looked down into her clear grey Eyes. Slowly, my dreadful Apprehensions drained away, like falling flood-Waters.

She was an Human Child, I thought.

"What is it?" I said.

"I do not truly believe your Sister is Match-making. I said it as a Joke. You would frighten Sophy to Death, and a long Way beyond it."

We proceeded up-Hill for a few Yards intimately connected; then we parted, as we were almost come upon the House.

Withy Grange was a tall, upright Building that seemed to me upon mine Approach to be more of a Means of Support for its high Gables and steeply pitched Roofs than a House to shelter Human Beings. The Walls were of white Stone interspaced with blackleaded Windows, and dark Woodwork that weaved across the Front of the Place in a Lattice. I judged it to be no more than two Centuries in Age, and therefore definitely younger than the willow Wood. I began to ask My Self whether Jane could be prevailed upon to disagree with Barnaby about his unobstructed View, and to fight for the Willows. It was a Pity she had such a gentle Nature.

Between the long Slope and the Lawn itself was a banked stone Wall, invisible from the House, but high enough to prevent Animals from wandering freely into the Gardens. A proper Ha-ha, I thought, unlike the one at Shirelands, which was in Truth nothing but an hedged Ditch. I called loudly for a Groom to come and attend my

Chestnut, and then, he being taken off mine Hands, I headed with Katherine thro' the wrought iron Gateway that led up to Withy Grange.

The Grass here, as we climbed the wall Steps, was new mown and somewhat dampe. Katherine pointed to the Hem of her Petticoat, which had grown bright green from the spilt Juice, and laughed. The Sound sparkled. I wished I could capture it in a Flask.

We crosst the Lawn together, yet apart, right up to the front Door, where we were met by Barnaby's Footman. He conveyed us to my Sister's morning Room, where she sate with Sophia.

"Allow me to restore to you someone you had lost," I said to Jane at once upon entering the Room, to allay her Suspicion. "Miss Montague, who was wandering the Grounds. Dear Sister, Withy Grange doth indeed possess the most enchanting Views."

Katherine sate down upon the window Seat, and feigning a compleat Lack of Interest in me, took up a slender Volume of Sidney's *Astrophel* and concentrated all her Attention upon it. Her Dissemblance is masterly, I thought.

Jane's sitting Room was in its Furnishings as delicate and light as she was. The smooth Walls were painted in a faint Shade of green that was echoed in the Upholstery of the Chairs and high backed Sophas. The main Colour was provided by the Curtains, which were an hopeful and enduring pea Hue that turned the silver tea-Stove copper green, and cast a sickly wash upon the leaded Countenances of the Ladies. I imagined that Jane, in ordering the Curtains, had not made any Allowance for the Quality of morning Light thro' her Windows. Nevertheless, the Room was pleasant enough, and I smiled to see Jane so happily enthroned Mistress of it.

"Oh, I am so glad that you approve of Withy Grange!" Jane said. "For then you will visit often. And thank you for bringing Miss

Montague up, as Miss Ravenscroft is upon the Point of Leaving and would have been delayed."

I took this as my Cue to pay my Compliments to Sophia. Her Response seemed cold; I feared that perhaps she had seen too much of mine Encounter with Katherine. She had Cause, I supposed, to feel badly used.

"How doth Mr Barnaby?" I asked my Sister, quitting Sophia with a shallow Bow.

"Very well. He is presently inspecting the Work we are having done about the old Orchard."

What? I thought. Is he to grub that up, too? But I said: "You did not mention anything to me of any Orchard."

Jane looked puzzled. "I did, Brother. When I wrote to you at Christmas I told you all about it. Do you not recall the Trouble poor Mr B. had in evicting those Vagabonds who had taken up home in it?"

"Why, no," I said.

"Did not you read my Letter, Tristan?" Jane said.

"I did, Madam," I answered; tho' 'twas another Lie, for I knew well that I had not.

"Then you will know," Jane continued, somewhat crossly, "that Mr B. was forced to call in the Constable, and have the whole Tribe threatened with Arrest for Vagrancy; and that in the End 'twas only fear of Hanging that caused them to remove."

All of a sudden I apprehended her Meaning—more than her Meaning, in truth, for in my Sister's honest Eyes I could discern no Sign of any secret Intimation. Yet the Event stood now to me as clear as Dayelight. Barnaby, in his Strivings to improve Withy Grange, had evicted Nathaniel Ravenscroft.

"Did this all take place last Summer?" I asked.

"You did not read my Letter, did you?"

"I did," I said. "Truly, I did. Tho' I may not have read all of it."

Jane sighed.

"It is Time for us to go," Sophia said, rising to her Feet with great Abruptness. "Thank you, my dear Mrs Barnaby, for shewing me around your beautifull House."

I realised that this must be my Parting from Katherine, and my Ribcage clenched. I knew not when I should see her next; and altho' this had been the Case two Nights before, the Wrench seemed now the greater for the Morning's Reassertion of our Closeness.

Katherine looked up, and closed her Poems.

"La! I have lost my Glove," Sophia said.

The next few Minutes were all perplext in Sophia's Leaving, and in locating her Glove and pocket-Book, which she had droppt. Katherine stood still, her Gaze threaded tight thro' mine, and her lower Lip presst white between her crooked Teeth. Neither of us made Attempt to help Sophia.

There was nothing I could do. Nothing. In mine Heart, I should gladly have brought Katherine Montague straight away from the House and carried her to London; but it was not even possible for me to take Hold of her Hand. 'Tis not right, I thought, that we must be parted so! If only I were already of Age! If I but had an Income of mine own!

"I wish you the safest Journey, Miss Montague," I said.

"Thank you, Sir," said Katherine.

Sophy, having recovered her Belongings, took her leave of Jane, and wished me well, saying that she hoped to meet again come Christmas-tide. I offered my polite Farewells, and then Sophia departed the Room, taking my darling Girl with her.

The Aire snapped her Absence like a Whip.

I left the Grange at about four o' the Clock, before Barnaby returned for Dinner, and out of Curiosity rode home by Way of the old Orchard, from where I felt sure he should by now be gone. Mine Head was full of Katherine, but there was yet a little Space for Nathaniel, who, I was certain, had spent his last Weeks in the Parish in that Place. I was desirous to see the Sward upon which he had slept, the Trees beneath which he must have sheltered. Yet I was anxious too, for here, I guessed, Viviane had camped also.

I rode around the outside of the Gardens, keeping by the Wall. The Orchard lay some fifty Yards westward of the Grange. It, too, was walled, but from atop my Chestnut this presented no Barrier to my Sight. The Orchard looked to be very old indeed; older than the House, and even older than the Willows. The Trees grew twisted, and too tall to climb, and very few seemed to be bearing Fruit. Upon a few of the very oldest I could see Mistletoe spindling about the tallest Branches, like green Cobwebs.

The Grass below, where Nathaniel must have lain, was thick with Moss, and had been close cropped by three white Goats the Gardener grazed here for that Purpose. If I had expected to find any Trace of Nat, I was come many Months too late.

I looked to see what Works Barnaby had been inspecting. I soon discovered that the far Wall of the Orchard had been badly crumbled by Rain, and that there had formed a Gap, some thirteen Feet in Width, that had lain open to the outside Fields. This plainly had been Barnaby's Concern, for the Gap was now all but sealed, and the Men who had laboured the Daye upon it were packing up their Tools and preparing to depart. I wondered that he should have stayed so long about the Supervision of a Task that was suited to neither his Rank nor his Ability, and I imagined that he must have proved a great Annoyance to the Masons.

Trotting closer, I was readying My Self to question the nearest of the Men, when he, who had his Back to me, turned unexpectedly about, and spat deliberately upon the Grass.

To my great Dismay, I perceived that it was Joseph Cox, the Bull's Manservant. Dismisst, I thought with scorn, and sunk to take daye Labour wherever he could get it.

Immediately, I suffered the violent Recoil in my Gut that had afflicted me that Morning at the Bull. Evil rose from Cox in a Miasma. Even my Chestnut appeared to feel it. Stiffening, he began to prance upon the Spot, his ears pricked forward in a great Alarum as he surveyed the swarthy Goblin who stood swaggering insolent before us.

Cox looked me up and down, and his Lip curled. "Good afternoon," he said. "Sir."

"What do you here, Cox?" I demanded.

"I's buildin' a Wall, Sir," Cox answered, adding, again after a Pause, and in the most surly of Tones, "if'n that's all right wi' you, Sir."

"If your Work is finished, then begone with you," I said. "You are not to loiter here. Do you understand?"

"Oh, I do understand 'ee, Sir," said Joe Cox, with a low Sneer.

Instinct made me put my Heels to my Chestnut, and riding right upon the Man, I raised my Whip to strike him. The Crescent of my sunnelit Arm loomed stark against the Shaddowes.

Joe Cox fell backwards into the Wall, and lifted both Arms to defend himself against my Blow; but I did not let it fall. "Cross my Path again, Cox, and you shall suffer for't," I told him. "Take up your Workman's Tools, and leave."

I was prepared to have left the Matter there; I pulled mine Horse up short, and readied mine Heels to have cantered him away. But Cox scrambled to his Feet.

"Take up my Tools?" he growled. "That I shall; an' if 'ee do come at me again I sh'll use 'un to crack thy Head open, Squire's Son or no. I oan never takin' no Orders off'n you."

I caught my Breath. "How dare you threaten me? You are in my Brother-in-law's Employ, Cox! I will see to it that your Insolence costs you your Place." I drove my Chestnut forward again, and slashed my Whip, as hard and furious as I could, across the pig-Man's Face.

To mine utter Amazement, Cox did not flinch from the Blow. He merely wiped his Mouth upon the Back of his Hand, as if he had felt nothing at all, and stared up at me, his brutish Visage contorting into a contemptuous Leer. "Aye, Sir," he said. "You do that, Sir, and see what Answer 'ee do get; there's Few as'll work for Mr Barnaby, but there's Many wantin' Labour."

Enraged by his Defiance, I threw up my Whip again, but a sudden Recollection of My Self, and of my Station, stayed mine Hand. It should have been below me to have been arguing thus with such a low Creature as Joseph Cox. Instead, I did what I should have done before, kicked my Chestnut into a Canter, and without another Word to Cox, left him there standing.

My Lungs ached as if I had been breathing Poison. I had to gallop for a Mile or more before the clean Aire washed the Stench away.

Finally, my Passion began to subside; I slowed mine Horse to a walk, and patted his foamy Neck. Had he truly perceived, as I had, that Cox was evil? The Philosophers whose Works I had studied seemed generally to be in Agreement with Descartes that Creatures, being mere Automata, perceived nothing, even Pain. The Reverend Hales' haemostatick Vivisections had been performed upon Horses.

Yet Dr Hunter had impresst on me the Primacy of mine own Observations; and time after time these had appeared directly to contradict this Assertion. The Creatures upon whom I had performed mine Experiments had often shewn me Signs of extream Suffering, and I did not feel inclined to dismiss mine Observations as mere Fancy. I raised my Whip, in a Spirit of Proof, and brought it down smarting upon mine Horse's Flank. He broke at once into a Trot. Wherefore? I thought. Surely, he seeketh to escape the Pain. What would occur if I were to continue to beat him, until he reached the Limit of his Speed, and still he suffered it? What occurs in the Perceptions of an Animal in Pain? Is it in any Way akin to that of an Human Being? Verily, he sees, he feels; he hath a Mind, of a Sort.

If 'tis possible, I thought, that he may sense as subtile a thing as Pain, then surely the Creature must perceive Evil, which hath an objective Existence.

He had perceived it. We, both, had perceived it.

The Thought of Pain cast my Mind's Eye back within my Study, upon Katherine, and her sweet Blood flowing, pure and swift, an Exaltation in my Sight. All at once, Revelation shone, clear as if it wound in front of me: A subtile Chain, Perception itself; communicated intimately from one Mind unto another thro' the Impulse, the bodily Sensation; Pain. Pain needeth neither Language, nor Reason. It crosseth all Boundaries: betwixt Man and Beast, Monster and Angel, even between Sinner and God. Did not Christ Himself suffer the most enduring Agonies upon the Cross?

'Tis a Species of Love, I thought.

Arriving home, I retired to my Study after Dinner, and abandoning as beneath my Dignity any Idea of writing my Sister about the absurd Behaviour of Joseph Cox, went thence to Bed, where Dreams of Katherine, and Nightmares of Nathaniel and Viviane, delighted and tormented me in equal Measure, till the short midsummer Night was at its End.

CHAPTER EIGHTEEN

I returned to London on the following Morning. I was glad to be arriving in the old City, filthy and lousy as it was, and as the smokey Towers of Westminster hove in Sight against the blue Sky mine Heart near leapt for Joy. I had ridden, in Company with James the Footman, the whole Distance from Shirelands, and altho' mine Arse was sore, my Spirits were light. The Country between Berkshire and London had lain open before me like a green Cloth, embroidered with many little Woods and Cottages. Here and there thro'out the Counties, new-planted Hedgerows sprouted like Bristles upon a Brush. James and I, to pass the Time, played our own Species of travelling Piquet and I won, my Score consisting of twenty Persons walking, seven Flocks of Geese, twelve Carriages and one old hedge Whore, by which I won the Game outright. James laughed fit to burst, and said that I should collar the Parson next; but I never did.

I set about unpacking my Trunk, and was putting away my Convict's Skull, whilst pondering the Volume of its Brain, when I was interrupted by Liza at the Door with a Letter that Minute arrived for me from Berkshire. This Surprize at once put all Ideas of Surgery out of my Mind; I could only imagine the Letter to be from Jane, and I could not see why she should write to me so soon For a Moment, I was grippt by Dread. Then I perceived the unformed Handwriting upon the Address, and mine Heart jolted, for I realised that it was from Katherine.

I turned about, the Letter crushed against my Chest. I locked the Door behind me and sate down upon my Bed.

The Letter, I could tell from the Feel of it, ran to several Pages, and I wondered that she had been able to post it without the Complicity, or Suspicion, of anyone within the Household, and from whom she had learned my London Address. Perhaps, I thought, she had slippt it into a Pile of other Correspondence, hoping that it would go unnoticed. As there were always such Comings and Goings of Persons and Papers within and without the Rectory, this may not have been difficult.

With shivering Hands, I broke open the Seal. Then I stoppt. My Body had responded to the Thought of Katherine as readily as if she were in my Presence. Miss Montague, I thought, doth not object to my dark Skin, or to my black Hair. I tried for a Moment to calm My Self, then began again to unfold the Paper.

Dear Mr Hart

I hope that You are not too Displeas'd by my Writing to You. I am Here (at Collerton) for another Month, as Mama hath writ to say that she will not be Readye for me to go Home till July when my Brother Albert gets his Leave and he can fetch me from the Post in Weymouth.

I have tryed hard to Keep my Word to You and I will continue to Keep it. Aunt R. says I am not Quite the Savidge any longer and I am to spend more Time with Mrs B. because she is a good Influence. I hope You are Happy to hear this.

I know that You do not enjoye long Letters, so I shall not bore You with Newes and such that You will get from Mrs B. I have been Studying my English Composition and have written You a Story about Raw-Head-and-Bloody-Bones of which I hope You will Approve. It is not a Nursery Tale, for I have made it up out of my own Head, and it is a very fright-full Yarn, with Blood and Gore and Horrid Death in it.

Your Friend

Katherine Montague

The Tale of Leonora

Once, there were twin Brothers of Noble Birth, who were in all things the greatest of Rivals. Their names were Raw Head and Bloody Bones, because when the Sunne went downe they Transformed into Horrible Monsters. Raw Head had but a Scull from which all the Fleashe had gonne, so that his Haire grewe directly from the Bone as Seaweed doth upon a Rocke. Bloody Bones became a Skeleton with Bones as Redd as Fire and Eyes like burning Embers.

Bothe were Bad to looke upon, and Worse still to meet with, but Raw Head was the Worst; for whilst Bloody Bones could stripp the

Skin from a Man's Backe with his long Fingernailes, one Glance from Raw Head could smite him into a Pitch Black Madness from which there was no Return.

Now Raw Head hath gonne away to seeke his Fortune in the West, and Bloody Bones is left Alone upon his Father's Estate. One Daye Bloody Bones is walking in the Fields, appearing most Handsome and richly Dresst, for 'tis the Dayetime. There he meets with a Sea Captain's Daughter, who is called Leonora, and she hath eyes as Blue as Forgetmenots and is as lovely as the June Sky. They fell in Love and planned there and then to be Marryed after several Sundayes at the Church on the Hill. But Bloody Bones could not tell Leonora his Dread Secret, for he feared that she would Flee from him if he did.

So the Weddinge went ahead, and on their Weddinge night Leonora wonders why her Husband shuts himself away. Doth he not Desire to lie with me? she sayes.

Then one fell Night an evil Goblin stole into the House and carried her off to his Lair on the high Moor. And Bloody Bones, getting up the next Daye goes into his Wife's Chamber and cryes: O Woe! Alack! Where is my poor Leonora!

And the Maid says: She is Gonne, up on the Moor, for the Goblins have Stolen her.

So Bloody Bones pulls on his Cote and takes up his Pistols and his Sword, and he calls for his Horse and Rides up on the Moor to Hunt for Leonora.

When she Hears him, for his Voice can Carry for Miles and Miles, Leonora cryes: O, My Darling! My Love! My Dearest! **Forget mee not, My Bloody Bones, How I miss Thee! Tell mee what I must do,** *for these Vile Goblins have taken me Prisoner!*

So Bloody Bones puts his Spurs into his Horse's sides, and he gallops all the Way over the Moor towards where he hath heard his Leonora's Voice. But his Way was blocked by an Hundred Goblins with sharp Teeth who wanted to Capture him too and drink up all his Bloode.

Bloody Bones draws his Pistols and Shoots two full Score of them Dead as they come, and their Bodies lay vile and Stinking upon the Moor, rotting away till there was no more Sign of them. But many More attackt him and they pulled him Down from his Horse, which they slew most Horribly. So Bloody Bones draws his Sword and fights on right Manfully, Cleaving the Sculls of many Goblins from their Shoulders, and splitting still more Compleatly down the Middle, like Logs for the Fire. The Goblin Bloode was Terrible for it scorched Bloody Bones like ice-water, and his Fine Cloathes began for to Smoake. And still he cryes: O, Leonora, my Love, feare not, for I come, I come!

He fought so Long and so Furiously that the Goblin Hoarde fell apart, and ran Screaming for their Lives all across the Moor, scattering like Ashes blown before a Mighty Gale.

Then Bloody Bones strode up to the Cave where the Goblin Knight kept his dear Leonora Prisoner. And he is gonne in and Lo, before him is Raw Head himself, who hath become the High Prince over all Goblins. And Raw Head he hath bound Leonora to a Chair, and he is supping her Bloode from a White Baysin. But Bloody Bones hath such a Fearsome Phrenzy on him that he easily defeats this most Wicked of all Foes, and he stabs him thro' the Chest to cut out his Heart, but the Goblin hath not one. So Bloody Bones pulled off his Head with his bare Hands so that the redd Bloode spouted from his Necke. Then Leonora throws herself into the Arms of her Deare Husband, and they Kissed and Embrac'd each other, never to be Parted ever again.

Then the bold Sunne began to Sett, and Bloody Bones was transfixt by Mortall Feare that she would love him not. But Leonora had learned long ago to See beyond meere Appearances, and she knew him for her Husband whom she Adored right well, and she Promises to do Anything he Wishes. So they returned Home across the Moor to his Estate, and Never were they parted ever Again.

As soon as I had finished the Tale, I took it up again and read it thro' from the Beginning to the End. I traced the Shapes made by Katherine's Quill with my Fingers; here, and here, and here, she had lifted her Goose feathered Pen from the Paper and dippt it in her Ink, for these Stroakes immediately after were thick, and very black. Here, the Ink had drippt, and she had blown upon the Page to blot it. I held the Paper to my Lips to taste the Fragrance of her Breath. When I closed mine Eyes, it seemed as if her cool, soft Lips presst light against mine own.

I murmured her Name, again, again: Katherine.

Dear God, if she were but here with me, now, lying beside me on this Bed! Mine Hands ached for the Touch of her, the delicate Skin—as I imagined—of her inner Thigh—the blonde Curls—for they must be blonde—of her Mons Pubis—the warm Wetness between her opening Legs.

My God, I thought, if she were here—if she—

Once I had regained my Composure, I took up my Quill and settled My Self at mine Escritoire to pen a Reply. It was short, curt enough to deceive any of the Ravenscrofts who might lay Hands upon it, and in its old fashioned secret Italics, I hoped intirely to my Point:

Dear Miss Montague,

I *am happy to learn that Mrs Ravenscroft is satisfied by your improved Behaviour, and I trust that you will keep to your Word in this Matter as in all others. I greatly enjoyed your little Phantasy of the unforgettable Leonora, who hath overcome the terrifying Raw Head with the help of her loving Bloody Bones. However, there is still an occasional solecistic Rusticity in your Grammar and Phraseology which you must strive to overcome, and your Handwriting is childish and inelegant. One Houre's careful Practice every Daye, until your Fingers ache, should remedy this latter Deficiency.*

I am greatly concerned at your Suggestion that you will be travelling Post. I trust that your Uncle will make sure to send a Servant with you. If he doth not intend to do this, remark upon it to Mrs Barnaby, and she will have one of the Hall Servants accompany you.

Yours, etc,

Tristan Hart.

I sealed the Letter, and addressing it to Miss Montague, at the Rectory, Collerton, Berkshire, I unlocked my Door and called for Liza to send it by the Return of Post.

The Months after my brief Sojourn in Berkshire pulsed by in a steady Rhythm. The Hospitals kept me busy; every Morn I rose at six and hurried from Bow Street to Southwark or Smithfield, as I would work alternate Dayes at each Establishment. I assisted upon the Wards from seven until nine; then after a short Breakfast I would operate, after a minor Fashion, until eleven, when Dr Hunter would arrive and I would watch him operate, and fetch and carry for him until one or two. During the Afternoons, if I was lucky, I was able to quit the Hospital and follow Dr Hunter into his private Practice until five, after which I would return to check up on the Progress of mine own Patients. I dealt with Innkeepers, Merchants, Footmen, and Shoemakers' Wives, Beggars and Vagrants; clean Cases, dirty Cases—those suffering from any of the venereal Diseases, who were kept apart in their own Wards—Injuries, and sometimes, Incurables; altho' the Governors of both Hospitals refused to allow these to remain after three Months, and the City, in the Event of their being treated on its Purse, refused to pay. I became a confident Dresser of Wounds, Lancer of Boils, Manager of Whitlows and Resetter of Dislocations. I watched—and I envied—the Removal of Tumours, the Closing of Fistulae, the Amputation of Limbs above the Joint and below it. I did not usually return to Mr Fielding's House before nine.

Naturally, my Visits to Mrs Haywood's Establishment were no longer as numerous as they had been; most Weeks I was too busy to pay Polly more than a quarter-Houre's Call; but my reduced Interest was neither intirely due to Lack of Time nor to the Fact that I now had real Subjects for mine Investigation. The Truth was that in every Scream, in every Cry, I heard the tormenting Echo of that One which I had not: my Darling's own.

"Tell mee what I must do," she had written; and so tell her I did; weekly, twice weekly, at length daily, even tho' I had warned her not to expect many Letters. I wrote to her demanding petty and trivial Improvements to her Behaviour, to her Grammar, her Manner of Walking, and her Mode of Dress—which Improvements, once achieved, I invariably decried. She wrote to me every Morning when she arose to reassure me of her determined Efforts to succeed and her continuing Progress—and also, sometimes, to seek mine Approbation of some devious Means she had herself

devised for her own Punishment, if, and when, she should have failed to please.

I was falling in Love; and thro'out all my Limbs and Organs Joy flowed immeasurable. I did not know whether any of the Fielding Family had guessed wherefore. That I did not tell them was not due to any Fear that they might despise my Choice; for as mine Aunt had remarked, Henry Fielding, at least, could have nothing to say upon that Point. I feared rather that they might, in their collective Pleasure at my potentially altered State, let the Story slip to my Father, by whom it must certainly come to my Aunt; and she would be sure to interfere against me.

To Mr Glass, however, whose Christian Name, I soon learned, was Erasmus, I discovered My Self to be an open Book. Perhaps half-open, for altho' Erasmus' Wits were sharp and his Insight penetrating, he had led an innocent Life in Comparison with mine own, and if he knew of the theoretical Existence of my particular Vice, he did not think to connect its Praxis in any Way with me. He guessed quickly, however, at the Existence of someone dear to mine Heart, and challenged me upon it.

We had passed the Afternoon together in the Hospital, witnessing the Excoriation of three facial Tumours and an high Lithotomy performed at nigh Cheseldenian Speed. These had awarded a pleasing Distraction to mine Eyes, tho' the Lithotomy had left Erasmus rather pale; thro'out the long, slow Morning I had spent tedious Houres about the lancing of Abscesses, the Reparation of Ruptures, and the cleaning of Ulcers. At about half-past seven o' the Clock, we were both of us just upon the point of leaving to go home when Dr Hunter arrived unexpectedly, and called us to assist him in an emergency Resetting of a fractured lower Mandible. The Patient, who was a wealthy city Merchant, had had the Misfortune to have been kicked in the Face, according to his Wife, by his own Horse. This Custom was all to the Good for Dr Hunter, who was to be heartily recompensed for the Inconvenience; but I had been busy about the Hospital since Dawn, and I was tired and irritable.

The Injury, which had occurred within the Houre, was not threatening to Life, altho' the ragged Break was in a difficult and delicate Position on the lower Maxilla hard by the Trigeminal Nerve. Erasmus made certain that the night-time Theatre was exceptionally well lit, whilst I ensured Provision of Lint and Curette. Dr Hunter inspected the Area closely and then carefully removed a Quantity of bony Fragments from the torn Muscle, before turning the afflicted Area over to Erasmus and My Self that we should set, bathe, and close the Wound. By now it was nearing nine, and Dr Hunter, assessing our Progress to have been sound, left to seek his Dinner.

Erasmus and My Self being as ravenous as he, it did not take long for us to finish with the Merchant, who left the Hospital in Company with his Wife and Son and his Jaw bound up so tightly in a linen Turban that he could not speak. I warned his Family that it was unlike that he would be able to converse freely, or to consume anything more substantial than Soup, for a considerable while. To my Surprize, they seemed absurdly happy about this, as if his Silence had been an added Beneficence on my Part; but verily I could not have cared less whether I had bandaged Cicero, or Mr Punch.

The November Aire was foggy, a thick smoaky Dampe spreading all across the low lying City in a foul Cloud that all Daye had not lifted. It seemed to me to have been of that Species of Strength-sapping Cold which, tho' not freezing in itself, penetrates inward to chill the Lungs, and to congeal the Spirits. If Descartes had been right, and mine Heart's Function had been that of a Crucible, it should have had a Promethean Task in front of it.

The Atmosphere within the George Inn, tho', to which Erasmus and My Self retired, was warm and friendly, the Aire suffused by a wispy Haze of tallow-Light and the red Echo of the slowly burning Coals. The Place was busy; whilst Erasmus sought the Attention of the Landlord, I elbowed a Path thro' to a Table beside the Fire, and with a Nod and a few subtile Intimations, secured Possession of it. As we dried ourselves out over a brisk Dinner and a shared Jug of warmed dark Ale, Erasmus told me of his Fancy to take up a Position as a Ship's Surgeon bound for Kingstown, where he meant to set himself up as Physician to the Planters.

"Wherefore should you wish to do that?" I asked, sitting upright in my Surprize. "I have heard that the Climate is unforgiving, and the People not at all friendly. You would do better, Erasmus, were you to enter Business here as a man Midwife. You have a most confiding Manner, and the Ladies are soothed by you."

"Oh," said Erasmus. "But then I should be forced to compete with the good Doctor and his Ilk, who put me to Shame. I should have to practise outside of London to have any Trade at all; and I had leifer not be a country Surgeon, setting gentlemanly Splints all my Life. Dr Oliver hath intimated that he could mayhap find me a Position in St Luke's, but I have little fancy for that. I shall hie me to the Plantations, and at least see something of the World."

"Yet," I persisted, "'twill be a Wrench to leave behind your native Soil."

"A small Wrench," confesst Erasmus. " Truly, Tristan, I have little

Reason to remain. I have always known that I would have to make mine own Way in the World. My Father told me when I was six that he should leave his Business to mine older Brother, and naught for me. I am glad. I should have made a poor Apothecary." Erasmus took a long Swig of his Ale, and then, finding that he had emptied his Tankard, lifted the brown Jug and refilled it, foaming, to the Brim.

"You have poured that too quick," I said.

Erasmus smiled, and put his Mugg gently down to rest upon the Tabletop until the Storm within it should abate. "You, I think," said he, "have more Reason to stay than your Expectations."

"How so?"

"There is a Woman, is there not?"

I stared at him. "Egad. How did you know?"

"Your Features, Sir, are most expressive. Oft-times have I watched them soften and your Gaze become quite distant from the thing in front of you. Yours is the Countenance of a Man in Love, I'll wager."

My first Reaction to Erasmus' Words was to resolve better to control my Physiognomy in the Future. But as I opened my Mouth to speak, the Tavern's cellar-Man, his Expression as meek as his Action was disruptive, made impossible mine immediate Denial by the sudden rattling Discharge of half a Scuttle's worth of Coals into the Fire. The red Gleam vanished, and an heavy Bloom of Smoake billowed outwards from the Grate. I coughed violently, and in no uncertain Terms berated him for his idiot Clumsiness.

Then, in the Moment's Grace provided by this Irruption, I realised that altho' I had spoken to no living Soule about mine Understanding with Katherine, that as far as I had Power over the

Secret, it was compleat, I longed to speak of her to anyone who might listen. Erasmus Glass, I then perceived, was so wholly separate from the Affair that telling him would risk nothing. Moreover, he was naturally reserved, and ill disposed to Gossip even when the Case affected his own Interest. He was, in fact, the perfect Confidant; had I created him to the Purpose he could not have been better.

So, as the Flames began to overpower and then to consume their fresh Fuel, I began the Tale; and over the Passage of the next two Houres I revealed the intire Story—leaving out only some few vicious Details involving Blood and Pain that I knew would be jarring to Erasmus' Sensibilities. I told him of Katherine's young Age, and her Relationship to the Rector, and the potent Attraction that had sprung up, so unexpectedly, between us. The Inn was all but empty by the Time I had reached mine End, and the Fire had burned again quite low. Erasmus was somewhat shocked by my Revelation that I must keep the Truth from my Father.

"Do you fear that he will cut you off?" he asked. In the paltry Candlelight, his grey Eyes seemed darkened Wells, and his Voice was serious.

"I am unsure," I told him. "I think not, but I dare not attempt it for another Reason. There is no Engagement yet in Place and it would be the easiest thing for my Family to have Katherine hidden where I cannot find her. She is almost friendless; her Mother seems to have little Appreciation of her Value, and I have no Knowledge at all of her other Uncle. Certainly, the Ravenscrofts would sooner cast her off than lose my Father's Approbation."

"'Tis difficult," Erasmus said, with a Grimace. "You have my Sympathies, Tristan."

I thanked him honestly for that; then, since it was nearly eleven, and we were both expected back at Bart's in the Morning, we departed from the George, and headed thro' the dismal Streets to our individual Lodgings as rapidly as we could.

CHAPTER NINETEEN

Six Dayes after Christmas-tide, it being the Opinion of the Government that it could alter Time by legal Decree, the Yeare of our Lord seventeen fifty-one ended, to the great Confusion of the Uneducated; it was barely two hundred and eighty-one Dayes old, and ought not to have died so soon. The only immediate Consequence to me was that, as I had been born in late January, I had now seemingly to have gained an extra Yeare, and should by the reckoning of the calendar have turned two-and-twenty instead of one. Altho' I knew for certain that this clerkish Dislocation of Time by Human Agency could have no Effect upon Reality, I felt strangely uncomfortable, for it seemed to me as if my coming of

Age had taken place in a Time that was, in some peculiar Manner, outside of itself—and so I perceived that I had in some bizarre Sense simultaneously attained, exceeded, and failed to attain my Majority.

Because I had not, despite my Sister's Exhortations, returned to Berkshire for Christmas, I had not seen my Father or any Members of my Family since the previous June. Upon my Birthdaye I received, in addition to a very lengthy Epistle from Jane, a cursory Missive from my Father explaining his Intention to settle upon me an Allowance of four hundred Pounds a Yeare for as long as I should choose to remain in London, unmarried, and without the Necessity for any greater Sum. I was staggered by this, and a Kernel of Shame began to germinate within me as I considered mine Inability to face my Father. I regretted the cowardly Spirit that had prevented me from so doing, for it broke clear upon me now that my Father, despite his apparent Reluctance to have aught to do with me, was neither Villain nor Ogre. I remembered his muttered Words concerning me to mine Aunt in the Carriage, and I began to question whether, in Truth, we were not more alike than I had realised.

My Work about the Hospitals grew ever more exacting, and mine Houres ever longer. I did not consider My Self overworked, for the simple Fact that I was about the Practice of Medicine thrilled me beyond any Thought of Tiredness. But I had noticed that I could no longer recognise, with any Clarity, the Faces of my Patients. I told no one this.

I was engaged, very late one Afternoon, about resetting the dislocated Wrist of an Apprentice who had fallen from a Scaffold, when Erasmus came to find me. I had been, as usual, about the Hospitals since the early Morning, and mine Eyes and Head were devilish sore, but I greeted him as affectionately as I could, and asked what was the Matter.

"Dr Oliver," he said, "is this Evening to perform a Trepanation upon a Melancholic who hath intirely lost his Reason, and he sent me to inquire whether you might wish to witness the Operation."

"Why," I exclaimed. "I should be astonished if Melancholy, which is surely a Disorder of the Mind, will be cured by an Operation."

"Your general Instinct is sound," Erasmus answered. "But Dr Oliver believes that this Man's Condition hath its Onset in an heavy Blow to the Head he sustained some Yeares since, which hath resulted in the Presence of mortified Tissue beneath the Cranium, that he hopes Trepanation shall remove."

Immediately, I was reminded of Nathaniel, and his Story of the Labourer who could not perceive Left. Verily, cerebral Damage doth affect the Mind, I thought. Dr Oliver's Hypothesis may not be incorrect. Erasmus, mistaking my Preoccupation, said: "If you do not wish to watch, Mr Hart, then do not come."

"I have not said so," I replied quickly. "I would not miss it for the World."

Erasmus laughed, and answered that he had thought that would be the Case. I finished bandaging the Child, released him into the Care of his Master, and hurried after Erasmus.

I should have expected that the Procedure would be carried out at the Bethlem, or at St Luke's in Windmill Street, which was the new mad-House. This Operation, however, I supposed for Dr Oliver's Convenience, and certainly to mine immense Relief, took Place in the Theatre at St Thomas's.

I had not witnessed a Trepanation before, and I was greatly excited. The Operation was now rarely performed, even for an Epilepsy, for the foolish Superstition that had maintained that such Disease resulted from the Imprisonment of Demons and fuliginous Vapours in the Skull had, thankfully, been overturned. However, it was still undertaken on Occasion where there was Cause to believe that such a mental Disorder might have a treatable, mechanical, Origin. I was not surprized, however, that the Surgeon should be Dr Oliver, whom I knew to be profoundly interested in the Question of how Lunaticks might have their lost Wits restored.

Yet how, I thought, as I watched Dr Oliver, with the Assistance of Erasmus, secure the unprotesting Man upon the Table, and prepare the three-armed Trephine for its Application, can Melancholy result from morbid Tissue? It is not like an Epilepsy, that manifests in violent Shaking of the physical Body. Neither is it like a Paralysis, that may readily be assumed due to Damage to a Nerve. Nor even is it a Distemper of the Senses. Unless verily there be some Truth in the Doctrine of the Humours, it must be a Disease that is intirely mental, having more to do with a Man's Soule than Matter upon his Cerebrum. Yet Nat's Labourer had no physical Incapacity—and what of mine own nervous Illness, that seemed so like to very Madness? Had that, as I had pondered, even hoped, its Origin in some Insult to my Brain of which I had lost all Memory? Where doth the Body stop, and Mind begin? Doth the one become the other? Was I poisoned? Was I mad? Or was I evil?

Mine Head began to spin; I sate down, and for the next half-Houre endeavoured to give my full Attention to the Scene unfolding before me upon the operating Table as Dr Oliver painstakingly removed a circular Section of the Man's Skull about the Diameter of a Sovereign, and having exposed the thickened and pulsating Meninges of the Brain, endeavoured to stem the Bleeding from the Scalp. But my Concentration was elusive. My Ribs felt as if they had sealed up around mine Heart, and the exhausted Organ fluttered desperate as a Goldfinch in a Flask. I wished that I could have had something to eat before I had arrived. I wished that I could have gone home, to have slept the Sennight out.

I stumbled out of St Thomas's at perhaps ten o' the Clock, and took a Chair all the Way back to Bow Street. I would have eaten when I arrived, but in the Event Sleep was too quick for me, and I succumbed to Slumber in Mr Fielding's largest Armchair, where I remained until Midnight, when Mary chased me off to Bed.

The following Fortnight I passt in such a frantick Whirl of Work, much of which was about the dirty Wards, that I clean forgot the trepanning Operation and would never have learned its Outcome had not Erasmus, one Evening in the Shakespeare, remarked that the Patient was great improved. I found these Newes staggering, and plain said so. I did not tell Erasmus, however, that the mad Man's Face and Name were both as absent from my Memory as if he had never been possesst of either. He, like all the Cases I had witnessed and worked upon, had seemingly become but an ordinary nothing.

Katherine, to whom I did confess this strange Phenomenon, wrote that she was afraid that I was working My Self sick; but I did not heed her Plea to cut mine Houres.

Mid May, my Sister wrote to tell me that she was with Child and longing to see me before her Confinement. I tried to respond to her Newes in an encouraging Vein, but in the Event could think of naught to ask, save whether she had made out her Will, so I gave up the Attempt.

It being a Sundaye, I had taken a few Houres away from my

Work about the Hospitals for Church; and with Katherine's Concern for mine Health lying guilty on my Mind, I had also fashioned for My Self a Distraction, via the Person of Lt. Simmins, whose Address I had easily found out from Dr Oliver's Associate, and who seemed, to my continuing Wonderment, extreamly pleased to renew our Acquaintanceship. Over the past Fortnight we had exchanged a few Letters, and the Conversation seeming friendly, we had arranged to meet in Person that Afternoon.

Simmins was settled with several other young Lobsters upon an Inn beneath the Sign of the Dragon near Hampstead. This Inn sate on the main Road into London, and it was to my Surprize that I learned that despite his Emblem the Landlord had put up but feeble Resistance when these young Pillars of the Nation had been foisted on him. Certainly, he must have regretted them, for they did not bring in anything like to the amount of Money their Billet surely cost him.

I arrived at the Dragon shortly before Noon on Sundaye, and finding Simmins not yet returned, waited in the Tavern opposite the open Door, and took a light Repast, to the Landlord's Delight; tho' not to mine own. The Inn put me in mind more of the Bull than any London Establishment, and I thought for a Moment wistfully of Nathaniel. Its low Ceilings were thick with the brown Residue of pipe Smoake; the plastered Walls glittered with horse-Brasses; upon the still Aire lingered the fulsome Scents of Beer and Human Sweat. The Daye being chill, I sate My Self in the shaddowed Recess of a leather Armchair, by the smouldering Fire, and from this Location I watched the Activity in the inn Yard. Simmins returned shortly after Noon, by which Time I was almost finished with my Meal. I heard him before I saw him; that Hesitation, an Extension of Sound at the Beginnings of his Words, unmistakable, despite the Yeares that had passed since I had heard it. He was laughing with one of his fellow Officers over the Reason he had been delayed.

"There w-as a Fr-acas," he said. "On the T-yburn R-oad. Didn't you h-ear? All Passage was bl-ocked for twenty M-inutes, until Captain K-eane arrived with a f-ew of our Fellows and we joined F-orces and gave the Wretches Hell. The Hi-ghway's damned clear now!"

There was much Laughter, as Lt. Simmins accepted the Congratulations of his Company. Then came the Clatter of Boots upon the Flags, and the conquering Hero steppt smartly into the dim Tavern. He blinked and looked about him. "Mr H-art!" he cried. "'Tis good to see you!" Striding forwards, he threw his Arms about my Shoulders and gave me an hearty Buss upon the Cheek. My Nostrils filled with the stout Reek of dampe Wool and Gunpowder.

Little Simmins had grown and altered much in his Appearance, for all that his Stammer had not. He was now almost eighteen, and tho' he stood many Inches shorter than My Self, he seemed to have compleatly disowned that Aire of helpless Innocence he had worn as a Boy. Now he looked, at least, the Soldier to the Core; smart of Attire, strong and wiry of Build, with an intelligent Look to his Eye and a friendly and humorous Demeanour. His Eyebrows, tho', were still too wild, and still met in the Middle.

"What do you think of the F-ood?" Simmins said, noticing the remains of my meat Pie, which lay still upon the Table. "It is bad, is it not?"

"Yes," I said, with a Laugh. "It is very bad."

Simmins clappt me quite hard upon my Back, and grasped me again in an Embrace so intense it seemed not unlike to the Hugg

I had given James Barnaby. "So," I said, disentangling My Self with Difficulty. "You are with the Regiment. And an Hero, now, to boot."

Simmins laughed, but his Nose flushed a brilliant pink. "I am n-not really an Hero," he said. "Captain Keane is, I think. I d-on't remember very M-uch, in Truth; 'tis somewhat of a Blur. There was a great Deal of Sm-oake, and I – I – I'm sure I did s-omething, but I don't know what." He scratched the Back of his Neck, perplext. "What a F-ool I am!" he exclaimed. "I may have b-een Heroick, but if I was I re-member nothing of it! What is the Good of that?" He laughed.

"When did you join up?" I asked, to relieve Simmins' Embarrassment.

"Oh," Simmins said. "My B-enefactor, thro' whom you found me, bought me my Commission f-our Yeares ago. 'Tis b-etter by f-ar than Sch-ool."

"Indeed," I said. "It doth appear to suit. You have grown up, Simmins."

Simmins drew back apace, and in the stark doorway Light I could perceive how keenly he was taking stock of me. Had I changed, I thought, as much as Simmins had?

As if he had read my Thoughts—or more likely, my Features—Simmins gave a small one-shouldered Shrug, intirely like to that which had long been mine own. Then his Chin came up. "You were not kind to me," he said. "But it was n-aught I could not st-and. And after you—my F-ather used to b-eat me soundly, before; af-terwards he stoppt altogether."

Again that little Shrug. The Effect was eerie; for all the Discrepancy in our Heights and Appearances, I could have been watching mine own younger Self. Then, hard upon it, came the anxious Smile of the little Boy I had tormented. I realised that Simmins wanted me very much to like him. I did. I always had liked him, even when I had terrified him into scrubbing my Boots in the iron Cold of Winter.

"Do you wish that I should call the Landlord for some Food?" I said. "Perhaps his Steaks are better than his Pies."

"If you have a Taste for W-orms," said Simmins, with a Grimace of Disgust.

The Landlord's Cellar being far superior to his Kitchen, Simmins hollered for a Jug of Ale, and so we sate together in companionable Manner for almost an Houre. I asked Simmins his Opinion upon the Condition of the Army, and with what Degree of Success he thought the Country would be able to resist an Encroachment upon her foreign Territories by the French, as appeared imminent.

"I cannot a-nswer for the State of the Colonials," Simmins said. "But I know that in too m-any of our Regiments, Discipline is shockingly l-ax. Captain Keane says that this results from the over-Use of the L-ash for trivial Offenses, which leads to poor M-orale among the M-en. Our Colonel, however, is of the opposite Opinion, that Flogging is an intirely n-ecessary Means of C-ontrol upon the common S-oldier."

"And Lieutenant Simmins?" I said. "What thinks he?"

"Men do not join the Army for its K-indness-es," Simmins said.

He gave me a strange, sideways Glance. The Tip of his Tongue nestled against his Teeth, lightly, twice. All of a sudden, exactly as it had been with Viviane, I seemed to see Simmins before me, his Hands chained high above his Head, his soft white Back scourged raw and bloody. I caught my Breath.

Simmins smiled at me from across the Tabletop, and for an

half-Second there again was the abortive Embryo of that one-shouldered Shrug: the Devil may care; I do not. His slender Fingers played lightly about the Handle of his pewter Mugg.

For a Moment I closed mine Eyes, and tensed My Self against the Thunderbolt that must certainly fall from Heaven. But the Almighty did nothing, and of course I opened them up again to see Simmins, still smiling. In his brown Eyes there hovered still that curious Intimation, which seemed to me not unlike the sly Look of a three-Guinea Whore. Yet, as I met his Gaze, it seemed to vanish, as doth a Mist upon the early Sunnelight.

"Are you quite well, Mr Hart?" Simmins said.

"I am," I said. I thought quickly. "I was suffering a Moment of Regret. 'Tis almost an whole Yeare now since I saw the Girl whom I would fain marry."

Simmins' Expression registered Surprize, then Sympathy. "The Separation must be hard on you," he said.

"Indeed so," I answered. "Sometimes it becomes almost impossible to bear."

Simmins stretched out his Arm across the Table and covered mine Hand with his own. His Skin was dry and hot; I started; but a tiny Flinch; and hoped that he did not take notice.

"Let us drink to the Lady," Simmins said. Taking his Hand from mine, he got to his Feet. "An Health, to—?"

"To Miss Montague," I said, scraping back my Chair, my Tankard held aloft.

At that Moment, a small Number of Simmins' Fellows, in scarlet Coats and rowdy Spirits, tumbled thro' the inn Door, and our private Conversation came necessarily to a Close.

Lt. Simmins' Cohort were, I discovered, an amiable Crowd. I had no Wish to join them, but I could perceive how any young

Surgeon with a more sociable Disposition than mine own might find it a fine thing to be with such a Regiment. I decided that the vile Fancy of mine earlier, unsought, imagining must have been but a passing Phantasm; gave up the Afternoon to Dice and Cards and Drink, and left the Inn in much more chearful Spirits than I had enjoyed for many Weeks.

Returning to Bow Street, I wrote at once to Katherine, to tell her of my curiously re-initiated Association with Lt. Simmins, and the unexpectedly friendly Nature of the Sentiments we had discovered in each other. But reaching the Point at which, in Life, I had so wretchedly invoked her in a foul Lie, I stoppt abruptly, and put down my Quill.

Oh! I thought, if only you were here, my Love, then I might tell you all; but what dare I risk in a Letter, that another may steal?

The restraining Cord within me, which had maintained mine external Silence and my Patience, snappt. I knew at once that should I endure a Sennight more apart from Katherine I knew not what I might do; moreover, that I need not do so. I was very nearly come upon the Time in my Life at which I could, if my Father should withdraw his Support, maintain us both; tho' truly, as I had said to Erasmus Glass, it was not his Rejection that I feared, but mine Aunt's Interference. If the Wedding were quick, I thought, and secret, she would have no Opportunity to meddle. The only Consent I would need, besides Katherine's own, would be that of Mrs Montague; and surely she would not prove difficult to sway.

The Devil could care for Caution, I thought, and for Cleverness. I dippt my Nib into mine Ink and hoped my bald Words would communicate the Strength of my Passion, and the Urgency of my Question.

My dearest, darling Brat,

I can endure this Separation no longer. If it should still appear to you that Bloody Bones is Leonora's, and Leonora his, then say so again, and we shall put a lawful End to our Suspense. It is within my Power to procure a License and Lodging, and once we are married we will be better placed to confront any Misgivings my Family may express. If they prove implacable, I shall easily find Employment in London. Write me at once, my Love, with your Answer—forgive me the Precipitance of mine Offer—my Feelings have long been known to you—they are unaltered and as strong as ever. I love you; there, I have written it, without Disguise. And I shall continue to love you, Katherine Montague, or I pray Katherine Hart, whatever Alteration Time and Circumstance shall work upon us both.

My Girl, what say you? I run now to take this to the Post, that it shall be with you as soon as may be, in the Hope that soon you will be here with me.

I remain, as ever, your Friend,

Tristan Hart.

When no Reply to this Letter arrived within the next Daye and an Half, I was disappointed, but not at once alarmed, for there might, I thought, be any Number of Reasons for the Delay. It was possible that the perswasive Arguments I had used upon the Post had not proved as effective as I had thought; perhaps mine own Letter had not been dispatched before the Mondaye. I went about my Work, and wrote to Simmins, inviting him to join me at the Shakespeare when he was able, where I proposed to introduce him to Erasmus. It had occurred to me that it might prove useful to Erasmus to forge a Connexion with the Regiment, and thereby obtain an Employment. My Motive was not intirely generous; I had no Wish for Erasmus to decamp to the Colonies, for I might never then see him after. Also, I had fallen under a strange and powerful Yearning to gather my Friends together in one Place, where I might more easily keep mine Eye upon them. Simmins was more than willing to join us both in the Tavern upon Saturdaye Eve, if Circumstance did not succeed, as presently it seemed it might, in keeping Erasmus Knee-deep in Pox.

When, by the Thursdaye I had still heard nothing from Katherine, I began to fear that she was ill, or worse. There was no one to whom I could turn to inquire after her Health; if she were not ill, but merely prevented by some trivial Circumstance from writing, or if she had not received my Letter, then any Approach I might make to the Ravenscrofts would work against me, and my Fears regarding mine Aunt become a Reality. Then I thought that perhaps the Reason for my Darling's Silence was that we had been found out, and mine Aunt had exerted her Influence to break us off. I feared that perhaps Katherine had been forbidden to write, and was overlooked, or that she had been sent away without my Knowledge. Then, finally, there broke in upon my Meditations the aweful Conceit that perhaps her Silence was my Punishment for everything I had not told anyone: my Desire to hear Lady B.—— scream in Pain; mine Abuse of Annie; mine Attraction toward Simmins; as if the Thunderbolt that I had dreaded then had struck now in such a Way as to sever the Link between us. If that was the Cause, I thought, then truly Katherine's Silence was the Work of God—or of the Devil.

I wrote to her again, from the Hospital, at nine, when I should have been again about Magdalen Ward:

I am in Hell. If Leonora hath Pity for her Bloody Bones, she must straightway shew it, for in Truth he groweth weaker with every passing Houre, and is begun to dread that he will not live out the Month.

Darling Katherine, write, write! Even if—God forbid—your Answer should be No. Shew me Grace, and relieve me from this cruel and ruinous Misery to which your strange Reserve contemns me. I have neither eaten nor slept these three Dayes, and I can think of naught but you and of my Fears for you.

An Bloody Bones were cruel, then 'tis Leonora who should be the crueller, if she were deliberately to keep him in this Dark. I refuse to believe that she is capable of such; I am sure there must be good Reason for this Neglect.

Darling, please. Write me as soon as you can, or send Word why you cannot. Only save me from this desperate Agony.

Your poor, unhappy, Friend,

Tristan Hart.

Again, I sent away mine Heart; again, I fled into the Company of Erasmus Glass, seeking in Vain some Comfort and Distraction in harmless Entertainments. I would not even consider the Idea of visiting Mrs Haywood. I had, for the third Evening, refused to join the Fielding Family for Dinner, despite Mary's sweetest Entreaties; it would have been only a Waste to feed me, since I had no Appetite. She had placed her Hand upon mine Elbow and called me Chick, and said she could not stand to watch me starve, but tho' I kissed her kindly on her Cheek and thanked her, I would not be swayed. But having departed the House, I began to dread that she would comment upon mine Health to her Husband, and he to his Brother-in-law, who would certainly conclude that I was losing my Sanity.

By the Fridaye Morn, however, even the Presence of my Friends was more than I could stand. I ran like an Hare from Erasmus at the Hospital, and did not respond to the anxious Missive I received from him inquiring after my Welfare. I was not tired; I was not hungry; I was not ill.

If I had lost Katherine, I was nothing.

CHAPTER TWENTY

Katherine's Reply arrived upon the Morning of Mondaye, at precisely six o' the Clock. I was lucky, being in the Act of departing the House, to be able to take it straight from the Boy. At the Sight of her Handwriting, mine Heart leapt. My Darling was alive. My worst Fears melted at once to nothing in the Brightness of the early Summer Sunnelight.

I could not now resist, having the dear Letter in mine Hand, delaying my Departure for some Moments in order to read it. I stood upon the Doorstep, the front Door closed at my Back, and all the noisome Bustle of the Street mere Inches from my Face, and, breaking the Seal, unfolded the creamy Paper. To my Surprize I found that there was only one, large Sheet, and that Katherine had filled it to the very Edge—as Jane was oft inclined to do, but which had never been Katherine's Habit. Eagerly, I ran mine Eyes over her Words.

Dearest and most Esteemed Sir,

How I Wish with all my Heart that it were Possible that I could freely accept Your Offer; but it is not, for our Marriage would be a Lie—I cannot go on, my Love, excepting thro' another Tale of Leonora, who may at least Speake for herself, when I cannot—Kate the most truly Cursed—for whenever I try to Speak of it I am struck Dumb and I beginne to Think that Mama is right, and these Things did not Happen, except in a Nightmare.

Oh, my Bloody Bones, my Deare, if it is within Your Capacity, forgive poor Leonora! If when You have read her Tale, You would still wed poor Katherine, then it shall be so; but if You cannot, then I will bear Leonora's Shame and disappear for Ever from Your sight.

I thought: this cannot be. There hath been some Mistake. I lowered mine Eyes, and read the Title of her Tale:

The Tale of Raw Head and the Willow Tree.

Once upon a Time, before Bloody Bones the Lover of Leonora saved her from the Vicious Goblins, she had a strange and evil Dream—

Mine Eyes un-focused. I took a deep Breath, and forcing My Self to concentrate, continued reading to the End of the Paper. But as I reached the Finish, my Mind seemed to give a giant Kick, and suddenly I could no longer comprehend what I had read. I returned to the Beginning, which was the last I could remember; but I could not find the Place where mine Understanding had deserted me.

—In the Garden of the House, there groweth a Willow Tree—

—the Willow Tree is Leonora—

I became aware of an apprehensive, roiling Sickness deep within my Stomach, as if I were upon a small Boat cast loose in a raging Sea. I tried to read on:

—one Summer's Evening a tender Youth comes to sit beneath her Trailing Branches, and he is Dark and Wondrous as the Night Sky; and the Willow Tree hath fallen Utterly in Love with him. But tho' she Quivered and Shook, he noticed her not—

—upon Christmas Eve a Wicked Magician, who was really Raw Head in Disguise, came along and he—

—said to her—

My Senses began to spin. Mine Eyes ran wildly up and down, all over the Paper.

—"I will Make you into a Woman"—

"No," I said. "It is not so. No, no."

I turned mine Eyes again towards the Tale, but the Page seemed to be covered by an indecipherable Mess of Sigils and Runes, incomprehensible to me as Hebrew Script.

My whole Body began to sweat; yet I felt as chilled as if the Yeare were approaching its Midnight. The busy Street was silent as a Crypt, and my Vision had grown dark. I shivered violently, and fearing my Legs about to give Way under me, I steadied My Self against the Fieldings' heavy Door.

I raised my Fist and battered hard against the Wood. After what seemed an Eternity, it was opened by Liza. "Lud!" she exclaimed. "Mr Hart, are you all right? You look as grey as a Ghost!"

I could not answer, but elbowed past her into the Hallway and made my Way on shaking Limbs to my Chamber.

I staggered into my Room, and lurched towards the Fireplace, where I was violently Sick. The Effluxion was of only Bile, my Stomach being intirely empty of everything else, and made little Mess. The Grate had not been swept.

I wiped my Mouth upon my Sleeve; then I turned back to my Task. If I was to write to Katherine, I needed Paper, Ink, and Quill, but altho' the latter Items were in plain View upon mine Escritoire, I could not anywhere locate writing Paper, despite my Conviction that I had several Sheaves within my Possession.

I was perplext; I remembered clearly, and without mental Disputation, that I had seen several Sheets of Paper atop mine Escritoire before I had retired to my Bed at half-past two upon the previous Night. I knew that I had not put them away in their accustomed Drawer, and, moreover, that neither Mary nor Liza had entered my Chamber whilst I was asleep, for I slept light enough to hear a Feather fall.

I ran my Hands over the top of my Desk, making careful Note of the Positions occupied by my Possessions, but naught else had been removed. My Pen and Ink stood exactly as I had left them, and my Books also. But my Paper had gone.

Mine Heart began to thud within my Chest. Dear God! I thought. Who, or What, hath been within my Room? And why, why, should anyone have thought to have moved my Papers, and left all else untouched?

My Bowels twisted. I realised that altho' it might seem to me that nothing had been touched, the Truth was like to be that everything I held dear, everything I loved, had been in some Way meddled with, and then replaced lest it appear to me that any Interference had occurred. But the Robber, whoever he was, had made a grievous Error in forgetting to replace my Papers. But perhaps he had only the Time to move them during the brief Span between my Leaving for the Hospitals and returning to write to my Katherine. The Creature might be now within this Room.

Upon this Realisation, a deep, chymical Fury began to burn within mine Entrails. The Impudence of the Thing to have thus broken in, the Inconvenience he had caused me in moving my Papers when my Need was so immediate, mine Apprehension of his evil Intent, the Violation of it; Violation upon Violation; Betrayal and Loss unbearable.

"I will not suffer this!" I roared. I was determined that the hidden Thing, whatever he was, should comprehend the bloody Severity of his Mistake, and cower in Terrour at mine Intimation of the Consequences. "Shew yourself now," I said. "And I may yet be mercifull. Hide from me and I swear to God that when I find you I shall rip your Head clean off your Shoulders."

I stood stock-still, in the Centre of the Room, with mine Head cocked upon one Side, listening and watching, for the slightest Trace of Movement. There was none.

Determined that I should not be made a Fool of, I strode across to my Bed and hurled the Covers to the Floor. Finding nothing and no one, I seized the Mattress and threw it aside. Nothing. I ran to my Closet. My clean Shirts and Breeches lay, seeming untouched, in tight Piles upon the Shelves, but I knew better than to trust to this Appearance. Reaching to the very Back, I clawed the whole Closet-ful out upon itself, and let it fall higgledy-piggledy at my Feet.

Nothing, nothing. I held mine Head within mine Hands and pulled at mine Hair. For what was the Goblin searching? So subtile a Robber must be acting upon Order, to relieve its Victim of some special, precious Thing, some irreplaceable Treasure; but what thing did I possess that could fulfil such a Criterion?

The only thing to have been moved, for certain, was my writing Paper. Therefore, I thought, the Object of the Goblin's Interest must be some papery thing; some Diagram, some Sett of Notes, some Letter.

Oh, God, I thought, at once. He hath come in Search of my Darling's Letters.

I leapt towards my travelling Trunk, which lay locked at the Foot of my Bed; which had come to Bow Street containing Instruments; which now housed all mine anatomical Drawings, my Notes that I had made during Dr Hunter's Lectures, and beneath them, I had thought safely hid, Katherine's Letters.

Mine Hands trembling about the Key, I unlocked my Case. Throwing back the Lid, I stared within. Mine Heart beat faster than a galloping Stag.

My lecture Notes and all were quite intact; I pushed them to one Side. Below, Katherine's precious Letters lay in the muslin

Kerchief in which I had wrappt them. At once I untied the Ribband and examined, closely, every one, to make intirely certain that no Intrusion had taken place. I laid them out in the Shape of a Wheel, centred upon My Self; the Pages were so many that the Circle spun about me thrice. Not one seemed to me to have been disturbed, so I tried to replace them in their secret Niche. But as I lifted the first Pages, I was struck by the dreadful Apprehension that the silent, secret Goblin had been watching me. I droppt the Letter like an hot Coal. While they lay within their Circle they were beyond the Touch of any evil Thing, as was I, seated at their Hub; but now I realised that neither they nor I would be safe if I replaced them within my Chest. I placed the Letter back within the Circle, taking great Care, altho' mine Hands were shaking, that it lay exactly as it had done before. Then mine Attention fell within the Chest, upon the Object on which they, themselves, had been resting. It was the Sketch Mary had made a Yeare and an Half ago, of My Self cradling the infant Bat upon my Knee.

I took it from the Chest, and stared at it, and for a Moment I was almost incapable of comprehending what it was. Bloody Bones stared back, his Bat—his!—resting safe within his Grasp; winged Innocence, Life, not skeletal Death, protected by the very Devil.

Viviane's Pup, got by a Rape.

At last, I understood. Bat was truly my Child, and my previous Mathematic, which I had thought to have proved my Guiltlessness, signified naught. The Sum was broken. Witches and Faeries are not Subject to earthly Time; they have no Hearts to mark it.

Then I knew, with an indefatigable Resolution, that this, not my Darling's Letters, was the Thing the Goblin had sought. I folded the Portrait and hid it within the Pocket of my Waistcoat.

Finding the Portrait soothed me. As long as I keep it, I thought,

I have Control: all will be well. Sitting back upon mine Heels in the Middle of my Floor, I remembered that I was expected about the Hospital, and that I was already late. This Thought spurred my Wits; scrambling to my Feet, I snatched open the bottom Drawer of my writing Desk, and finding there Paper a-plenty, took up my Quill, returned to my Circle, and began forthwith to write.

My Dearest Miss Montague, I began.

I stoppt. I could not remember anything of her Tale. I did not dare attempt again to read it, for Fear of those daemonic Hieroglyphs; and whenever I tried now to recall what she had been trying to tell me, my Mind reeled away, as if from a Precipice.

After many long and fruitless Minutes during which I sate staring at the Back of mine Hand, movelessly poised over the blank White of the Page, I wrote, simply:

I remain
   As ever
      Your Friend
         Tristan Hart.

I sealed up the Letter, wrote upon it Katherine's Address, and placed it in my Pocket, safe beside the Portrait of My Self and Bat.

I was halfway thro' my Chamber Doorway when I heard a tiny, half muffled, scratching Sound that caused me to wheel about, and make at Speed for my Fireplace. Disregarding the Stench rising from the wet Ashes, I knelt down and put mine Ear to the Chimney-piece. I held my Breath.

A faint Scrabbling, like a trapped Rat, echoed down the draughty Chasm.

So, I thought, 'tis a Gnome! A Gnome, within my Chimney!

Gripped by an outraged Fury at the Notion that my personal Effects had been touched by so mean a thing as a common Gnome, and Shame at mine own idiotic Fear, I scrambled across the Floor to my bed-Cloathes, and took up a well-stuffed feather Pillow. Returning to my Fireplace, I thrust the Pillow with all the Force I could muster into the sooty Opening and then stood back. The Pillow appeared to be securely wedged. There is no Chance, I thought, of any fuckster Gnome finding its Way back into my Chambers by that Route.

"Die there," I said.

Cramming mine Hat upon mine Head, I pushed past Liza, who was stupidly standing just within my Doorway, and fled the House in the Direction of the Post. I ran as if the Devil were snapping at mine Heels. It was not fast enough. The Throng upon the Thoroughfare was thick and slow; in Places I was forced to stop, and swear, and strike out wildly with my Cane. Mine Heart beat frantick with Exertion, and with Guilt. While I was running to the Post, St Thomas's Hospital lay in quite another Direction, and I was needed there.

The Post was busy; I was forced to wait. My Chest thrummed with a Pain so furious I felt it had become a Fire-box, and all my Limbs shuddered so that I half believed I should fall down. A ringing Noise, high and sharp as a silver Pin, had begun to sound within mine Ears. I shook mine Head to dispel it, but in vain.

Then, over both the Ringing and the ragged Noise of mine own Breathing, I heard a Voice behind me. I knew it instantly.

> "The Goblin Knight stood by the Bedd
> The Curtain tore and one was dead.
> The Goblin grubbed up th'Willow Tree,
> The Blossom ruined, that bloomed on mee."

I spun abruptly about. I could not see her. Whose Words? Were they Leonora's?

"Raw Head, Raw Head, in the Dark
While All the Family lies Asleepe."

"Where are you?" I whirled this Way and that, in an Attempt to catch a Glimpse of her.

"I am amazed at you, Caligula," Viviane said.

"Where the Devil are you?" I shouted. "Stand still and let me see you, you damnable Witch!"

"Whose Fault is it, Caligula?"

I twisted my Neck; I hunted for her everywhere. Perhaps she had become a Sparrow, or a Blackbird, or a Thrush. I knew she had not flown from me, this Time, for all that I could not see her. I would not deny her, no; I had proved my Crime now to My Self and I was ready to answer for it. I called her Name, over and over, as Nathaniel must have done that May Daye in the High Field. But she would not come to me.

I became slowly sensible then of the Presence of an Hand, grasping mine Elbow, and a Face, not Viviane's, floating before mine Eyes as if upon a Cloud. I desisted from my frantick searching Gyre, and blinked; within a Moment or two the formless Face assumed the Proportions, and Identity, of Dr Oliver.

"For God's Sake, Sir," he was saying. "Calm down."

"Dr Oliver!" I said. "Where hath she gone? She would not permit me to see her. Did you see where she went?"

"Did I see where who went, Mr Hart?" said Dr Oliver.

I drew back. I knew that he had seen me with Viviane. The Notion was alarming; I did not care that anyone besides My Self and Nathaniel should know of mine Association with her. "Nobody," I said.

"Who are you looking for?" said Dr Oliver.

"Nobody!" I cried. "Believe me, Nobody!"

"I do believe you," Dr Oliver said. "But now you must come with me, before the Constable arrives."

"The Constable?" I said.

"My dear young Man, you have been the Cause of a Disturbance to the Peace."

"I do not see how," I said.

"No," said Dr Oliver. "That I realise, Mr Hart. Nevertheless, it is better that we leave—and quickly. Come, let me accompany you back to your Lodging."

I permitted Dr Oliver to lead me from the Post-house into the bustling, Sunne-filled Street. The Sunne was very high, and the Shaddowes that had stretched a quarter-way across the Road when I had entered the Office seemed shrunken now to blackened Slits.

I turned in Amazement and Dismay to Dr Oliver. "What Houre of the Clock is it?" I asked.

"Near twelve," came the astonishing Reply.

"No!" I said. "Then I have wasted an intire Morning, when I should have been about my Studies, and my Work! I must hie me to St Thomas's, and quick."

Dr Oliver did not release his Grip upon mine Arm. "No, Mr Hart," he said. "I do not think that you should be todaye about the Hospitals. You look as if you have walked from a Battle, Sir."

I frowned. "Thinkst so, Harry? You should see me when I am come fresh from an Amputation." I laughed.

"You forget," said Dr Oliver, "that I have done so, many Times."

"Do not," I warned him, "think me mad. I am not; I am quite as sane as you."

"I never imagined that you were mad," Dr Oliver said. "But you are undoubtedly very tired. When did you last sleep, Sir? Or eat?"

"I am quite well," I said.

"My dear Sir," Dr Oliver said. "The most brilliant Physician may, in diagnosing his own Case, prove to be the biggest Fool. Permit me to tell you that you are not well, that you must go home, and that you will not be returning to the Hospitals until you have recovered both your Colour and your Wits. I shall inform Dr Hunter of your Illness."

I drew back from him. Something in his Tone reminded me of my Father.

"Take your Hand from mine Arm, Dr Oliver," I said. "Or by God, I shall make you do so. I will go nowhere with you, Sir. I am not ill. I am needed at St Thomas's, and the longer I delay the worse the Consequences will be."

"Sir, do not threaten me," Dr Oliver said. "I speak to you as a Physician, and as a Friend."

"If you speak as a Friend," I said, "then speak to me no longer of my being ill, and remove your Hand."

"As you wish," said Dr Oliver, and he released his Grasp upon mine Elbow. I studied his Expression. His Concern, that truly I had lost my Mind, was writ plain upon his Features. At once it became as starkly clear to me as Sunnelight that I must escape his Company. Even if he was himself, he was surely an Agent of my Father's, and his Design could only be to keep me from both my Work and my Responsibility towards Viviane. I bowed, steppt backwards into the busy Thoroughfare, and put my Heels into Flight. The Road was crowded with Horses and other Traffick, but by the Grace of God, I crosst it.

I did not now dare, after what Dr Oliver had said about apprizing Dr Hunter of his Belief regarding me, approach the Hospital lest I be seized; nor did I think it prudent to return to Bow Street. With a most heavy Heart I bent my Steps toward the River.

Reaching the northern Bank of the Thames, I sate My Self upon a rickety wooden Jetty out of the Way of everything, and watched the Progress of the Waters.

"Marry, Madam," I said. My Voice sounded strange to mine Ears—as if I wept. "Are you come with a Warrant to arrest me? I will go with you, and welcome. I mean to see Justice done; by you, and by my Daughter. If that means mine Head, then so be it. The Blame lieth upon me."

A cold, varying Breeze sprang up after a Time; it chilled my Face, but it was not enough to blow away the sour green Stench of the river Mud. My Thighs grew clammy and cold as the Dampe seeped thro' the thin Linen of my Breeches, and my Back began to ache, but I did not move. I did not mind it. After some while longer, the Noises of the City faded.

CHAPTER ONE-AND-TWENTY

Eventually, I was roused from my Coma by the Chiming of some Southwark Church, echoing across the Water. A small brown Rat, who had perched contentedly upon the Tip of my right Shoe, left off washing herself with an outraged Squeak, and skittered safe beyond my Sight. I called to her to wait, and scrambled to my Feet. Staring around me in Surprize thro' the encroaching Dusk, I remembered suddenly the Appointment I had made to meet with Erasmus Glass and Lt. Simmins in the Shakespeare. My Breeches were quite soaked from my sitting for so long upon the wet Jetty, and I thought must appear as soiled as if I had been a Boat-man at Work about the Quay all Afternoon; my Coat, moreover, had somehow become shrouded in filthy Cobwebs. The lace Cuff of my Shirt reeked of Vomit. I recoiled from My Self.

The Rat had not stoppt running. She had recoiled from me, too, when she had realised who I was; recoiled from me as did all wild things; as they were wise to do. Only an Hero or a Fool would happily lie with Vivisection, Death, and Bloody Bones.

"I am so sorry," I called out. I did not think she heard me. I turned, and steppt briskly away from the black Thames in the Direction of the Garden. Why, I wondered, had Viviane not ordered me to jump?

When I reached the Shakespeare, I discovered to mine Embarrassment that I had no Money, for my Purse had gone a-missing from my Coat. The Thought struck me that I must have been robbed whilst I was sitting upon the Jetty, but I had seen no Sign of anyone except the Rat, and surely the Jetty would have collapsed beneath the Weight of another Man besides My Self. I felt my Face drain of its Colour; any Thief must have been either a Goblin, or some other evil Scion of the Faerie Race. Mine Hand flew to my Waistcoat, but to my great Relief I discovered Mary's Sketch still safe; and, tightly folded in front of it, the Letter I had desired to send to Katherine.

How could it be that I had not sent it?

Thank God, I thought, that Viviane had not desired my Death! If she had told me: Jump, I should have lost my Katherine, and been lost to her for ever. Whatever my Transgression, and however just its Punishment, how could I have been prepared to abandon Katherine? My Stomach turned cold at the Thought, and my Limbs began to shiver. Afraid again lest I fall down, I fought my Way thro' the Crowd and sate by the Fire. Tears itched mine Eyes.

For surely, I thought, Katherine hath not refused me; not in the common sense.

The Tavern was exceeding full, and in the shifting Mass of Figures I could discern neither Simmins nor Erasmus. I swallowed, my Throat suddenly dry, and scrambled up on to the Seat of my Chair, the better to see over the Heads of the bubbling Crowd. From this high Vantage I was like a God, like a Red Kite poised to dive into a golden Field of August Grain. Far below me, the Tavern seethed like a viperous Pit. What, I thought, are they all Viviane's Minions?

No Gypsy, no Raw Head, no Goblin Knight can threaten me here. I will bite off his Head. Viviane hath had her Chance with me; she did not take it; I shall not give another.

I will protect them all: my People, my Land, mine Home, my Willows, my Sister, my Simmins, mine Erasmus, my Bat; most of all, my Katherine. I shall swaddle them within my Wings, bind them safe within my Circle; and neither Viviane, nor Goblin, nor any other, shall dare attempt Harm to us.

All of a sudden I perceived within the massed Huddle the Figure of Erasmus, beating his Way thro' the Mobb with an Hand outstretched. I jumped down from Olympus and threw both mine Arms about his Neck. I was so delighted to see him that I kissed him over and again on both his Cheeks.

"Erasmus!" I cried. "My dear Friend! But where is Isaac?"

"Isaac?" said Erasmus.

"I am sorry," I said. "I have Vomit on my Sleeve. Where is Isaac? I fear that Viviane will try to steal him from us."

"Peace, Tristan," Erasmus said, patting my Shoulder. "If by Isaac you mean Lt. Simmins, he is here. There are few Redcoats in this Tavern, and it was easy for me to single him out. Sit down, Man; so; there is no Cause for Agitation."

"Indeed not," I agreed. "I am the Kite, who smiteth the Evildoer with one deathly Blow." I laughed aloud, and clapping Erasmus firm between the shoulder Blades, kissed him once again. Then I sate down again and Erasmus joined me, with only the Table to divide us.

"Where is Isaac?" I asked.

Erasmus, in Reply, beckoned into the Crowd, and after a few Seconds' Confusion, Lt. Simmins steppt out of it.

"Simmins!" I shouted, springing to my Feet. "Come here, and quickly! You shall be safe from these Curs if we stay together."

"Tristan," Erasmus said, in his quiet Voice. "Listen. It is imperative that you return to your Lodgings. We have been searching for you all Daye."

"You have been speaking with Dr Oliver," I said. "You must not trust his Word. He would have me locked up as an Experiment in St Luke's."

"My dear Friend," Erasmus said; and there was a Sadness in his Voice. "That is not the Case at all. Your Brother-in-law is at Mr Fielding's House."

"Wherefore?" I said. "What hath happened? She hath not taken her Revenge by harming Jane? I told her I would suffer my Punishment My Self!"

"Lord, Sir, no! No." Erasmus came to my Side of the Table and, putting his gentle Hands upon my Shoulders, pushed me down once more into my Chair. "You are urgently required at Shirelands, Sir."

"I cannot and I will not go to Shirelands," I said. "Mine Aunt and her Schemes can go to Hell. I leave for Dorset tomorrow to wed Katherine. I have proposed to her and she hath accepted me."

Viviane, beneath the Hawthorns on May Dawn; the Fault is mine.

"Mr H-art," broke in Simmins. "The R-egiment is tr-ansferring to Weymouth within the W- W- Sennight; if you wish, I can carry a Letter of Ex-planation to Miss Montague, and c-call upon her to explain the Si-tuation. Surely, the Lady will n-ot obj-ect to what must ul-timately be a short Delay, when the C-ircumstances that demand it are so pressing?"

"Circumstances be damned!" I shouted. Then I smiled upon Simmins, who had jumped several Inches backwards. "Truly," I said, "you are a Blessing to me, Isaac. Todaye I was unable to send the most important of Letters to Miss Montague, for I was waylaid at the Post by Viviane. But now you shall take it."

I reached inside my Waistcoat for the Letter I had written, and failed to send; and feeling there several folded Pages, withdrew and presst them into Simmins' warm Palm.

"The Address is written," I said. "Ride with Speed, and do not miss your Way. Miss Montague must not fail to receive this Letter."

Simmins unfolded the Papers.

"Your Father is ill, Tristan," Erasmus said.

"This other is no L-etter," Simmins said. And then, before mine Eyes, he seemed to undergo some eldritch Shift; verily I saw him blink, and blink again, as might a Man awakening from a Spell. "My God, Hart; I have s-een this Ch-ild!"

"What?" I snatched back Mary's Sketch, and crushed it deep within my Pocket, before any Faerie could behold me with it. My Fingers stung as if they had grasped a Thorn.

"Truly, I have s-een such a Ch-ild!" Simmins said. "It was that Sundaye, when we met, Mr Hart, in the Dragon, and I was delayed. I r-emember now. The Highway was blocked at Tyburn by an whole Tribe of Gypsies—one of their People had been hanged the S-aturdaye, and they were out for Blood. They did not want his B-ody to be taken for Anatomy. And s-everal of our Muskets had been f-ired, and all was Sm-oake and Rage; and then there she was—that Child—running towards me out of it all; and I picked her up, for F-ear she should be trampled. How could I have forgot her? Almost weightless, she was, like a Butterfly—and underneath her little Cloak, those W-ings!"

Simmins seemed as if he could not stop. Words tipped from him like Oil. "Then the Man appeared. He steppt out of the Smoake—a beggarly R-ogue, like all the Rest of them, but with long, silver H-air, like Mercury. And such strange Eyes! Green as Sn-akes, and with such a terrible Look!"

My Blood caught fire. "Nathaniel!" I whispered.

"Mr Hart?" Simmins ventured. "I—I am sorry, Sir—you put the P-aper into my H-and. I did not m-ean to touch it." He was staring at me with a strange, fearfull Expression upon his Countenance, and I suddenly apprehended the Possibility that he had neither Memory nor Comprehension of aught he had told me.

"It was Nathaniel!" I cried, leaping once more to my Feet. "Where did you see him? Take me there!"

Erasmus leaned aside, and shaking his Head, said, *sotto voce*, to Simmins: "Did not Dr Oliver warn us that he must not become excited?"

"Dr Oliver!" I cried. "What? Do you mean to betray me to him?"

It was a Trap. A Trap, invented and laid by mine Aunt, and Dr Oliver. Simmins, quite by Accident, had sprung it, and it had closed upon him; and on Erasmus. A yellow Horrour, antient, unclean, uncoiled in the Pit of my Spine.

"No!" said Erasmus. "No, Tristan, I beg you, listen to me!"

I had no Time to listen. I had to ride to Dorset straight away; and Nathaniel Ravenscroft was ranging somewhere about the City, my Bat somehow in his Custody; and here stood

Erasmus—mine own Erasmus—conspiring with Dr Oliver and my Father to keep me from him. Little Simmins started to his Feet and began to edge away. "No, no," I said. The Gypsies would steal him. "You, at least, are innocent in this." My Fingers encircled his Arm, and I dragged him roughly behind me, out of Danger. My Chair broke his Fall. I heard it splinter on the Flags. Then I turned to deal with Erasmus.

"So!" I shouted. "You would see me taken and contemned! You, whom I have loved as dearly as a Brother!"

With my right Hand I flipped the Table out of my Way. Raising my left Fist, I sprang towards Erasmus.

For one painted Second I could see naught but the Expression in Erasmus' Eyes. Horrour and Sorrow mixt. Then a giant Forehead, ugly and woolly as a Bull's, loomed startling fast in front of me. Rough Hands arrested my Shoulders. Mine Head seemed to have hit a Wall; mine Eyes flashed white. I fell upon my Knees.

Within Seconds, before I had any Chance to begin a Fight-back, I had been dragged to my Feet. My Wrists smarted from the sudden Clap of cold Iron. An harsh Voice, which seemed to me as if it might have one Time been familiar, shouted at the Mobb that it must "Clear the Way, Sirs – back about your Business!" and before I had even regained my Vision I found My Self being forcibly marched thro' the tavern Door.

The Instant the cold Aire hit my Lungs I was quite awake, and I began violently to resist, screaming to anyone who might hear me to run for the Constable. My Kidnapper cursed as I dealt him a sharp Kick upon the Shin, and his Grip upon me weakened slightly. Quickly slamming back mine Head into his Nose I flung My Self forward to escape him; but he was too strong, and he knew better than I how to fight. We fell hard into the Gutter, he on top.

I would have opened my Mouth to scream again, but for the Foulness that surrounded it. I held my Breath and struggled with all my Might against the cruel Weight that presst down upon my Spine and Shoulders.

"Jesus Christ, he's as strong as the Devil," panted mine Attacker. I felt a split Second's Satisfaction at the Thought that he was having quite as hard a Time of it as I; but the Thought passed faster than a Breath. And I could not breathe.

The Strength of Terrour empowered me. I had no Intention to suffocate in Shit. Despite that mine Hands were shackled behind me, I thrust my Face up out of the Mire and with a great Heave threw the Monster from my Back.

I scrambled to my Feet. It was clear to me now what this was, this Attack; it was the Murder that I feared to have happened to Nathaniel. The Gypsies loved him; they would forgive him anything, anything; but not me; no, not me. Viviane was not thro' with me yet.

Mine Instinct was to run; yet it was plain to me that the Brute would pursue me if I did. I had only one Choice. Mine Hands are chained, I thought, but I still have my Teeth. I will rip out its Throat.

Somewhere deep within my Skull, the Drums had started.

Baring my Teeth, I whirled about, and sprang.

The Brute was bloody-Faced, and huge, and it was ready. An heavy, hefty Blow straightway slammed the left Side of my Jaw, so hard it sent me spinning sideways into the stone Wall of the Shakespeare. My Mouth filled up with Blood.

"Right, Mr Hart," came a Voice, and it sounded, for a Moment, half like to that of Saunders Welch. "You're coming with me. Mr Fielding and Dr Oliver are very desirous of speaking with you." The Voice was faint; as if it echoed from a thousand Miles away.

I felt something hard and unexpected upon my Tongue, a minute Pebble tumbling in a bloody Sea.

I spat the Object out upon my Knee, where it lay, small and incongruously white against the befouled Cloth. It was mine eye-Tooth. As I stared at it, it seemed to wink.

The Drumming became louder. It thumped within my Body, a steady, incessant Throb, deafening mine Ears to every single Sound that was not it. My Liver and mine Heart began to quake. I tried to stand, but my Senses were still reeling. I could not control my Limbs.

Panick consumed me. Not Panick of the Kind that could have given my Legs the Force to leap or my Mouth to scream, but a low, despairing Agony that wrappt mine Arms about my Waist and rocked me slowly back and forth, and back and forth, while the Monster that had stolen the Speech and Appearance of Saunders Welch steppt forward to execute its killing Blow.

"God help me," I cried. "God protect us! My Brat and Bat; separated by an R. Thou shalt not kill me, Raw Head. I will not die."

I felt My Self being once more roughly seized, and forced to walk; but tho' I would have resisted, I had not the Strength. All my Fight had deserted me. Mine only Hope lay with the Almighty, if He had not turned His Back upon me in Disgust.

After some while I realised, to my great Surprize, that I had been brought to Bow Street, and that I was sitting, shackled Hand and Foot, upon the heavy wooden Armchair in the below Stairs Room that both Messrs. Fielding used for hearing Cases.

Gradually, I became aware of the Babble, around me, of many different Voices.

"No!" said Erasmus' Voice—at least, I thought it was Erasmus'

Voice, tho' it seemed cracked and brittle. "I demand that Mr Welch be made to leave. He hath treated Mr Hart extreamly ill, and I shall not suffer him to receive any more of the same. Mr Hart is no Criminal, but a Gentleman, and a Genius."

"A Gentleman and a Genius, Mr Glass," came the angry Reply, "who was presently about to take your Head off!"

"Mr Glass," came Mr Henry Fielding's Voice. "I shall reprimand Mr Welch. It will, however, be easier for Dr Oliver to attend to Mr Hart if he is not in mortal Fear whilst so doing."

"With Respect, Sir," replied Erasmus. "I do not perceive that Mr Hart is now like to pose the least Threat to anybody. He is barely conscious."

I opened up mine Eyes a little. In the flickering Candlelight I could make out, quite clear, the little Figure of Erasmus Glass, standing bullishly between My Self and the immense Bulk of the High Constable for Holborn. Behind Mr Welch, against the black Doorway, stood Mr Henry Fielding, with Dr Oliver.

"Erasmus," I said. My Voice was a Spillikin of itself.

Erasmus turned, and his Face was filled with such a Mix of Sentiments: Fury, and Hope, and Fear, that I could scarce bear to look upon it. "Don't let them take me," I said.

"Indeed, they shall not," Erasmus said.

"Tristan," said Mr Fielding, in a Tone that seemed to shake the very Timbers of the House. "No one shall take you anywhere without your express Consent. You have my Word on that, as Magistrate, with Dr Oliver and Mr Glass as Witnesses. You are overwrought, Sir, and you have become unwell, and you will either permit Dr Oliver to administer his Treatment or you will be forced."

"I am not mad!" I bellowed, beginning to thrash against my Restraints, despite the Pain this caused me.

"Hush, Tristan," Erasmus said, dropping before me on one Knee, like a Courtier. "Indeed, and truly, you are not; your Nerves, merely, have become overstrained. You have been studying much too hard. Dr Oliver desires only that you take a soothing Draught, and then retire to your Bed."

"Why didst thou betray me, Judas?" I said.

"I did not," Erasmus said, and to mine Astonishment I saw plain Tears shining in the dark Wells of his Eyes. "I did not know that Mr Welch would become involved."

"You listened to Dr Oliver," I said.

"I did, 'tis true; he told me of his Worries regarding your Health. I share them, Tristan. But neither I, nor he, nor Mr Fielding thinks that you are mad."

I examined Erasmus' Expression. He was telling the Truth, I discerned, in so far as he could know it; which was to say that he gave Credence to mine Affirmation of my Sanity and he believed that the others did too. Whether he was right or wrong in this Belief, I could not verily tell, altho' I doubted much that he was right. Dr Oliver would not have used him as Bait if he had thought that I was amenable to rational Argument.

"There you are deceived," I said. "For the Doctor would have me locked up; I know not why; perchance it hath to do with the Lady B.———. But before God I meant her no Insult. I struggled against the Passion but it would not go away; it doth not; the Evil is always there, always. I could not contain it. I tried."

"Mr Glass," came Dr Oliver's Voice. "It doth Mr Hart little Good for you to befuddle the Facts. I do believe that you should be better if you were to be in St Luke's, Sir, for there I should be on hand to deal with your Case. As to whether you are incurably mad, that I do not know. I pray that you are not, for as your Friend says you are a brilliant young Man, and 'twould be a tragic Loss to our Profession as much as to your Family."

"I will not go," I said.

"You cannot remain here, Sir, in your present Condition," said Dr Oliver. "Mrs Fielding cannot be expected to care for another Invalid—begging your Pardon, Henry. And I do not see how the Barnabys can take care of you, given their current Circumstances."

"I am no Invalid!" I said. "I need no one to take care of me! I will not go. By God, you must not try to take me."

Dr Oliver shook his Head.

I turned, desperate, to Erasmus. "Help me," I said.

"I shall," Erasmus answered. "I shall not leave you, Sir; I shall stay for as long as you shall need me."

To be fair to Dr Oliver, I must admit that St Luke's was not an Institution in any Way akin to the hideous Bethlem. The Ethos of the Place, with which I had fully concurred when I was sane My Self, was that Madness was as curable a Disease as any other; and its Practices were intirely designed to further the Restoration of Reason to a Mind temporarily bereft. But that Night, sorely bruised as I was from my Fight with Saunders Welch, and trappt in a Nightmare of mine own Making, I could not comprehend this.

Erasmus finally having perswaded me to take the Doctor's Prescription, I was unshackled from the Chair, and taken with more Gentleness than had been heretofore accorded me into the drawing Room, where waited James Barnaby.

At mine Entry, Barnaby leapt from the Seat upon which he had been sitting and placed himself square behind the Sopha on the far Side of the Room. I had no Power to pursue him, even had I wanted to, yet despite my somewhat pathetic State his evident

Terrour amused me. Aye, I thought, you have Reason, Hypocrite; but I said nothing. Erasmus assisted me to sit in an Armchair, and then turned to confront him.

"Mr Barnaby," he said, "it hath been suggested that your Brother-in-law must be confined in an Hospital for the Duration of his Illness. I have argued, and will continue to argue against this Course of Action as I do not doubt that it will make Mr Hart's Condition much the worse. However, the Decision is yours; owing to his Father's Incapacity you are his Next of Kin. What will you do?"

"Lud," said Barnaby at once, with a slight Squeak in his Voice. "If Mr Hart may be taken to an Hospital, then for God's Sake he must be therein committed."

"But consider," Erasmus retorted swift as Lightning, "the Shame of that."

This Bolt hit direct upon Barnaby's weak Spot; he could not abide the Thought of publick Ridicule, and the Spectre of the Neighbours discovering that Jane, who was with Child, had a mad Brother, threw him into quite a Funk. Insanity, they say, runneth in Families. "I'facks!" he cried. "Let him then remain where he is!"

Mr Henry Fielding, who had walked into the Room at my Rear, then pointed out in a most cutting Tone that if I was not to be committed, I must instead return to Shirelands forthwith. Barnaby turned very white at this Proposal, and cried out that he could not possibly allow it; I would most likely murder him upon the Road, and could there not be found some other Solution?

"Indeed, Mr Barnaby," exclaimed Mr Fielding sharply. "Do you know nothing of your familial Duty? He is your Brother, Sir!"

"As I have given Tristan my Vow that I will not abandon him," Erasmus interrupted, "then I propose that I shall accompany him to Shirelands Hall My Self, and take charge of his Care until he be well again."

"And who, Mr Glass, shall pay your Bill?" Barnaby cried out, in a frantick Tone.

"Good God!" exclaimed Mr Fielding again. "You shock me, Sir!"

"I would do't for nothing but my Board and Lodging," Erasmus snapped. "Mr Hart is a good Man; and he is my Friend."

This Offer seemed to mollify Mr Barnaby, and he began to talk tentatively of my Return to Shirelands under Erasmus' Supervision. As he still expresst some Reservation as to the Expense, it was eventually suggested that Erasmus' Keep was to be paid out of my Father's Purse; unless of course my Father died, when it should fall upon me. To this final Proposal, Barnaby, happily, agreed.

Shortly after this I fell asleep, and I do not know what occurred after; but in the Morning Erasmus made me to understand that we were straightway to leave for Berkshire, and that we should not be very soon returning.

"Your Father hath endured a Stroake," he said. "He hath been left unable to speak, and hath lost all Sensation upon the right Side of his Body. Your Family needs you, Tristan. It hath been arranged that I shall accompany you, to give whatever Assistance I can in the Matter, for it is quite beyond the poor Skill of the local Physician."

I had been greatly soothed by my laudanum-induced Sleep, and even more so by the subsequent Draught which Erasmus had presst upon me before Breakfast, so despite my Knowledge of the previous Night's Conversation with Barnaby, I did not query why Erasmus was to attend upon my Father. It seemed peculiarly appropriate that he should. I suggested to him that we confer closely together on the Case.

"So shall we," Erasmus said. "But you must remember that you go home, in the first Instance, to rest." He encouraged me to drink a further Draught, to ease my strained Nerves, and then, before I had properly to register what was afoot, we had said our Goodbyes to Mary and the Brothers Fielding, and departed together in Mr Fielding's Coach.

I recall little of what happened on the Journey. Some Miles, I suppose, outside of London, I remember realising that Erasmus had taken off the Shackles that had bound my Wrists and Ankles, and that we had stoppt for a short Meal at a roadside Inn. I noticed nothing of the Meal, or of the Place.

I saw my Father once upon mine Arrival at the Hall. He lay helpless in the semi-Darkness of his Chamber, a Room into which I had not penetrated since mine own Infancy, attended by Mrs H., who was spoon-feeding him some Soup from a porcelain Bowl. The Strangeness of the Sight reminded me of Mary with my Bat, and made my Bowels churn. I did not go near him after. I kept Bat's Sketch safe in my Waistcoat, by mine Heart, and only changed its Position when I changed my Cloathes. No one saw it.

CHAPTER TWO-AND-TWENTY

I consider it Memory's greatest Strangeness, with what Ease a Man—even a sane Man—may forget for Yeares a small thing heard, or seen, which later, upon appropriate Stimulus, presseth so intently upon his Awareness that it seem almost more real than that present Moment which hath so recalled it. For almost five Yeares I had utterly forgot that Ballad of the Goblin Knight Nathaniel had sung to me beneath the August Sunne. Now, that Memory was revived; at first so softly that I had not noticed, then gradually with greater and greater Force, till now, upon my first Evening back beneath the Roof of mine ancestral Home, it rang in mine Head more loudly than any Hunting-horn. And as it rang I realised, with a great and sudden Clarity, that this Goblin Knight intended great Evil to mine intire Family. I saw truly that he was Raw Head, and the would-be Ravisher of the Woman I loved; and with his Goblin Army he prowled nightly thro' the Gardens, watching for his Chance. I had the Suspicion he should be identified with some unknown Individual who had yet neither Name nor Countenance; but tho' my Mind strove to make the Connexion, and provide him with both, it could not. Raw Head, Raw Head, in the Dark. Whether he had aught to do with Viviane or not, I was unsure; but what, I thought, would be more like than that a gypsy Witch should consort with an evil Fay? Why should not she, having baulked at her Revenge herself, discharge that Task upon him?

Against this Threat, it became mine habitual Duty to prowl at Dusk from Room to Room, demanding that every Door, every Window, every Crack, thro' which even a mere Mouse could creep, be stoppt fast against this Legion of Monsters who dwellt outside in the Dark. Mrs H. went with me, when she was not nursing my Father. Erasmus, at first, would not; but after a few Weeks he too began to accept the Ritual's Importance, and then he would follow at a Distance with a Candle whilst I checked, and checked again. I tried to explain to him the Severity of the Threat which Raw Head surely posed, but unfortunately he did not appear to comprehend it. He seemed more distressed by my Caution than by the Danger itself, and, fearing, so he said, that I should overtax My Self, fed me Paregoric by what seemed the Tankard. This frustrated me; I was not distressed, nor like to be, as long as all the Gaps remained fast. I went not near the Windows, lest I be seen.

I wrote, and wrote, on all these things, to Katherine. She did not respond. I did not know why. Erasmus assured me that she was well, and that she loved me still, and that Lt. Simmins had given her my Answer, and my final London Letter. She had gone, he said, to stay with her maternal Uncle for the Present, and I was not to worry My Self with unhappy Fears for her. But it was so compleatly unlike my dear Katherine to fail to answer me that I was forced to dread the very Worst, and had Erasmus not continually repeated his Reassurances I should mayhap have sought out mine own Death. Sometimes, I thought—and hoped, for Hope made the Possibility seem real—that she had not responded because I had not yet composed mine own Letters, and therefore what I remembered was the Future. Time had become a Mystery to me, its intimate Workings incomprehensible, for all I knew that eight supposedly followed seven o' the Clock. I determined to leave the Safety of Shirelands Hall and make the deadly Journey to Dorset to see her; but when I was brought up to Scratch I dared not to cross the Threshold of the House. Mine Impotence enraged me. I broke things. Other Dayes, deep in Despair, I became certain that she had replied, and ran to my Trunk to read again the Letters she had sent to me in London, and each one was as fresh as if it had been written yesterdaye.

One unthreatened thing remained to me: my Studies; for, despite Erasmus' Insistence that I must spare my Nerves, I had refused to desist from all Work. I bade my Father's Gamekeeper bring me live Subjects for Experimentation and Study, and within a Fortnight of my Return my Cages had begun to fill, and my Laboratory to rustle. Yet, despite my stated Design, I found My Self incapable of performing a Dissection upon any one of these, for the mere Effort of preparing Board and Instruments seemed beyond me. Left thus unmolested, my Captives gradually and against all Reason transfigured into my Companions and Friends, and after several Weeks I could no more stomach the Notion of killing one of them any more than I could have killed Erasmus, or Katherine. So I hid my Tools from view, and buried My Self within medical Tracts and Works upon the Theory of Knowledge, spending Houres upon my Sopha beneath the vacant pitying Eyes of my Skulls, my silently scampering Skeletons, finding therein a slight and fleeting Comfort.

One Afternoon, towards the End of the Summer, I made the unwelcome Discovery that Erasmus thought my Father very sick indeed. He had not been in the Habit of discussing the Case overly much with me; but when he did, he seemed quietly optimistic, and expresst a firm Belief that Time would ease a great many of my Father's current Difficulties. But shortly after full Moon of August, I overheard him talking quietly with my Sister. It was a rainy, blowy Daye, as drear as ever late Summer can be, and not fit for travelling; yet my Sister, who had remained devoted to my Father despite her Marriage, had made the Trip in Barnaby's Coach, and asked that Erasmus take Tea privately with her in the drawing Room, that she might hear his Opinion.

"I will not deceive you, Mrs Barnaby," Erasmus said, as they sate within, and I hovered secretly and silent without the unlocked Door. "He hath made some tremendous Progress. The Sedative is keeping him calm, and as long as he remain so there is a Chance that his Rational Self will regain control. But it is my Fear that, from this Point, we will not see much more of a Recovery until many Months pass; if, indeed, we see any at all. I must ask you to prepare yourself for the Possibility that he will continue indefinitely in his present Condition."

"But he is calm," Jane said. Her Voice was somewhat slurred, as if she had been sobbing. "He was never calm, before. Always he was agitated, and so terribly afraid."

"Yes," said Erasmus gently. "He doth not suffer, I think. But, from what you have told me, he hath never before been subjected to a Regime based upon the modern Principles of Rational Suggestion and appropriate Medication."

The August Rain lashed hard against the House. "It must be a good Sign," Jane said. "I will not give up on him, Mr Glass."

I was furious. Poor Jane! I thought. Great with Child as she is, she should not be encumbered with such Cares, nor should Erasmus be so discouraging to her Hopes. The Prognosis is not so very poor. 'Tis true my Father makes but a slow Recovery, but the Assault was a massive one. I would have burst in upon them, and my first Impulse was to do so; but a Concern for the Effect this might have upon Jane prevented me. I restrained My Self.

I had a Number of Ideas regarding my Father's Illness which I had not yet broached to Erasmus, and for Jane's Sake I retired to my warm Study and sitting at mine Escritoire attempted to write them into a coherent Theory, the which, I thought, would have effect both upon his Treatment and on that of others. I knew that the most likely Cause of an Apoplexia was that of an Aneurysm within the Brain. This being so, it had been an acute Crisis which my Father had survived. I remembered how Thomas Willis, in his *Cerebri anatome*, had argued that cerebral Lesions could produce Hemiplegia. Could such Lesions result from cerebral Haemorrhage? Could they be the Cause of my Father's Incapacity? Musing upon this, I lifted my Convict's Skull and turned it over, to peer within the brain-Case. If so, I thought, then perhaps a thorough Regime of the active Stimulation of the Nerves might induce the broken Fibres to re-grow, the Lesions to heal, and Sensation to return. I had an Image in mine Head as of the Hand of God, reaching down from Heaven to grasp the Hand of Man, but my Words could not make Sense of it. The Ink would not stay still upon the Page.

At half-past Seven I shouted for Erasmus, as I wished him to accompany me upon my Rounds, but Mrs H. informed me that he had gone to see my Sister safe back to Withy Grange, where he was expected to stay for Dinner. I told Mrs H., in no uncertain Terms, that I thought this exceeding inconsiderate, and refused to take the Palliative he had prepared for me. When she presst it on me, I snatched the Glass out of her Hand and threw it with all my Force into the drawing Room Fireplace. She had more Sense than to continue after that. I refused her Peace-offering of a dinner Tray, and lit up all the Tapers in my Study, where I remained, by their Light studying Dr Hunter's lecture Notes upon the System of the Nerves.

After a while the Rain moved off to the North, and the Night had become still and cold. I had covered up my Creatures, and the Quiet of my Study was that of warm coal-Light, and Sleep. All of a sudden there came a Ring upon the front Door of the Hall, and after about half a Minute, I heard the Sound of angry Voices, echoing up the dark Stairwell from the entrance-Way beneath. Mine Heart missed a Beat. I lifted mine Attention from my Page and held my Breath, focusing all mine Hearing intent on the Stairs.

There were, I could discern, two Speakers. The one was Mr Green, the Butler, shouting in an exasperated Tone that this was the third Time in as many Weeks; that Beggars were not to call at the Front; and the Caller must ask Alms at the Kitchen or begone. The other Voice I could not quite make out, for it seemed somewhat muffled, as if its Owner stood within the Porch and yet without the front Door; but it was desperate in its Tone. The Row continued, Hammer and Tongs, for a full Minute; then there was a loud Slam, and a faint Cry, and Mr Green's Footsteps clacking sharp across the marble Floor; then Silence.

I thought: 'Tis no Beggar. They have come; they are at the Door. Trembling, I got quietly to my Feet, and was about to tiptoe down-Stairs to ransack my Father's Library for his Gunne, when there resounded an harsh, rattling Crack against my window Pane.

I froze in mid Step. I did not dare to breathe. There came a second Tap upon my Glass. Immediately, I droppt upon my Knees. My Limbs shook as violently if I were caught in an Earthquake.

I thought: 'Tis Viviane.

A third, sharp Crack; and from somewhere below, a loud, fierce, surprizing, Human, Curse.

The Voice was familiar – and 'twas not Viviane's. Mine Heart began, slowly, to beat again. My Courage rose. Perhaps, I conceived—with a sudden rash Hope, and despite that I had thought it a Woman's Pitch—it is no Demon, it is Nathaniel! Who else would ever stand so bold throwing Stones at my Window?

I crawled under my long Table to my Window and knelt beside it, keeping My Self out of Sight, lest it be not Nathaniel at all, and peered carefully between my Shutters down upon the moonlit Gravel that lay directly outside it.

And then mine Heart did truly stop; for the Person I beheld was neither Nathaniel, nor Viviane. It was Katherine.

She was standing alone upon the Gravel, her Countenance uplifted and her Expression wild. Her blonde Hair, loose in the swirling Wind, whippt up a radiant Halo about her Head, and her Skin shone in the silvery Light like Alabaster. About her delicate Shoulders, she wore a thick, grey-green felted Cloak, of the stile Ladies commonly wear for travelling; beneath it, a dark coloured Gown of some Scots Cloth, or Linsey-woolsey, that hung heavy with Wet, and looked to be compleatly muddy from the Knee to the Hem. Her small Shoes and her Stockings were so filthied they were fit for nothing but the Fire.

She was the most beautifull thing I had ever seen.

Within her white Fist, she clutched a fourth Stone, and as I stared, too astonished for the Moment to do anything else, she drew back her Arm and hurled it at my Window with sufficient Force to have cracked the Glass if it had hit; but it bounced harmlessly off the Ivy.

I leapt to my Feet and scrambled to unlatch my Shutters before she should throw again, and thrust up the Sash. Cold Breeze snatched at my Face.

"Katherine!" I shouted. "Is't you, or do I dream?"

"Oh, Tristan! Tristan! Yes, 'tis me, my Bloody Bones, truly it is! Have someone let me in before I freeze! Your Butler would not—I think he mistook me for a Vagabond!"

"Come to the Door," I told her. "I shall let you in My Self."

I pulled my Window down, and fastened my Shutters tight. There would have been little Point in bringing Katherine in to Safety if Raw Head and his Goblins could have got in also. We would have been Mice in a Trap. This done, I ran quick and silent down-Stairs to the front Door, and slid back the iron Bolts. I opened the Door.

Katherine hurtled up the Steps. If I had yet had any lingering Doubts that she was anything but her own, real, Self, they vanished into nothing as I enfolded her at last within mine Arms. She was solid, and alive. Her blonde Hair smelled of Oil and Rain, there was a Leaf upon her Shoulder, and her Lips were warm against mine own, despite the bitter Coldness of her Hands and Face, the clinging Dampe of her Mud-bespattered Cloathes. At once I brought her within the House, and fastened shut the Door. Then I took up her quick Body once more into mine Embrace.

"Egad," I said, when I had Chance again to speak. "How far have you walked?"

"Only from Highworth," she answered, breathless, kissing me a few Times more upon my Chin. "I travelled with the Post from Weymouth. Oh, you are grown so terribly thin, my Love! Mr Simmins told me you were not well, but I could not come before. I would have, but—"

"Alone?" I said.

"Yes, yes, alone! I have run away. Mama hath not the slightest Notion where I am. Nor doth she care, I am sure! When Mr Simmins arrived with your Answer to my Letter, and I told her of your Offer, for you know I had not said aught of it before, she would not believe at all that you were honest. She called me a vicious Slut, and worse, and cast me out. I stayed a few Weeks with my Uncle Whitcross, but he only wanted me for an Housemaid, so as soon as I could I took my Wages, which he would never have given me otherwise, from his Purse; and I got a Lift in a Farmer's Cart as far as Weymouth, and for the last Part I walked here. Tell me true; really have you read all of my *Tale*, and really it is still your Desire to marry me?"

Mine Heart beat hard and fast within my Chest. "Yes," I said. "I have never had any other."

"Then I will marry you, I will! I love you," Katherine said.

I scooped her off her Feet. The dampe Slub of her Dress was coarse against mine Hands, and tho' she was light as a Butterfly, her Skirts hung Curtain heavy against my Thighs. My Loins, for the first Time since I had left London, began to rouse.

"No doubt you are tired," I said. "And hungry."

"I am hungry! But not so very tired, now I am with you."

I was aware of nothing but the Grasp of her slim Arms about my Neck; the Pressure of her Skull against my Shoulder; the sour Perfume of her Scalp; the moist Warmth of her Breath upon my Throat. I carried her up-Stairs to my Study, and placed her carefully upon my Sopha, where the medical Tract I had been reading lay yet open to her unobstructed View. I slippt it quickly out of Sight, and turned to stoke the Fire. The red Coals burned extreamly hot, but Katherine shivered.

"Sweet Heart," I said, kneeling before her on the Rugg and chafing her chill Hands briskly between mine own. "You must eat at once, and bathe. Make no Noise. Stay there."

Springing from the Floor, I caught up my Bell, and ran out of the Room to the Top of the Stairs. I rang hard and loudly for Mrs H., and I did not let up until I saw her slowly mounting the lower Staircase, a Candle in her Hand.

"Mrs Henderson, I will take that Tray!" I called out. "And bring me red Wine, and Chocolate, and Comfits; bring me sugared Plums! And have a Bath prepared in my dressing Room!"

Mrs H. sighed. "I shall tell Mr Stevens that he will be needed, Master Tristan," she said.

"Stevens? No, no, no; Mrs H.; I require a Bath, not a Valet. Let Stevens remain where he may do some good; with my Father. Do you believe I know not how to wash?"

Mrs H. opened her Mouth as if to speak again, but then shut it up.

"For God's Sake, Woman," I said. "Dost think I plan to drown My Self?"

Mrs H. having departed, I returned to Katherine. She had taken off her muddy Cloak and her wet Shoes, and settled herself as

318

closely by the Fire as she could. Faint Wisps of Steam rose from the sodden Hem of her Skirt, and her pale Features had grown ruddy with the Heat.

I bit my Lip. The Brightness of her almost hurt mine Eyes. So vivid; so present; so intensely alive. She is here, here, here. I remembered how I had used to dream her Presence beside me, how I had imagined, so many Times, the Velvet of her untouched Skin beneath mine Hands, the Curlew's Whistle of her Scream.

Am I dreaming now? I thought. If 'tis a Dream, I will not wake.

"Art well, Love?" I whispered, settling My Self beside her upon the Rugg. She smiled, without speaking, and leaned her slender Body close against my Chest. I put mine Arms around her and buried my Face in the dampe Silk of her Hair. She was more real than anything in mine Existence.

"Why must I make no Noise?" she said.

"Because I intend to keep you to My Self," I said. "I will not hurt you."

"Ah," she breathed. A Sliver of Excitement sparkled in her Voice. "I would not dislike it, Bloody Bones."

I brushed my Fingertips against her naked Throat. "Why did not you write?"

"Oh, Tristan, I could not," she said, angry; tho' not with me. "Mama would not let me, and my Uncle keeps his Paper under Lock and Key against anyone stealing it. But be damned the both of them. You have me now, and will not ever lose me."

I thought then to have asked her what she had intended in asking whether I had read her *Tale*, and what she meant me to have understood from it, but my Courage failed me; the Words would not form.

Katherine wriggled herself around within the Circlet of mine

Arms until her Mouth was a mere half-Inch from mine own; but we were interrupted by a soft Tap upon the Door. I swore, and tho' with some Reluctance, scrambled up to answer it; for it had dawned on me that it must be the dinner Tray I had required. I found that it was not Mrs H. herself, but one of the Chambermaids, so recent in her Employ that I had not yet learned her Name. I opened the Door just enough to take from her the Tray, which was exceeding full, then retreated rapidly into my Sanctuary, closing the study Door and locking it.

Katherine sate up straight, and Hunger coursed thro' all the fine Bones of her Face. I carried the Tray across and laid it on the Floor in front of her. "Eat," I said. "Drink."

She was hungry, far too hungry, to have any Use for Manners. She ate like a Savage, or a Child: tearing off great Chunks of Bread and dipping them in Wine, clawing up Handfuls of rich sugared Fruits and cramming her Mouth till it was almost too full for her to swallow. I lay back and watched as her white, uneven Teeth sliced fierce into cold Chicken and boiled Ham, stripping the Bones. Eventually, as her ravenous Fit began to be appeased, she slowed a little; and then I joined her, to sip the red Wine from her Goblet, and share in her broken Crusts, and feed her Comfits from the very Palm of mine Hand. She laid her fair Head in mine aching Lap; and then she smiled.

I leaned over her. Her Lips parted, and with an increasing Hunger of mine own, I slowly slid my Tongue deeply into her Mouth. She tasted of Sugar and Wine.

For the second Time, I was prevented; now by the Maid's Voice thro' my study Door, informing me that the Bath I had demanded was got ready, and was awaiting me in my dressing Room. I gave a low Growl of Frustration. Katherine sate up, and put her Hands about mine Head, kneading the croppt Hairs upon my Neck between her Fingertips and seeking to pull me close again. But I had by now recollected mine original Intent. I stood up, and held out mine open Hand.

"Your Bath is ready," I said.

Candle Flames gleamed in her Eyes. Suddenly, as if she had not been intirely sure that she should do it until that precise Moment, she caught hold of mine Hand.

Pausing only to unlock, and to make fast again, the Doors between, lest some Gnome or anyone else intrude upon us, I led Katherine thro' the House to my Chamber, and thence to mine adjoining dressing Room, where the hot Bath lay wreathed in silvery Steam, despite the new-lit Fire.

I made her to lie down upon the Floor, and kneeling astride her, took from my coat Pocket my small Etui. A sharp Breath escaped her, and she swallowed. I felt her Breastbone shiver beneath mine Hand. "Shh," I whispered.

Her Eyes grew very wide, and glimmered in the Firelight like Mercury. I leaned over her, pinning her down, tho' there was no Need, with mine Hand, and breathed in deep the rich Scent of her Flesh. The Fragrance spun thro' my Blood like alcoholic Vapour.

Katherine whimpered. I twisted my Fingers into her wind-tangled Hair. Will I bleed her again, I thought? I turned her Arm within mine Hand, feeling for the puckered Scars that crosst the thin Silk of her inner Elbow. I found them easily. Many were fresh. The Scabs felt hard against my Fingertips, like rough sewn Thread.

"I am sorry," she whispered.

I sate up again, and removed my Lancet from its Case. Yellow Light glinted sharp upon the Blade.

Then with one Movement, I stretched out mine Arm, and slashed thro' all the Lacings of her Bodice. The tight Stays fell open and tumbled away, falling Veils. Katherine gave a shocked Shriek, but I muffled her Cry within mine own Mouth. When once again she was quiet, I sate back, and still straddling her, I swiftly dissected every Article of her Dress that posed any Barrier between her Body and mine own, and threw the Rags behind the coal Scuttle.

At length, her Body lay undisguised upon the Floor, her unblemished, translucent Skin glistening in the Firelight. Soon, I told My Self, with a Stab of Guilt, oh, soon, that beautifull Fabric will be marked; and it shall be into a Pattern of my Design and Making, with Proportion and Grace: a Work of Art.

I restored my Lancet to mine Etui, and then carefully I rolled down the filthy Stockings that covered each Leg from the Thigh to Toe. Beneath the blue Worsted, which was too thin to have been of any Use, her Feet were bruised and blistered, tender to my Touch. I kissed them both.

Such Wonder now possesst me at the Idea that this Joy, this Marvell, could be mine, that I was forced to catch my Breath. I had presumed that the animal Urge, to fuck, had been quite dead in me; but at the Sight and Scent of her, shivering beneath me, I was struck by the Suspicion that it had, perhaps, been only sleeping. Could I? I thought. Will I?

I looked into her Eyes and she stared back, without Fear.

"I have loved you," Katherine said, "since I was nine Yeares old."

I suddenly remembered the small, blonde girl-Child sitting so still, her unwavering Gaze so disconcerting, underneath the Willow Tree. "Morris off, Kitty!" Nathaniel had shouted.

"You sate watching me," I said.

"I was always watching you," she whispered. "I loved you."

I gathered her nude Form into mine Arms and lifted her gently into the still warm, steaming Waters of the Bath. Then I removed my Coat and Waistcoat, that neither they nor my precious Sketch should become wet, and rolling up my Shirt-sleeves to mine Elbows I dippt mine Hands deep beneath the Surface, and washed away from her all the Uncleanliness of her long Journey, and of her Servitude in her Uncle's House. I poured out lavender Water upon her Head, and washed her beautifull Hair, that had been so dulled, until it shone again like fire-spun Gold. At length, I assisted her to rise, like Venus, and wrappt her sweet Frame in an embroidered Turkish Towel I had left to warm before the Fire. I carried her from the dressing Room and laid her down upon my Bed.

"Lie still." Carefully, I dried her Milk-white Skin, her slender Arms, her Breasts, her little, blistered Feet. I tasted the lymph Salt of her Heels; I kissed her Knees, her Thighs, the golden Mound below her Belly where the Fleece grew, dampe, and soft as Lambskin. I ran my Fingers over her downy Curls, that for so long I had yearned to caress, and then probed farther.

She opened her Mouth; upon an Impulse, I put mine other Hand hard across it, and looked down upon her. Her Eyes opened wide. I lifted mine Hand. She caught, and presst it between her own, her Palms upraised as if in Prayer.

"Hurt me," she whispered, breathlessly. "Please, hurt me, Tristan."

All the Spirits in my Body surged towards my Loins with such a Violence that for an Instant, I was convinced that my Passion would over-run its Cup. I put mine Hands about her Throat.

"You did not obey me," I said. "You cut yourself."

Her Pulse fluttered beneath my Fingers. "Yes."

I remembered how I had stood outside the Church at Collerton upon the Daye we had met, trying in sorry vain to numb my Mind to the Desire to beat her slender Body until the Blood spurted. Then I remembered too, and with a horrible Stab of black Guilt, Annie; and mine Heart quailed within me. But this was Katherine, my Katherine, my Leonora; and no more could I deny her than the very Breath of my Lungs.

Gloria in excelsis Deo: Let me expiate my Sin; *Deo*: the Stroake falls; *Deo*: the bare Breath catches in her Throat; *Deo*: she struggles, desperate as a netted Curlew; *Deo*: and she screams out; Oh, Oh, Oh!

Then Memory shewed me again how perfect she had appeared to me, lying at peace upon my laboratory Sopha. Beautifull, and wonderfull.

Before God, I realised, there is neither Evil in that which we desire, nor in that which we do. No unnatural Lust, no Insult to His earthly Creation. This is an Act of Beauty.

I took mine Hands from her Neck. "Do not move," I said.

I scrambled from the Bed, and retrieved mine Etui from the Pocket of my Coat. Opening it, I searched thro' it for the very Blade I had used on her those many Months ago. Withdrawing it, I placed it in readiness upon the bedside Table and returned to Katherine. She shivered, like a Flower in a slight Breeze. Mine Excitation again increased. I took a deep Breath, struggling to restrain it. "Give me your Hand," I said. "Why did you return to cutting yourself? Answer me truly."

Her Eyes flickered like Stars. "I was frightened," she said. "I thought—I was afraid that—that I could not have you, Bloody Bones."

"Listen," I told her in a grave Tone, cradling her delicate Carpal Joint within my Palm. "You are mine, Leonora. Katherine. You belong to me, and with me, and as you have sworn to me that I shall never lose you, so the same is true for me. I will never permit that you be lost. I love you."

"Oh!" she said, her slender Wrist beginning to tremble. "Are you angry with me?"

"No; but you must not doubt me."

"It is not, verily, you I doubt," she cried. "I fear that I am dreaming, and shall wake, and find that I am still at home, and that we did not ever meet; and I am wicked, wicked!"

I parted her Legs, and made her to lie compleatly still, and then I raised both her Arms level with her Shoulders, as in Vitruvius. Her Body in the Firelight became as shining Marble. *O, Thou art Beautifull, O My Love; as Tirzah*. I lifted my Scalpel. My Loins ached. The Moment sang.

What is this? Love: I love, I love; each Word, each Note curtailed by a Kiss. I reached for my Lancet.

"Keep open your Eyes," I commanded her. "And watch."

I turned Katherine's Wrist, so that the Back of her Hand was uppermost, and pinned her bent Arm firmly against my Knee. White Excitement spun mine Head, and I was almost undone. I steadied My Self, took in a deep Breath, and applied the Blade to the ivory Epidermis of her Forearm. She gasped. One upward, diagonal Stroake, and then a downward. *T*. Her Skin was fragile. I lifted her Arm to shew her. "Shall I stop?"

"No." Her Eyes were radiant. "No."

I paused, breathless, waiting for the Cut to clot; then focusing mine Attention intensely upon my Work, I wiped away the Blood and lowered the Scalpel once more to her delicate, velvet Skin. Mine whole World had clarified, all Time and all Sensation, into the right Angle between her Body and my Blade.

A new Strength flooded into me as if from Heaven, or from her, dispelling all Anxiety. In that Moment I understood that to possess Power such as this meant to be irreducibly alive, utterly present, to the very Core; and this angelic Presence, this Awareness raced thro' every Atom of my Flesh, quickening mine every Nerve, mine every tiny Muscle till my Body sang with an Alertness beyond anything I had before experienced. It rushed thro' me, thro' my scrolling Scalpel, and thro' Katherine. Then I felt as if she and I were, in subtle Quintessence, become one Being; and her Mind was my Mind, her Sensations, mine; her Pain, mine own.

Steel thro' Flesh. And as I had known that she would not, she did not struggle to escape, but lay still, breathing fast, small mewling Whimpers catching in her Throat; of Pleasure or of Pain, and I could not tell for which, and it did not matter; until at the final Cut, her whole Body trembled, and my Fingers shook. I slippt my Scalpel back within its Case and flexed mine Hand. Her Forearm was wet with her Blood. Carefully, I presst the Towel against it, soaking up the little Flow until the rich Embroidery was dyed quite red, and the Bleeding had almost ceased. Then I removed it, and beheld mine Handiwork.

Upon the virgin Parchment of her Wrist I had inscribed two Letters: *T.H.*

"Look," I told her. "Look, look."

Beautifull, and wonderfull, and mine, mine. I presst my Lips against her Arm. "Do not ever doubt me," I repeated, enunciating each Word clearly, as the Tolling of a Bell.

I bathed the Wound in Brandy; then I tore a Strip of Linen from mine own Shirt, and bound it up.

I laid me down upon her, my still cloathed Body close against hers, mine Hands resting each Side of her Head, my Fingers entangling in her Hair; and no sooner had I done so, than to my Surprize the mysterious Extasie, which I had sought and then repulsed, caught me up into its highest Rapture. My Limbs shuddered; I collapsed, helpless, atop her.

Tears blinded me. I did not know for why. As I lay, spent, silently weeping, she turned her Head, and I felt her feather-soft Lips brush my Fingertip. Mastering My Self one final Time, I summoned the Power to lift my Body from Katherine's and roll into a Position from which I could look upon her Face.

Her Eyes were wide, and wondrous. I pulled her towards me, and our Lips met in a deep, lingering Kiss, as if each sought to reassure the other of who we were.

"I am not a wicked Slut," Katherine whispered.

"No," I answered her. "Indeed, no."

CHAPTER THREE-AND-TWENTY

I awoke, as I had done every Morning for many Weeks, before seven. Mine immediate Thought was of Katherine; and at first it was to dread that everything that had gone on between us was a Dream. Then I became aware of the Weight of her Cranium upon mine Arm, her wild Hair tickling my Breast, her warm Palm pressing soft upon my Stomach. I realised that she was real, and that our extatic Connexion had been real also; and mine Heart swelled with the excited Wonder of it till it scarce allowed my Lungs the Space to breathe.

I had an urgent Need to make Water, but I did not dare to move lest she should wake during mine Absence and be distressed to find me gone. Nevertheless, I had no Choice; with great Caution I withdrew mine Arm from underneath her, and fled from the Bed.

As I stood, shivering over the Pot in my dressing Room, and trying hard to think of anything but Katherine, I found that my Perceptions were as clear as new cut Glass. The Cold upon my Skin seemed more acute, the Relief of my Body more compleat, even the Darkness in the shuttered Chamber more tangible than I had experienced at any Moment since my Return to Shirelands. The hot Stench of Piss caught my Throat, and made me cough. I put mine Hand to my Mouth, and was startled to find a Roughness on my Chin. I had not shaved since yester-morn.

I crosst the Room and opened up the Shutters. The morning Light splashed like pink Wine across mine Hands, and into mine Eyes. Half blinded by the Brightness, I stared, awestruck, astonished, into the beauteous Countenance of rising Dawn.

Beauty, however, brought no Warmth. My Legs grew weak, and my chilled Stomach churned. Shaking, I crept to my Bed, and wrappt My Self as close around Katherine as I could, tucking my Face into the Hollow of her Axilla, and twining my Legs over and under hers, as Ivy groweth about a Tree. A strange Yearning had possesst me; for Laudanum. For a Moment, I craved the Drugge, desired it more than Aire or Food, or the sweet Sound of a Scream. The Desire was so strong I was nigh compelled to struggle again from my Sanctum and seek out Erasmus; but as I half commenced to withdraw, Katherine, rousing, wrappt her Arms around my Neck. I put out mine Head from beneath the Covers to see that she had opened her Eyes, and was smiling at me with an Expression of Wonder that surely had been copied from mine own. At once, my Stomach calmed, tho' my Limbs were trembling like the Leaves upon an Aspen Tree; a reviving Warmth flooded into my Chest. We embraced each other, our Delight as intense as it was innocent; and as we conversed, I felt me becoming once again mine own Self. I understood then that my sudden Sickness had most probably been connected with the Onset of the alien Longing for Paregoric. The Thought that I could be in Thrall to any unnatural Substance disgusted me. I held nothing against Erasmus; but I vowed quietly to My Self that, whatever convincing Arguments he might present, I should never take his Prescriptions again, for certainly their Effects were to my Detriment.

I dresst, quite quickly, and locking Katherine for Safety in my Room, I descended carefully down-Stairs in Pursuit of Sustenance for us both. I had not descended below one Flight, all the while pondering this pharmacological Discovery, when I ran across Erasmus himself, severe of Expression and accompanied by a prattling Mrs H. Encountering each other, we stoppt abruptly, and stood as, I thought, might two Generals of contending Armies, each assessing the apparent Strength of his Opponent.

"Tristan," Erasmus said, in an oddly cautious Manner. "Are you well, my Friend?"

"Erasmus," I answered. "I could not be better, tho' mine Head hurts like the Devil. I would ask something privately of you. Mrs H., I know not what Errand you may be about, but must delay it; I require Breakfast sent straight up to my Chamber."

I steppt towards Erasmus and caught Hold of his Elbow. Erasmus frowned, and peered, searchingly, into my Face.

"Step into my Study," I said, since we were hard by the Door. "What I have to say is not for anyone's Ears."

I unlocked my Laboratory and drew Erasmus quickly within. Erasmus half closed the Door, but did not bring it intirely to. I slowly shook mine Head and tugged it shut, quite violently; the Woodwork rattled.

Nobody, plainly, had been in here since late last Night; for altho' the Remains of Katherine's evening Meal had been taken away, no one had lifted the night Cloths from my Cages, and my Specimens languished in Darkness. Erasmus un-shuttered the Windows, and I cursed the slip-slop Neglect of the Hall's Servants, for as long as they were living my poor Creatures required Light and Aire, even if they were never to see the outside World. Muttering furious Obscenities beneath my Breath, I hurriedly disclosed them one by one, and took careful Time to ensure that every furred and feathered Inmate had sufficient Food and Water.

"Tristan," Erasmus said, "I am happy to have seen you. I had wished to apologise for mine Absence last Night. Mrs H. told me you were seriously upset by it."

"Your Absence? Pshaw, that matters naught. Why should I have been upset at your accompanying my Sister home? I should rightly have been annoyed if you had not, for 'twas foul Weather. 'Tis all Barnaby's Fault, that he did not come with her; but he cares little for the Comfort of others." I crosst to my long Table and raised the Cloth from the Cage of my cock Goldfinch, which I kept upon it.

"Why," said Erasmus, in Surprize, "you seem in fair Spirits, todaye, Sir."

"Aha!" I said, opening the cage Door and removing both Bowls. "There are two Reasons for that, and you shall hear both; tho' one I must ask you keep silent upon, for the nonce. First, I have decided that I will imbibe no more of your damnable Opium, for it doth nothing but dull my Mind and bestill my Bowels; and second, tho' 'tis of far greater Importance, I have passed an intire Night and Morning in the Arms of Katherine Montague."

Erasmus' Reaction to these startling Newes was not quite as I had anticipated. "Indeed?" he said, slowly. "What makes you think so, Tristan?"

"Do you jest? I did not dream it! She arrived last Evening, while you were at Dinner with the Barnabys." I opened my Window sufficiently to throw out the filthy Water, and refilled the Bowl from the Jug. My Goldfinch began to preen its Tail.

"She arrived last Evening. By herself?"

"Truly, so. She hath fled her wicked Uncle, having neither Money nor Cloathing; and that is partly what I desired to charge you with, Erasmus: the Task of secretly procuring for her suitable Apparel. She is very slight, and I doubt that any of Jane's old Cloathes will fit, unless they be nursery Dress; and that will not do."

"Where is she, now?"

"I have secured her in my Chamber against anyone's learning that she is here, as yet. You know my Fears, Erasmus."

"And yet," Erasmus said, "you have told me."

My Goldfinch left off its Preening, shook its Wings and began loudly to chirp. The pretty Sound made me wince. I shut my Window.

"I have no Distrust of you," I answered Erasmus, smiling, despite my Goldfinch, and headed to the Closet wherein I kept my Supplies of Muslin and of Lint, that I might apply a proper Dressing upon Katherine's Arm. "But I feel disinclined to face mine Aunt's Displeasure, or even my Sister's. Would that we had been of equal Station! But enough of that. My Point, Erasmus, is this: I have every Intention of remaining in my Chamber until tomorrow, you may easy guess wherefore; so do not expect me down to Dinner, and if anyone should ask for me, spin them some Yarn to account for mine Absence. Will you lie for me?"

Erasmus regarded me closely, his Brow furrowed.

"Egad, Man!" I said, secreting several Rolls of the soft Cloth within my Frock. "'Tis but a little Lie! I don't ask you to swear on Oath!"

Erasmus ceased his Scrutiny, and smiled. There was a strange Expression in his Eyes. "I shall tell no one anything," he said. He looked up at me with a Perplexity that made me feel exceeding uncomfortable. I did not question that he should wonder at Katherine's unexpected Arrival, which I should have scarce credited My Self; but I could not comprehend why there should be, mixt in amongst his Admiration, so much Sadness.

"'Sdeath!" I cried. "Anyone should think from the Look upon your Face that I had got a Wound! I will not brood upon the Difficulties."

"Tristan," said Erasmus quietly, touching me gently upon mine Elbow. "Perhaps a small Dose of Laudanum will soothe your Head, and your Nerves."

"I will not take your Medicines, my Friend." I pulled mine Arm away, having no farther Time to waste, and hastened for the Landing to intercept Mrs H. before she could begin to mount the upper Stairs.

"Tristan, stay; talk with me more upon Miss Montague."

"What more needs be said? Whatever 'tis, must wait, Erasmus," I replied.

Katherine, when I returned, was standing by my bedroom Window. She had cloathed her Nakedness in my red night-Gown, and stolen her small Feet inside a pair of my Slippers, all of which were so many Times too big for her that she had the Appearance of a Child playing Dress-up in its Parents' Closet.

I lowered the Tray onto the Table and crosst the Room to stand behind her. She leaned against me, and putting her own Hands atop mine, pulled them to her left Breast. The dizzying Pain in mine Head began at once to ease.

"Tristan," said Katherine. "You cut my Cloathes to Rags. What am I to wear?"

"Naught," I said.

"I cannot wear naught."

"Assuredly, you can," I told her. "Naught becomes you better than the finest Satin, and is ever to be preferred above that demeaning Costume, that filthy, repulsive, beggarly Attire; that Dishclout; which was never fit to wipe your Feet, let alone for you to wear. Come from the Window."

She did not begin to move. I kissed the Satin of her Neck, and freeing mine Hands from hers, lifted her as easily as if she had been made of Gossamer. I carried her to my Bed and forbade her to move a Muscle or to look whilst I inspected my Work and replaced the Bandage upon her Wrist. The Incisions were clear, precise, and darkly scabbed, but fresh and sweet smelling, with no Trace of Infection or Disorder. Pleased, I threw away my makeshift Dressing and replaced it with clean Muslin. Then, she and I together set about my Breakfast. Mine Headache had vanished.

As I was finishing my Meal, Katherine sate up. "If any Woman dares even look at you," she said, vehemently, "I will poke her Eyes out."

"That would prove most inconvenient, for what about the Maids—and Mrs H.? Antient tho' she is, she is a Woman, I believe."

I wiped clean mine Hands on the linen Cloth and placed the empty Tray upon the Floor.

"As long as they be Maids, not Jades, they have naught to fear," Katherine said.

A profound Happiness pulsed thro'out my veins at these Declarations, as if that angelic Presence that had descended upon me during our previous Night's Delights were still living within mine Heart. But as I experienced it, I found that this Happiness, tho' powerful, was not immaculate; as it grew, there grew, parasitic upon it—as Mistletoe upon a willow Tree, half beyond Sight—an inchoate Terrour, that twisted and shifted in Colour and Proportion, until eventually, and with a dreadful Clarity, it coalesced into a Shape I could perceive. It was the White Owl.

I must unwittingly have tightened mine Embrace, for Katherine cried out that she stifled, and struggled against mine Hold with a Vehemence that had naught to do with Passion, and all with Aire. I released mine Hands at once, and she turned to me, her Expression concerned.

"Oh, my Dear," she said, putting her gentle Hands up to my Cheeks. "What is wrong?"

'Twas nothing, I pretended.

At about ten o' the Clock, Mrs H. sent Molly Jakes to empty the Bath and to light the Fire. I hid Katherine behind my bed-Curtain, and nothing was suspected. Eventually, the bright Sunne dippt, and Dusk crept into the Room; and I realised that the Houre had come for me to make my Patrol. I slippt from Katherine's Side, intending, for she had fallen into a light Slumber, to try to leave without waking her, but at my Movement, she roused, and sate upright.

"You must not worry," I said, lighting the Candles, and shuttering the Windows fast. "I must make sure that the House is safe. I will return as quickly as I can."

"Tristan—"

"Be careful of the Hearth, there may be Gnomes—but they will not trouble us whilst the Fire is lit."

I kissed her upon her Forehead, and reluctantly departed.

I was greatly surprized to find Erasmus waiting for me in the Passageway without my Door. "What, Sir?" I said. "You have been up and down my Stairs todaye more often than Goosey Gander. Yet, I see, to no Effect; you have not brought me what I asked."

Taking his Arm thro' mine, as Nathaniel had used to do with me, I held my Candle high and we began the painstaking Circumnavigation of the House.

We had compleated the uppermost Floors, when Erasmus, whose Habit it was, upon these Occasions, to press me hard upon the Topic of Goblins in general, and Raw Head in particular, said: "Tristan, do you recall the Writings of Mr Locke?"

"I know them well," I said.

"Then do you recall his Words upon the wrong Association of Ideas? Specifically, these: 'The Ideas of Goblins and Sprights have really no more to do with Darkness than with Light; yet let but a foolish Maid' – or a Mrs H., perhaps – 'inculcate these often on the Mind of a Child, possibly he shall never separate them again so long as he lives, but Darkness shall ever afterwards bring with it those frightful Ideas, and they shall be so joined he can no more bear the one than the other.'"

"You are suggesting," I said, as we began our Descent of the upper Staircase, "that mine Ideas are mistaken, and from Mrs H., to boot."

"Yes, Tristan. I am."

"I would that you were right, Erasmus!" I replied. "But they are not, my Friend. I have the Proof of that."

"Do you, Sir? Where? What is the Evidence that may be confirmed by our common Observation?"

"I cannot shew you," I answered.

"What Conclusion should we, properly, draw from that Omission?"

"If it were the Case that I could shew you no Proof because I had none, your Skepticism would be justified; but that is not how 'tis. I cannot shew you because—" I broke off.

"If it please you, Sir, continue," Erasmus said.

"It is a private Matter."

We reached the Landing. I turned towards my Study and led Erasmus within for the second Time that Daye—which I knew to be exactly half as many Times as he had been between its Walls since we had arrived from London. I had not made him unwelcome; but I perceived that Erasmus had very swiftly taken the Measure of the House, and my Family's Habit of Separation and Withdrawal soon became his own. Because of my Father's Incapacity, his Library, which for so many Yeares had been his private and uncontested Territory, had been left vulnerable to Incursion; so Erasmus had taken up a temporary Residence therein, almost as if he had been mine older Brother. The strangest Effect of this, from my Point of View, was that I had over the past Weeks spent more Houres among my Father's things than I had done in twenty Yeares; and the Stranger who now inhabited it seemed closer to me than Flesh and Blood.

Erasmus was good enough to assist me with my Creatures, whilst I saw to the Closure of my Shutters, and poked up my Fire.

"Wilt tell me once again about Raw-Head-and-Bloody-Bones?" Erasmus began again, as he drew the Cloth over my Cage of Squirrells.

I stood up, and returned the Poker to its Stand with perhaps more Vigour than the Act demanded. "Egad, Erasmus!" I said. "What more dost require me to say? I have told you all I know. Raw Head is the Prince of Goblins, Ravisher of Maids; and Bloody Bones the Keeper of the Dead. They are two, who tho' seeming Twins, are really the bitterest of Enemies."

"Would it amaze you," Erasmus said, "if I told you that I grew up in mortal Horrour of a Monster exactly alike to your Raw-Head-and-Bloody-Bones? My Mother convinced me that if I was disobedient, Lambskin would carry me off and skin me alive. There are many such nursery Fiends, Tristan, but none of them are real; and as we grow older, rational Men must cease believing in them."

I laughed bitterly. "Verily, thou art wrong," I said. "Our Cases are not alike at all. Raw Head and Bloody Bones are not one, but two; and they are no mere Boggarts fit only to terrify little Children out of Sleep. Raw Head is the Goblin Knight."

"The Goblin Knight is a Character in a Ballad, and I can think of no Song in which he is also Raw-Head-and-Bloody-Bones."

"Pshaw! Those Balladeers are wrong also; I know the Truth."

"Balladeers," Erasmus said, "sing a mere Tale, which hath no Power in this World to be wrong or right. Our rational Understanding, however, hath the Capacity to discern Truth from Fiction, and guide us away from Superstition. There are no Goblins, Tristan."

I felt a great Annoy at this, but not wishing to lose my Temper with my Friend I cast around for something with which to distract My Self. The Flames were licking upwards within the Fireplace, and as the Heat increased, it occurred to me that now was as good a Time as any to burn Katherine's ruined Slippers. I searched about in the Vicinity of the Hearth, where she had kicked them off upon the previous Evening, but to my Surprize found nothing. I straightened up, and cast my Gaze over the whole Room, lest the Items had been placed upon my Desk or in some other inappropriate Place; but I did not see them. Then I noticed that her woollen Cloak, also, was gone. Mine Heart chilled beneath my Breastbone.

The most likely thing, I knew, was that Molly Jakes or any other of the Maids had taken the Cloak and Slippers away to Laundry. But I remembered, suddenly, horribly, and as if I were remembering a Nightmare, how a Gnome had stolen my Papers in Henry Fielding's House.

"I have left her alone!" I cried. "I have left her; I should not have done that!"

"Tristan," Erasmus said, lowering the red Cloth he had held in his Hands and hastening swiftly to my Side. "Calm yourself, my dear Fellow; there is nothing to fear."

"You are wrong," I said. "There is everything to fear." I pushed past him. "I have left Miss Montague alone; the Monsters may break in while she is unprotected. Her Cloathes are missing; her Cloak and her Shoes. Raw Head may have learned already of her Presence here."

"Tristan, Tristan," said Erasmus, taking hold of mine Elbow. "Please—wilt not entertain a different Explanation?"

"What might that be? Unhand me, Erasmus; I must go to her."

"Is it not possible," Erasmus said, "that her Cloathes are not here because they never were; because Miss Montague is still safely in Dorset with her Uncle Whitcross?"

"What?" I whirled to face him.

"What is more like to be the Truth?" Erasmus asked. "That Miss Montague, who is but fifteen, hath crosst open Country by herself, and hath broken into the Hall against everyone's Knowledge but your own; or that you have been once more cruelly deceived by your perceptual Faculties; that you have been half dreaming, perceiving the Event you yearn for to have been, against all Probability, made manifest?"

I shook free mine Arm.

"She is not here, Tristan," Erasmus said.

CHAPTER FOUR-AND-TWENTY

Now, it may be supposed that this Assertion by Erasmus Glass, that Katherine was not here, and that all I had experienced with her in the previous Houres had been the Work of mine Imagination, would have been deeply hateful to me. In Truth, however, it was not. In mine Heart, as in my Mind, as in my very Loins, I knew that Katherine was every bit as real, and every bit as present as mine own Body; and one tentative Suggestion from a Man who, however respected, had not seen her had no Power to shake my Certainty. Neither was I angry to hear the Assertion voiced, for it appeared to me that Erasmus spoke neither in Jest nor out of any Desire to alarm me; he believed what he said, absurd as his History was in the Face of my Reality. Moreover, and finally, it seemed to me an highly amusing thing that he was so mistaken, and that he should probably think himself most comically stupid when he discovered his Error. All these Thoughts flashed thro' mine Head in less than half a Second; then all were gone from mine Awareness, displaced by the overwhelming Fear that I had left Katherine in Danger.

Abandoning Erasmus, I fled from my Study and ran pell-mell up the Stairs to my Chamber. I was distantly conscious of Erasmus calling out my Name, and beseeching me be calm and resist falling into Panick, but I paid no Heed to him. Reaching my Door, I fumbled for a Moment with my Key; it was with Difficulty that I fitted it into the Lock, for mine Hands were shaking, and my Candle had been extinguished in my mad Rush. Finally, I was able to turn it. I threw open my Door and flung My Self into the Room.

Katherine appeared before me sitting on the Bed, bathed in golden Firelight. I ran to her, and took her sweet ivory Form straight up into mine Arms. "Are you well?" I asked her. "Hath there been aught Mishap? I thought Raw Head had stolen in—I was frightened for your Safety."

"I am well, my Love," she said, soothing my Terrour with a Kiss. Mine Agitation began, slowly, to subside. I kissed her again upon the Crown of her Head, and then, hearing Erasmus upon the Stairs, bade her wait my Return but a little longer, and left the Room as precipitantly as I had entered it, almost bowling over my poor co-Physician, who had just arrived at the Door.

"Peace, Tristan, Peace!" Erasmus exclaimed, catching at mine Elbow as I bounded into the Hallway. "For God's Sake, there is no Danger. Be easy, Sir."

"Verily, Erasmus, you are right," I said, my Voice a-flood with Relief. "Miss Montague is well. There hath been no Incursion. We shall proceed down the Stairs."

"Miss Montague is not here," Erasmus insisted. "Is she, Tristan? Is she? Answer me, truly."

I shook mine Head at him, tho' not, as he may have supposed, in Answer to his Question, and then continued my Circum-ambulation of the House, which, after I had thoroughly shut up the lower Floors, eventually led me to my Father's Library. Here I paused, and looked toward Erasmus. I could not to my Satisfaction conclude mine Inspection without venturing within, and this he knew. After a Moment during which I apprehended he should refuse me Entry, he reluctantly opened up the Door.

My Father's Library was on the ground Floor of the House, almost directly underneath my Study. I suddenly remembered how, in the early Dayes, when I had been new in Possession of my little Universe, it had sometimes pleased me to imagine that I sate upon the Crown of a Tree that had its Roots below, in his Soil. I had not indulged this pretty Phantasy for Yeares, and its Revival shocked me. The Furnishings were warm, and comforting red. Rich damask Draperies shielded the cold Glass of the Window, and the dark panelled Walls reflected the dancing Flames within the Grate. The Aire hung with the Fragrances of old Paper, and leather Binding.

In a great Rush, I recalled the Thoughts I had had regarding my Father's Treatment; and tho' I somewhat hazily recalled how I had been unable to write them down, I remembered the Ideas them-selves as clearly as I remembered the Touch of Katherine's silken Skin beneath my Fingers.

"I have been composing a Treatise," I announced, suddenly, "upon the likely Cause and appropriate Treatment of my Father's unhappy Condition, which we commonly designate Stroake, despite that of all things that may have occasioned it, a Strike from an Elf-Arrow is the most unlikely."

Erasmus put down his candle upon my Father's Escritoire, and regarded me, his Eyebrows lifting. "Indeed," he responded, slowly. "I concur; the Condition is poorly named. But our superstitious Forebears had no Way of knowing that 'twas not the Work of evil Elves, shooting the Unwary from behind old Trees. So, what are your Ideas regarding it?"

"I conceive," I said, "that the sudden onset of the Paralysis doth imply a sudden Cause; but that my Father's continuing Affliction doth suggest some more permanant Rupture of the nervous Connexion between the Brain and the afflicted body Parts, whatever they may be. For doth not the nervous Web extend thro'out the whole human Flesh, and is not its Purpose that of ensuring that such Communication take place?"

"Verily," Erasmus said, slowly, "I think it is; but if 'twere merely the Case that the Fibres were broken betwixt, say, Limb and Spine, then why should there also result the general Incapacity of Speech and Movement that hath afflicted your Father?"

"I have not finished," I said. "'Tis mine Hypothesis that the Injury lieth within the Brain itself, and therefore hath a more general than specific Effect. Do you not recall the Exploration that we made of the Brain and Spinal Cord during the Dissection we performed with Dr Hunter? Do you remember how the Brain itself appeared to be largely composed of nervous Tissue, wrappt in Fat and well supplied with Blood?"

Erasmus paused, and I saw in his Eyes an Uncertainty, perhaps as to my Purpose in introducing the Topic. I could not guess. But within Seconds, his Surgeon's Instincts seemingly took him over, and he said: "Do you suggest that your Father hath sustained a Blow to his Head that hath caused Injury to his Brain? There is no Sign of any such Insult."

"I suggest," I said, "that his Brain is injured. Whether he sustained a Blow or not I cannot say, for tho' it seems reasonable to suppose it, I suspect the proximate Cause to be a cerebral Aneurysm, which may be in itself the Result of some Failure of Regulation within the Body itself."

"Certainly, that is possible," Erasmus said.

"'Tis merely an Hypothesis," I answered him.

Erasmus began to pace the Chamber in front of the Fire. I watched him closely, awaiting his Response, and as he continued to pace and to ponder, became somewhat concerned that he had discerned some severe Flaw in my Reasoning that would collapse mine whole Theory. Finally, he looked up, and giving an anxious Smile, as one might to a Person to whom one must deliver difficult Newes, said: "Tristan, I know not whether to speak to you upon this be intirely wise, but I believe I must chance it. Sit down. Sit, and listen, if you can. Is it still your Desire to return to London, and study under Dr Hunter at the Hospitals?"

Seeing no Reason to refuse, tho' I was somewhat perplext by Erasmus' Aspect, I sate My Self upon one of the high backed Chairs that were propped up against the chimney Wall of my Father's Library. "Naturally, I do," I said. "Why would I wish otherwise? I must work, especially if I am to marry."

"As to your marrying," Erasmus said quietly. "Neither would your Family permit you to marry, nor your Marriage be considered valid."

My Mouth fell open. "Why not?" I demanded.

"You are not well, Sir," Erasmus said, in a soothing Tone. "If you were to wed now, your Family would presume that your Marriage resulted from your being not in your right Mind, and God alone knows what Confusion would result from it."

"What?" I stared at him.

"Pray, be easy," Erasmus said. He paused, studying me closely, and then resumed, speaking this Time with no less Care, but quite quick, as if he wanted to be done with the Words as soon as possible: "We have spoken of this more than once already, but I fear that you do not remember. Your Family, Mr Hart, would presume you mad because, for many Weeks, you have been so far out of your Senses that 'tis only because of mine own extensive Efforts that you were not put into a private mad-House."

This was too much. I leapt to my Feet, clattering over my Chair in mine Agitation. "What?"

"Sit down!" Erasmus said, to mine Amazement leaping up also and catching hold of both mine Arms. He stared intently into mine Eyes. "Sit down, Tristan! 'Tis the Truth, painfull as it is for you to hear it. Yet I must tell you, and tell you now, whilst you are in your Senses; for right now you seem yourself, and shewing a Rationality that hath been hidden all Daye, behind your constant Worry upon Raw Head. You have been very ill, Sir, more ill than you know; and you are not well, yet, despite your Conviction." He gave mine upper Arms a short, bracing Shake. "But you will be. You will be, Tristan. Sit down, for God's Sake; please, sit down."

He took his Hands from mine Arms and patted them, like a dairy-Maid about the Butter. Then he bent, righted my Chair, and seizing mine Elbows again exerted upon me a firm, gentle Pressure to make me sit; and I was so profoundly surprized by all of this that slowly, I complied. Fascinated by this new Erasmus, who might leap up, or shout out without warning, I began to watch him very closely.

There was no Question of my crediting his Assertion that I had been insane. Did my Family verily believe me mad?

"If you are to return to Health," Erasmus said, "and to your Work, then you must convince yourself of the non-Existence of Faeries, and Raw Head; and the Truth regarding Katherine Montague. Miss Montague cannot be here, Tristan, because I had her informed that you had suffered a severe nervous Collapse, and bade her stay away."

"What?" I exclaimed. "You did what?"

"I acted only for the best, Sir, and I stand by my Actions. I have had always your best Interests at Heart, and I have them still."

"'Tis not all one thing," I cried. "To say thus, and yet to tell Miss Montague that I am mad."

"I have never told anybody you were mad," Erasmus answered. "I am convinced your Illness hath to do with your Senses, not your Reason. I have explained this over and again to Mr and Mrs Barnaby, and to you, yourself, when you have been well enough to hear me. Please, Tristan, try to remain calm. I have neither the Skill of Dr Oliver, nor one tenth of your own Talent; but I have tried my best and more cannot be asked of any Man."

"If you are my Physician, you must pronounce me sane," I said. "'Tis the least you can do."

"I would like to," Erasmus said. "But I cannot, yet."

I drew a deep Breath, and folded mine Arms across my Chest. "If you were not my Friend, I should break your Head," I said, thro' clenched Teeth.

"I conceive," continued Erasmus, after a Moment, when he perceived that I kept my Temper under my Control, "that it would

be beneficial if you were to pay a Visit to your Father. You have
been ill, but your Physician's Instincts are, I vow, as sharp as ever.
It may be that altho' you can prove nothing regarding the Causes
of Apoplexy, you may well advance the Efficacy of our Methods
of treating it. Moreover, if you can succeed, by rational Effort, in
maintaining your Awareness wholly within this, real, World, I will
declare you to be as sane as My Self. If you will give me your
Word, now, that you will make this Attempt, I shall do everything
in my Power to establish a positive Opinion in the Minds of your
Family toward your Affection for Miss Montague, and with their
Co-operation she shall be sent for out of Weymouth and you shall
be formally engaged. An you agree, I will write upon't to your
Aunt this very Night."

I was inclined to laugh at this Notion, and a little to weep, seeing
that I knew full well that Katherine was already in my Bedchamber,
safe away from Raw Head and my Family besides, at least for the
nonce, and all the Delusion was upon the Part of poor Erasmus;
but I did neither, and instead, decided to give him what he desired:
the Appearance of my playing along.

"Thank you, my Friend," I said. "But do not write mine Aunt.
She hath declared an Interest for herself in my Marriage, and will
savagely mislike the Notion of my marrying Miss Montague. She
will create an Uproar."

"In that Matter," said Erasmus, "your Illness doth aid you, for if
your Aunt formerly intended you to marry a Wife of her choosing,
she expresseth no such Expectation now. I conceive she will accept
the Newes without Quarrell; however, if you prefer, I shall write
instead to your Sister."

I did not know what to reply to this. My Preference, naturally,
was that Erasmus write to neither; but I had decided to play up to

his Phantasy, and there seemed to be so much riding upon my Co-operation – Egad! My Sanity! Mine Ability to marry, and to order mine own Affairs, as I saw fit! I stood up to leave. "If writing to Jane is what 'twill take to have you call me sane, do as you will," I said, with extream Reluctance. "But be sure to tell her that I will not be swayed, no Matter what Intelligence she thinks she might have heard from Sophy Ravenscroft or anybody else. I love Miss Montague and always will."

I turned, and would then have departed the Library alone, but to my Surprize and somewhat to mine Irritation Erasmus insisted on pursuing me all the Way to my Chamber, attempting to direct my Conversation firmly towards mine Hypothesis. In this Effort he was unsuccessful; I had seen thro' him clear enough to guess that he feared mine apparent Rationality would vanish like Smoake in Mist the Moment I departed his Society. I found this Motive objectionable enough to keep my Lips tight shut upon my Thoughts, tho' they were bounding like a Stag.

As soon as my Chamber Door was closed, Katherine fell on my Neck. "If I get with Child," she said, "will you swear that you will not force me to give it up?"

"What cruel Fancy is this?" I exclaimed in Astonishment, dis-engaging My Self from her Embrace and holding her at some small Distance, the better to observe her Expression. "We have done naught that you should conceive. But I would not do so. We would wed at once."

Mine Heart reeled, despite my Bravado. If I was ill—nay, worse, if I was mad—for all that Erasmus had refused the Word—not only could Katherine and I not wed, but I could not work. I trusted that Erasmus would not break his Word, and would declare his Confidence in my Sanity as soon as I had convinced him of its continued Fastness; but beyond that Time, what Hospital would employ a Surgeon who had been considered insane? I must remain dependent on my Father. On top of this, I did not concur with Erasmus in his Estimation of mine Aunt Barnaby, and I wished I had forbidden him to tell a Soule. I had only the slightest Hope that Jane would not reveal the Newes to her Mother-in-law, and it seemed too remarkable to believe that mine Aunt had given up her Desire to see me connected with a Woman of good Standing, and her Choosing. She would demand my Father disown me if I married Katherine; and I could not trust that he had Strength of Will to resist her, particularly in his present Sickness. Whither could we run? Nowhere.

That Night, I sate up in my Bed for many Houres pondering the Question, but I found no Answer. Shortly before Dawn I gave up the Assay, and to distract my Mind took up instead my Quill, Ink, and Paper that I might begin again upon that Treatise upon Apoplexy that had proved so far beyond my Capabilities. And I know not wherefore, or how, for surely I should have been in no fit State to think, let alone to write, but despite the Poverty of the Light and the Difficulty inherent in the Attempt whilst sitting up in Bed, I managed to compose a coherent Intention.

After I had been writing thus about an Houre, or little longer, I heard a Noise without my Chamber: a Grunt, obscene and gluttonous, like a Pig in the Mud. Puzzled, and alarmed beyond Measure, I arose, and pulled on my Breeches and Shirt. I took my

Cane from behind my Door, and my lighted Candle in mine other Hand, and barefoot, crept from my Bedroom.

The crude Sound came again; it was close, I realised, but not within the House. 'Tis at the front Door, I thought. And it is not Viviane. I strode thro' mine ancestral Home, my Mettle quickening.

My Shaddowe stretched out behind me, long and narrow and unfathomable black; and, as I walked, I gradually sensed, at the Extremity of my Perception, a Mobb of twisted Horrours: Gnomes and small Goblins and Devils, crawling out of the blackest Recesses of the House and making swift Sorties across the Light, to hide themselves within it. I shuddered in Disgust, but this Attempt to frighten me was futile; I continued after the Sound, determined to track down and set about its Maker.

But as I came into the Hall, the Candlelight flared, suddenly, supernaturally bright. I threw up mine Arms to shield my Face, but in vain; the Brightness was blinding. It penetrated mine Head, mine Heart, my very Bowels, pulsing, drumming upon mine Eyeballs, a purging Brilliance of Pain.

It was mine Heartbeat, it was Nathaniel's Snare; it was the Drumming of Hooves underneath the Surface of the Earth.

After a long Minute, the Agony finally receding, I lowered my crosst Arms from mine Eyes, and looked about me. Raw Head's Goblin Multitude stood in the Centre of the Hall, jibber-jabbering in the Candlelight. I could see them all, as clear as if it had been Daye. I stared upon them, shocked, amazed. Monsters, they were; green as Toads, red as Liver, black as ditch Water. Many had the Shapes of Pigs erect upon two Legs, with Trotters and bristling Hair. Some had two Heads, like the old Raw-Head-and-Bloody-Bones of Nathaniel's Jest. I began, out of Revulsion, to back away; but then the Cane kicked sharp against my Palm.

I am not one who needeth fear the Dark, I thought, suddenly. I am Bloody Bones.

In that Instant, I finally perceived that Raw Head, Goblin Knight that he was, had made a grave Mistake in sending this foul Army to torment me. I sprang forward, and I slashed as ferociously with my Cane as if't had been a Sword. Head after grotesque Head fell bloody to the Floor, scarlet upon white and black; until before I comprehended it the Monsters had begun to flee towards the Door, which they passed thro' as easy as if it had been Aire.

Unprepared to let the Matter end thus, I chased to the Portal and flung it wide. Starlit Cold flooded the Step. In the blue starLight I could still determine the twisted Forms of Goblins galloping across the dark Grounds of the Hall. Without even thinking against it for one mere Second, I steppt barefooted onto the Gravel. To my Surprize I suffered no Discomfort. I swiftly crosst it, and ran over the velvet Grass, away from the House. The thrilling Aire stung my Throat. The Sky vibrated. I was not fearfull, no, not I. I was angry.

Before long I found My Self at the locked iron Gates of Shirelands; and there I stoppt, and wondered at my Battle and fruitless Pursuit, until in my Wondering I had half forgotten both and begun to think I ought to return inside; and then into mine Head there soft began to encroach, upon the very Edge of mine Hearing, a Song:

"*Young Tom he was a country Lad, a country Lad was he.*
He's gone up into London Town the City for to see.
With a Whack! Fol al a-diddle, al a-diddle o!
He's gone up into old Cheapside, a fair Maid for to meet
He's taken her by the lilywhite Hand and given her Kisses sweet.

She's ta'en him to her Mother's House, she's rung low on the Pin
They've opened up the wide front Door and let young Thomas in.
With a Whack! Fol al a-diddle, al a-diddle o!
And they've had Beef and they've had Wine, and to the Bed
  they've gone
And Poll says Tom I've lost my Muff, and 'twas my only one.

Young Tom he says I'll help you Poll, your Treasure for to seek.
They say 'tis under my Apron, if thou wilt take a Peek.
With a Whack! Fol al a-diddle, al a-diddle o!
Fair Polly 'tis too dark below, I can no longer see.
O Tommy use your pretty Hand, to find my Muff for me.

So Tom he use his pretty Hand, and find her Muff forsooth
O Tom your Fingers are too cold, pray warm them in my Muff
With a Whack! Fol al a-diddle, al a-diddle o!
So Tom he slips his Hand within, right up unto the Wrist
Fair Polly 'tis too small inside, I fear 'twill break my Fist

O Polly why so faint and pale? Why dost thou moan and cry?
Why do thine Eyes turn in thy Head, thy fair Breast heave and
  sigh?
With a Whack! Fol al a-diddle, al a-diddle o!
I have found out your Precious Muff, I wot you sit astride it.
I cannot move my Hand at all, it is stuck quite inside it."

What? I thought. Both Voice and Song were wondrous familiar; the one as pitch perfect as a Nightingale, the other as filthy as a London Gutter.

Peering excitedly thro' the iron Gates, at last I saw, upon the

Road beyond, approaching at an easy Pace out of the rising Sunne, Nathaniel Ravenscroft.

Nathaniel looked, to mine Eyes, exactly as I had seen him appear upon the Daye of his Departure; as if not even one Heartbeat had passed betwixt that Morning and this. His Hair shone silver in the breaking Light, and his smooth Skin was as fair as Buttermilk. Yet his Attire was altered: at his Hip hung a tooled Scabbard, atop which was visible the Hilt of a silver Sword; upon his Back he carried a Bow which I knew somehow to be of finest English Yew, and Arrows of straight elm-Wood. He was cloathed in Frock and Breeches of grass-green Satin, adorned with golden Braid upon the Cuffs and Hems. His Waistcoat, also of green, was decorated with a rare and most intricate Embroidery of white Hounds chasing a snowy Stag. As I stared, and I stared most closely, I realised that the Design was no mere Tapestry; both Hart and Hounds were really running, Hooves and clawed Pads pounding, Limbs weaving in and out, Flanks heaving, Foam flying; yet as neither could draw farther or nearer to the other, both Hunter and Hunted were condamned to Chase eternal, with no Chance of Capture or Escape.

"Nat!" I shouted. "Nathaniel Ravenscroft!"

I flung My Self upon the Gate, stretching mine Arms thro' the wrought-iron Work as far as I could reach, but I did not attempt to open it. Nathaniel came close; I put mine Arms about his Shoulders and bussed his Cheek.

"So," said Nathaniel, stepping back and studying me critically all over, like a Magpie appraising a Trinket. "Tristan Hart. How comes it that every Time we have lately met you have been half-dresst and covered with somebody's Blood?"

"I have been slaughtering Goblins, Nat," I told him.

"Ah," said Nathaniel slowly, and a curious, catlike Smile began to play about his Lips. "I know you have."

"You spoke truly," I said, excited, "when you told me, that Daye in the High Field, about Faeries, and I thought you madder than I; you spoke true."

"Naturally," Nathaniel said. "What I say is always true, tho' 'tis not the only Truth. It is no Fault of mine if my Listeners are deaf, or stupid."

"Which was I, Nat?"

"You?" Nathaniel narrowed his Eyes. "You were stubborn, for you both heard and understood, but you would not verily perceive; even and exactly as you are doing right now."

"Egad, Nat!" I said. "I have missed you!"

"You should have come with me," Nathaniel said.

I shook mine Head.

"Don't try to pretend that you do not regret it," Nathaniel said.

"I regret that I lost my dearest Friend. Will not you come back to us, Nat?"

"I will not, even for the Love I bear you. I have escaped my Shackles, Tris; I will not put them on again."

"'Tis no Shackle," I protested, "to live a good Life amongst those who love you. What can those damned Gypsies offer you that we cannot?"

"Tristan," Nathaniel said, suddenly catching hold of mine Elbows in a Grip so strong it would not have shamed Saunders Welch, and staring hard into mine Eyes. His Gaze was Firework bright. "Come with me now. Unfasten this Gate, and walk thro' it."

"Oh, Nat! I can't," I said.

"I suppose there is a Mistress." Nathaniel broke his Stare, and rolled his Eyes toward the Sky. I could not help but smile at his

Contempt. "There is inevitably a Mistress. Who is she, Tris? Some Horse-arsed Wench with Dugs like saddle-Panniers and a Cunt like a wool Stocking, out of Shape from daily Use?—or a London poxy-Doxy who hath so skilled her Hand in th'erotick Arts she can no longer unflex all her Fingers? Whoever she is, she doth not deserve you and you should have no Scruple in abandoning her. She will crack your Heart like an Egg over your Head and spear both Testicles upon a toasting Fork; and still she will declare herself unsatisfied."

"There is a Woman," I said. "But she is not at all as you describe."

"Women all," Nathaniel said, "are precisely as I describe, unless they are unnatural Examples of the Species, and the Sex. And all are worthless to you, in the End."

"Who says so?"

"I do; I—along with the sorry Majority of Men upon this stinking, Wench-infested Earth."

"I am not one of them," I said.

"So," Nathaniel said, at last, relinquishing his Hold upon mine Arms. "You will not come. Who is the Lady who holds such Sway over your Prick, and your Heart?"

"I will not give her Name," I answered.

"Cunning, Tris! Cunning! Ah! How I miss your Madness—and your exceptional Wit! But—" he sighed, and stepping backwards from the Gate, regarded me with a Look of affectionate Sadness. "Do not forget," he said, "if ever you have need of me, send Word, and I will put a Girdle round the Globe in forty Minutes."

Exclaiming thus, Nathaniel spun about upon his Heel, and, whistling as merrily as a Goldfinch in the Spring, he began strolling Devil-may-care along the Road, his silver-hilted Sword glinting upon his Hip, and his Hair so dazzling white in the dawn Sunne it could have been spun out of bleached Silk.

"Nat!" I shouted. "Stay! Oh, please, Nathaniel, stay!"

Hearing my Cry, Nathaniel halted, and turned back to regard me with the same amused, exasperated Pity. "I cannot stay," he said, addressing me patiently, as if I were an Idiot or a small Child. "And you will not come, so I must go. There are Laws."

"I don't care a Fig for your damned Laws!" I shouted.

"They are not mine," Nathaniel said. "I must away, and you—you must wake up, Tris."

"Why must you always teaze me? Don't! I am awake!"

Nathaniel shook his Head. "So much Study, yet you remain as great a Booby as you were when you were six. Wake up, Tristan Hart."

He turned from me again, for the final Time; and as he did so, the yellow Sunne upon his Face seemed to me as if it had given it the Appearance of a bare, white, antient Skull. My Senses began to fail. My Surroundings slippt away from me, like Water.

CHAPTER FIVE-AND-TWENTY

I woke to blue Morning. For a Moment, I lay motionless, perplext and confused to have found My Self in Bed, when I had been but Seconds previously in the Grounds. I had not Time to wonder at the Marvell that I had been outside, whither I had not dared set Foot for what seemed to me an Eternity, before the Notion struck me that perchance I had collapsed there, and been brought hither by the Servants, in which case 'twas lucky I had not succumbed to Pneumonia; at which Thought I realised that Katherine had been sleeping in my Chamber, and that if the Servants had brought me within she must have been discovered, and the Game was up. I sate up, casting my Gaze wildly, around me. "Katherine!"

After perhaps a Second, I perceived her, and my panicked Heartbeat slowed in my Chest. She was sitting upon the window Seat, attired once more in my red dressing Gown, and holding in her Hands an open Book. At my Cry, however, she started up, and letting the Book fall to the Floor, she crosst the Bedroom at a Run, arriving at my Bedside with some Violence. "Tristan, you are awake at last!" she cried, throwing her Arms tight about my Neck.

I caught hold of her Biceps, before she could throttle me, and made her to let go. "My Darling," I said. "Let me breathe! What mean you by 'At last'? It can be no later than seven o' the Clock."

"'Tis nine; but you slept so deep that I was afraid . . ." her Voice trailed off.

"I was sleeping? Not gone from the Room?"

"Not that I know of, Bloody Bones."

I rested my Cheek against Katherine's Hair. The Fragrance of the lavender Water, in which I had washed it, perfumed it yet. I could not credit the Likelihood that I had dreamed my Meeting with Nathaniel—but what else could it have been, if I had never left my Bed?

Memory took me to Erasmus' Confession upon the previous Evening: he had told Katherine that I had suffered a nervous Collapse. I thought hard about this, and after a while found My Self wondering at her Loyalty; she had never given up on me in spite of everything, and she had crosst the Country to be at my Side. Had she been frightened, then, when I had seemingly failed to wake? Had she secretly dreaded that I might not?

"Mine Illness," I said eventually, "is most unlike to kill me, excepting that I forget to eat and betimes cannot sleep. I do not believe that I have ever done aught truly dangerous, as have some, who have imagined themselves able to walk on Water or to fly thro' th'Aire. Sometimes I am uncertain in my Senses, and perceive one thing as if it were another; but the Misperception is temporary. When my Senses return, I can see very clearly what is real, and what is nothing but mere Phantasm." I lifted up mine Head. The Morning was clean and sharp against mine Eyes.

Perhaps an half-Houre later—I cannot be certain, for perhaps due to the odd Nature of mine Awakening, Time that Morning seemed to me as formless as a Bone in Vinegar—Katherine, who had returned to her Seat in the Window, ventured: "Tristan, I would love to walk in Shirelands' Grounds. Do you know that I have never properly seen them? When I arrived on Saturdaye it was already dark, and when I came to Dinner the Carriage travelled at such Speed, and Sophy was so provoking, I was able to see almost nothing."

I startled at this Request. "But you cannot leave the Room," I exclaimed.

"I can't stay hidden for ever, 'tis impossible; and anyway, I would hate it in the End."

"You know well I have no Wish to share you, yet," I said. "And my Family will try to send you away."

"But you will not let them, will you, Bloody Bones?"

"I cannot walk outside," I confesst, all on a Sudden overcome by a Panick. My Words tumbled one upon the other.

"Why?" Katherine asked. "Do you fear the Goblins?"

"Worse," I said. "The Goblins are in Pay of the Land, and the Land is what I fear. It knoweth me for a Monster, and hates me accordingly."

"Tristan," Katherine said, circling her Arms about my Chest and looking me direct in mine Eye. "You are no Monster, my dear Sir."

"Not to you, perhaps."

"Well," she said, straightening up. "If you can't go out, then so be it. But I know that the Valley hath no Enmity 'gainst me, and so why might not I walk abroad as I wish?"

"I fear you may be taken in my Stead."

Katherine did not drop her Gaze. "It is my Understanding," she said at last, with surprizing Authority, "that in such Matters no one can be punished for another's Misdeed unless all Parties have agreed it."

"What? How dost know this?" I exclaimed, astonished.

"Somebody once told me. They—you know who I mean when I say *they*—they have Laws. Not Laws of our Kind, that can be broken at will; their Laws are like those by which the Sunne always rises and sets, and doth not turn around halfway; or how falling Objects fall always downwards."

"You speak of Natural Laws," I said, thinking of Newton.

"Yes; Laws that cannot break. And this is such a Law, just such."

"By that Argument," I said, my Rationality becoming engaged by the Debate, despite mine extream Surprize, "you are safe; never would I let Harm come to you, even to save my Life."

The Goblins are gone, I remembered, my Victory coming back to me in a Flash. Gone from Shirelands; whether in Dream or in Body, I have slain them; they mayn't rise again; and as for Raw Head—well, whoever he is, he is not here. And I thought: If Katherine and I are to marry, then I cannot continue to behave as if I were a mad Man. Erasmus Glass hath made that plain enough.

"If you wish to walk in the Gardens todaye, we shall," I forced My Self to say. "I have not dragged you to my grisly Den, that you be never seen again."

Immediately had I these Words spoken, I knew in my Gut that

I was free. Whatever Enemy brooded against me without Shirelands' Gates, it could no longer enter unless I agreed it do so. I was free to walk in mine own family Home, to open up my Windows and breathe in the outside Aire; to step out thro' the great front Door, to tread the Lawns and pass between the high Hedges without Danger, without Fear. I crosst to my Window and on a Whim flung up the Sash. The morning Light danced green and gold upon the Valley of the Horse. Across the Land whispered a soft autumnal Wind, and it carried to me on its Breath the mewing Screech of a far-off Buzzard, high above the many-flowered Chalk. Even if it were unfriendly, I thought, still, 'twas beautifull. Great Joy and great Sorrow, equal in Measure, melted together in my Breast. In my Months-long Terrour of Raw Head, I had forgotten what a Wonder my Valley was, and how deeply I had loved to wander it, with Nathaniel; and the Reminder was like to the Pressure of a Lover's Fingers on a Bruise.

I had sorely missed mine Home, for all that I had thought My Self returned to it.

Turning from the Window, I touched with the Toe of my Shoe that Book which Katherine had previously let fall on the bedroom Floor. I picked it up. To my Surprize, however, I saw that it was not mine at all, but had come from my Father's Library. I dimly recalled that I had carried it hither. But when, and wherefore? I knew the Title; I possesst mine own Copy, locked behind the glass Door of my study Bookcase. It was the Poetry of Donne.

"It falls open by itself, at *The Extasie*," Katherine said. "I like it very much—but it is hard to understand it."

I turned the Volume over in mine Hands.

As 'twixt two equall Armies, Fate
   Suspends uncertaine victorie,
Our soules, (which to advance their state,
   Were gone out,) hung 'twixt her, and mee.
And whil'st our soules negotiate there,
   Wee like sepulchrall statues lay;
All daye, the same our postures were,
   And wee said nothing, all the daye.

On a swift Sudden I seemed to hear my Mother's Voice. Its
Accent was warm and brown as Cinnamon, playful and joyous as
a summer Breeze above the High Chalk. I closed mine Eyes. The
Poëm, in mine Head, continued on. Mine Infant Face lay buried
in her blue, silk-rustling Breast.

This Extasie doth unperplex
   (We said) and tell us what we love,
Wee see by this, it was not sexe,
   Wee see, we saw not what did move:
But as all severall soules containe
   Mixture of things, they know not what,
Love, these mixt soules, doth mixe againe,
   And makes both one, each this and that . . .

When love, with one another so
   Interinanimates two soules,
That abler soule, which thence doth flow,
   Defects of lonelinese controules.
Wee then, who are this new soule, know,
   Of what we are compos'd, and made,

For th'Atomies of which we grow
Are soules, whom no change can invade.

I opened mine Eyes. For a Moment, I felt as if I had intruded upon an Intimacy. My Mother had known this Poem; she had loved it; she had read it aloud by Sunneshine and by guttering Candlelight to my Father, as he sate listening silently, unable to meet her Eye; yet unable still to unthread his own Eyes from her.

Only many Yeares of close Attention could have caused the Pages to fall thus apart. How many hundred Times since her Death had my Father opened up this Book, that he might hear again her Voice? Had she the merest Comprehension of how compleat a Change would invade when she had gone?

My Mother could have lived. Why had she chosen otherwise?

I snapped shut the Book and put it high upon my Mantelpiece.

Having dresst, I went down-Stairs to find Erasmus, with the Intention of explaining to him that as Miss Montague was now to be taken for a Walk about the Gardens, it was imperative that he compleat the Task I had yesterdaye allotted him; viz, the Acquisition of a Sett of Garments appropriate to her Sexe and Station. I found him seated at Breakfast.

He looked up at mine Approach, and smiled. "'Tis good to see you, Tristan. Do you join me?"

"No; I will break my Fast in my Chamber, as usual." I paused, then feeling my Refusal to have been somewhat churlish, I said: "Thank you, Erasmus."

"I was most impresst last Night by your Ideas upon your Father," Erasmus said, before I could say another Word. "If you have any

Suggestions to try with regard to his Care, as you implied you might, I should be interested to hear them."

"Verily, I should be glad," I replied. "But 'tis not the best Time for the Discussion; I am about—" I stoppt abruptly. I knew that Katherine was within my Chamber. I was certain of it. And yet there was some curious, subtile Warning in Erasmus' whole Demeanour that made me to reconsider the Wisdom of my mentioning her to him again. Best I find Cloathing for her by My Self, I thought. Erasmus need not concern himself about the Business; 'twould be a waste of his Time, that is better spent upon my Father. Taking first a deep Breath, I began instead to elucidate my firm Conceit that my Father would respond more positively to Stimulation than to its Lack. I did not succeed in convincing Erasmus that I was right. However, having heard me out, he made the Suggestion that since I was in mine own Self manifestly improved, it might be helpful for us all if I were to visit my Father in his Chamber this very Noon. "There," he said. "You shall make your own clear headed Assessment of his present Condition, which you have not yet done; and you may find that your Ideas are thereby altered."

"I may equally well find them given Encouragement," I said.

We parted company shortly afterwards, Erasmus heading up-Stairs to my Father's Chamber to appraise him, and Mrs H., of my intended Visit; I to my Sister's old Closet. Katherine might look askance at a back-fastening Gown and leading Strings, but since her Choice was to be that or Nakedness I had little Doubt that she would ultimately concur.

However, to my rational Dismay, when I came to the Point of letting Katherine go from my Chamber, I found My Self as incapable of it as I had previously been of leaving the House. My

Disappointment was profound; and Katherine, perceiving from the Intensity of my Passion that mine Inability was neither Test nor Trick, eventually allowed me the Daye's Grace and said that she would see the Gardens on the Morrow, to which I readily agreed.

"I do not wish," I honestly told her, "to keep you Prisoner; but I think I am afraid that you will vanish like Mist in Sunnelight when you depart this Room."

She looked at me very strange at that, and with much Anxiety, and told me in no uncertain Terms that she would not vanish, as she was a flesh and blood Human Girl; and that whoever had put into mine Head the horrible Idea that she might not be deserved the severest of Scoldings, which they would get once she caught up with them. In short, she was exceeding angry; her grey Eyes flashed like folded Steel, and for the first Time ever in her Presence, mine Heart did quail a little in my Breast. I promised most sincerely that I would let her leave my Chamber the following Morning, come what might; and then, it being near to twelve o' the Clock, I departed about my new assumed filial Duty.

Arriving at my Father's Door, Erasmus knocked once to alert Mrs H. The Door opened almost immediately; she must have been listening for us. She stood across the Opening, peering outwards and blinking in the hallway Light as if it were painfull to her old Eyes, and I could not help but think of the Gargoyles upon Collerton Church, keeping timeless Watch over the antient Dead.

The Chamber beyond her was much too dark for me to perceive much, for the Curtains were drawn and the Shutters closed, and the only Light emanated from the one wax Taper that Mrs H. was

clutching in her scrawny Claw. Seeing me, she dippt a small, perfunctory Curtsey, and said: "Good Afternoon, Mr Tristan. Your Father
is ready to see you." Her black Eyes looked quick-sharp to Erasmus,
as if seeking Guidance, and it was not until he had given her a
quiet Nod that she steppt out of the Doorway and I was able to
pass free over its Threshold.

The Aire within was stuffy, tho' quite cool. I pondered with
considerable Distaste what it must have been like over the Summer,
and wondered at my Father, shut up now regardless of his own
Will, intirely away from Light and Aire. Did he perceive the Degree
to which he had come closer to Reunion with my Mother? The
Instant of Death, it seemed, was all that now had Power to divide
them, for both lay entombed. Yet therein I perceived a terrible
Irony, for my Father was not dead, and was not, by Erasmus'
Reckoning, very soon to be so. Instead, I thought, he will persist
in this dimmed Limbo, as good as dead, but neither able nor
permitted to die.

If my Father be conscious, I thought, and cogent, he should by
no Means continue in this daily Situation, lest he become unable
to remember being alive. How can such interminable Silence be
aught but a Barrier to his Recovery?

I took the proffered Candle from Mrs H., and, Erasmus closely
following, moved toward my Father's Bed.

I had expected that he would be lying down, as he had been
upon that horrible Daye when I had seen him spoon-fed, but to
mine intense Relief he was sitting proppt up against a Quantity of
soft Pillows. He was not dresst, but wore over his night-Shirt a
cambrick dressing Gown, and atop his Head a linen Turban in
whose careful Application I discerned the tidy Fingers of his devoted
Nurse. His Countenance appeared askew, for the left Side of his

handsome Face had been severely afflicted, and the Flesh hung limply off his Cheekbone and Jaw. His Skin was tallow white.

For the merest of Instants I felt a Stirring of Fear; then out of mine Anxiety emerged the strange Truth that this Father, however fearfull and freakish he might look, was really far less terrifying than he had been in good Health, and seemed to me all the more human for his Deformity.

"Sir," I said, approaching my Father, as if he had been my Patient. "Sir, it is your Son. It is Tristan."

My Father did not speak; I would not have expected him to do so even had he been in full Health; but his Eyes turned quickly upon me. For a long Second, as they lingered upon my Face, I met his Gaze; for the first Time in my Life I looked properly into those green-grey Orbs that withheld so many Secrets. Then, as always, his Attention slippt away, and hovered in its accustomed Place somewhere over my left Ear.

"You know me," I said. "Canst speak, Sir?"

My Father blinked; a lop-sided Contortion of Distress accosted his Physiognomy. I put the Candlestick down, on the bare Table that stood by the Bed. "You understand me, at least," I said. "Mrs H., doth ever my Father speak?"

"He cannot easily speak, Mr Tristan." For a Moment, Mrs H. appeared somewhat confounded. "He hath Difficulty in forming his Words; tho' sometimes he uses very short ones."

"If he can comprehend and communicate, albeit with Difficulty," I exclaimed, "then he remains a rational Being, and should not continue to be shut away in this Manner. He is an educated and thoughtful Gentleman. Mrs H., why do not you, in all the Houres you spend closeted at his Side, read to him?"

"Lower your Voice, Sir," Erasmus said, interrupting. "It is my

Belief that your Father's Hearing hath become extreamly sensitive. Mine Opinion hath been that he requires total Rest, in order that the Damage that hath been done may have Chance to repair."

"Indeed," I said. "And hath this Stratagem achieved aught?"

"It hath, Sir. His regained Speech. Until recently he could not speak at all."

"Probably," I said, ignoring, in mine Enthusiasm, the plain Fact of my Father's Paralysis, "he refused to speak, for Shame at finding himself crippled, and now hath begun to speak as a Defense against Despair; for that is what this Pitch and Stillness would inspire in me, and I am better used to suffering Illness than he, who hath never endured aught as long as I remember; nay, not even the Influenza."

"Draw Breath, Tristan," Erasmus said, gently, but with a warning Tone. "You shall make your own Assessment, and welcome; but do not upset your Father."

"Egad," I said. "I know not how I am to make any physical Assessment in such Darkness, for I can barely see. Mrs H., for God's Sake pull back those damned Draperies and let in a little Light!"

Mrs H. looked toward Erasmus, who shook his Head. I remembered then, with a small Jolt, how he had stood up for me against Dr Oliver, when the Latter would have pursued a Path of Care that would have proved injurious to mine Health. Now he stood up between me and my Father, and I knew both that he believed that he was right and that he would never back down without substantial Change in that Conviction. But I was equally convinced of the Rectitude of mine own.

"Erasmus," I said quietly. "There is much to be said in Favour of Containment and Rest. I do not dispute that at the Onset of his Affliction these were appropriate Treatments. But I am certain that my Father's Recovery will now be advanced by an increasing Contact with the real World."

I stoppt abruptly. His Recovery from what? I thought. From this Stroake, or that of my Mother's Death?

"Well," Erasmus said. "What Forms, Sir, do you propose that this Contact should take?"

"Lord," I exclaimed. "I suggested Reading, which hath always been his Pleasure, so let us begin with that. Mrs H. shall select a Number of Volumes from his Library, and read to him. Moreover, there must be an End to this oppressive Darkness. Bring back the Light as gradually as you will; but bring it back, even if at first he is resistant to its Introduction. I do not ask that you be cruel, Sir; but sometimes, as you certainly remember from our Time together in the Hospitals, it is neccessary to cause Discomfort or even Pain in order to help heal an Injury."

Erasmus regarded me thoughtfully; then his Gaze shifted to my Father. Mine followed.

That Gentleman's Expression, or as much of it as could clearly register in Eyes alone, I perceived to be as full of Dread as had been that of Lady B.—— before Dr Hunter had begun his Operation. Suddenly, an astonishing Conception dawned upon my Faculties. My Father was afraid of me.

Verily, 'twas so; verily, I apprehended that it had been so for a good many Yeares, and I, caught up in mine own Preoccupations and distracted by my Fear of him, had never once discerned it. Yet it was so. I realised that my Mouth had fallen open. I shut it up. My Father, afraid of me? It was a compleat Reversal of the natural Order of things. Surely, I knew well that the Child ought to fear his Parent, but I had never thought that a Parent might fear his Child. Why should he?

Had the Rector feared Nathaniel?

"I think it Time this Visit ended," Erasmus said. "Tho' if you and Mr Hart are both willing, Tristan, you may return the Morrow, or the Daye after. I will give Consideration to your Ideas regarding the Light. But as to Reading," he smiled, "I think that is a Task better suited to yourself than to Mrs H."

"My Self?"

"Without Doubt," Erasmus said. "I am sure Mrs H. doth not disagree; I very much doubt, Madam, that you have any Knowledge of Latin, or Greek?"

Mrs H. sniffed. "I should think, Mr Glass, that I most certainly do not!" From the Tone in which she answered, Erasmus might, I thought, have been suggesting that she had been a Prostitute.

Erasmus and I made our Excuses to my Father, who made no Attempt to speak, tho' I was certain he had understood. Then we left the Chamber.

"So, Tristan," Erasmus said, turning to me with a Smile as we progressed down the Stairs. "Tomorrow, if you will, you may begin your Treatments, and we will discover what their Effects, if any, shall be."

Verily we shall, I thought. Upon my Father's Recovery, and upon mine own.

CHAPTER SIX-AND-TWENTY

As the Government, unsatisfied by its Remove of New Year from March to January, had in its infinite Sagacity decided surgically to excise eleven Dates from the Month of September, the next Morning fell that many whole Dayes after the Evening preceding it. It remained, however, still Thursdaye. On this Occasion, however, the Dislocation did not disorient me one Whit, and I felt a certain Pleasure at the Thought that Human Time, at least as it was ordered by the present Calendar, was in its own Stile quite as flexible as that of the Faeries.

Katherine awoke in a tetchy Mood, and dashing away mine Attempt to share mine Enjoyment in the Mutability of the Date, demanded I tell her straightway when she should be permitted out of her Cell. When I could not answer to her Satisfaction, and warned her, moreover, that I must leave her alone again for another Houre or so whilst I helped Erasmus with my Father, she became thoroughly vexed, and raised her Voice. I tried to suppress her with mine Hand over her Mouth, but in the End I had to vow to leave her in Charge of my Keys before she would be shut up.

"Don't worry, Bloody Bones, I will not vanish," she said, with some Scorn. "But I can't bear this Incarceration any longer. Merely the Thought that I might now leave the Room if I wished will ease my Mind sufficiently that I shall willingly stay and bear your Absence until you see fit to return. But then, my Dear, you must let your Household know that I am here and introduce me to Mr Glass, you must. We shall tell him I am new arrived from Weymouth."

The Altercation being thus concluded, I returned, with Erasmus, to my Father's Chamber, and with very little ado settled My Self to read to him by the Light of the Candle. Mrs H. departed about her other Duties and a Quietness fell. I looked into my Father's Face and watched with a peculiar Relief as his Eyes stubbornly refused to meet mine own and settled, as ever, above mine Ear. I opened the *Aeneid*, and began to sing Arms, and the Man, exiled by Fate from the Shores of Troy.

The Houre till Noon passed peaceably. I could not tell for certain whether my Father was attending to Virgil, or even to the Sound of my Voice, but I felt very strongly inclined to believe that he was, and said so to Erasmus. Mine Instinct that he would benefit from the Stimulation was encouraged. Moreover, I thought, with great Relief, I had not seen any Sign of that Apprehension that had convulsed his Countenance upon my previous Visit. It had begun to matter to me marvellous much that he should not endure any such Sentiment. I read on, well past Noon, until I heard the hall Clock chiming the three quarter-Houre. Then, I stoppt. The Clock's Bell having restored me to mine own Century, I had suddenly become aware of another Sett of Sounds: a violent Disturbance, of a female Nature, echoing from the down-Stairs Portion of the House. Erasmus had heard it also. He frowned, and rising to his Feet, suggested that he should go down to uncover the Cause whilst I remained with my Father.

"No, no," I said. "Whatever 'tis, it is within mine House, and is therefore my Responsibility. I shall go."

But as I spoke these Words, the Noises below increased in both their Pitch and Volume, and of the Identity and Source of the Discord there could no longer be any Doubt. My coward Heart quaked within my Breast.

Mine Aunt Barnaby was come, the Evil I had so greatly dreaded was upon us; and she was shrieking at the top of her shrill Lungs at my poor, ill-deserving Katherine.

"Marry, shall you? Marry, you shall not! Oh, I shall see you in a Bridewell first. Thou vile Wench, thou jumped-up Hussy, thou wicked Fortune-hunting little Minx, I shall see thee dead before I let thee touch a Farthing of my Family's Money, a Farthing, dost attend?"

There was a brief Hiatus, as mine Aunt, presumably, was forced to draw Breath. Her Voice had been growing steadily louder during this Harangue, and suddenly I realised, to mine intense Horrour, that this was not because she was screeching any more loudly, but because she was rapidly drawing closer. Her Footsteps rattled the Staircase.

Erasmus stared at me. "Surely she cannot be—" he began, astonished.

Then I heard Katherine's Voice, sharply upraised in Anger. I froze, like an affrighted *Manes*; and Erasmus could not help but do likewise, for it appeared to both of us that we heard a very Fury.

"How dare I? How dare you? You evil minded Hag, I would wed Tristan Hart without a Farthing, and be twice as quick! How dare you think you can insult me, because you have Money, and I none? You call me low, you dare to call me Creature—Bah! It is you who are low, for all your Silks and Wiggery, with your filthy Accusations and your foul Names. Faugh! You make me puke! If I thought you were a Lady, I would never want to be one—and if 'tis Money that hath made you the low Creature that you are, I would rather die a Pauper!"

"Wicked Strumpet!" screamed mine Aunt. "What, chide thy Betters, bold as Brass? Oh, every Name I have called thee hath been richly deserved—there is none bad enough! Thou shouldst not presume even to tell me todaye's Date! Thou Slattern, thou Whore, thou vicious, conniving little Bitch!"

"She is here?" Erasmus cried. "Verily, Katherine Montague is here?"

"Why hath she left my Chamber?" I cried. "She promised that she would wait!" I leapt to my Feet. "She will strike her, for sure!" I meant that I feared mine Aunt would strike Katherine; in truth, I ought to have been more afraid that Katherine might readily, and with justifiable Provocation, have struck mine Aunt; but my Concern was only for her.

Erasmus had the Look of a Man who hath been struck by Lightning. Nonetheless, by sheer Force of Willpower mastering his Amazement, he took a deep Breath and got to his Feet, and saying: "Stay where you are. I will put a Stop upon this," he started towards the Doorway.

Mine Aunt, however, prevented him. Precisely as Erasmus

reached the Door—which I felt certain he was bitterly regretting that he had not locked—it collapsed with such Violence that it might have been blown inwards by a powder Keg. Mine Aunt Barnaby filled the Frame.

She had, evidently, received the incendiary News of mine Attachment halfway thro' her Toilette, for she had come away with her Face whiteleaded but her Wigg un-stiled, and the Effect was as startling as it was ridiculous. The squat and shapeless thing that writhed untidily upon her shaven Head resembled, to mine Eyes, a Nest of Serpents, writhing and bound in bloody Fillets about a Visage as stark white as a death Mask. She had, however, succeeded in getting herself fully dresst, and was clad in a red damask Gown of such extream width that she was broader than she was tall.

Erasmus stood petrified for a Second, quite aghast; then, automatically, he fell back as mine Aunt turned her terrifying Gaze upon me, and keeping her Head intirely still, swivelled her Body so that she might enter side-ways thro' the Doorway, which was otherwise too narrow for her Hoop. She pushed her Skirts into the Room, followed, and then, raising her index Finger to point it straight at me, she screeched: "Tristan!"

I stared at her, mute with Astonishment. Then a Movement behind her caught mine Eye; Katherine, determined not to be left out, appeared in the Frame. Our Eyes met; she opened her Mouth to speak; then all at once she disappeared, as if pulled thence by an unseen Hand.

"Madam!" said Erasmus, recovering himself and stepping between mine Aunt's imposing Finger and My Self. "This is a sick Room. You must leave immediately."

"Leave!" exclaimed mine Aunt Barnaby, drawing herself up to her fullest, and looking down upon Erasmus with unmitigated

Contempt. "Who dost thou, little Man, think that thou art to order me to leave? This was my Father's House! I grew up here! I will neither leave, Mr Glass, nor will I be given Instruction by a mere Servant. Lud! 'Tis high Time there was Order in this House! Tristan Hart, mad tho' you are, you shall not marry with this Vixen, this Chit, this ill-bred Pauper! I did not intend, when I admitted that you were not like to marry well, that you should marry badly! You shall not marry at all! I will not have it! First my Brother, and now his Son, bringing God knows what Creatures beneath my poor dead Father's Roof, polluting mine Home, bringing Disgrace and Shame upon my Family's Name. I will not have it, do you hear? I will not have it!"

Mine Aunt had thoroughly lost her Temper. She was angrier than I had ever seen her, and I was certain that beneath the Whitelead her Face was as scarlet as her Dress. Nevertheless, I could tell that she was not even one half-Quart as furious as was Katherine, whom I could now see again, within the Doorway but blocked from entering the Chamber by the enormous Hoop, violently struggling with Mrs H., tho' her Eyes were fixt upon me. The Housekeeper had seized hold of her Arm, and appeared to be remonstrating with her in an urgent Manner.

"Oh," exclaimed my Father, quietly. I looked down. In the Confusion occasioned by the sudden Arrival of his Sister, mine Attention had been all upon her, not upon him; and I had not known that he had opened wide both his Eyes and turned his Head full to behold the Spectacle currently in Performance at the Foot of his Bed. His Expression was not clear to me, but despite that I sensed, radiating from him as if it were invisible Light, a sudden, terrible Anger.

For one panicked Second I thought his Anger to have been with me. He fears me, I thought; and suddenly that aweful Fact loomed with a Relevance and Import that I had hitherto ignored. Surely, he will cast me off. I will lose all: my Station, my Fortune, mine Home, my Family. Katherine and I will be forced onto Charity; and her Relations hate her, and have naught anyway to give. Oh, pray God, no! No! I must work. I will go to Dr Hunter and plead with him to find me an Apprenticeship despite mine Illness. I will do anything, anything. I will not send my Katherine away.

Katherine appeared again, quiet now, tho' her Face was anything but still, within the Doorway. Our Eyes locked. How I love her, I thought anew.

My Father drew Breath. Then, into the brief and fragile Silence which succeeded upon mine Aunt Barnaby's Outburst and his small Exclamation, he pronounced three, very short, Words; the clearest I had ever heard him speak.

"Fuck off, Ann."

There was no doubting his Sincerity, or his Comprehension. Verily, my Father understood, and understood compleatly, what he meant; and he spoke, moreover, with such ferocious Profundity that it seemed as if the Words had sate frustrated on his Tongue for Decades. So great was his Clarity, so undeniable his Force, that I was, at once, the more astonished by his habitual Silence, for it seemed to me an Impossibility that a Man possesst of so potent a Spleen would have been able, much less would have chosen, to constrain it.

A long Silence followed my Father's Words. Then Erasmus, as always the first to recover, cleared his Throat. "Mrs Barnaby," he said. "With all due Respect, you must do as Mr Hart directs."

Mine Aunt's Mouth had fallen intirely open; she did not appear to be able to hear Erasmus. I did not suppose, given her previous

Choice of Words, that it had been my Father's Vocabulary that had proved so very shocking. It had been the mere Fact of his shewing Resistance; as long as I could remember, he had never before stood up to her once she had begun to set about him. Then the Thought struck me that she had not, in truth, set about him; her Ire had been directed quite at me, and he had stood up to her on my Behalf.

"John?" whispered mine Aunt.

My Father made an incomprehensible Noise that might have been an Attempt at complex Speech, but, equally, might not, and turned his Attention stubbornly toward the Wall.

On my Behalf! Mine Heart began to pound. "My Father hath nothing to say to you, Mrs Barnaby," I said. "Nor have I. I shall not forswear mine Understanding with Miss Montague and I heartily detest and repudiate the Insult of your Conduct toward her, of which, Madam, I must tell you that I am deeply ashamed."

Mine Aunt's Expression, which had seemed something sorry, and perplext, when she had looked upon my Father, hardened instantly at mine Interruption. Her blue Eyes turned turquoise; she did not speak.

All on a sudden mine Imagination perceived, with an aweful Certainty, what it was that mine Aunt, in that same Instant, perceived in me; and I knew without Doubt that it was neither her Brother nor her own beloved Father, but someone alien: my Mother. I looked like a Jew.

Mine Aunt was Lady B.——, was Foremother to every Woman in my Life who ever had turned her Countenance from me in Distaste of my dark Skin, mine Hair, mine Eyes. She was Nero's Mother, as surely as she was James Barnaby's. Hers were the Perceptions, hers the Prejudices, that had encouraged Joseph Cox to demand of Margaret Haynes whether I was all over stained with tawny. And I remembered, without Shock or Sadness, but with a Flash of Comprehension, the numberless Punishments to which she had subjected me when I had been a Boy. Childhood, she had insisted, was the State of Original Sin, and the Devil must be beaten out else he refuse to leave; but it had not been Sin she had perceived upon my Physiognomy. Because mine Hair was black, mine Eyes also, because my Skin was olive and my Nose hooked like an Hawk's, I had been falsely condemned straight out of my Mother's Womb, and with no Hope of a Repeal.

But my Father, my shy, secretive brown Wren of a Father, who could not bring himself to meet another Man's Eyes, who could not, in normal Circumstance, speak above a muttered Monotone, felt no such Prejudice. If he feared me, he feared me not for that. Because when he had been but one-and-twenty he had shewn the Courage to look beneath the Surface, and to love the Quality he had therein discovered, and I was the Result: Eugenia's Heir, with her Looks and her Perspicacity; and whether for that, or for mine own Sake, my Father, also, loved me.

It was a stunning Thought.

"Get out," I said to mine Aunt Barnaby. "My Father hath every Right never to allow you to set Foot within this House again. Mr Glass will see you to your Carriage."

Mine Aunt made me no Reply; but her Position being intirely without Defense, she perhaps thought it better to attempt none. She bestowed one last, bewildered, outraged Look upon her Brother, and then, recalling something of her Dignity, she rotated slowly upon the Spot and steppt crabwise into the Hallway, to which Katherine had retreated, still in Mrs H.'s protecting—or restraining—Embrace.

Mine Aunt Barnaby stared at her; a slow Stare of such pure, petrifying Venom that mad Discord might momentarily have become the Medusa. She raised her right Hand high, as if to ring a Blow about Katherine's Ears.

"You will not!" I shouted.

I did not know whether she had heard me, or if merely she thought the better of her Inclination, but mine Aunt lowered her Fist. "Marry!" she spat. "A fine Wife she will make you, I am sure!"

"What is todaye's Date, Miss Montague?" I said. "Wilt tell Mrs Barnaby? She thinks you are not good enough to tell her. I tell you, 'tis the fourteenth."

"I shall," Katherine said. "Truly, Madam, it is the fourteenth of September."

Mine Aunt drew herself up to her greatest Height, once more, and turned her Stare upon me in Disgust. "Ridiculous and absurd Boy," she said, with withering Contempt. "I see you wilt choose a Shrew who is as crazy as yourself! Katherine indeed! You must make her avow the Sunne the Moon and stamp upon her Cap! Any one of sense would have known 'tis the third." Turning sharp on her crimson Heel, she strode out of my Sight.

Erasmus, after a Second or so, bowed in an hurried Manner to my Father and quitted the Room, presumably to do as I had directed and see mine Aunt Barnaby securely off the Premises. I hoped that she would not abuse him; the whole Affair was none of his Business, much less any of his Fault. Katherine, seeing him and mine Aunt both departed, tore herself at last free from Mrs H.'s Arms, and ran into the Chamber. Then, at the Foot of my Father's Bed, she stoppt, all of a Sudden caught by an hesitant Uncertainty. Her Gaze met mine, and for an Instant I thought that she would throw herself upon me; but then her Eyes fell instead upon my Father.

That Gentleman had turned his Head again that he might look with Ease upon the Doorway and all Proceedings thither, and his Attention seemed to have impresst itself upon a Locus some six Inches from Katherine's left Hand. His Mouth moved, silently, wordlessly, as he battled to form his reluctant Countenance into the Shapes he desired of it. Finally, after an half-Minute or more of terrible Struggle, he gave it up; his Strivings ceased, his Features fell still.

Katherine looked at me in silent Horrour, her Fingers presst close against her Lips, as if she were stifling a Cry. Mrs H. took her by the Arm. "Come away, Miss," she said. "You must not see the Master in such a State."

"Damn good Piece," said my Father, with dazzling Clarity.

Mrs H. started violently. Her Lips blanched, and the Muscles of her Cheekbones became instantly as rigid as if she had been upon the Spot turned into Marble.

Very short Words, I thought. "Mrs H.," I said, sharply. "Doth he always communicate in such Vulgarities?"

Mrs H.'s fixt Expression crumbled. For a few Seconds I thought that she would give me no Reply. Then Tears welled up in her old Eyes, and she nodded, furtively, as if she did not want to acknowledge her own Experience. "Oh, Master Tristan," she said. "He doth, and I am sorry, so sorry, to have to hear them—for as long as I have known him, he hath been the very best of Gentlemen, and hath held himself so far above any Profanity as I had thought him to have been beyond their Knowledge."

"Plainly," I said, "he is not. Release Miss Montague's Person and let her come to me."

I held out mine Hand for Katherine to join me. My Thoughts were working, furiously, and fast. As she approached, I turned mine

Attention to my Father, and studied his Eyes. As I had hoped, they followed her, fluttering about her left Hand in the Manner of an half-wild Bird, that knows Nourishment to be contained within the closed Palm, but hath seen its Fellows in the Clap-Net, and is thus too wary ever to become tame.

Katherine reaching my Side, I took up her left Hand firm within mine own, and pressing it to my Breast, looked from my Father's ravaged Face into her beautifull one.

Mine Heart leapt up in my Throat. I swallowed, and cast my Gaze once more unto my Father. "Sir," I said, "this is Miss Katherine Montague, whom I love most dear, and with whom I would be married, as soon as shall be. May we have your Blessing, Father?"

For a long Moment, he was silent. Then I discerned within his Look the Beginning of a second Struggle, of the same Kind as the first. He tries to speak, I thought. He tries to use the Language and the Terms to which he, as well as we, have been accustomed; but he cannot, and the Difficulty lies not only in his Paralysis; no, no; the Ideas themselves are too subtile, and the damaged Channels in his Brain cannot contain them; yet when he useth the vulgar Tongue, the Words do not escape him, being made of coarser Stuff, and therefore he is capable of Speech. He doth not intend Offense; he doth not intend aught but to communicate.

At length, and as before, the Battle ceased. My Father's Gaze took Flight from Katherine's Hand, and brushed, soft, like a wing Tip, over her Face. "Bang up," my Father said. "Hellish fine."

"Thank you," I said. "Thank you, Sir."

CHAPTER SEVEN-AND-TWENTY

Less than a Minute after this wonderfull Dispensation, Erasmus Glass returned, and insisted that we quit my Father's Chamber, which had seen, he said, enough Excitement for a Month, let alone an Houre. Refusing to let Mrs H. be the Exception, he conveyed us all down the Stairs in one Party and straight into the Library. He crossed to my Father's Desk, and immediately poured himself a generous Measure of Brandy from a large Flask.

"Madam," he said, addressing Katherine. "What, for the Love of Heaven, are you doing here?"

"She is new arrived from Weymouth," I returned quickly.

"That, Master Tristan, is a Lie," said Mrs H. She turned to Erasmus, her Words spilling out in a great Flood. "I am very sorry, Mr Glass, but Miss arrived three Nights ago, at least, for Mr Green told me then he'd sent away a Beggar from the Door, and I thought nothing of it until Jakes found her soiled Cloathing the Morning after, and knew not what she ought do about it. Where she hath been hiding since then I don't know, but 'twas somewhere within the House."

"Mrs H.," I said, sharply. "Prithee, do not call my Bride 'Miss' or we shall have a Quarrel, in which you will come off worst. Miss Montague hath been . . ." I hesitated, for I had already told the Truth to Erasmus, who was now staring at Katherine as if he were now as much inclined to disbelieve the Evidence of his own Senses as previously he had been to discredit mine. "She hath been in my Sister's Chamber," I finished.

"My Good God," Erasmus murmured.

"Well," I said, with a Shrug. "There is the whole Matter of it."

"Lud!" exclaimed Mrs H., shaking her grey Head. "For Shame, Master Hart! And as for you, Miss—Miss Montague—but never mind. You must be hungry and thirsty, having been hiding out for half a Week living on Scraps from Master Tristan's Plate. Why did not you come to me? I wouldn't have turned you out."

"I must repeat my Question to Miss Montague," Erasmus said. "Miss Montague, were you not informed, by Lt. Simmins, that Mr Hart had become extreamly ill, and told of the Nature of his Affliction?"

"Yes," Katherine answered.

"Yet you saw fit to leave your Uncle's Guardianship and travel here, alone, knowing that you must put yourself into grave Danger, to arrive without Warning and—I need not continue. I should like to know your Reason, Madam, for compleatly disregarding my clear Advice to remain precisely where you were?"

"You are not my Master," Katherine said.

"I am Mr Hart's Physician."

"Yes," she answered, jutting out her Chin. "And a pissing poor one!" Her lower Lip began to tremble.

"Hush, Brat," I said, putting my left Palm on her Shoulder.

"And Mrs Henderson," Erasmus said, his Tone increasing in Incredulity with every Word. "When—when was it, two Dayes ago?—you realised that there was a Stranger hiding in the House, why, for the Love of God, did you not come at once to me with your Suspicions?"

"I'm sorry, Mr Glass, but I didn't know what to do for the best," Mrs H. replied, wringing her Hands. "I guessed—I thought—I hoped, Sir, it must be Miss Montague. I know how Master Tristan adores her, Sir, for hasn't he spoke of little else all thro' his—his Wanderings? I thought that mayhap if it were Miss Montague, then having her here might make Master Tristan well again. I thought there was no Harm in playing along with them for a Daye or two, and that I should find her before there was any Trouble."

"Trouble?" Erasmus laughed harshly. "As to Trouble, the Fat's in the Fire now, and no Mistake. Not only may Mr Hart get married, but he must, or Miss Montague's Reputation shan't be worth a Fig. By God, Tristan, you ought not to have done this."

I felt this Accusation to be deeply unfair. "I told you Miss Montague was here, Erasmus," I reminded him. "You would not believe me. And this Row with mine Aunt Barnaby is no Fault of mine. You wrote to apprize her of my Wish to marry, did not you, even tho' I warned you how she would react?"

This Memento appeared to give Erasmus Pause, and he sate down, very suddenly, upon an heavy Chair behind my Father's Escritoire. "I wrote your Sister, not your Aunt," he sighed. "As we

agreed I should. But you warned me, yes; both things; you did."
The Wind had droppt out of his Sails; he fell silent.

"Might I go, Mr Glass?" Mrs H. asked, somewhat timidly. "I
daren't leave the Squire for long, Sir."

"Yes, Mrs H., you may leave." Erasmus ran his Hand distractedly
thro' his Hair and took a deep Draught of my Father's Brandy. He
looked up, and seeing My Self and Katherine still standing, all on
a sudden cried: "Begone too, Tristan, and Miss Montague besides!
All of you, go, go! Egad! If there is one sane Person in this whole
Household, it is not any one of us!"

I took Katherine's small white Hand in mine own, and we hastily
departed.

It transpired that Katherine's Disobedience in leaving my Chamber
had not been her Fault, for, several of the Maids arriving to strip
the Bed in mine Absence, she had almost been discovered, and had
fled in the Direction of my Study. Upon the Stairs, she had unfortunately been intercepted by Mrs H., and then by mine Aunt, who
had been at that Moment ascending them in a furious Passion at
the Newes of mine affectionate Attachment, which Barnaby had
brought her whilst her Abigail had been dressing her Wigg. I did
not scold her, for her Action had brought about a marvellous
Result. For the first Time in my Life I had clear Proof of my
Father's Love; and Katherine was to be my Wife within the Week.
Wild Excitement, irresistible as elfin Musick, whisked me up, and
forced me to caper to its Strains; a fast and complex Dance of
Doubles and Setts and Turns as each Phrase was repeated twice,
and then began anew, as in *Argeers*; until I had danced Katherine
off her Feet, and driven Mrs H. to Distraction. The Houre being

then late, Erasmus quietly insisted that I take a Dose of Laudanum, and go to Bed.

My Conviction being unchanged toward that Drugge, I refused. Erasmus persisted, and eventually wrung out of me the Concession that I would return to my Study with the declared Intent of there remaining as silent as a Mouse; altho' I did not expect that I should be. I took up Locke, but finding it impossible to concentrate upon him, fetched Quill and Paper—tho' I confess I did not expect any more Success in this Endeavour than the other. I let my Mind run free and mine Hand scribe whatever Ideas might associate in mine Head, and I gradually fell into an intense Consideration of my Father's Case: the plain and evident Fact of his Cogency; his immediate Acceptance of Katherine; his disturbing Inability to express himself in the Language of civilised Men.

What, I scribbled, is happening within his injured Brain when he begins to speak?

I could not understand how one Manner of clear formed Thought, to wit, the Words my Father desired to use, could not arrive upon his Tongue when coarse Vulgarities came as ready as the Rhetoric of Cicero. I was certain that his Ejaculations were not as the Barking of a Dogg, automatic, as Descartes would have it. My Father knew what he was saying, and, moreover, what he meant. His Reason was undamaged. And yet, I thought, was it not evidence of an Injury to the Mind that he could not pronounce the Words that, I thought, took shape within it. Was it truly Words in which he now thought, or simply Ideas, unchisselled, unformed? Yet these Ideas, surely, were not brutish. My Father had never been, and surely was not now, a brutish Man. Moreover, there was the terrible Struggle I had witnessed him undergoing every Time he had been forced to speak—except todaye, when he had dismisst mine Aunt. Plainly, his Ideas were civilised, but the Stroake had deprived him of the Language by which he might have expresst them. It seemed to me somehow to be a thing of profound Import that, if civilised Speech was beyond him, but not civilised Thought, the vulgar Tongue was become the Medium in which he made manifest his Ideas. The Notion put me in Mind of the Almighty's Creation of Adam out of base Matter; if such thing, I thought, had ever taken place.

I looked down. I had written: What is Thought? What is its Substance?

At once I noticed, thro' the nocturnal Silence, how loudly ticking was the Clock upon my Mantelpiece. I recalled my long ago Conversation with Dr Hunter about the Workings of the Nerves, and my Perception that the Cadaver in front of me was naught but a broken Clock; my Conclusion that a living Man must be somehow more than this; that he had a Mind, a Soule. I remembered Dr Oliver applying his Trepan to the Skull of the Lunatick, saying: "Once the corrupt Matter hath been excised, we can hope that the Corruption in his Reason shall have been also, and his Mind set aright." I remembered my grave Doubts regarding Trepanation, and my later Conversation with Erasmus in which I had learned this rational Doubt had played me false. I recalled my Notion regarding Pain, and its Existence as a Mode of Thought; mine Hypothesis that sensitive Thought may run thro' the intire Body along the nervous Filaments; and I realised that never, in all this Doubting and theoretical Questioning, had I queried Descartes' Conclusion that the Mind is a non-material Substance.

Now I wondered at it; now I asked, how could it be? Mine Heart began to pound so hard within the Casement of my Ribs I feared it should break free; for I perceived at once a terrifying Answer.

Thought hath, or Thought is, a material Substance. How else could it be shaped into a Word? How else could it be affected by a physical Event such as a Stroake?—for if I am certain of anything it is that Stroake is not the Work of Faeries. Being material, it exists in a material State within the Brain, and runs indeed thro'out the Nerves of the physical Body, and it may materially be disturbed by Injury or by Sickness or by the Workings of some Drugge. La Mettrie was right; Man is a Machine. Reason hath Extension, Form, Shape. It hath Limit.

Can Reason, God-given Reason, have Limit? My Limbs began to shake. Ink spattered the virgin Paper.

If, I thought, Reason hath Limitation, then a Man's Reason hath no more special a Significance than his Digestion, or the Circulation of his Blood. And if Matter may think, if Matter may be conscious, or may have Conscience, who is to say that a Tree might not possess Awareness, or even a base Rock? What separateth an Human Being from a Red Kite, or a Willow? 'Twould be naught but a Question of Degree.

Cogito, ergo sum, Descartes said. My Thoughts prove my Conscience, prove mine Existence, Moment by Moment, to My Self. Surely, the Mind did not equate with the Soule. But if, I thought, there is no non-material Mind, it may be that there is no Self, no non-material Soule to which this may be proved; for nothing material may imply the Existence of anything other. If the Soule truly were non-physical, the material Mind would not be able to interact with it at all; it might as well be nothing; for from nothing mental, neither Pain nor Conscience nor Love, might be drawn any Inference that a non-physical thing exists. But the Soule cannot be a physical thing, for then it could not survive physical Death.

I droppt my Quill.

Abandoning my Scribbling, I curled My Self into a small Ball on my Sopha, and hid my Face behind my Knees. The Candles, untended, burned down, and the Room fell into Darkness. My Creatures were still. Dr Oliver, in my Memory, lifted the bone Sovereign from the Cranium of the Melancholick. The Clock ticked on.

For a long Time I lay curled thus. The dreadful Implication permeated my Veins. If there was no non-material Soule, then there was no Place, no Place at all for God or Christ or Religion the whole World over; 'twas a great Lie; Christ's Sacrifice was without Meaning, for there was nothing that might be saved, and neither Heaven, nor Hell. Perhaps, verily, really, there was no Soule, and no God, none, none. I felt the small Hairs rise up on the Nape of my Neck.

Mine Heartbeat began to grow stronger, louder, until it drummed in mine Head, each Beat one with the Clock. Blood circulated thro' the Tissues of my Body, swishing in mine Ears like the distant Echo within a Seashell. I thought upon its Progress thro' the Channels of my Liver and my Brain. Is Man a Machine? Is Thought nothing but the Sounds made by the Movement of the Mechanism?

As the Minutes passed, I began slowly to remember those Thoughts I had entertained the other Daye, about my Father, and the Love he had shared with my Mother, in which God had played not the merest Part. That Love had been, and still was, real, despite her Death; and even tho' John and Eugenia might never meet again in any sort of Heaven, it remained of itself a wondrous thing, a thing that seemed to give me Hope that there was some Species of Soule in Man, even if 'twere not the immortal one of Christian Catechism. Surely a Machine was no more capable of Love than of experiencing Pain?

Could the Soule exist without God? How could it? And wherefore should it?

My Forehead throbbed. Carefully, I stretched out mine Arms and uncoiled my Spine. My Frame cried out in Protest at this unexpected Release from its Confinement; Elbows cracking, loud as snapping Twigs upon a Lightning-scorched Oak.

Katherine and I were married on the Saturdaye Morning, before my Father, Erasmus Glass, and as many of the household Servants who could be spared their Duties for the Duration. Neither my Sister, nor her Husband, nor mine Aunt were in Attendance. I was not surprized by this, but I sorely regretted Jane's Absence, which I had no Doubt was her Mother-in law's doing, despite the facile Excuse that Jane was too near to her Confinement to risk travelling even the shortest Distance from Withy Grange.

To everyone's Amazement, two Dayes after he had given me his Blessing, my Father made it striking clear that, notwithstanding the Difficulties such a Venture must entail, he was determined to be present at my wedding Ceremony, as he had been at Jane's. It being impossible that he should visit Church, and neither Katherine nor My Self desiring that our Nuptials should take place in his sick Room, we fixt upon the Idea of holding the Wedding in the drawing Room, with the Curtains drawn and a few small Candles burning for the Benefit of those of us whose Eyes were not so painfully sensitive. This Particular having been thus settled, and the Rector having consented to perform the Service, I spent much of the intervening Time in encouraging my Father to quit his Bed for an Armchair. Erasmus voiced Reservations regarding the likely Success of this Enterprize, but he had reckoned without my Father's Stubbornness, and to everyone's Delight, upon my wedding Daye he was able to sit, nigh invisible in the dimmest Corner of the drawing Room, dresst all over in his customary Black and with his Virgil open on his Lap as a Defense against anyone who might have tried to speak to him.

I knew My Self to be deeply happy that I was to wed the Woman whom I loved. But I could not rouse My Self to experience in my Body and mine Heart the Joy I knew within mine Head, and which I witnessed upon Katherine's Face every Time she looked into mine own. I struggled hard to comprehend the Reason for this Lack, and even harder to conceal it, but I was afraid that in neither Assay was I quite successful. I could not put away those Suspicions I had formed regarding God and Matter; and everything, when illumined by their low burning Lampe, seemed somewhat flat, like the Aspect of a Landscape underneath a leaden Sky. The more I pondered upon this obscure Disconnexion betwixt my Feelings and mine Heart, the wider it grew; until for Fear of mine own Sanity I determined that my Ponderings must surcease.

Some little while after the short Ceremony, I was standing, a Glass of Burgundy in mine Hand, by the Fireplace, where my new Bride and I had been receiving the humble Congratulations of Shirelands' Servants. My Father had retired to Bed; the Curtains had been pulled open, the Windows thrown up, and the Candles put out. I had declared the Afternoon a Holidaye, and the middaye drawing Room was empty apart from My Self, Katherine, Erasmus, and the Rector. The Rector having been, in accordance with Tradition, first in Line to have offered his stilted Compliments, I was suspicious of his Choosing to linger after my Father had gone. I suggested to Katherine that I would like it very much if she were to play *Greensleeves* on the Harpsichord, and she, suspecting nothing, went happily to.

Perceiving now that my Bride, his Niece, was out of Earshot, the Rector Ravenscroft once more came forward, his portly Shoulders rounded beneath his Cassock, and square Jaw thrust forward like a bellicose Bulldogg. Altho' the Weather was not excessive warm, he appeared to sweat. His Jowls quivered, and I remembered, once again, the savage Thrashing he had given me in his Orchard, so many Yeares before. Staring down into his Eyes, I seemed to feel again the pudgy Clamp of his left Hand upon my Neck, to hear the laboured Heaving of his Breath.

"I disapprove," the Rector said, "of these irregular Marriages, and 'tis only out of Regard for your worthy Father that I consented to officiate at yours. No Good will come of such a bad Beginning. Mr Hart, you have chosen, in my Niece, a thankless Bride, and demonstrated by the hurried Nature of your Union a grave Want of Judgement and of Character. Had you sought my Counsel I would freely have given it; but 'tis all to no good now; you are married. I wish you well, as I must. When it is time to christen your first Child I hope that you will not delay, as your Father did, and risk the Child's Soule to the Devil. Good Daye, Sir."

Altho' the Rector's Scolding was not altogether unexpected, I was surprized by its Harshness. "Stay, Sir!" I said, catching my Breath, and his Forearm, as he turned to walk away. Rage at the Slander he had cast against my Wife swept over me like a Wave. "You do not seem considerate, Sir, of the Honour I have done your Family by marrying your Niece; and whatever Countenance she hath shewn to you, I do not discern in it that of a thankless Bride. Mayhap, Rector, if you had proved kinder to her, who is after all your Flesh and Blood, she might have demonstrated to you a sweeter Temperament."

"Unhand me, Sir," the Rector said. The Colour was rising swiftly in his fleshy Face, and the Thought came to me that perhaps he too was remembering the Occasion of our last private Encounter, in his apple Orchard. I imagined, with Pleasure, what Pantomime might ensue should I retain my Grip upon his Wrist, and he lose his upon his fierce Temper. My Grasp tightened. Let him! I thought. His Reputation will be besmirched, and he will have only himself to blame. Let him make an Enemy of me, his Benefactor's Son, upon my wedding Daye, when I have just graced his Family with a Condescension of which they had never any Hopes. Ah! But that surely is the Nub; the Ravenscrofts must all be most put out that, if I was to have chosen any of them, I did not choose their own Sophia.

I stared, hard, at the Rector Ravenscroft. The Man was shorter than me by a Foot, many Yeares older, and certainly no Jack Broughton. Nevertheless, I could feel in mine Hands how much I should have enjoyed giving him a sound Beating; if not for the Slight he had issued against Katherine then for the Insults he had laid upon my youthful Back. Hypocrite! I thought. You are really no more a Servant of God than I am. But Pity, or something akin to it, moved me. I released mine Hold upon his Arm. "Control your Contempt, Sir," I said. "It doth you ill Service." The Rector shook his Arm, as if attempting to restore the Blood to its Extremity, tipped his Hat, in abrupt and perfunctory Manner, and then departed from the Room.

Egad, I thought, suddenly. He hath nothing whatsoever in Common with Nathaniel. The Rector Ravenscroft is not Nathaniel's Father.

At once I saw, with my Mind's Eye, the Gypsies. Kin, Nathaniel had called them. He had meant it; they were truly his blood-Kin, in a Way that the Ravenscrofts were not; and there had been, present and evident to my then unperceiving Eyes, a familial Resemblance between them all: their savage Teeth; their brilliant, slanted Eyes; their sharp Cheek-bones; their translucent Skins; their pointed, foxes' Ears.

He was one of them, I thought. And I refused to recognise it, even tho' I saw't with mine own Eyes. I wondered at the Strangeness! How could this Cuckoldry, which had resulted in such an obvious Cuckoo, have been imposed upon such a Man as the Rector? Surely, I thought, he had suspected. How it must have teazed him that his best beloved and beauteous Son was not his Son at all, but an Outsider; a Stranger, hatched, without consent or warning, in the Rector's Nest to prey upon his own, brown, Chicks.

Nathaniel Ravenscroft. Why was I thinking of Nathaniel now? Mine Heart felt suddenly as shocked as if I had seen him enter unexpectedly within the Room. I took a deep Swallow of my Wine, and sate My Self upon one of the Sophas, until the Shuddering that had taken over all my Limbs had ceased. The Musick from Katherine's Harpsichord glided over mine hot Forehead like Ripples from a swimming Swan.

I did not want Nathaniel on my Mind upon my wedding Daye. Yet even as I thought this, I apprehended, with a dreadful Sinking in my Gut, that Nathaniel's Intrusion upon my Thoughts was most like to be a thing I must experience every Daye of my married Life.

I found My Self remembering the Words of Katherine's final Letter.

Oh, my Bloody Bones, my Deare, if it is within Your Capacity, forgive poor Leonora!—but if You cannot, then I will bear Leonora's Shame and disappear for Ever from Your sight.

What Shame? I thought.

"I will Make you into a Woman".

Nay, I thought, that cannot mean anything; I know 'tis from the faerie Tale she wrote me of Raw Head and Leonora.

Katherine, seeing that I had been forced to sit down, left off her playing and came over to me, her Expression poignant with Concern. She put her Hand upon my Shoulder and sate herself at my Side. Her blue Silks rustled.

"What hath he said?" she asked me. "Oh, he is a rotten old Man, my Uncle Ravenscroft! He would ruin Happiness at a Glance for naught but to brag that he hath done it."

"The Rector hath said nothing that I could not easily repudiate," I answered, catching up her sweet Hand in mine own and pressing it against my Lips. Nathaniel is gone, I thought, and for once the Thought was a Comfort. I looked into her grey Eyes and mine exhausted Heart lightened a little. "He is a Fool to have tried to annoy me; 'twill only make his own Life harder, in the Event that my Father die and I be left to deal with him."

"Mr Hart may not die for Yeares," Katherine said.

"Will not, I hope; I do not want to lose him now, when we have at last discovered each other's Affection."

"Is that what he said to you? That your Father shall die? He is a foul Pig."

"No, no, he did not. His Talk was rather of Christenings than Funerals. It was his Implication that gave Offense. Let us not speak of it any longer."

"No," she said. "Let us not, Tristan." She squeezed my Shoulder, and her Expression brightened. "Let us please be merry instead! I think our Breakfast is ready; afterwards, if you will, I shall send to ask James if he would play for us, for Mrs H. hath told me that he is no poor fiddle Player."

"Indeed?" I forced My Self to sit up. "Then do so, and we shall dance until our Feet fall off."

"I hope," she answered, with a sly Smile, "that we shall not dance until we are quite as exhausted as all that, Bloody Bones."

After many long Houres it was Time for Bed, and with the smallest Pother and Fuss Katherine and I took ourselves to what was now our marital Bed; and for the first Time, lay down together as Man and Wife.

But to my Shock, and bitter Disappointment, I found that even tho' Katherine had plainly no Intention of being aught but willing, I could not dare attempt Consummation of our Marriage. I was not physically tired, and, as we had prepared ourselves for Bed, my Loins had sprung into Life with an Intensity so vital that they had hurt; but as soon as I allowed My Self to make any carnal Approach upon Katherine, the Image of Nathaniel entered my Mind, and my Flesh at once sank flaccid and purposeless. I tried to fight it; but no sooner had the one Image been banished, than it was succeeded by th'Apprehension of the two-faced Goblin Knight of his Ballad, and half remembered Words from Katherine's last Tale fluttered about mine Head like Bats.

—upon Christmas Eve—who was really Raw Head in Disguise—
"I will Make you into a Woman"—

Katherine made no Complaint, but when after some little while it became apparent to us both that we were not to enjoy a Union of that Nature, at least not upon that Night, she wrappt me tight in her Arms and laid mine Head upon her Breast, whispering: "I do not mind, my Love." I could not help but wonder at her Patience, and the Thought struck me that she might, secretly, be relieved by mine Incapacity. At this, mine Heart sank lower. Verily, I thought, the Rector's Words possess a sorry Irony. There will never be a Baptism to delay, if I cannot get Katherine with Child.

I slept fitfully, and light; until sometime in the Houre before the Dawn, rousing, I left my Bed and walked circuitously thro'out the Hall, eventually to find My Self standing at the great front Door. I moved to unlock it, thinking that perhaps the night Aire might banish my Sleeplessness, and steppt forth on to the sandstone Step. The Night was cold; Boreas rattled the old-berried Branches of the hawthorn Hedge. I took a deep Breath and turned about, intending to close the Door, and return me to my Bed, but then, from quite near, came suddenly that barbaric, porcine, Grunting I had heard before I had banished the Goblins, and I froze upon the Step, and turned again.

This Time, I thought, I must do everything I can to rid me of that Sound. I steppt back thro' the Doorway, staring out across the dark Gardens, and listened. The Noise was emanating from the Ha-ha, from the slippery black Ditch where I had attacked Viviane. I knew, in mine Entrails, it was Raw Head.

Plucking up my Courage, I walked toward the Ha-ha. The Grunting, and its pulsating Echo, filled up mine Ears, deadening the Wind. Mine Head began to hurt. But mine Heart was pounding faster than a Drum, and my riding Whip, which I supposed I must have picked up along the Way, appeared by some Magick in my right Hand. I steppt thro' the thorn Hedge, and as I did so the yellow Cold of Dayebreak flooded the Ditch; and all that had been hidden within Darkness burst into foul Clarity.

Raw Head, if indeed it was Raw Head, did not appear at all as I had anticipated. Before me, to mine immense Amazement, crouched Cox, the pig-Man. His Skin was darker than mine own, and hairy as a black Beast. Beside him, in the Mud, sweated an enormous, black Sow, deep in the last Throes of Labour, her great tusked Jaws working furious upon the Femur of a Man.

A savage, all-compassing Fury leapt up within mine Heart at the Sight. I perceived that the Sow's Labour was come of her Ravishment by the Man, and from it would spring all Manner of unclean and evil Things, countless and unending, until all the World lay Fathoms thick in Vice, and all Virtue, all Beauty, was forgot.

I screamed. It was the primal Howl I had heard in mine Head before I had tortured Annie. I leapt forward, and laid about the pig-Man and his repellent Sow with all the Ferocity I could unleash from within My Self. The foul Brute, bawling, fled bleeding from the Ditch and hurtled wildly along the Driveway toward the iron Gates. I gave chase, determined that he should not endure this World, or any other, for one more Minute. But to my Dismay, altho' I ran so fast that I near took to Flight, I could not catch him.

CHAPTER EIGHT-AND-TWENTY

Now I was married, I could no longer perceive the Force of any Argument by which Erasmus might continue to plead for Moderation in my philosophical and scientific Researches; for as far as I could discern, my mental Equilibrium was compleatly adequate to sustain my plunging My Self fully into my Studies. In vain too did he suggest that I should give at least some Attention to sealing the Breach that had opened up between my familial Household and mine Aunt's. In mine Opinion, this Alienation would function to my Benefit, as it must portend fewer Interruptions to my Work, and to mine Honeymoon.

On the Morning after my Wedding, I returned, with a renewed

Interest and Vigour, to my Treatise upon Stroake, and while Katherine sate beside me on my study Sopha, with a clear and critical Faculty I read thro' it a great Number of Times. I was convinced of the Rectitude of my central Assertion, which I held in common with Willis, that the hemiplegic Paralysis associated with Stroake is the Result of an Injury to the nervous Tissue of the Brain. All that was to be done, as far as I could ascertain, at least for that Part of the Theory, was to prove a causal Link between a cerebral Aneurysm and the cerebral Lesions responsible for the Paralysis. As mine Excitement grew, I discerned the Possibility of rewriting my Treatise into a scientific Paper to be submitted before, and approved by the Fellows of the Royal Society.

I immediately discerned a Difficulty, however, in that this theoretical Paper must, I knew, be supported by practical Evidence, which I did not have. I thought upon this Notion repeatedly, and the more I thought upon it the more essential it appeared that I have Dr Hunter's Assistance, for I could think of none other who might be in any Position to secure for me those Corpses I particularly needed: namely those that had died, tho' not immediately, succeeding upon an Apoplexy. Making my Decision, I leapt up from Katherine's Side. "We go to London," I said.

"What?" cried Katherine at once. Catching my Coat, she tried to detain me. "Oh, Tristan," she said. "I would not go to London, not for anything! I would despise it!"

I gently removed her Hand and hastened to my Escritoire. I spread my writing Paper and dippt my Quill in its Ink, when all on a sudden the Realisation came to me that my Researches were not, in fact, in nearly as advanced a State as they must be if I were to be taken at all seriously by Dr Hunter. I was so startled by this Revelation, and the Thought of the publick Ridicule to which I had almost subjected My Self, that I droppt my Pen as quick as if't had been a-burning. Before I even dreamed of approaching Dr Hunter, I ought to have acquired a supporting Body of Evidence by which to prove beyond Doubt that Willis himself had been correct, and that Damage to the cerebral Tissue did indeed cause Paralysis; and, beyond that, the Disturbances in Speech and, perhaps, in Thought, that had incapacitated my Father.

I looked up, and mine Eyes fell upon the multifarious winged and furred Specimens with which I had seen fit to populate my Sanctuary. At last, I thought, their Presence hath a discernible Purpose; as any living Creature is capable of experiencing Pain as an Human Being might, so it must possess a nervous Net and Brain that is in every Sense analogous to that of a Man.

I stood a while in Thought. "Nay," I said to Katherine. "We stay here for the nonce."

I began mine Experiment that very Afternoon. Leaving Katherine to occupy herself as she saw fit, I returned to my Study to spend the Houres until Dinner in close Examination of the uninjured Brain of a freshly killed male Rat, which I intended to set up as a Yardstick against which to measure those Specimens upon which I hoped to create Lesions. The Creature squeaked when I killed it, but I believe it felt no Pain, for my Knife was swift. I dissected out the Brain and having washed it, sate it before me in a porcelain Dish and took extensive Notes regarding its Shape and Condition. I now purposed to inflict upon another Rat an Haemorrhage beneath the Cranium, in the Hope that this would induce the Formation of Lesions upon the Tissue. Remembering Dr Oliver's Operation upon the mad Man, I decided that the best Method was to drill a small Hole thro' the Cranium and then suppress the Bleeding, which I intended would be re-directed inwards. Selecting a second Rat, similar in Size and Proportion to the first, I attempted to render it immobile ready for Vivisection, but the thing escaped while I was tightening the Straps and I was obliged to chase it all about my Study. When finally, after much Cursing, Confusion, and Delay, I achieved mine Aim, the Animal died immediately.

This second Frustration caused me to ponder whether I was rushing the Pace of my Research, and ought not first perfect the Art of causing Paralyses by inflicting Damage upon particular Nerves; which Procedure, tho' it tell me little about Stroake, would reveal much about Communication betwixt Brain and Limbs whilst at the same Time greatly refining my Skill. This took me back to mine unnerving Intuition that Thought itself must be a material Thing; but I thrust it aside. It signifies naught, I told My Self, whether the Message that is supported upon the Nerves is material or mental. It matters not whether Pain is a corporeal thing, or whether it consisteth more in its apparent Meaning; no, what hath Importance to my Thesis is that it subsists upon Matter, and that the Nature of the Brain is thereupon disclosed.

I disposed of both bloody Corpses, washed mine Hands, and joined Katherine at Dinner.

This great Work absorbed mine Interest so thoroughly over the succeeding Weeks that I neither noticed the Time passing about me, nor mine own natural Hair growing thick upon mine Head; until one Morning I awoke to find that it was Christmas Eve, and two Yeares since Mary Fielding had taken in my Bat. This sad Anniversary put me again in Mind of London, and the Necessity of my Returning thither; but I judged that it was not likely I should reside again with the Fieldings, with Katherine or—Fortune forfend—without her.

My Marriage was everything I could have desired, except in one Area: it had remained unconsummated. Altho' I had found My Self to be intirely capable of Emission when torturing my Darling into Agonies, when I considered performing any Act of natural Intimacy the Thought of Nathaniel would flash across my Mind, and mine Excitement wither on the Vine like poisoned Grapes. I had refused to allow this to matter. Katherine and I had, after all, our own Notions of Intimacy.

We passed Christmas Eve in playful Fashion. I secured Katherine firmly, by Means of several Coils of thick silk Rope, to the left Post at the Foot of the Bed, and slowly inscribed an attractive Euclidean Pattern upon the white Flesh of her upper Buttocks with mine ivory handled Lancet.

It was pure Delight to me to treat her thus, and to have her thus restrained, because when she was fastened upright, her welling Blood drippt down across her upper Thighs like melted Wax, and formed beautifull Shapes upon her Legs. This was all our Pleasure; I had never whippt her. I had still to hear that most magical Sound, that full throated, immoderate, wanton Scream that would have told me I had taken her to her Edge. I sometimes regretted this; but I had no more Desire to rush her than my Researches. The Memory of Annie pinked me still; I wanted to hear Katherine scream, not see her faint.

I had compleated the Outline of mine Inscription, and, seeing by Katherine's Expression that she had descended deep into that State she treasured most, I kissed my Blade clean of her Blood and prepared to begin upon the lengthy Procedure of its Illumination.

There came a gentle, scuffing Knock upon my chamber Door.

It took me perhaps a Minute to realise that I had heard anything; Katherine did not appear to have noticed it at all. I turned, as if in a Dream, upon the Spot and stared at my Door, half unsure as to whether verily I had heard what mine Ears had told me. The Scuffing repeated, hesitant and soft, as if the Scuffer were afraid of my Response.

I rested mine Hand upon the Small of Katherine's Back. "What is it?" I asked quietly.

"Mr Hart, Sir," replied a muffled Voice, which I recognised as belonging to Molly Jakes. "Your Sister, Mrs Barnaby, is come, Sir."

I stroaked Katherine's velvet Skin; it rippled soft and pliable beneath my Fingers. A low, sighing Moan escaped her Lips. I would have been an unnatural Monster, or Man, if I had been able to break off at this Point. Moreover, I was still very cross with Jane.

"Tell Mrs Barnaby that she may wait," I told Molly. "We will be an Houre."

"Yes, Mr Hart." I heard retreating Footsteps beyond the Door, then Stillness.

Once Katherine and I had brought our Game to a satisfactory Conclusion, I explained to her the Nature and Purpose of the earlier Interruption, of which, as I had discerned, she had at the Time been oblivious. Together, we dresst and headed down the Stairs to find my Sister.

Jane was a-waiting in the drawing Room, where Katherine and I had been married. The Evening was well advanced, but the curtained and shuttered Room was warm, and, owing to the reluctant Chimney, which refused to draw, its Aire was redolent with Ashes and holly Smoake. Katherine, in Defiance of Shirelands' Tradition, had perswaded Mrs H. to deck the intire Hall from Floor to Cornice with an hundred Sprays of fresh Pine, and with ivy Tendrils long as driving Reins, all newly harvested from the Grounds and fragrant with Sap and Turpentine. In both drawing Rooms she had sparked a vivid Explosion of Leaf and Branch upon the Walls atop the Panelling, and winter Greenery chased round the dado Rail in a mad Saturnine Riot. Needles were dropping near the Hearth.

Upon our Entering the Room, Jane, who had been sitting at some Distance from the Fire, leapt to her Feet, then stood still, helplessly wringing her Hands, her Countenance tortured.

Jane did not look, to mine Eyes, exceeding well. She was very well attired—I should have been astonished if't had been otherwise—but she had lost a lot of Weight, and her whiteleaded Features appeared drawn and haggard. Perhaps, I thought, 'twas all the Strain of her Pregnancy and recent Confinement, or perhaps 'twas from the Worry of our Father's Illness—and mine own; but whatever its Cause, the Effect was alarming. On a sudden, I recalled the private Warning I had given to Barnaby upon the Daye he had married Jane. If he abused my Sister, I had said, I would take it upon My Self to snap every Bone he possesst, beginning with the smallest Phalanges and the Metacarpals, and progressing of course to the critical Vertebrae at the Base of the Cranium, whence the Spinal Cord began its Exodus.

It struck me that this was the first Time my Sister and I properly had met since my Departure for London, which had taken Place mere Dayes after her Wedding. This Realisation was so odd, coming direct upon the other, it made me pause and shy, like a Stag, surprized by an hen Pheasant starting suddenly from Cover. I had not been properly My Self in Company with Jane for one and an half Yeares.

She hath caused me an Hurt, I thought. But I cannot hate her for it.

I held open mine Arms. "Sister," I said.

Mrs Barnaby let out a miserable Wail, and breaking her Freeze, rushed across the Room and flung herself upon my Neck.

When Jane had ceased Bawling, I had Katherine summon Mrs H., to tell her to bring up hot Toddies to soothe all our ragged Nerves. Then we sate in an Huddle hard by the Fireplace and Jane became able to relate, slowly, and with a great amount of Hiccoughing, the Particulars of her current Existence at Withy Grange, and her extream Contrition at her Absence from my Wedding, which had resulted from too avid an Attention to the Opinions of her Mother-in-law.

"'Twas a Shock, Tristan," she said. "I knew nothing of your Attachment, naught at all. And Sophy had seemed so certain that Miss Montague was a—a shameless Flirt." My Sister hid her Face in shaking Hands. "Oh!" she suddenly cried, tossing up her Face to reveal to me its desperate beseeching Look. "Can either of you ever forgive me? I had to explain Mr Glass's Newes to Mr Barnaby, because he is my Husband, I felt 'twas wrong to keep it from him. I knew he would tell all to our Aunt, but I did not imagine—I could not—that she would behave in such a dreadful Manner. He wrote her first thing in the Morning and she was caught by Surprize. Now she is quite distraught at the Rift that she hath provoked between our Families, but she is such a proud Woman that she knows not how to apologise. Oh, Tristan! I did not ever want to lose my Brother, or our dear Father, for you both are dearer to me than mine own Life, or Mr Barnaby's!" Her Hands flew once again to stop up her Mouth, as if she feared what she might say next.

"Sweet Sister," I said, catching hold her Hands and bringing them away from her Face. "I forgive you intirely your Part in this; I know your Character well enough never to have suspected any Unkindness behind your Actions. As for mine Aunt, I shall forgive her nothing till she hath apologised, on her Knees, to my Wife. But she must still remember, e'en so, 'twas my Father forced her leave, and I can venture no Guess as to how his Pardon might be obtained."

At this latter Statement, which I plainly conceived as being naught but Fact, Jane began violently to weep anew, and gave over only when Katherine put both her Arms about her, as Mary Fielding had done betimes to me, and dabbed her Tears away with her own Handkerchief. I felt an odd Discomfort at the Sight, and, knowing not where to look, directed my Gaze towards the crackling Hearth.

"I am not Mistress in my own House!" Jane sobbed. "In every Decision I am overruled. I perswaded Mr Barnaby to spare the willow Wood, but Mrs Ann said to leave't would be untidy, and not like Stowe, and would not do. A fine View Mr Barnaby will have if the River floods, as I have been told, on good Authority, it will, if the Willows are grubbed up. And I am not permitted to hire my own Servants, or to dismiss them, even if they are sloppy and lazy, and rude, and will not do one thing for me unless they hear it from Mrs Ann. And they would not let me come and make Friends with you, till now, and I do not know why todaye they agreed that I might. I try to be a good Wife, Miss Monta—Mrs Hart; I do not seek to oppose my Husband's Will; but it is cruel when he attends only to his Mother, and cares not a Whit for me!"

"You must call me Katherine, Mrs Barnaby," said mine own Wife; and the Notion struck me like case-Shot how much more, from a certain Point of View, she had to put up with than did Jane; how much more unreasonable, verily how extream were my Demands compared to those of Mr Barnaby. Yet Katherine did not contemn them as such. Therein lieth the Difference 'tween our Houses, I thought. When James Barnaby married Jane, Jane understood, or thought she understood, the Conditions of their Contract; and either she was then deceived, or he hath since arbitrarily altered them. I would never do such thing, and Katherine is fully cognizant of that. My Sister is correctly sensible of an Injustice.

I pondered briefly whether this particular ill Usage of my Sister constituted sufficient Grounds for my breaking Barnaby's Ribs, but decided, regretfully, that it did not. I thought, however, that it must necessitate a private Conversation with my Brother-in-law upon some future Date, when we were upon amicable Terms again. It annoyed me, also, that the immediate Cause of Jane's Distress was the Destruction of that pretty Copse at the bottom of her Property— or her Husband's—which had enchanted me upon that Daye when I had ridden over from Shirelands—the Daye when Katherine had flown down-Hill to meet me, a grass-stained Angel.

"When doth Mr Barnaby intend beginning the Trees' removal?" I said.

"He says in the Summer; when the River is at its lowest."

Mr Barnaby had thought me insane. "So, doth he imagine that 'twill never rise again?" I exclaimed. "Egad, Jane, your Husband is a Fool. A squalling Milksop, clinging to his Mother's apron Strings and whining to her whenever his Will is challenged. I shall speak with him about your Willows, and your rightful Expectation to be Mistress in your own Abode. 'Tis wrong that Aunt's Word should outweigh yours. You are Barnaby's Wife, and his Child's Mother. He will listen to you; or he shall answer to me."

This Statement was met by a Look, from Jane, of mixt Skepticism, Longing, and Fear; but she did not speak.

"Please, might I see your Baby, Mrs Barnaby?" said Katherine, uncommon timidly, into the long Hiatus that followed.

Almost at once, Jane brightened, smiled, and said certainly,

Katherine might, as she was the Infant's Aunt by Marriage; and even if't had not been so, Jane so enjoyed shewing off her dear Amelia it would have made no Difference; she would have had her fetched immediately.

Both Women then looked inquiringly toward me, as if I might raise an Objection to this proposed Introduction of a Babe amongst our Party; but I had none. I shrugged my Shoulders. "By all Means, have the Child brought up," I said. "'Tis mine own Niece, after all. I only hope, Jane, that you do not have it swaddled. Swaddling doth, I conceive, more Damage to the Infant's developing Skeleton than it prevents."

Jane looked astonished. "Truly, Brother," she said. "I did not expect to find you so knowledgeable."

"I am not without an Interest in Children's Bones," I said.

"Oh!" exclaimed Katherine. An hungry Apprehension echoed in the Caverns of her Voice.

Little Amelia was accordingly sent for, and less than five Minutes later had been passed from the not unkindly Arms of her Wet Nurse into the kindly ones of her Mother; and I had my first clear Glimpse of this small Snippet of mine own familial Cloth.

The Baby was light skinned, bald headed, and round faced, with dark hazel Eyes exactly like her Mother's. She had a small Mouth, Lips like a tiny Rosebud, and a miniature Tongue that wriggled repeatedly between them, as if she were suckling upon an imaginary Tit. She did not cry, or mewl, or wheeze; neither did she kick, or make any wriggling Movement that might have made her at all difficult to hold. She was not swaddled, but had been rationally dresst in a Petticoat and light Gown of green Muslin. I hoped this Dress, at least, had been at my Sister's Instigation and not that of her Mother-in-law.

"Hath she Teeth?" I asked.

My Sister laughed. "No," she said. "Babies do not grow their Teeth so young!"

The holly Log sparkled in the Grate, and fell upon its Side. I reached for the Poker. There was no Need to bother James, I thought. In Mr Fielding's House, I had rarely troubled My Self with calling for the Servants.

A pretty enough Child; but perfectly common.

"She is beautifull, Mrs Barnaby," Katherine said, as I raked the drab Ashes incarnadine.

"Please call me Jane," said my Sister, with remarkable Warmth, and sororal Affection.

I selected two large holly Logs from the Fire-box and positioned them carefully atop the glowing Embers. After a Moment or so, a small, citrine Flame began to curl about the cylindrical Body of the nearest, then a second fluted Column of golden Fire spurted between them both, and stood, surprizingly erect, and unwavering.

"Do you want to hold her?" Jane said. "She is very placid."

"Might I?" cried Katherine.

Jane got to her Feet, and somehow turned the Child about in her Arms so that she could easily transfer it. Katherine also stood, and took up the Babe with a confident Ease that confounded me, even tho' I knew she had Siblings younger than herself, with whose Care she had doubtless been charged. I remembered mine own inexperienced Handling of my little Bat, and my Stomach lurched. Where is she now? I thought. My poor, pretty Freak, stolen back by Viviane, wandering the Country with a Mobb of Gypsies and Nathaniel Ravenscroft.

Nathaniel Ravenscroft, I thought. A Stab of Anger, overwhelming,

412

incomprehensible and savage, caused me to catch my Breath. Nathaniel Ravenscroft. Whither didst go?

Katherine stroaked baby Amelia's Head, and then, to worsen my Confusion, bent her Neck and snuffled at the Child's bald Crown like an hound Bitch identifying a Pup.

"Oh, yes," said Jane, delightedly. "Is she not delicious?"

"What are you about?" I asked. "Is this some female Mystery, or have you both lost your Wits?"

Jane laughed again; it was good, despite my Perturbation, to hear it. "It is the Infant Scent, Tristan," she said. "Young Babies have a special Odour. 'Tis hard to describe it—but 'tis sweeter than the Primrose."

"Indeed?" I thought back again to my Bat, but the only Smells I could recall were those of oyster Sauce and Christmas Spices. If Bat had smelled of anything, I thought, it would have been of highway Dirt, and Mistletoe, and the old Gypsy Hag.

I looked upon Katherine's rapt Expression as she beheld the Babe, and I could think of nothing but Nathaniel; and mine Heart stoppt.

Much later, when my Sister had departed, I straightway took Katherine to my Chamber, and helped her to undress. I did not anticipate that things could change between us in the important Way that they must, but as her Corset came away, like a Ribcage, in mine Hands, the Skirt of her Gown shivered to her Feet and took with it the linty Bandage I had earlier applied about her fresh Cuts. I bent down to pick it up, and as I did so Katherine shifted her Body slightly. Golden Candlelight fluttered across the Scars, both livid and pale, that adorned her Buttocks.

413

Beautifull, beautifull. "Place your Arms behind your Back," I said.

She laughed, lightly, innocently, and folded her Arms behind her. The blue Veins pulsed in her exposed Wrists. I took her left Arm in mine Hand and twisted it so that, just visible above the laced Fretwork was mine own Name, like to the Signature upon an Artist's Masterwork. *T H.*

She belongs to me, I thought. She is mine, and there hath never been another who hath had, in Truth, any Claim upon her Body, and her Heart.

An I do not, I thought, then by the Letter of the Law she will not be my Wife.

T. H.

"You belong to me," I said. "To me, and not Nathaniel Ravenscroft."

"What!" Katherine shuddered, and deep Revulsion twisted her Mouth. "I was never his!" she retorted. "Never! How dare you to suggest it! Before God, with my whole Heart, I was only ever yours, even when you refused to recognise that I existed!"

"Indeed?" I felt her Carpal Ligament slide beneath my Thumb. "So you say. How am I to tell whether you speak the Truth?"

"Believe me! I put Meadowsweet in your greatcoat Pockets once. I was eight. Do you remember? You did not know who had done it, and you flew into a Passion, and told Nathaniel that it was Sophy. And he pretended to believe you, and he teazed Sophy so bad she wouldn't come out of her Room for a Sennight. And you never noticed me, never, never!"

The Inscription of my Name lay beneath my Fingertips. Mine Hands began to relax their fierce Hold. "I truly thought 'twas Sophy," I said, slowly remembering. "And I took little Delight in meadow Flowers."

"I should have used Bones," Katherine hissed.

Without letting My Self reflect for one Moment upon the thing I was about to do, I freed My Self from my confining Breeches, and with my Gaze still fixt upon the lettered Script, clappt fast her Wrists in my one Hand and the Base of her Cranium in the other, and roughly forced her to lie Face downwards upon the Bed.

I had held Polly Smith thus, and others; I had overpowered, and ravished each Girl as easily as if she had been a Plum ripe for the picking. I had done so; verily, I would do so again.

Katherine cried out in Astonishment. I did not think. I did not dare to think. With my Knee, I parted her Thighs. Her carpal Bones, plastic to the Point of Dislocation, shifted some little Way beneath my Fingertips.

My Loins began to stir. I kept mine Eyes fast upon mine own Name. Katherine, I thought. Mine, mine.

I was forced to let go her Neck, but she did not move, only trembled, violently, as I opened her. There was no Impediment. A red Gauze fell across mine Eyes. Mine Excitement increased; within my Chest a wild, frantick, spiralling Vortex. At last! I thought. Then Lust began to move me; I thrust again and again, with increasing Violence and wild Rapidity. With each savage Movement Katherine cried out, a mewing Scream of Pleasure or of Pain, I did not know which. It did not matter. I felt my Torso shudder; I spiralled down, into the sweet, welcoming Darkness of Oblivion.

I had fucked Nathaniel Ravenscroft compleatly from mine Head.

CHAPTER NINE-AND-TWENTY

Now that I had overcome my Dread that if I used the Body of my Wife after the natural Manner of Men she would run away in Horrour, I discovered that I had License to repeat the Liberty whenever I so wished. She was my America, my new-found Land; and the novel Freedoms that I had disclosed in her sent me into such an Extasie that for a full Sennight I wished them repeated several Times in every single Daye; until upon the first of January she objected, and pleaded with me in God's Name be still and leave her be. After this petty Rejection, which I understood to have been not unkindly meant, I took care to moderate my Demands, and we fell into a more comfortable conjugal Routine in which our other Delights resumed Precedence; for betwixt Katherine and My Self, Pain was really a thing of greater Satisfaction than mere Pleasure.

The Seasons turned, and the Yeare of our Lord seventeen fifty-three progressed from Winter toward Spring. The River rose into full Torrent all along the Periphery of Barnaby's obstructed View, and then, at last, began to recede. Still the Breach between my Father and mine Aunt remained unspanned. Jane, in contrast, began a new Habit of travelling the few Miles from Withy Grange to Shirelands four Dayes out of every seven, often staying in her old Room over-Night instead of returning to her Husband's. None of us raised any Objection to this except, surprizingly, Erasmus, who seemed most discomforted by her continued Presence, altho' when I challenged him he denied harbouring any Dislike toward her.

In early March, as the Dayes had begun noticeably to lengthen without Shirelands Hall, my Father requested that the Light slowly be returned also within his Chamber; and once his Eyes had accustomed themselves once more to the Rhythms of Dawn and Evening, he began again to read, and to receive private Correspondence from an Aquaintance within the Government in whose Support he previously had been active as an Agitator. He perused his Letters silently, by himself, and made no Mention of their Contents. I could only suppose that the Sender had Intelligence, by some Means unbeknownst to me, that their Recipient was not in any Condition to write a Reply, for I was never called upon as an Amanuensis.

His Paralysis, however, continued undiminished. I was not surprized by this, as it was what I would have expected in accordance with both mine Hypothesis, and my previous Knowledge of Stroake. I continued in mine Efforts to induce an analogous

Condition in a living Creature, but the Task proved extreamly difficult, for like Human Subjects of Trepanning, either the Animals died at once or they appeared largely unharmed, dying afterwards of some other Cause. During the first Fortnight of that Month I killed five and twenty Rats and seven Coneys before I had one Survivor. This Animal endured three Dayes in a paralytic Condition before it expired; I dissected the Brain, but could not detect any Lesion upon it. These practical Failures were frustrating, but I determined to persevere in mine Attempts, for they proved naught against my larger Theory. I often wished I could have healthy, Human, Subjects, who might be able to apprize me of any subtile Changes in Sensation or Perception that were impossible for me objectively to discern in an Animal, but I knew this was mere Fancy.

Between mine Experiments I returned to the Poems of Mr Donne, thro' which I had heard, whispering across Death, my Mother's Voice. Donne wrote of Love, and Disappointment; and of his frustrated Longing to submit intirely to the Will of a God whom he could not fully perceive, and who would not exercise his Power upon his tortured Cleric. That was inevitable, I thought, for Donne's Christian God was surely composed of nothing but his Phantasy. There was tragic Absurdity in this; yet as I returned again to those Poems which, by their thumbed Appearance, had best interested my Mother, I began to imagine that there lay, concealed within them, Hints toward the potential Existence of something that was real; some Genius more coherent than the omnipotent, omniscient good God of Christ, and wholly as powerful as Love. I knew not whether it was Reason or Delusion that made me suspect it so.

★　★　★

On the nineteenth of March I received a Visit from Lt. Simmins, whose Regiment had been posted to Abingdon, and who had arranged that he might stay at Shirelands for the Night before rejoining his Commanding Officer for the remainder of the Journey upon the Morning. It had been raining hard all Daye, so I had expected that our Guest might be thereby delayed, and it was after six before he arrived, which by our country Standards was very late for Dinner. My Father, unable to tolerate the Delay, had dined already and retired, but Jane, Erasmus, Katherine, and My Self patiently awaited Simmins' Arrival in the front drawing Room, whose Window had a good View of the Driveway. As the hallway Clock chimed the quarter-Houre, Katherine, who had been sitting on the Sill, cried out that she could see a Rider approaching, and a short Time later Mr Simmins was introduced.

I had not set Eyes on Lt. Simmins since our last Meeting in London, upon which Occasion I had not been intirely My Self. Simmins, however, gave no Indication of remembering this. He looked to me to be in that enviable State of being in Possession of both Happiness and Health; Life in the Army was plainly suited to his Constitution and his Temperament. Still short in Stature— tho' taller than Erasmus—and cursed with the Hesitancy that afflicted his Speech, he had grown as lean and muscular as a Monkey, and carried himself with a swordsman's Grace. He had evidently ridden thro' the Weather; his scarlet Frock was wet, and his white horsehair Wigg, in the Places where it had not been under his Hat, had begun to curl out of its proper Shape. The overall Impression, I thought, was more that of Rapscallion than of disciplined military Man. I was glad.

Introducing Simmins to my Wife, I was briefly surprized to discover that they were already known to each other.

"But, Sir," Katherine reminded me, gently, "you, yourself, charged Mr Simmins with the Duty of watching over me when he was posted to Weymouth."

I shot a questioning Glance toward Erasmus. "Did I?"

"Which Duty," Simmins said, "I di-scharged most f-aithfully, until Miss M-ontague made it impossible by her D-isappearence."

Katherine smiled at this Admission, and Simmins, shyly, smiled back. They reminded me of Children engaged upon a Conspiracy.

"I charged you with a Letter," I said, suddenly remembering. "But that was all."

"You must f-orgive me, Mr H-art," said Simmins. "I exceeded your O-rders. I thought Miss Montague, as she was then, to be in grave Need of a Fr-iend."

"And I was, and a Friend you were, Sir," Katherine said. "My only Complaint is that you hid from me exactly how ill Mr Hart had become; for if I had known, I should have fled the sooner."

Simmins' Gaze flickered from Katherine to Erasmus, and then to me. "I-ndeed," he said. "I am s-orry for that D-eception. It seemed for the B-est, at the T-ime."

"Enough of this Palaver," I said, putting mine Arm amicably about Simmins' slender Shoulders and giving him a bracing Shake. "I take it, Mr Simmins, that you would prefer to change your Cloathing before Dinner. You are very dampe."

"Indeed, I will," Simmins said. He made no Effort, however, to leave, and his Eyes flickered, hesitantly, toward Jane, whom I had neglected, in my Confusion, to introduce.

My Sister made an impatient Noise. "My Brother is exceeding rude," she said. "I pray you will forgive our rustick Manners, Mr Simmins. You and I remember each other well, I am sure, from our Childhoods. My Name is Mrs James Barnaby."

Simmins, somewhat taken aback, as indeed we all were, by my Sister's uncharacteristic Forwardness, bowed respectfully, and then made a swift Exit.

"Why should I not?" said Jane loudly after we were alone again. "I remember him from Yeares ago; and I am a married Woman, who may speak to whom she please. Do not you agree, Mr Glass?"

"Indeed, Madam," Erasmus said, quite evenly, yet in a Tone that bespoke no small Irritation at being thus addresst. "I am in no Position to opine; as I have said before, there is a considerable Difference between our Stations, which would make any Comment I might make impertinent in the extream."

Jane tossed her Head; a Gesture she might have caught from Katherine. "Impertinent?" she said. "I think not, as I have expressly requested it."

To mine Amazement, this Statement produced, upon the Visage of Erasmus Glass, a Glare so fierce he might have been the Sunne itself. "I repeat," he said: "It could only be impertinent, and improper for me to comment."

"Do you not think Mr Simmins is handsome?" Jane said to my Wife.

Katherine's Eyes widened. "I do not find him especially handsome," she said. "Tho' he is not unpleasing of Countenance."

"I think that he is, indeed, very handsome," Jane said. She turned, yet again, toward Erasmus. "Mr Glass, will you express any Opinion upon that?"

"Excuse me," Erasmus said, stiffly. "I have some Business I must conclude before Dinner." He bowed shortly, and left the Room.

"La," said my Sister. "I care not. Wherefore should I care aught for Mr Simmins, or for Mr Glass either, and his Opinions!" She rose abruptly from her Chair. "I must dress," she said, and whirling rapidly about, she left the drawing Room in a rose satined Flurry.

I turned, not comprehending, to Katherine. "What in Heaven?"

"Is't not evident?" Katherine sighed. "Mrs Barnaby is desperately unhappy."

Over Dinner Simmins entertained us with Anecdotes of army Life, and we were a chearful Party, despite the prickling Rancour that hung in the Aire like impending Lightning betwixt Erasmus and Jane.

Seeing Simmins again, after so many Months, was most pleasing; and yet at the same Time quite unsettling, for my Mind would not refrain from casting its Eye of Memory back upon that fragmented Evening of our last Encounter; and with every Recollection mine Heart sank lower in my Chest. Had I struck Simmins? I thought that I had; but he said naught upon the Matter and my Recollection was so unsure that had I not known that I had been ill, I should have dismisst it as a mere Dream.

After some while the Conversation turned to London, and Simmins, Eyes sparkling in the Candlelight, disclosed that he was, in one Month's Time, to return thither to be made Captain. This Newes we all agreed to be most exciting, and my Sister ordered at once the Opening of a fourth Bottle of Burgundy, that it might properly be celebrated.

The Notion that little Simmins might become a Captain, with Authority over those Officers who ranked beneath him, struck me as more than passing strange. I could not repel the Thought that, should I desire it, I could command that he kneel before my Feet, and he would instantly obey. I possesst, I knew, no legitimate Power over Lt. Simmins; but the Conviction persisted, and with every subtle Twitch of Simmins' Lips, every careless Shrug of his Shoulder, it strengthened.

James opened the Bottle and we toasted Simmins' Promotion with a good Will. Simmins accepted our Congratulations with a broad Smile and an heated Cheek, and then turned the Subject at once from himself by asking after my Father. "I am glad," he said, "to hear of the Squire's returning H-ealth. Tell me, what is his View upon Mr P-elham's Bill? Is it that it shall be p-assed, or no?"

"Egad," I said. "I know nothing of it—our Father's political Affiliations and Interests are a thing of which Mrs Barnaby and I have little Intelligence."

"Oh!" Simmins' furry Eyebrows lifted in Surprize. "That amazes me, Sir, for Mr Hart's N-ame is well r-espected among those of Mr P-elham's P-arty."

"Which Newes," I said, "astonishes me the more; but as I consider it, I do recall my Father having mentioned Mr Pelham's Name in mine Hearing."

"The Bill in Question," Simmins said, speaking with great Care, "is to do with granting Nationality to the resident J-ews."

"Why! I have heard of it!" exclaimed my Sister. "Mr Barnaby hath a strong Opinion against it, and hath spoke up about it often."

"He is n-ot alone," Simmins responded. "C-aptain K-eane says that there is such violent O-pposition, especially in the Sh-ires, he doubts that it will get thro'. But had I any P-olitics, I would s-upport it. With all due Respect to your Husband, Mrs Barnaby, I believe that there is little Ch-ance the J-ews will all c-onvert to our Ch-ristian R-eligion; and Britain hath enough D-iff-iculty in m-aintaining her C-olonies abroad, without su-ffering a f-oreign C-ommunity to persevere within her Sh-ores."

"The Bill hath been much talked of," Erasmus said. "For my Part, Mr Simmins, I agree with you; but I think for Reasons of Justice rather than the national Expediency, which you cite."

"Mr Glass is intirely right," said Jane. "I have never agreed with Mr Barnaby. I find his Opinions distasteful, and his strong Avowal of them provoking of Offense."

"Can it be," I said, "that everyone hath heard of Mr Pelham's Bill but I?"

"I had not heard of it," said Katherine at once.

"You have had m-ore i-mportant th-ings to think of, Mr H-art," said Simmins, his shy Smile returning once more to play about his Lips.

He meant my Work, and recent Marriage; but nevertheless, my lamentable Ignorance of the Jew Bill, the Controversy in which it was mired, and most of all my Father's Interest in its Proposal, made me feel sharply vexed at My Self; and to imagine that both he, and my Mother's Ghost, must be sore disappointed in me.

"Our Mother," I said suddenly, "was of the Jewish Faith, and were it not for the Fact that we were christened, my Sister and I would have been subject to all the Restrictions those People commonly languish under. I am unsurprised at my Father's Connexion with it."

"Fie, Brother!" Jane exclaimed, her Features reddening. "Our Mother was a Christian, Aunt hath always said so."

"Fie yourself, Jane, she was not. Aunt Barnaby is telling Lies. Our Mother never converted. You may succeed in pretending she was English, having, as you do, our Father's Countenance; but all the Whitelead in the World cannot alter the Fact that I spent my Boyhood running from those Fellows who would have cracked mine Head and thrown me in the River to see how well I would float. I shall be delighted if the Bill is passed." I thought suddenly of Mr Henry Fielding, and of how as we had first entered into the City of London he had spoken of his Ambition to see Society improved, and improved at a Depth more profound than that of mere Landscaping, by the Enforcement of just, incorrupt, Laws. "These petty Tyrants," I said, "who pull a Child by the Ears because they reckon him insufficient English for their Liking must be held accountable. There is no Reason whatsoever why our Country should privilege one Religious Sing-song over another, when all are errant Nonsense."

My Companions stared at me, astonished by mine Outburst, Indeed, I was surprized My Self, for never before had I thought such things mattered to me one Whit.

In that Instant I made the Resolution that, upon the morrow Morning, once Lt. Simmins had gone on his Way, I would betake me not to mine Experiments, but to my Father's Library and thoroughly acquaint My Self with him. I would read all the Works of those Thinkers who had convinced him in his Atheism, and presumably in his Politicks; I would find him in Philosophy as I had found my Mother in a Poem, and then, when I knew him neither as Father nor Patient, but as an intelligent, feeling Man, I would at last know My Self able to address him, without secret Fear that if I spoke to him he would turn his Eyes from me, and send me sorrowing away.

Simmins went early to Bed, as he had to be up at Dawn to join his Commanding Officers at Highworth. The Ladies having retired before eleven, his Departure left me alone with a preoccupied Erasmus, and mine own Thoughts, which echoed around mine Head with an increasing Loudness and Intensity.

Over the Course of the Evening, my Suspicion that Simmins

would obey me, even against his own Inclination, had hardened with every Glass into a Certainty; and my Yearning to prove my Certainty against Fact pricked me beyond Endurance. I made My Self believe that mine Urge had neither to do with Pain, nor Lust, nor Beauty; nor had it anything in common with that rare Species of Love that I shared so willingly with Katherine. The Desire seemed to me instead to represent the ineluctable Consequence of our Beginning; a Progression of our Friendship that was as proper as it was inevitable; and, this Time, I knew neither Guilt nor Terrour at its Promptings.

I thought hard upon what I might ask Simmins do, and for a long while no Inspiration was forthcoming. I had not the least Desire to whip him, and no Chores to set; and I could not see how he, with his Lack of scientific Training, might be of any Use to me in my Researches.

Then the shocking Possibility occurred to me that he might be of some Purpose as a live Human Subject for Experimentation; much as Polly Smith had been, whom I had tortured in the Name of scientific Investigation. Perhaps, I thought, I might be able to use Simmins to determine something of the Experience of Paralysis in a Subject who was still capable of describing its Progress, as my Father, with his more general Sickness, could not aid me any more effectively than my Rats. The Notion, that my Phantasy might become real, troubled me deeply; I thrust it forcefully away.

Finally, as the Clock struck one, and Erasmus, draining the last Drops of his Burgundy, rose to his Feet and bade me a firm Good Night, into my Mind came creeping the unwelcome Memory of Lady B.——, and Annie; and I understood at last what Service I must require of Lt. Simmins; for truly I knew no one else to whom I might have trusted it.

After Erasmus had gone, I picked up the Light from the Table, and made my way quietly, tho' I was somewhat unsteady upon my Feet, to my Study, and thence to the guest Chamber in which Simmins had settled himself to sleep, and I knocked, hard, thrice, upon the Door.

The Night cracked open. I jumped back. Out of the chasm'd Silence came an irrational Impulse to fling My Self against the vibrating Wood, as if I might thereby muffle the Intrusion, and undo everything that I had done, or that I might yet do. Nonsense, I thought. I am not about to harm him

There was no immediate Answer, but after three Minutes, or thereabouts, I heard Footsteps upon the Boards beyond the Door, and Fingers scrabbling at the Latch, and then the Door swung inwards, and open. Lt. Simmins stood blinking in white night-Shirt and yellow taper-Light.

"The D-evil?" Simmins said.

"Be easy, Lieutenant Simmins," I said, taking him by the Shoulders and pushing him backwards into the Room. "I mean you no Harm. I would speak with you, now, in private."

I closed the Door behind me, and made Simmins put his Candle with mine upon the Mantel and sit upon his Bed, whilst I took up the only Chair, wrapping my Frock tight against the springtime Chill. Simmins' Face was a pale Lamp in the midnight Darkness. The Chamber seemed to spin slowly about me.

I had intended to reveal almost everything to Simmins: mine uncommon Proclivities, and how my pressing Need to inflict Pain upon another Human Being had led me, before my Marriage, into Vice. I had planned to tell him how the repeated Satisfaction of my vicious Lust had caused it not to slacken, but to grow beyond mine Ability to contain it; of the horrible Operation upon

Lady B.—— and my Mortification at Dr Oliver's Suggestion, as we had walked together afterwards across Covent Garden, that I needed to fuck. I do not know why I had intended this; perhaps I was hoping that to have confesst, to have baptised Simmins into my Darkness, would have brought me a preliminary Form of Absolution. I could never, after all, have spoken of these Horrours to Katherine. But as things fell out, I could not bring My Self to Scratch. I told him only, and in much truncated Form, of the Abuse I had inflicted upon Annie.

"This," I said, when my Narrative had reached this Point, "is what you must do for me, and 'tis a Charge I would entrust to none other. When you return to London, you shall seek out Miss Annie Moon, otherwise called Antoinette, and present her with this Purse, which contains one hundred Sovereigns, with which, you are to tell her, she is to pay off her Debt to Mrs Haywood. Once she is free, she is not to return to the Whoring, but is to take up an honest Profession."

Simmins took my proffered Purse, but his Expression was one of unquiet Perplexity. "Mr H-art," he said, slowly, turning the kid-leather Pouch this Way and that several Times in his Hands. "F-orgive me, but I cannot see why you should shew such G-enerosity toward a common Pr-ostitute, who hath done naught to deserve it."

I watched my candle-Shaddowe flicker up and down the plastered Wall. "We may call it Purgatory," I said, at last. "I would pay for the Insult I inflicted upon her Person."

"S-urely the P-urgation of Guilt," Simmins ventured tentatively, "is G-od's Affair; and I do not believe that He—" he flushed, and swallowed, and his Voice droppt until it was barely above a Whisper, "would j-udge you with any great Degree of H-arshness, Mr Hart."

"My dear Simmins," I said. "I care naught for how I may appear to any God; what matters is how I appear to My Self; and I am not—I will not be—any Kind of Monster."

"B-ut you are not," Simmins said. "I do not kn-ow, in Truth, whether it is possible to r-ape an Whore; and even if it is, you did n-ot. I do not u-nderstand, Sir." He held out the Purse to me, as if desirous that I take it back.

I pushed his Hand away. "I do not require your Understanding," I said gently. "Merely your Compliance. Will you give me that?"

Little Simmins looked up at me, his brown Eyes those of my most faithful Hound. At last he gave that little Shrug, so familiar to us both, and put the small leather Bag beneath his Pillow. "I shall, Sir," he said.

I leaned forward, and taking hold of his Shoulders with mine Hands, softly bussed his Forehead, like an Emperor with his darling Slave, or a Father his beloved Son. "Thank you, Isaac," I said.

When I joined Katherine in our marital Bed, some little while later, it was to find her still awake. "Where the Devil have you been?" she demanded, as I slippt beneath the Counterpane, and prepared to snuff out my Candle, which had burned extreamly low.

Surprized by the Vehemence of her Question, I sate up. Her Face had upon it the same Expression it had worn when I had made false Love to Sophy. "With Mr Simmins," I said.

"Oh."

"Art jealous?" I exclaimed.

Katherine glared at me. I felt mine Heart wither, like a Violet transplanted all on a Sudden from an English Bank unto the scorching Desert-lands of Araby.

"Tristan," she said. "Put out the Light."

"Oh, banish me!" I cried. "But kill me not! I am not so unworthy!"

"You are hideously drunk," Katherine said. She turned her Back toward me, and pulled the Counterpane up to her Chin. "For God's Sake put out the Light, and let me go to Sleep."

CHAPTER THIRTY

Three Mornings after Lt. Simmins' Visitation, I was busy about my Work when Katherine came unexpectedly to speak with me. I had decided that the Time was right to draft mine Epistle to Dr Hunter requesting his Support, even tho'—in fact, largely because—mine Efforts to reproduce the Effects of Stroake upon a living Animal had proved inconclusive. I could see no Way forward now for mine Endeavour unless I performed the Human Dissections I had previously considered, and proved thereby that a significant Injury to the nervous Tissue of the Brain was, at least, consistently present in these Cases.

I had begun to compose a Letter to the good Doctor detailing my small Successes, when there came Katherine's soft Rap upon my Door, and it opened, and she steppt within, holding a lavender scented Handkerchief up to her small, straight Nose.

Instantly she gagged; my Study reeked with the Odour of a fox Cub, the Dissection of whose Spinal Cord I had been out of simple Curiosity engaged upon the previous Night. This Cub had been trapped by my Father's Gamekeeper, and had been dead a Sennight; but nevertheless, the Corpse was in a fair Condition, despite the Decay that had already set in, and I was confident of being able to set up the Skeleton in my Display Case when I had compleated mine Investigation, after mine old Habit: Bloody Bones, Collector of the Dead. My Study was quiet, the Fire low in the Grate; the spring Aire remained cold, and was still. Of all my Creatures, only my Goldfinch now remained to me, and he, toward whom I harboured no experimental Intent, fluttered freely about my Study, perching oft-times on my Shoulder as I worked, and twittering his pretty Melodies into mine Ear. I found this mildly annoying, but I could not bring My Self to cage him for it.

I was somewhat surprized; it was not Katherine's Habit ever to intrude upon me during mine Investigations, for she found the Sights and Smells of a Vivisection or an Anatomy greatly distressing, and on the only Occasion when she had caught me thus, she had run away at once to vomit.

"Tristan," she said, in the Voice of one who hath a great Secret. "I have Newes."

I pushed back mine Hair from my Forehead. "Wil't not wait?" I asked.

She tosst her Head. "No," she answered. "No; it hath waited too long, already."

Her Determination was, it appeared, greater than mine. Curious, I put down my Quill. Her Expression was not at all grave, and from this I deduced her Newes to be of a profound, but not terrible Nature. In respect of her Sensibilities, I drew a white Shroud, the which I kept solely for the Purpose, over my open dissecting Board and came out from behind my Table, in order to attend her properly. She looked me over in Silence for perhaps ten Seconds, biting her Lip, her grey Eyes sparkling; then she smiled, and the Words came spilling forth.

"Tristan," Katherine said. "I am with Child!"

Not terrible? Not? I had been wrong!

I had hoped for such Newes; I had expected them. But, to my immense Dismay, I discovered, now, when it was too late, that I was wholly unprepared to hear it. My World reeled about me and I clutched the Corner of my long Table for Support. My Goldfinch, alarmed, gave one sharp Whistle and fluttered to the very Top of my Bookcase. My Thoughts ran wild, incoherent in mine Horrour. "Alas!" I cried. "'Tis too soon! How long hast known? Oh, when was it conceived? At Christmas?"

"What?" Katherine exclaimed. Her Jaw droppt, and began to quiver. She crosst the Room, and put her slender Arms about my Ribcage, pressing her Cheek against my Sternum. "No, no; I do not think so; no."

Her Answer did not signify. I knew that there had been neither Time nor sufficient Occasion for the Child to have been conceived, and for Katherine to have confirmed its Existence, unless it had been during that relentless Week. Yet, had not that been what I had wanted? I did not know; verily, I did not. Still shivering somewhat, I relaxed mine Arms and folded Katherine in against my Chest. At least, I told My Self, if it were so, the Child would be born healthy; my Vigour had at that Time been so singular in its

Intent, and so relentless in its Force, that there could have been no Dissipation of the animal Spirits involved in its Conception, and if anything, it would be born under a lucky Star.

Lucky? Lucky? Mine Heart felt hollow. How could any Child of mine be lucky? The very Violence, I thought, of that Sennight's Passion must surely have begot a Freak. Such was the Condition, after all, of my poor little Bat.

"It will be dark!" I cried.

"You are dark, and I love you for it."

"The World doth not, and will not!"

Katherine put her Hands about my Face, and with some surprizing Violence turned my Chin, so that I was forced to look her in her Eye. "Then," she said fiercely. "I shall despise the World, if it love not you, my Bloody Bones, my Dear; and if our Child prove black as a very Bear, I shall not love it any less than if't were fairer than a Swan. Nay, I shall love it more. I did not choose a Man who was white, and fair. I chose you, Tristan; you; and I am truly happy for our Child. I want you to be happy for it, too."

But my Thought was: the World will call it Jew.

I wrote to Dr Hunter that Afternoon, and I did my best to put before him the Details of the Case: mine Hypothesis, mine Experiments, my Findings, and the Frustration which I currently faced. I begged him, in Tones that I considered suitably respectful and yet cautionary of the Implications to Science of his Refusal, for his Aid in procuring for me both appropriate Cadavers and Time within his anatomical Rooms. I suggested to him that, if he would see fit to assist me in my Research, we might together identify and isolate the physiological Cause of Stroake. I suggested, too, that I had already formed a Notion regarding its Treatment which might open up the Possibility of a Cure.

434

Having concluded this Epistle to my Satisfaction, and dispatched it, I then returned to my long Table to compleat the Dissection of my fox Cub.

I waited eagerly for a Reply to my Letter, but to my Surprize and Disappointment none arrived. I could not easily credit that Dr Hunter judged mine Hypothesis to be of such little scientific Worth that it deserved not even the merest Consideration; moreover, I thought it most unlike that he would not, if that had been the Event, at least have written to have told me so. But dampe March turned into damper April, and April progressed onwards, and still I had received no Word from him.

I began, in mine Anxiety, to have some Difficulty in sleeping; and out of Compassion for Katherine—or thus I perswaded My Self—who was otherwise kept awake, I began spending Nights alone in my Study upon my Sopha. I felt that this occasioned no great Loss to her; since she had disclosed her Condition to me I had not dared to be intimate with her in any Way for Fear of causing Injury to her increasing Body, or the Infant within. Sometimes it seemed to me that I perceived upon her Face an heart-sore Plea for the Sensation of sweet Pain that in our first Dayes would have sent me scrambling for my Knife; but I did not respond, and she did not provoke. Every Time I closed mine Eyes, I seemed with Horrour to see before me the Series of Sketches Dr Hunter had produced depicting the Foetus nestling within the pregnant Womb; the expanding Muscle of the Uterus, the stretching Ligaments, the thickening Veins. *Uteri humani gravidi.* Little Questions, peremptorily dismisst.

So it was an immense Relief to me when I received, out of the

435

Blue, a Letter that appeared to throw the Initiative squarely back into mine own Hands. It was from the newly gazetted Captain Simmins, acquainting me with his Address in London and issuing an open Invitation to visit him at my Convenience. Within the Sennight I had written back to accept his Invitation, and despite both mine own Misgivings at the Thought that I must leave my Katherine, and those expresst by the various Members of mine Household, I began to make Preparations for my Departure.

"I wish," burst forth Katherine one Evening, as we ate, the two of us alone, in the panelled dining Room, below the ever ticking Eye of the mantel Clock. "I wish that you would not go, Tristan!"

"'Twill not require of me a Stay of any lengthy Duration; but I must somehow speak with Dr Hunter. Perhaps he hath not had my Letter."

I had no Desire to be parted from her; and yet I had, I had.

The stiffest Resistance to my going was, however, and to my considerable Surprize, put up by my Father. I wondered greatly at this; for though it was still mine Intention to take over his Care once I had the Workings of a Cure for his Condition, I had not of late been overmuch in his Society.

"Doth he think I intend to fail?" I said to Erasmus, as we departed his sick Room. "If I come back having identified the Method by which he shall be made whole, he will be grateful for my going."

"Even so," Erasmus said. "But consider, Tristan, that you have not heard from Dr Hunter. You must allow the Possibility that he will not help. He is a busy Man, who hath his own Practice and School to run, and tho' he may yet wish to assist, be unable. I am concerned for the Effect on your Nerves, should you find that to be the Case."

"Erasmus," I said, looking him square in the Eye. "Dost consider me well, or no? Because if, as you have previously agreed, I am truly recovered from the nervous Fit, then I may suffer and overcome such Setbacks as masterfully as any Man. Tell me, am I sane, or no?"

"You are sane enough," Erasmus said, "to know that I have no Power to compel you to stay or to do otherwise. But you would be wise to listen to mine Advice. I offer it in Friendship, and not as your Physician."

"Thank you," I said. "I shall not attend it, but I appreciate its Sentiment."

There was a long Pause. We walked along the Passage together, he in the Direction of the Library, I, my Study; at the Door to which Erasmus stoppt, and turned to me. "Perhaps," he said, "as you are set upon returning to London, I shall do the same, and see whether the Offer Dr Oliver made that I should join him in St Luke's is still open. I cannot continue to live idly upon your Hospitality."

"Egad," I said. "I would prefer that you should stay! Wilt not take full Charge of my Father, as you were supposed to do?"

"Tristan," Erasmus said gently, "I must work, my Friend. I have no country Estate."

I remembered then, as I had never done before, that Erasmus had taken on my Care, which I had then imagined my Father's, owing to his Affection for me, and his fervently expresst Desire to keep me out of St Luke's; and that he had never properly been paid for his Services, owing to Barnaby's Affection for his Purse.

"Erasmus," I said, "if you will stay as my Family's Physician, I shall offer you whatever Pay you deem appropriate; and no one shall object if you practise among our Neighbours also. Our local Physician is no Man of Science, and his Treatments, I am certain, kill as many as they cure. Why, my Sister—"

"Stop there," Erasmus said. "Mrs Barnaby dislikes me."

"Indeed, she doth not!" I exclaimed. "She hath an high Regard for you and hath often expresst it."

"Not before me," Erasmus said. "She hath contrived only to demonstrate a singular Distaste for me in my Society."

"Her Husband, I grant you, is an hypocritical Coxcomb," I said. "But my Sister is the sweetest tempered Woman anywhere, and if she hath been unkind it must be because she is striving to conceal the Extent of her Affection."

Erasmus looked at me in plain Astonishment. "What dost mean, Tristan?"

"Egad," I said, shrugging my Shoulder. "Mine Offer is before you, Erasmus. Do what you will. We should all be happier an you stayed."

"Well, Tristan," Erasmus said, looking at me very queerly. "I shall consider your Advice. But I wish you would consider mine, your Father's, and that of your Wife."

Shortly before the Daye I was due to leave, about the Week the Hawthorns began, that dampe Spring, to bloom, I told my Sister about Katherine's Pregnancy. Mine Announcement had an un-expected Consequence: Mr Barnaby, no Doubt at the Promptings of strict Propriety rather than those of his Wife, who was now so many Nights at Shirelands it was hard to see when she might have found an appropriate Moment to prompt, issued a grudging Invitation to Katherine and My Self to visit at Withy Grange upon the following Saturdaye. I did not expect this Visitation to be a chearful one, but out of Curiosity and a mean Desire to see Barnaby squirm, I scrawled a curt Acceptance upon the Back of his own

Missive and sent it back forthwith by the same liveried Hand that had delivered it.

Upon making this Decision, however, I discovered an unexpected Difficulty. It had not occurred to me, when I had elected to return to London, that to do so I must leave mine Estate and cross enemy Territory; for tho' I knew that I had banished Raw Head's Goblins from Shirelands, Viviane ruled in the Valley, and I felt certain that her Hatred for me must be as strong as ever. Even this short Journey to Withy Grange, I thought, must present Opportunity for her to strike. I considered writing to Barnaby and withdrawing mine Acceptance of his Invitation; but then it appeared to me that doing so might convey to my Family some false Impression of Insanity, if my Reason should be guessed at, which would cause Confusion sufficient to threaten mine whole Project. I dismisst the Notion.

Instead, upon the Morning of the Visit, I dresst up My Self and Katherine in sad coloured Cloth, that our true Selves be thereby disguised, and instructed my Father's Coachman, who wore no Livery, to tell no one of his intended Journey, or what Passengers he carried. He was forbidden to stop, even in the Event of Robbery. I had suggested to Erasmus that he accompany us on this Visit, but somewhat to my Disappointment, my Suggestion met with so flat a Refusal that I could have played Bowls on it. We travelled with the Blinds down, and I refused to heed Katherine's Protestations that she wanted Light and Aire. We were as two Grouse, in matching Plumage. Our Cage, out of Necessity, remained covered.

We reached Withy Grange after an Houre or so, and on hearing the Carriage-wheels slowly crunching to an Halt upon Barnaby's Gravel, I was upon my Feet and opening the Door. The crimson Interior of the Coach immediately quickened with an agile Light, and the stuffy Aire itself seemed to draw Breath.

"Thanks be to God!" cried Katherine, at once.

"As there is no God," I precipitantly responded, "you must rather return Thanks to me, it being My Self that hath unclosed the Door."

"In that Case," replied Katherine, acidly, "thanks be unto thee, great Tristan, whose mercifull Kindness knoweth no Bounds, and falleth as freely upon us as the winter Rains." She bared her Teeth at me; it was not, by any Measure, a friendly Look.

"Too much," I said, stepping down onto the Driveway. "Shut up thy Mouth; that is a Smile so sweet the whole Wealth of the Africk could not buy't; and I am but one Man, who hath not yet come into Possession of his Fortune. Take mine Hand; I will assist you from your Seat."

"So ought you, Bloody Bones; you put me into it," Katherine answered, her Voice a low Growl.

She placed her Palm upon mine own, and descended carefully the three Steps that divided us. For a Moment, as she stood there before me, her Eyes fixt upon mine, it was as if the Distance betwixt us had never intervened. All we had, verily all we were, was contained in the Space between her Body and mine own: Katherine and I; My Self and Katherine. Then I put mine Hands about her Waist, and startled at its increased Thickness.

"Come," I said, lifting my Fingers from her as if from a burning Brand, and swivelling on mine Heel toward the magnificently roofed House, whose bright painted front Door, compleat with ready Footmen, stood open in seeming Welcome. "We must not linger here, for all it seems fair. Let us disclose what Mr Barnaby hath to say for himself."

"Oh," said Katherine. "Indeed, Tristan. Let us at once within." Instead of waiting for mine Arm, she lifted her Skirts above her

Ankles and propelled herself forward at almost a Run, treading hard upon my right Foot. I called her back, in some Alarm, but she ignored me, and vanished, like Eurydice, within the grey Vault of the Portico.

Barnaby received us most politely, with Jane at his Side, in the long drawing Room of Withy Grange that shared with my Sister's sitting Room a View over the Valley toward the River. The Room was splendid and well lit, but not lively; the crimson Curtains, the Chippendale Sophas, the Chairs against the Walls, the central Italian Rugg and paired Grecian Vases that stood beside the white veined Marble of the Chimney-piece had all to mine Eyes the Appearance of having recently worn Sheets, and the cool Aire reeked of Emptiness.

Barnaby could not have been in any Doubt as to my Familiarity with the Condition of his Marriage. However, he had evidently ordered Jane to co-operate in some Pretense of conjugal Unity, for both were stood up together, and steppt forward in a Welcome which was meant, with equal Sincerity, by neither. Jane was got up in a flea-coloured satin Sacque and white Stomacher of expensive Flemish Lace, and with her Physiognomy disguised under a thick Layer of Whitelead, and her Wigg piled high atop her Head, she appeared so greatly altered from herself that, had I met her in the Street, I might never have known her for my Sister.

Barnaby, for his Part, was dresst as sober as a Parson. His tight woollen frock Coat was dark blue, and buttoned high beneath his vulturine Chin, which appeared ill nourished, despite his great Wealth. He looked me over with Disdain, and ill-concealed Apprehension, as a lesser Lordling might an Hero of the boxing Ring. I remembered, with a nettling Sting, how it had been by his Consent that I had been brought home instead of being confined in St Luke's. I misliked full sore the Idea that Barnaby had been

Witness to me in my nervous Mania, and if such thing had been possible, the Notion would have induced me to love him even less than I presently did. Perhaps it was a good thing, therefore, that my Contempt of him was already so damning that it would have taken a Miracle for him to sink lower in mine Estimation.

We sate and played at Cards, until Katherine and I had thoroughly routed the Barnabys, and my Patience with the tedious Pantomime had utterly run out. Before Jane could suggest another Hand, I turned the Subject of our Conversation toward Barnaby's willow Wood, and the Sentiment I shared with Jane upon its intended Removal.

"That Wood," I said, "is like to have stood for many hundred Yeares, and if it is left unmolested, it may stand hundreds more. Moreover, it is beautifull, and Jane is fond of it. Will not you, Mr Barnaby, alter your Intention in respect of your Wife's Affection?"

"La, Tristan, I care not!" put in Jane at once, before her Husband could draw Breath. "It is the Fashion! Mr Barnaby may make whatever Improvements he pleases."

This Response was so unexpected, so compleatly different from the sorry Complaint Jane had made, privately, to me, that I was briefly stunned. "Sister," I stammered, when I had recaptured my Wits. "Did we not agree that the Destruction of the Willows would be dangerous, as it may result in the River's overspilling its Banks?"

"Mr Barnaby," said Jane pacifically, "tells me that Argument is peevish Fiddle-faddle, and that neither our Lawns nor the local Farms are in any Danger of Submersion."

"The only Fiddle-faddle," I answered, "is in your saying so, when—" I broke off. Katherine had kicked me, very hard, upon my shin Bone. Barnaby's Nostrils flared.

"Mr Barnaby's hired Men," Jane said, "have already begun about the Works. They are very efficient. Mr Barnaby is very pleased with the Repair they made to the Wall in the old Orchard."

Doth he beat her? I thought, suddenly.

I presst the Knuckles of my right Fist into my Palm until they cracked. The Sounds rang out surprizing loud in the still Room, a Battery of small Shots.

CHAPTER ONE-AND-THIRTY

It was with both a leaping and a sorry Heart that I quit Shirelands at the End of that Week, in, once again, a plain Carriage, with its Blinds drawn fast against all spying Eyes and its Horses swift. My Sorrow, and more than a little Guilt besides, was all at the Thought that I was leaving Katherine, and should not, if all went well in the City, see her again for several Months; but mine Ambition, and the great scientific Advancements that this, our second Separation, might make possible, made me to put all such Regrets aside. I told My Self, as I had repeatedly told Katherine, that as long as we continued to write, as we had done during my previous Travail in London, we would be happy enough. It had, after all, been only when Katherine had failed to answer the Letter presenting my Proposal, that the Scheme had gone awry; and I knew that, this Time, there would be no meddling Mama or misguided Erasmus to effect any similar Catastrophe.

I still had heard naught from Dr Hunter, but my Fear that he might have no farther Interest in my Career, or in mine Hypothesis, had been greatly allayed by my Receipt of another Letter from Mr Henry Fielding himself, in which—it being tacitly understood that I would not, this Time, be lodging at Bow Street—he first extended an open Invitation to visit, and second, acquainted me with the Fact that Dr Hunter had but recently inquired after mine Health and my present Circumstances. The Implication of this Inquiry seemed to me quite clear. Dr Hunter was querying the Likelihood of my being able to compleat my Work without his Support, which must mean that he was seriously considering extending it. Mine Heart leapt, therefore, with Hope; and as the closed Carriage rumbled thro' the dampe Morning, taking me away from Katherine, from my Father, from Erasmus, my Sickness, and the Memory of Raw Head, I recited in mine Head the Words with which I intended to perswade him.

I arrived in London early upon the following Afternoon, and having established My Self in the musty little Room known as the Hound, in the Red Lion on St John's Street—which Inn had been suggested to me by Captain Simmins, as nearest to his own Lodging—I sent Word to Bow Street of mine Arrival. Mr Fielding replied at once with, as I had intended and hoped, an immediate Invitation to Dinner.

Acutely conscious of the unhappy Condition in which the Fielding Family had last beheld me, I dresst carefully for the Occasion, in my grey silk Frock with Brocaide Embroidery, Waistcoat and Breeches of matching Stile, white Stockings and buckled Shoes, Hat, and silver handled ebon Cane. Thus attired, I examined my Reflection in the Mirrour.

At once, I startled. It had been so long a Time since I had paid more than the slightest Attention to mine Appearance that I had not properly become aware of how significantly I was altered from the callow young Man who had argued the Case for Fashion against Mr John Fielding. But my Frock, tho' it had been extream smart when I had had it from my Tailor, was now new in neither Cloth nor Cut; my buckled Shoes were Pinchbeck; and whereas I had been used always to have worn a stilish Wigg, mine Hair now was mine own, black as Coal and reaching to my Collar in an heavy Curtain, before which the Bones of my Cheeks, and mine hooked Nose, stood out in stark Relief. I look a Freak! I thought. My Stomach twisted with a shocking Fear; and for the first Time in mine whole Life I was grateful for my dark Skin, for had I been fair I should verily have looked an Apparition of approaching Death.

But before this Panick had the Chance to set its Course into my Bowels, it suddenly occurred to me that there was a very good Excuse for mine appearing as I did. I was now a Man of Science, not Fashion. Mine Ideas were my Cloathing; they, not my Dress, would be the Measure of my Standing and my Reputation; and thro' them, and only them, should I garner Respect. The Cut of my Frock, the Absence of my Wigg, were not things that ought to matter to me one Moment longer. I had steered my Feet on to an higher Path; truly, I was to become a Man of no mundane, superstitious Sort, but one of Reason.

I chose not to walk the Distance to Bow Street, tho' it was not far. The Weather was dampe; the London Highways and Lanes were filthier than the main Road into Highworth, and the Traffick was great; tho' I would dearly have loved to wander again thro' their clamorous Ways, it seemed wiser to call upon the Chairmen. I kept the Chair's Blinds open, however, and feasted mine Eyes upon the Multitude of excitatious Personages crowding, shouting, hurrying, leaping, fighting, busy about their own Affairs and intirely oblivious to mine Admiration. All this Noise, and phrenzied Activity seemed to me strange after the Peace of Berkshire; yet after no more than five Minutes, my Surprize, and the slight Disquiet that accompanied it, faded away. This City, I realised with a Jolt, this wretched, noissome, filthy, wondrous City, had been mine Home, every bit as much as Shirelands was; perhaps even more. Here, I had been happy; here I had been safe, at least until the End, from Viviane. Here I had not only my Work, but my very Purpose.

I ought to stay, I thought, suddenly. If I can convince Dr Hunter. Even if I cannot.

Would Katherine be able to stay, to live properly, in London? I had never once considered it. I pondered it, now, and with serious Intent. Would Katherine, who had never been to any Town larger than Weymouth, adjust to the Pace and Excitement of London? I feared, in my Bones, that she might not.

Bow Street was well lit up within, it being now seven o' the Clock; and its candled Windows cast a soft ivory Sheen upon the murky Street. I paid off the Chairmen and alighted on the front Step, Anticipation tingling in my Blood.

Straightening first mine Hat and then my Coat, I approached the Fieldings' Door and rang low on the Pin. The Hall beyond erupted with those once familiar Sounds, still dear to me: Children shouting, Dogges barking— and, I fondly imagined, knocking over the Children in their Surge towards the Door—and finally Mrs

Mary Fielding's own Voice, commanding that everyone be still and let her unfasten the Door that Mr Hart, if it be he, might enter.

"It is indeed he, Mrs Fielding!" I shouted thro' the solid Wood. I tried to compose my Features into an Expression that betrayed no Hint of my tumultuous Sentiments, but I was not, I think, successful.

A Key turned; Mrs Fielding opened up the Portal, and smiled.

"Mary!" I cried out, before I could stop My Self; and I fought back the sudden Impulse to catch her up in mine Arms, as I had done once before. I coughed, ashamed of the Impropriety, and correcting My Self, said: "Mrs Fielding, how good to see you!"

"Come inside, Mr Hart, don't linger on the Step," Mrs Fielding said quickly, with a broad Smile of her own and an hastily aborted Curtsey, the which I was certain I ought not to have noticed.

I steppt over the Sill, and stood in the Hallway, while Mrs Fielding locked the Door and drew across it several heavy iron Bolts.

"There are some," she said, seeing my querying Expression, "as do not take too kind to Mr Fielding's Progress with his Runners."

"I see," I said. "There have been Threats?"

"There have, Mr Hart," Mary said. Her Countenance was grave. "Mr Fielding says the best Way to find out how many Rats are in a Nest is to stick a Pitchfork into it; and he is doing it. London hath Rats aplenty, Sir."

It had begun to dawn upon me, slowly, that something had altered in Mary. It was nothing in her Appearance, which was as it had ever been: an agreeable, round cheeked Face beneath a linen Cap; open, honest Eyes, and a clear Skin, unspoilt by the small Pox. I considered her closely, thinking that perhaps she might be with Child again, but her Shape and plain Dress gave away no Sign. Finally, I realised what it was. "Mrs Fielding," I exclaimed, with a Laugh. "You have found your 'H'!"

Mary Fielding smiled, and held forth her Hand, quite as if she had been a Lady of Birth and Fashion. "I have," she said, aspirating the Letter with considerable Pride. "I have."

Mrs Fielding led me thro' the Mobb of Dogges into the sitting Room, and then departed, leaving me in Company with both Brothers Fielding, who were sitting one to either Side of the slow burning log Fire, their Faces ruddy in the Heat. It struck me suddenly, seeing them thus together after such a Time apart from both, how unlike they were. Mr Henry Fielding was very tall, well built but not corpulent; his long Nose, the most prominent Feature of his Face, appeared above a sensuous Mouth, while his Eyes sparked with Wit and ready Temper. He was dresst in a dark brown Frock, a Wigg of middling Length, buff coloured Breeches and, due to the Gout, one Slipper, upon his less affected Foot. His other, which he had stretched out before him upon a softly cushioned Stool, was bound up in Muslin and Lint.

Mr John, in contrast, was somewhat shorter, but much more heavily built, a veritable Bull, with a wider, fleshier Face. I saw with a Start that he was tonight wearing neither black Band nor Glasses.

"Mr Hart!" exclaimed Mr Henry Fielding at the Sight of me. "Come in, young Man, and sit down. Liza, a Glass of Claret for Mr Hart."

I found a Chair, settled My Self beside the side-Board, some small Distance across the Room from the Brothers, and happily accepted the Glass Liza poured for me. "Good Evening, Mr Fielding; Mr Fielding," I said, addressing my Words first to Mr Henry Fielding and then to his Brother.

"You will pardon me, Mr Hart, if I do not rise," Henry Fielding said. "My damned Foot hurts like the Devil tonight, and Dr Hunter hath told me that I must rest it or suffer much worse the Morrow. However, I have pledged both John and Mrs Fielding that I shall endeavour to forestall the Pain's disrupting my good Humour. Well, Sir, it hath been a while, a good while—and a great Deal hath happened. Here you are, a married Man, no less!"

"I am, Sir," I answered.

"Where is your Bride? Can it be you have left her behind, so very soon?"

"I did not think that she would enjoy London, Sir." I felt my Cheek grow warm.

Henry Fielding sank back into his Chair, chuckling in Amusement at my Predicament. This gave his Brother John an Opportunity to Speak; and despite the Affection I had developed towards this Mr Fielding over the many Months of my Residency at Bow Street, I felt a Queasiness in my Gut at his addressing me.

"Tristan," said John Fielding. His sightless Eyes, for once visible to my Gaze in the Absence of his customary Lenses, turned a little Way in my Direction. As if he could still see, I thought, as I had always thought, when he turned those Eyes upon me, hidden or no. A chilling Shiver ran the whole Length of my Spine. "I am glad," continued he, "to find you thus recovered from your Nerves. I hear that you are eager to recommence your Apprenticeship under Dr Hunter's Tutelage."

"Tutelage?" I frowned. "I know nothing of that, Sir. I have written to Dr Hunter to ask whether he would consider offering his Support to me in a scientific Inquiry of mine own Devising."

"Your own Devising?" Henry Fielding exclaimed. "An ambitious Project, Mr Hart."

I leaned forward. "I know it, Sir," I said. "And yet my whole Aim is ambitious; I seek to identify and explain the Cause of Stroake, the better thereby to discover a Means of curing the Disease that hath crippled my Father."

John Fielding gave a Grunt. He appeared, to mine heightened Sensibility, to have been propelled deep into Thought; tho' scanty Trace of his Deliberations appeared on his forbidding Countenance. "Tristan," he said, at last, in a serious Tone, "I know you for an exceptionally intelligent young Man, who might even yet become a brilliant Physician. Your Ambition is commendable and I wish you, ultimately, all Success. But it is my Duty to warn you, as one who hath your Welfare close at Heart, that I have grave Doubts as to whether Dr Hunter will allow you to resume your Studies until you have been consistently well for some considerable Time; if, indeed, at all. Moreover, even if he consent to help you in your Scheme, it is unlike that with all his great Skill and Knowledge at Hand, you will uncover a Cure for Apoplexy that you can use to help your Father."

At these Warnings, mine Heart sprang into my Throat and clung there, as a terrified Cat leapeth into the Branches of an Ash. "Yet," I said, forcing My Self to ignore the former Part of Mr Fielding's Speech as if he had never given it, "am I not Honour bound to try? And even if I cannot help my Father, I shall set my Findings before the Royal Society, and advance the Currency of my Name enormously amongst our Men of Science."

"Indeed," said John Fielding. A dark Frown creased his Forehead. "To advance yourself is an understandable Desire," he said. "And one that every young Man of Ability should share, after his Talent. You would be a second Paracelsus, I perceive. But such powerful Ambition, Tristan, is a two edged Sword, and you must be cautious, lest you cut yourself in its Wielding."

At these Words, my Breath caught afire in my Chest. I realised just how passionate was my Desire and Hope of such an Outcome; and conversely, therefore, how terrifying the Possibility that I might fail. To be a second Paracelsus! What might I not sacrifice to become such? I did not know; and this Awareness, that I did not, frightened me.

"Blasted Pain!" Henry Fielding cursed, savagely, half silently, and quite to himself.

I left Bow Street by Chair at about half-past ten o' the Clock, and arrived, without Incident, back at my Lodging shortly before eleven. The inn Yard was exceeding busy, owing to the untimely Arrival of the Leicester Mail, so in the general Bustle I did not at first perceive, standing patiently in the Doorway, his Hat and Coat quite dampe from the spring Rain, the wiry Figure of Captain Simmins. In all Innocence, therefore, I lighted from my Chair, paid my Shilling to the Chairmen, and headed forth into the Inn. Then I felt an Hand catching at mine Arm, and without even turning mine Head, I knew in my Bowels that it was he.

"Good Evening to you, Captain Simmins," I said.

"Good Evening, Sir."

"Hast been long waiting for me?"

"No, Sir," Simmins answered. "Th-ree Houres, Sir. No longer."

"Some might consider that a long Time, Mr Simmins."

"I – I do not, Sir."

I turned mine Head to look at him. His Face shone golden in the Light that spilled out from inside the Building, as his Breath wisped, cloudy upon the drizzling Aire, thro' his parted Lips. His dark brown Eyes were fixt upon my Face.

I looked sharp around, feeling for an Instant as if I were committing a Crime. Everyone's Attention was upon the new arrived Mail; no one shewed the slightest Curiosity in My Self or the slender young Adonis who had suddenly accosted me.

"Come," I said; and without more ado, I strode across the slate Doorstep and proceeded swiftly to my Lodging. I knew that

Simmins would follow me. Had I commanded it, he would have followed me into the Mouth of Hell.

I let Simmins before me into my Room, lit the Candle and fastened the Door before rounding upon him. "Have you found the Whore?" I demanded.

"No, Sir."

"No? How can you thus answer? No? I gave you firm Instruction, Mr Simmins: find Miss Annie Moon and bestow upon her a certain Sum of Money. How can it be that in all these Weeks you have not found her?"

"I could not, Sir. I asked at Mrs Haywood's Establishment, but all say she is no longer there."

"Indeed?" Mine Heart sank. Surely, I thought, she hath not already bought her Freedom of Mrs Haywood? Mayhap she is dead. How can I, if Antoinette be dead, ever redeem My Self concerning her? "Then," I said, "you should have redoubled your Efforts, and searched elsewhere, beyond Covent Garden. I am disappointed in you, Mr Simmins."

"I kn-ow, Sir. I am s-orry. I will m-ake better E-ffort in the F-uture."

Simmins hung his Head. I studied, close, his Expression, his Shape; the smallest Movements of his Hands and Feet. "Mr Simmins," I said, "you are an Offense to my Sight. Your Coat is wet and your Shoes are muddy. How is it that every Time we meet you contrive to drip, Mr Simmins?"

"I st-ood in the Rain," Simmins whispered.

"That is no Excuse," I said. "Get out."

I did not permit my Mind to linger at all upon the Intimation Mr John Fielding had given me regarding the poor Likelihood of my

Return to Dr Hunter's Favour. The following Morning, I wrote to Katherine, to assure her of my safe Arrival, and to tell her I had visited the Fieldings. Then, having Quill in Hand, I composed a second Letter to Dr Hunter, to acquaint him with my London Address, and to ask of him whether he had considered my Proposition. I gave both Letters to the Pot-boy, with a Shilling for his Trouble, and then fell to considering how I might todaye further the Progress of my Theory, for I did not judge the Room of the Hound conducive to maintaining a studious Frame of Mind. There was, for one thing, no Desk, but merely a side-Table; for another, the Chamber was so diminutive that it was quite impossible for me to have unpacked compleatly lest I fall over mine Equipment, or scatter my Notes in the Clutter.

I thought that I might go to one of the Taverns I had frequented in Erasmus' Company during our Tenure at the Hospitals, and there discover what Newes I could of Dr Hunter himself: whether he had made any new Discovery pertaining to Aneurysm, and what Progress he had made in bringing his obstetric Etchings toward Publication. I began to dress; but Recollection of Dr Hunter's Depictions of the gravid Uterus put me in mind of Katherine, and mine Hands began so violent a Tremble upon my Cravat that I could not tie it, and was forced to sit upon the Bed until I had regained my Composure.

The Walk to St Thomas's Hospital – for by this Means it suited me to travel, when I had at last restored both Will and Power to my quivering Limbs – took me past Smithfield, St Bartholomew's and the antient Horrour of Newgate Prison thro' Cheapside to the London Bridge, below which snailed the thick Thames, while small Boats queued for Passage thro' the narrow Arches. I glanced down, at the green and silent Waters, and then steppt in a lively

Manner onto the Bridge, losing Sight of the River behind its Buildings.

This main Road into the Boro' was the most crowded and busy of Southwark's Thoro'fares, yet I knew nothing of the Fear that impelled most Men of my Station into Carriage and Sedan. I knew not wherefore, nor do I even now comprehend the Reason, but those Gentlemen of Highway and Alley, who might have perceived in me an easy Mark, and treated with me accordingly, kept as respectful a Distance from my Person as had the youngest of the Collerton Maids.

By the Time I reached the George Inn I was intensely thirsty, and my Feet were aching from my long Perambulation. I steppt quick thro' the Doorway. Perhaps I had been too long in Berkshire, for the Establishment seemed at once too crowded and noisy for my Taste, and the dark smoake Reek caught in my Chest. I made my Way to the far Corner, where I hoped I might not be disturbed, and called the Landlord to bring Food and Ale. This done, I sate with my Plate and listened in upon the Conversation of the Students and Physicians who frequented the George, straining my Hearing for any Mention of Dr Hunter.

Perhaps I had timed mine Arrival ill, for although I pricked mine Ears as intently as a Coney apprehending Dogges, I caught no Newes of Dr Hunter, the Progress of his Lithographs, or his Researches. Moreover, none of those Individuals presently conversing in the George was familiar to me from my Time in the Hospitals or anywhere else. I wondered at this; how could the Studentship of St Thomas's have altered so compleatly in the Months I had been absent from it? Then I remembered, with a small Jolt, that with the Exception of Erasmus, I had never taken the slightest Interest in my Companions upon the Wards; and I realised that I had perhaps been surrounded by these Fellows for many a Sennight, without exchanging Word with one of them. The Notion saddened me; then I felt, all on a sudden, violent Anger at the Notion that these mediocre Clerks had been able to pursue their medical Careers when I had not; and I fervently wished each one of them at the very Bottom of Hell's fiery Pit before I remembered that I no longer believed in Hell, nor Devil, neither; and I ground my Teeth, and sate on in fruitless Silence.

After some fifteen Minutes, mine Attention was captured by a Conversation some little Distance to my Right, between two I had thought to resemble the humblest Members of the Clergy and had dismisst therefore as having nothing of Interest to impart, concerning the medical Use of the electric Fluid.

"The electrical Machine," the Speaker was saying, with such Enthusiasm in his Tone I could easily imagine him to have been an antient Prophet, "may be used cheaply, for 'tis only required to make a Purchase of the one, that may be used over and over; and therefore it may be offered free to the Poor, who cannot afford these Physicians. We may thereby bring about great Relief to the Ills of those Wretches so abominably afflicted with Palsy and with other vile Complaints; and this must be a good thing, and pleasing to the Lord; for once their Bodies are made whole, their Soules may be better able to attend His Word."

"Aye, they may get Relief, Mr Wesley," the other said. "But what of the poor Practitioner, who must spend Houres a-cranking th'Wheel and delivering the Shocks? Seems to me that any Benefit to the Poor from that Device will be at high Cost to ourselves. What Proof have we the thing will work as you say? Mayhap their clever Talk is naught but Puff. And how do we know, besides, that the Machine, in all Truth, causeth anything but pure and simple

Pain? 'Tis not God's Will, I'm sure, that we torment the Poor to make them well."

"No, no!" answered the other, striking the Table with his Fist. His Passion surprized me, and I jumped. "'Tis verily a Motion of the electric Fluid, from the Machine to the Body of the Afflicted; this Motion, like Lightning from the Clouds, hath a significant Effect within the Body. Lightning may kill a Man, as we all know."

"Which Fact alone implies," the other retorted, "that there is little Good that can come from electrical Application."

"Electricity is not harmful, in itself," replied the first. "'Tis dangerous only by its Quantity; the Amount that is stored in a Leyden Jar is insufficient to do Harm. For My Self, I am convinced of its Potential; and when 'tis commonly understood, even by our medical Men, who are set against it, that Electricity may relieve Palsy, or cure Blindness or Cancer, I shall be vindicated, to the Glory of Almighty God who hath created it for our Use; and my Detractors shamed."

Naturally, I had heard, during the Course of mine Habitation in London, of such Electrostatick Machines, and such unscientific Ideas; but, todaye, something in the Quality of mine Attentiveness, or in the Pattern of my Thoughts, caused the Notion suddenly to leap out before me as an Hart from an Hedge: what if the curative Effects of medical Electricity were real, but did not derive from the electric Fluid *per se*, but purely from the intense Pain that such Shocks produced—as the second Speaker had, indeed, suggested. For Pain, I was certain, was a Mode of Thought, a physical Motion in the nervous Web of the Body immediately perceptible and comprehensible to both Body and Mind, in a Way that mere Electricity was not. Could I, by the appropriate Infliction of Pain upon my Father, encourage the Lesions in his Brain to heal, and cure him of his Paralysis? The Action would not, after all, be very far removed from that of opening up the Curtains and letting in the Light; it implied only an Increase in the Intensity of his Stimulation. Could not it help him? At very least, I thought, it may ease his Condition. And then the Thought struck me that if that were the least, then at most—at most, such a Discovery might not only secure my scientific Reputation, but alter the Course of Medicine for the next Century. If it were indeed the case that Pain itself might be used to heal, that Pain was not necessarily the abominable Scourge of Mankind that commonly 'twas perceived to be, but might be an Aid to Recovery, then what Difference might be made to future Practice of the medical Art! The more I pondered upon this Revelation, the more it seemed to make great Sense to me; for had I not already reasoned that Pain, alone among Human Sensations, had the Capacity to leap betwixt two Persons, when in sufficient Sympathy? Again I thought, as I had done before: 'Tis a Species of Love.

I could have taken this Insight home and applied it straightway to my Father's Care; but I did not. I applied my Reasoning instead to how it might be proved.

Verily, I must acquire Time in the dissecting Room, I thought. 'Tis now a Matter of most pressing Urgency that I demonstrate causal Relationship betwixt cerebral Damage resultant upon an Apoplexy and the Paralysis of the Limbs that my Father endures. Oh, why hath Dr Hunter not responded to my Letter?

I returned to my Lodging on foot, as I had come, and upon arriving there inquired whether I had received any Correspondence or Visitor, but I had had neither. I was greatly disappointed. I returned to my cramped and musty Chamber and composed a

Letter to Katherine in which I poured out my Frustrations as freely as Oil from a Cask. This accomplished, however, there seemed little I could do except to wait.

On the third Daye after this I received a Letter, but 'twas not from Dr Hunter. It was from Katherine, telling me naught of Bloody Bones or Leonora, but that she herself had injured her right Shoulder whilst reaching for the Sauce; yet I must not worry, for Erasmus had succeeded in clicking it back into place. I was somewhat concerned as to what she could mean by sending me this Intelligence, for she described precisely a minor Subluxation of the Os Humeri. I was naturally familiar with the excessive Pliability of her Joints, and had often wondered at the Ease with which I might have pulled her Limb from Limb, but I had never heard of such an Event's occurring spontaneously. I thrust firmly from my Mind the wondering Dread that had leapt up at her Newes, and the shameful Thought that it should have been I, not Erasmus, who had put her together again, and forced My Self to conclude against mine Instincts that her Report was greatly exaggerated. I wrote in Reply to scold her for reaching like a Savage across the dinner Table in the first Place.

I continued thus frustrated and helpless for another Sennight before my Forbearance cracked. I wrote again upon the Mondaye Morning to Dr Hunter, asking him wherefore he had not responded to mine earlier Epistles, and alerting him that unless he give me strict Instruction to the Contrary, I should call in at the Little Piazza later in the Daye, to discuss my Proposition with him in Person.

Within one Houre of my dispatching this Missive, I received this Reply.

Dear Mr Hart,

I regret that it is quite impossible for me to attend to you this Afternoon, for I shall have a Class of Paying Students, whose Educational Advancement I must, regretfully, put before yours. Moreover, I am unable to offer you any Manner of Support, Financial or Otherwise, in your Endeavour, despite its very Commendable Aim. I trust that you are still minded of the Caveats I rigorously apply in Respect of Anyone who would seek Entrance to the noble Profession of Surgery. I wish you well, but I must politely request that you do not contact me again until such time as we may both have Reassurance as to your State of Mind.

Dr Wm Hunter

Upon reading this cruel Dispatch, I found my Legs begin to quiver beneath me as intense as if Hades had been about to swallow me. My Knees giving way, I collapsed upon the hard Floorboards of my Chamber. A Puff of black Smoake billowed from the smouldering coal Fire. Dr Hunter would not assist me. Worse, he desired no future Contact, as if I had caught the Plague, or were a Person of such low Character it would be improper for him to associate with me.

Doth Dr Hunter consider me mad? I thought in a Panick. But mine Hypothesis is sound, and my Method also. 'Tis unlike he could have mistook them for the Ravings of a Lunatick, however unwell I might previously have been. Hath he simply dismisst them, doth he dismiss me, because he thinks that I have been mad? I am not! I am a sane Man, as sane as he; and mine Hypothesis is right! Wherefore doth he disown me?

Struggling to my Feet, I threw My Self bodily upon the Door and wrenched it open. I had it in mine Head to disregard Dr Hunter's Instruction and demand of him what he thought he was about, to abandon me thus and contemn my Research to rank Oblivion before 'twas even birthed.

I had regard neither for mine Hat, nor my Greatcoat, nor my Cane. I thought nothing of mine Appearance, which must have been at that Moment akin to a Spectre a-rising from the Tomb, the Letter crumpled in my shaking Hand, mine Eyes wild and staring and mine Hair untended; nor did I consider what I ought to say to Dr Hunter when eventually I confronted him. I ran down the Stairs fast as an Hare, and thro' the Door into the inn Yard, where for the second Time I collided, to my present Shock and Annoy, with Captain Isaac Simmins.

CHAPTER TWO-AND-THIRTY

Simmins, being so much smaller in Stature than My Self, and having not a Fraction of my Momentum, was immediately knocked from his Feet and tumbled upon his soldierly Arse on a Patch of the wet Straw that lay here and there in Heaps about the muddy Flags. The violent Collision having broke my Flight, I stoppt abruptly, to determine who, or what, I had run into. Perceiving at once who it was, I realised that I could not immediately continue in my Pursuit of Dr Hunter, and I was overcome by a Disappointment and Anguish so great my Legs began anew to tremble feverishly. I put out mine Hand to assist Captain Simmins to his Feet, but to mine Horrour perceived that it was shivering. Simmins did not take it.

"Mr Hart," he said, staring up at me from the Dirt with an Expression of Concern. "Are you in some Difficulty, Sir?"

"No, Mr Simmins," I replied, but my Voice betrayed me, "I—"

Simmins scrambled to a standing Position. "Mr Hart," he said. "F-orgive me if I speak out of T-urn, but you have the Appearance of a M-an whose Courage hath sustained a severe and shocking Blow. Wilt return within? Some st-iffening Sp-irit will not do you ill, and if I can offer you any A-ssistance, I put My Self intirely at your D-isposal."

"I—" I said. I could not continue. I could not say the Words that echoed, more and more loudly, within mine Head: I have been thrown away.

"Come inside, Sir," repeated Simmins, putting his Fingers gently upon mine Arm and making some tentative Movements toward the inn Doorway. A greyish Rain had begun to fall. Tho' 'twas near Noon, the Sky was dark. Simmins' brown Eyes, glistening in the desolate Gloom, seemed suddenly to me to represent the only Points of Light in the whole World, twin Lanthorns like those that adorned the Door of the Collerton Bull, or like marsh-Lights dancing over the slow River. I reached out, and graspt him tight by his Elbow. He did not flinch.

"How is't," I said, "that you know precisely when, and how, to comfort me, Isaac? Hast some magical Glass that tells you when I am in Need?"

"No, Mr Hart," Simmins whispered, his Eyes fixt upon mine. "'Tis but f-ortunate Co-incidence. I have the A-fternoon off."

The Strength was now returning to my Limbs. I tightened my Grip upon Simmins' Elbow, seeking to insinuate my Fingertips into that tiny Crevice betwixt the Bone and the Ligament, to make Simmins yelp, to make him pull away. His Greatcoat, however, was too thick. Simmins only gave a little Smile, and cocked his Head upon one Side, in a Gesture that would have seemed unnatural and improper if performed by any other Man, yet appeared curiously correct in him.

Turning about on the Spot, I pulled Simmins sharply in that Direction in which he had hitherto attempted to guide me, back into the Inn; disregarding everything else, I dragged him into my Chamber, locked the Door, and secreted the Key in my Waistcoat Pocket along with Mary's Sketch.

"Sit down," I said.

I did not know precisely what it was that I desired to do to Captain Simmins, except that it was to hurt him viciously, sorely, cruelly. I wanted to exorcise, by making Sacrifice of his strong, beautifull Body, the Demon of heartbreaking Despair that seemed even this very Second hovering above me like a carrion Bird, its black Wings whispering that all mine Ambitions were as Dust.

I looked down at Isaac Simmins, my loyal Friend, beloved Slave, and some darkly hidden Thread in mine Heart seemed to snap. At last, I understood the Nature of the Service he must render me, and its Event seemed as inevitable as Night after Daye. I knew now that the Sensation I felt for him was not carnal Lust, as I had feared it might be; not as it might have been for Annie, or even, to my Shame, for the bound and naked Lady B. It was indeed Excitement; but despite the Spark in my Loins and the Fire in mine Entrails it was an Excitement of an intellectual Kind, brilliant as blazing Sunnelight, clean and sharp and intractable as a very Blade. Damn you, Dr Hunter, I thought. Ah, damn you! I shall prove mine Hypothesis—all mine Hypotheses—without your Patronage.

"You say you put yourself intirely at my Disposal," I said, removing my Coat, and Waistcoat, and tucking in the Ruffles of my Sleeves.

"I accept your Offer, Mr Simmins. I have Need of your Assistance in my Studies. Remove your Shirt and your Boots, but otherwise you may remain cloathed."

"What, Sir?"

"I do not desire to bugger you," I told him. "Do as I say."

Remembering how tightly it had been necessary for Dr Hunter to restrain Lady B.—, I searched thro' my Belongings until I found Items suitably strong and flexible to tie down Mr Simmins to my Bed, and then Instructed him to lie supine upon the Counterpane. This Simmins did, quite readily, his Expression one of simple Curiosity rather than any dread Apprehension. I lifted his Arms above his Head and tied his Wrists first together and then to the vertical Bars at the Head of the Frame, so that his bent Elbows rested each above one Ear. To prevent his moving much during the intended Operation I bound also his Feet firmly to the Posts, and would have secured his Trunk to the Mattress, but I had insufficient Cordage. Once I had thus rendered him securely immobile, I steppt hurriedly across to the Grate, for the meagre Fire was now fading from Hunger and I had to feed it, ere we both catch a Chill. Having coaxed the fresh Coals to Flame, I lit from them first one wax Candle, then seven others, which I placed about the Room in a near perfect Circle, so that wherever I should stand sufficient Light would fall upon Simmins, and upon my Table, for me to perform mine Experiment and record my Findings. My Theatre thus established, I returned to the Bed and sate My Self beside Captain Simmins. He smiled.

"I had assumed," I murmured softly, stroking Simmins' Head, "that I should find some unfortunate Inhabitant of Seven Dials, and pay him handsome for his Service. But now you, my dearest Isaac, have put yourself quite literally in my Path, and offered yourself up to me. So I shall explain all; for 'tis only right that you know what, and wherefore, you shall suffer. It is mine Intent to prove upon you the Rectitude of an Hypothesis I have lately formulated regarding Pain, and its Potential to cure Paralysis. My dear Father, as you know, hath recently endured a crippling Stroake; I have spent countless Houres and Dayes in searching for a Method to replicate it upon a living Animal and thereby prove its Cause, which I am certain is an Insult to the Tissue of the Brain. All by the by; I do not intend to inflict upon you—as yet—any Manner of Insult within your Cranium, for I could not be at all certain that you would survive the Process. That may come later, when I have perfected my Method. I do, however, require your Co-operation in an Investigation of the Effects of Pain upon a previously induced Paralysis."

Simmins' Eyes grew wide at these Newes, as well they might; he stared at me, perplexed, and to my Mind somewhat skeptical, and gave a little Laugh. Ignoring this Response, I continued: "My present Interest is in that Portion of the Net of Nerves that weaves thro'out the Body, and connects the Extremities with the Spine. A Sennight since, I was sitting in Southwark listening to a Conversation— the Detail of it matters not, but it put me in Mind of something I used to notice between-whiles at Mrs Haywood's. I told you something, I think, of mine Experiences there. I will now confess that I was not intirely truthful. I did not fuck the Whores, Isaac; I do not like to do that. But neither am I like you, as you seem to have assumed; the Bodies of Men do not much entice me either. My Pleasure was to bind those Women as I have bound you, and to torture them severely, until they could no longer endure the Agonies. Now here comes the Point, which I hope will prove to be of great Significance to Science: upon a Number of Occasions,

I noticed that upon my releasing them from Bondage they would complain of a Numbness in their Hands, which did not persist long. Then, I merely considered this to be indicative of my Tying them too tightly, and compromising the Circulation of the Blood; but now, I think I had not interfered with their Blood at all, but rather had injured a Nerve. This, Mr Simmins, this Induction of nervous Paralysis, is what I intend to do to you; then I shall inflict such Pains upon the senseless Part as are necessary to restore its Feeling, sufficient possibly to make you faint if you were properly to sense them—which of course you shall not, for a while. And we shall see whether, as I am utterly convinced it must, these healing Pains restore Sensation quickly, or take a longer Time."

Simmins' perplext Expression lingered a little while longer; then as he began to comprehend that I was in earnest, his meagre Smile vanished, and the Colour drained slowly from his Face. He made a strange, incoherent Sound. I placed mine Hand quickly over his Mouth.

"Do not cry out," I said. "I require your Co-operation, Mr Simmins, and I do not want to have to gag you; but if you cry out we will be overheard, and interrupted."

Simmins, to my extream Surprize, was not quieted by this Admonition, but became a great Deal more agitated. He began to struggle hard against his Bonds and fight to free himself from mine improvised Gag. I presst down with mine Hands upon his Mouth and Shoulder to restrain him, and chided him, reminding him sorrowfully of his Failure to carry out mine Errand regarding Annie, and pointing out to him the Depth of my Disappointment in that Matter; which, I told him, his Sacrifice todaye would greatly mitigate. I sought, with an increasing Desperation in my Voice, to impress upon him my Conviction that the Paralysis would be of a limited Duration, and easily cured, for I had no Intention of cutting him or employing any Method in its Induction other than this simple Immobility, but he would not be calmed, and I found My Self forced to use much more aggressive Force upon his bound Arms than I desired.

"Isaac," I said, trying to reassure him. "Isaac, desist!"

But Simmins did not desist; he struggled harder, and caught me hard about the Chin with an Elbow. And suddenly, as unexpectedly as I had understood his Purpose to me, I lost Patience. Damn you! I thought. You and Dr Hunter both! You shall co-operate, you damnable little Goblin; and if you sustain Injury to your Brain, so much the better; why should I waste my Time upon the nervine Net when it is that which lieth within the Cranium that signifies? Damn you! I will prove mine Hypothesis, I will make My Self a Giant of Natural Philosophy, I will have my Will! Suddenly I was hurting him, smothering him, pinning down his Elbow with mine own; tightly covering his Mouth, his Nose, with my left Hand; pressing with my Knee upon his Chest, crushing with mine other Hand his slender Wrists, feeling the Ligaments and the small Carpals shift and crunch beneath my Fingertips; watching his Eyes roll backward in his Head as he battled to draw breath; his Neck desperately twisting this way and that, his Skull wrenching violently to one Side as he sustained a rough Blow from mine own Elbow; and suddenly Simmins had fallen silent, and lay quite still, except for a subtile Quivering that ran like Electricity thro'out his whole Body; and I took away mine Hands from his Body and, automatically, put my Fingers soft against his Carotid Artery.

"Isaac," I whispered. "Isaac."

He did not respond.

Have I broke his Neck? I thought.

Suddenly overcome by Horrour at My Self, and at what I had done, I sate back upon mine Heels. Damnable Goblin? Damn Simmins? Wherefore damn Simmins? He was—or he had thought himself—my Friend.

"Oh, Isaac," I cried. "I did not intend to harm you thus!"

I could not for the Life of me begin to understand wherefore Simmins had resisted. Why, why had he attempted to cry out, why had he begun to struggle, when all I had demanded of him was his peaceful Compliance? Had he not made me the Offer of Assistance? Moreover, was he not my Slave, who would do for me anything that I requested, without Question, without the merest momentary Consultation of his own Desires? Why should not I expect him to submit, and submit willingly, to Vivisection? There seemed no Logic to the Business, no Sense at all.

Suddenly, Simmins drew in a ragged and half-hearted Breath, and this brought me back to My Self. His Pulse was fluttering beneath my Fingertip. His Eyes opened, but they held no Intelligence, and appeared as vacant as if I had trappt him in an Aire Pump. Panicking now as I had never before, I took his Hands in mine own and squeezed them; they felt as lifeless to my Touch as those of a Corpse. Yet Simmins was now breathing; neither dead, nor, I prayed— tho' to what Concept or Manner of God I knew not—dying; but he lay quiet, still so quiet; and his Quietude was so terrifying wrong.

"Fool!"

I knew that I could not, for Humanity's Sake, if not just for Simmins', continue beyond this Point with mine Experiment, so with shivering Fingers I carefully untied the Bonds I had so tightly applied and gently brought Simmins' Arms down to lie flat upon the Bed at both Sides of his Body. I ran mine Hands over the wiry Muscle of the Biceps and the *Supinator longus*, to what Purpose I do not know, unless it was to attempt restoration of the Feeling and Circulation I feared, now, had been genuinely lost; and the wild Notion struck me that mine whole unplanned and ill-designed Experiment had been as much vacant Phantasy as had been my misplaced Confidence in Dr Hunter, and that verily I had never wanted to injure Simmins in any Manner, temporary or otherwise. My great Worry, my terrifying Dread was that I had done him an unknown Injury that would prove incapacitating, and permanent.

After some Minutes, during which my Terrour mounted to such an Intensity that I began to believe I must run to seek Assistance from some Physician other than My Self, Simmins turned his Head in my Direction, and flexed the Fingers of his left Hand, and then the Elbow quite independent of all my Kneading and Cajoling, and his brown Eyes came into steady Focus on mine own.

"I am s-orry," he said. "I p-anicked, Sir. I did not understand. I h-ope I did not—was I—did I—g-ive A-ssistance?"

My Mouth droppt open, and my whole Body began to Quake. I could have kissed him, like a Woman, hard upon the Lips. The pure and beautifull Relief, flooding over and thro' me at this marvellous Recovery: Simmins apparently unharmed, able to see, and speak coherently, and move his body Parts of his own Volition when I had feared all was lost, was so powerful a Wave it was some Seconds before I could speak. "You did," I stammered. "You were— you assisted—most helpfully, Captain Simmins."

"Your W-ife," Simmins said. "Mrs H-art. Does she kn-ow what Kind of M-onster you are?"

"Yes," I said. I collapsed beside him, unable yet fully to comprehend the Narrowness of my Squeak, my Limbs shaking far too much for me to stand, or even to sit erect. My slowing Heart felt as if it had never thumped so furious, never pumped so much Blood.

"'Tis t-errifying," Simmins said.

"I love Mrs Hart, and she loves me. We married in full Cognizance of each other's Interests, and Tastes."

Simmins made no Response to this. I imagined him to be digesting the Intelligence, and for some Minutes lay exhausted beside him, glad of his Silence. Then he spoke.

"I cannot f-eel my right Arm," he said. "That is the P-aralysis you were sp-eaking of, isn't it? It will p-ass, will't not?"

Over the next six Houres I did everything that I could think to do in order to restore the Sensation to Captain Simmins' Arm, but all for naught. I stroaked it with Silk, rubbed it with warm Fat; pinched, scratched, pricked, jabbed with the Point of my Lancet; applied Pressure, cold Water, extream Heat, and Theriac; repeatedly flexed and un-flexed the Arm, and let it lie still; but either mine Hypothesis regarding Pain was quite wrong, or the Damage I, in my careless, ruthless Violence, had inflicted upon Simmins' vulnerable nervous Fibre was too serious to be swiftly restored by any acute Treatment. Perhaps I had rippt the brachial Nerve from its Anchor at the Base of the Cranium. Or perhaps in those Moments during which we had struggled, he without Aire, I verily had injured his Brain, tho' I had committed no direct Assault upon it. Perhaps I had, by Accident, induced a small Stroake. I had no Method of knowing, none. Yet tho' it appeared to me quite soon that my Treatments were ineffective, I persisted with them; for to have given up so quickly, to have admitted the horrible Enormity of the thing that I had done would have flung the shattered Remnants of my Courage into the deepest Pit, and I knew not how I would have got them back again; so I continued to administer mine attempted

Agonies, and still Simmins felt nothing; until finally he placed his sensible Hand upon mine own, and bade me quietly and calmly to cease.

I already had untied him; now it fell to me to dress him, as one might a Child or a Cripple; and then I walked with him the small Distance to his Quarters, where finally, we parted.

Simmins took two Steps thro' the Gateway and then, pausing, turned back toward me. "I shall tell the S-urgeon that I was fi-ghting," he said. "I w-as in-toxicated, and I got My S-elf into a Brawl. There may be s-omething he can do."

There was not; but I said nothing.

"Do not w-orry, my d-ear H-art," Simmins said. "All shall be well." He got up on his tiptoes and bussed me, feather light, upon my hot Cheek; then he was gone.

I would then have wept; but I could not. A strange Coldness had taken Possession of mine Heart, and verily I believe I felt nothing; neither Pity, nor Remorse, nor Loss, nor Grief. I knew that every-thing was over, everything. Mine Ambitions were as useless, as beyond Recovery as Simmins' Arm. Dr Hunter had abandoned me and without his Assistance I could not make any Progress whatso-ever upon mine Hypothesis. My Dream was broken. I did not permit My Self the merest Contemplation of Simmins' Prognosis. The Truth was that I did not know, I could not know, or with any Confidence predict, how soon, or even if ever, he would regain the Sensation I had raped from him in my Carelessness.

All at once, into mine Head came the Memory of that Moment when I had stood, with Nathaniel, at the Door to the Bull, and all the Light had vanished, and the whole World had appeared as if to shrink to the Size of a Pin-head. Perhaps 'twas not Memory, but Vision; for as I stood at the Gate I seemed to stand again at

Nathaniel's Side; and yet it must have been I, not he, who had the Look of a coiled Spring strained as if to snap; for Nathaniel turned to me, and putting the Palm of his left Hand softly upon my Cheek, said: "The only Way out is to smash the Clock."

I blinked. The Vision disappeared. The quarter-Gate Lanthorns blazed bright in the wet Darkness; around me the night Street drippt.

I turned at once and fled ere I was robbed.

CHAPTER THREE-AND-THIRTY

"I am going home."

Thus Nathaniel had said. And it was exactly, precisely what I desired to do, now. I wanted to be back with my Katherine in mine own House, where everything would make Sense; but I knew that even were I to pack up all my things and bargain my way aboard the very next Mail, I should not arrive home in less than two Dayes time.

I could not stand to return to my Room at the Red Lion, where the Horrour of my failed Experiment yet lingered in the Scent of Simmins' Body. Instead, numbly, almost blindly, I hastened thro' the dark London Streets toward Bow Street. I did not glance to my left or my right, but only in the one Direction: forward.

I arrived at the Fieldings' House all out of Breath and muddy from my Shoes to the Hem of my Greatcoat, and mounted the front Steps to hammer hard upon the Door. To my Surprize, it was opened almost at once. I pushed past Liza and made my Way to an hall Chair, into which I collapsed, mine Hands shaking as if with a Palsy.

"Mr Hart!" exclaimed Liza. "Mrs Fielding! Oh, Madam, come quick!"

"I am not injured," I said at once, cutting off the Misunderstanding I perceived mustering, like Xerxes' Army, beyond the Pass. "Nor have I been robbed, Liza. Do not sound any Alarum, there is no Necessity."

Drawing a long Breath, I permitted My Self slowly to relax into the Fieldings' high backed Chair, becoming gradually conscious of its bracing Support against my Spine, my Weight descending thro' its sturdy Legs into the solid Floor.

Why have I come here? I thought. I can tell the Fieldings nothing of my Misadventure; there is nothing they could reply in any Case that might restore me to My Self, or the Feeling to my poor Isaac. Oh, what have I done? I have sacrificed him on the Altar of mine own Ambition, and for what?

I had not been sitting long alone when Mary Fielding appeared out of the Kitchen, pulling off her Apron. She took me thro' into the sitting Room where previously I had met with her Husband and her Brother-in-law; tonight, however, the Room was empty.

"Where is your Husband, Mrs Fielding?" I asked, surprized.

"He hath been called out on some Business, and Mr John with him," Mary said.

"Business to do with his Police Force?"

"I suppose so," Mrs Fielding answered. "He doth not tell me very much, as you may imagine. But I am certain if you want to see him, he will be back soon, for 'tis very late. Would you like something to drink, Mr Hart? If you don't mind my saying so, you look as if you have met with a Ghost."

I did not refuse, and so Mary poured me a Glass of Wine, and patting me gently upon mine Hand, insisted that I sit on the Arm-chair nearest to the dying Fire, whilst she began energetically to stoke its Embers.

Perhaps, I thought, I was waiting for the Brothers to return; but if I was, it was with a desperate Trepidation, for I knew not what I should say if either one of them were to challenge me.

What will I do? I thought. I did not wish to abandon my little Simmins, as—I now perceived, with sinking Heart—I had abandoned my Katherine; but I knew I would be unable to endure one Minute longer in the Hound, nor even in London itself, for I would have to do both in the Knowledge that my continued Residence was futile. Reason, Duty, Shame and mine own sudden, desperate Need all told me that I must return to my Wife, and tend to her; indeed, that I ought never to have left her. I had not been a Brute, but in mine intellectual Arrogance and vain Ambition I had fairly impersonated one; and the Situation in which I now found My Self was the Consequence of that. I had wilfully ignored every Plea and Protestation she had made; and she had been right.

"Mary," I said, watching her. "I have reached a Decision. I shall be returning to Berkshire upon the Morrow."

Mary Fielding turned, the Poker in her Hand a black Crease against the blue flowered Linen of her Dress. "Oh, Mr Hart!" she exclaimed. "I am surprized. But I shall confess that I am very glad to hear it!"

"What?" I said. "Wherefore?"

Mary gave a little Laugh. "I speak merely as a Woman, Sir. I know how hard it must be upon Mrs Hart to be left alone at such a Time, and I can only think how happy she will be at your Return. For my Part I shall be sorry to see you go, but my Sorrow is a small thing compared to her Joy. That is all."

"You are too good, Mrs Fielding," I said. "Indeed, you are too good."

Mrs Fielding coloured. "You confuse me with mine Husband, Mr Hart," she said. "I am not good, altho' I have tried to be. To be truly good requires Strength of Character, and I am weak, and ignorant, and make foolish Mistakes. I am an Embarrassment to Mr Fielding, and he should not have felt himself obliged to marry me."

"Whence comes all this!" I exclaimed, astonished.

Mrs Fielding sighed unhappiily, and returned the Poker to its Box.

"Mary," I said, rising and crossing the Room to grasp Mrs Fielding squarely by the Shoulders. "You are truly one of the best Women I have ever met. Why, what other Housewife would have taken in a freakish Gypsy Brat, and nursed it a full daye out of naught but the Goodness of her Heart, when she had her own Children to consider, and Christmas, and an Husband whose waspish Temper doth him no Credit, tho' he be the finest of Men in every other Wise. I will not allow you so to demean yourself."

Tho' I had spoken kindly, Mrs Fielding's Eyes opened as wide as if I had given her the harshest of Scoldings, and she drew back from me half a Pace before saying, in a careful and measured Tone: "Mr Hart, I do not know what you are talking about."

"Egad," I said. "What meanst by that? Surely, you must remember the Babe?"

"Sir, I do not remember ever taking in any Gypsy, at Christmas or at any other Time. I am certain Mr Fielding would have had much to say upon it if I had."

"What?" I exclaimed.

"I have no such Recollection, Mr Hart," Mary repeated, patiently, as if I had been a Child—or a Lunatick.

"Madam," I responded, when I had got back my Tongue. "Either your Memory holds with all the Permanence of Sand upon a Beach, or else you lie; for the Incident was extraordinary, and hard to forget. I recall it as vividly as I recall the Words you spoke five Minutes since. It amazes me if you do not."

"I do not, Mr Hart."

I studied her Face, a cold Panick stirring within my Gut. I could not ascertain from her Expression whether she was lying or verily had no Memory of my little Bat. Then I realised that I had upon me that Sketch which I always carried in my Waistcoat, and mine Hand flew to it. "Mrs Fielding," I said. "Mary. Here is a Portrait of the Child, done by your own Hand upon the Night of her Stay. Dost not see? Dost not, now, remember?"

Mary pulled away from me, quite violently, and crosst brusquely toward the sitting room Door. "Look at it," I pleaded, catching her by the Hand and thrusting the Paper before her Eyes. "Mary, look."

"Oh, Mr Hart," Mary cried. "Please, do not insist!"

"I do insist," I said. "Nor shall I desist until you have told me exactly what you see upon this Paper."

Mary tried once more to pull away and then, to my great Relief, turned and cast her Gaze once over the Drawing. "I see you, Sir," she admitted, reluctantly. "Holding a Babe."

"The Babe, yes; the Gypsy Babe, the Bat." Mine Hands shook upon the Paper. "Do not you perceive her Wings? They are quite clear."

"No, Sir," Mary answered, levelly, and turned her Face away. "I do not see any Wings."

"What? But they are there—look!"

"They are but the Corners of the Blanket," Mary said.

"'Tis quite evident," I said, growing angry at her Refusal, "that they are no such things. Do you at least agree that the Picture sheweth the Gypsy Babe?"

"I do see a Babe," Mrs Fielding cried. "But, oh, Mr Hart, I am sure 'tis mine own Child."

Her Hand flew to her Mouth; stifling a Sob, she pushed roughly past me, and fled from the Room.

I returned to Shirelands Hall via the Oxford Mail forty Houres later. I did not see Mrs Fielding again before my Departure, neither did I have the Opportunity to take my leave in Person of the Brothers. I left my Card. This seemed, and almost certainly was, from me, enough.

I sent a Message by the willing Hand of the Pot-boy to Captain Simmins, in which I explained the Change that had come upon my Circumstances in result of Dr Hunter's Dismissal of mine Appeal, and told him that I no longer deemed it fitting that I should remain in London. I concluded the Missive with my warm Affection, and issued an Invitation to Simmins to call upon me at home whenever he should be so able; but altho' I could not deny that I still felt a great Pull toward that tender Youth, my Repulsion from him was now greater, and I hoped in mine Heart that he would not accept it. The Thought that I had injured him was nearly more than I could bear; but the Idea that I was compleatly powerless to put right this Injury was so far beyond my Endurance that I did not let My Self consider it at all. I told My Self that his Paralysis was certainly trivial in Nature, and undoubtedly temporary in Duration, and that I, now, had more urgent Matters waiting upon mine Attention at home. I had abandoned Katherine; I had betrayed her; and all when she had been in her greatest Need of me.

And yet, I thought, I have not abandoned her at all, nor would I; and my Fingers found again the folded Corners of Mary Fielding's Sketch. Mary might have proved herself Peter; I never shall.

The Oxford Mail was uncomfortable, the Journey long and the Company rude, but I cared naught for any of this. I averted mine Eyes from the Goose throated Woman with the haughty Stare, who was without Question some kind of upper Servant, and I blanketed mine Ears to the Lectures of the Parson seated opposite, who may, for all his seeming Lack of such Qualities, have been an honest and a compassionate Man.

I looked only upon, and listened only to, mine own Heart, beating within my Chest like a battle-Drum; and it appeared to me that 'twas as dark and hollow as a very Cave.

I left my Luggage at Oxford, to be sent on or collected later, and for the Sake of Speed purchased a fast grey Mare to ride alone across Country as far as Faringdon, which Town was, as far as I could judge, at the distant Edge of Viviane's Influence. I planned from there to send a Letter to Shirelands asking for the Coach, and continue thus. Packing only my Money, my Papers, and my surgical Instruments inside the Mare's saddle Bags, I quitted the City at a brisk Canter along the high Road, which thankfully had not been rendered so boggy by the six Months of constant Rain that it could not be travelled at above a Walk. Thus it was that within an Houre of my first Arrival at Oxford I was among Fields again, the clouded midsummer Sky flickering unbroken over mine Head.

Arriving after a long Time at Faringdon, I took a Room in the Town's largest Inn, and after stabling my Mare in the Back settled My Self in the well-lit publick Room to compose my Letter. The Room was quite busy, it being early in the Evening, and I perhaps ought to have taken My Self up the Stairs for this Purpose, but the spitting log Fire drew me close, as the Fire at the Bull had seemingly drawn Nathaniel, and would not let me go; so I sate quiet upon the Chimney-seat, my Paper upon my Knees, and wrote my Newes, whilst about me the country Conversation ebbed and flowed.

By these Means, I learned that My Sister's Husband Barnaby continued, in Spite of the sodden Condition of the Chalk and the swollen Nature of the River Coller, to disturb its Course; and that his Actions were no more popular among his immediate Neighbours, and their Tenants, than they were with me. There was a general Apprehension that the faster flowing River being created by Barnaby's supposed Improvement would do great Damage to the Farmlands that lay opposite it and downstream; and since these had recently been made subject to Inclosure, Livelihoods could be lost. I quickly discovered that the Men working for Barnaby had been drafted in from as far abroad as Wiltshire, with the Exceptions of two who, living upon Grange Land, had no other Landlord to appease, and survived by taking casual Labour. Of one of these, a Man by the Appellation of Matt Harris, I knew nothing, good or ill; the other was Joseph Cox.

Cox, I discovered, had married that Rebecca Clifton whose moon-faced Bastard was supposed Nathaniel Ravenscroft's. The Pair did not agree. I heard many Reports of Joe's excessive Drunkenness, and the rough Music to which Rebecca was often subject. These Newes came as no great Surprize to me, for I had ever thought Cox capable of Evil, but I disliked them none the less for that, and Cox the more.

I compleated my Letter and, having addresst it to my Wife, gave it to the Landlord of the Inn to have it sent as soon as possible; then, mine Ears ringing with Gossip, I retreated to my small Chamber.

I sate beside mine open Window, listening to the low Thrum of Insects in the Ivy, as the Sunne set in the western Distance, lost behind the glowering Thunder-clouds, and bethought me that the Morrow's Scouring of the Horse, and all its associated Revells, must surely be undone.

As I sate, I became slowly aware that I could hear, thro' the Window or perhaps only in mine own Head, the Sound of one, lone, distant Drum, beating regular as a Fist upon an heavy Door, a doubled Blow; one-one, one-one, one-one. I put mine Hands to mine Ears, but the Sound was not extinguished. By this, I understood that it must be extant within my Mind; it was an Hallucination of the Kind that had tormented me so many Times before. Yet strangely, perhaps, I was not afraid.

An hunting Horn sounded; loud, loud, yet far off in the Vale below the Horse. The triumphant Fanfare wound spiralling thro' mine Hearing like Eden's Serpent thro' the apple Tree, like Mistletoe upon the Ash. Forgetting everything I had been thinking about, I leapt to my Feet. The Atmosphere, suddenly thunderous, choked me. I must leave, I thought, at once; and there seemed to me nothing strange at all that I had thought thus. I must away, outside, away, in search of some Location where I might refresh my sore Lungs with an Atom of cold Aire.

The Light was failing. And yet—and yet—I stared out thro' the Window. The Sky was leaden grey, darkening to the Southwest above the High Chalk, but the View was oddly clear, and thro' the softening Veil of evening Light, that rendered everything to mine Eyes diffuse and unsure, I perceived, atop the far distant Ridge, a flittering Line of brilliant Lights, bright and sharp as Stars.

I caught my Breath. The Gypsies had returned.

I stared across the Valley. Nathaniel! I thought. At last. And in that blinding Moment, as indeed for some long while afterwards, I thought only of the Possibility that I might see him again, my Friend; alive, present, solid, warm; that I might hear his magpie Laugh, and watch his green Eyes glint and spark like Emeralds in the lanthorn-Light; that I might stand Shoulder to Shoulder with him again, and feel his Hand upon mine Elbow, the Touch of his Skin on mine like Fire on Tinder. I looked across the Vale whither the Owl had flown, and I forgot Viviane. I forgot Leonora, Raw Head, and Bloody Bones. I forgot everything I ought to have remembered, and I knew not that I had forgotten.

Without pausing, without a Moment's Thought or an Instant's Delay, I caught up my saddle Bags and ran as hard and swift as I could to the stable Block, where finding, by some Stroake of Fortune, the Lad still at Work, I had my grey Mare bridled and her Saddle thrust upon her Back. Like a Djinn under a Spell, I vaulted straight upon her and put mine Heels roughly to her Flanks. She leapt forward; and it seemed to me as if she knew, within her own, animal Mind, whither we must go, even tho' I did not. Her iron Shoes crackled on the granite Flagstones of the Yard.

I had some unformed Notion of crossing the Valley toward the Ridge Way, that I might intercept, or at least follow, the Gypsies' Caravan; but when I at length arrived within Sight-line of the High Chalk, the starry Procession had vanished, and I could not make any Guess as to the Direction in which the Gypsies might have gone. I reined in my sweating Mount and surveyed what I could see of the darkening Landscape. In the fast falling Twilight, the Valley of the Horse was becoming by the Second harder to perceive; soon, I realised, with a Stirring of Panick in my deep Bowels, even the Road ahead of me would be compleatly black. Could my Mare still see in such Darkness? I knew that I could not.

I should turn back, I thought. But I did not do it. Mine Heart was pounding so fiercely against the membranous Wall of my Ribcage that I could not still mine Hands upon the Reins. Mine Ears ached with the Echo of its Drumming. One-one, one-one; neither a Drum, nor a Phantasm, but mine own Heartbeat. And now I was out, out in the blackening Middle of Viviane's Country, alone and undisguised, defended only by this one beautifull Servant, my grey Mare, of whom I knew so little and who had served me so well.

I must not dismount, I thought. That is the Answer. Whilst I am out of Contact with the Earth, Viviane cannot harm me. This Notion, which gave me some small Comfort, immediately was followed by another; that in fact my Katherine's Love might provide me with a Rampart and Protection against Viviane and her Goblins that Viviane, who knew naught of Love, would find it a wearisome Task to break thro'. Whilst Katherine loves me, I thought, I may be safe. This Thought, Conjecture tho' it was, put great Spirit in my Vitals. I might still, I thought, survive this Night. I might meet with Nathaniel again.

"Damn you!" I shouted out into the Night. "You will have nothing of me! Nothing!"

I closed my Knees about my grey Mare's Sides, sending her forward once more, but this Time more carefully, that she might pick the Way for both of us, into the pressing Darkness underneath the Storm.

I rode thus onward for Houres, I conceive. I had not any Idea where I was going, but, after some while, I realised that I had come as far as the Crossroads whereupon stood the wayside Inn where Nathaniel had held his farewell Revellries; that Inn of the Bull, where I had first seen Viviane, and had been vilely insulted by the pig-Man, Cox. A weak tallow-Light shone from the paired Lanthorns that hung, supposedly for Illumination, over the oaken Door. On a clear Night, such as it had been upon that May Eve, they were scarcely needed; but in this thickening Blackness they glowed like twin Beacons, promising Sanctuary within to any Human Soule in need of Companionship, and of Light.

But I knew that I would not discover Nathaniel in any such Place as this; he would be as strange, now, to its Comforts as any other Man must be to those of the Moon. Besides, I thought, the Landlord Haynes will never admit those Vagabonds upon his Premises a second Time. He only admitted them the first because he owed Nathaniel a Favour, and he feared too the sore Consequences should he fail to repay it.

I presst on. From far off in the southern Distance came a low, throbbing Growl. So I had been right: Thunder.

It seemed that I must head towards the Ridge Way, and the Chalk Horse, and I turned my Mare along the Road that led thither, by Way of Withy Grange. We had not gone, however, more than seven Paces when she, until then so steady, perceiving some Terrour—a Movement upon the Road, or in the Hedge, or our own Shaddowe falling on the carven Way-Stone—shied, and lost her Footing in the Dark. She stumbled, and went upon her Knees. I, taken by Surprize, and already as tense upon the Saddle as a wooden Doll, lost my Balance and plunged Head first over her left Shoulder. As Fortune fell, along with me, the Ground was soft from the continued Rains, and I got therefore as gentle a Landing as one might wish. But I had fallen off, and lost the Reins besides; and my Mare, affrighted perhaps as much by our suddenly broken Connexion as by the Monster in the Dark, got unsteadily to her Feet and began to sidle away, her Eye wary.

Shaking, I staggered to my Feet and reached out for her, but she shied from mine Hand and all I managed to do was to grab hold of my saddle Bag. I held on tightly to it and spoke to her gently. At this most unusual Contact, however, my Mare finally panicked. She reared, and I felt the saddle Bag's leather snap. My Mare let out a ringing Neigh, put her Hindquarters hard to work and set off at a flat Gallop along the Road toward Faringdon, leaving me alone, the torn-off Pannier still in mine Hand and mine Arse planted once more full-square in Viviane's Earth.

I called my Mare to come back, but she did not. Shaking, I staggered to my Feet. My Cloathes stuck tight about mine Arms and lower Quarters, and my buckled Shoes—for I had not, in mine Hurry, thought to change them—were heavy with the clinging Mud. I feared that I was surely stuck, and a sitting Duck for any of Viviane's Hunters, should they recognise me, but a few Seconds' vigorous Agitation freed me from the Ground's Embrace, and tho' my Shoes were ruined, I did not lose either—which, in the Circumstances, I counted a Victory.

But I was alone, and a fair Distance beyond home, even in Dayelight. Moreover, I was nowhere near to where I imagined the Gypsies might be camped. I turned mine Eyes toward the Inn of the Bull, whose pale Lamps glowered in the Gloom, and the Thought presst in upon me that I ought to seek Succour there, as I had been forced to do once before; but I could not abide the Humiliation of admitting to the Landlord Haynes that I had lost my Seat. Besides, I knew that once I had entered within, I should have abandoned all Hope of encountering Nathaniel. I continued instead to walk toward the South, in Hopes that I might follow the Track on Foot as far as Withy Grange, and there borrow a fresh Mount, if need be.

Reasoning that the grassy Verge that ran alongside the Road would probably give a firmer Footing to my Tread, I put my saddle Bag under mine arm, and stumbled up out of the Mire. Slowly, it seemed, I approached Withy Grange. I had no Method of judging Time, for the Moon, if it had risen, was utterly invisible behind the Clouds, and I had no Clock about me save mine own, measureless Heartbeat, which pounded on against the dampe, brooding, nocturnal Stillness. Perhaps I had been walking for some Houres, when I trippt upon some indeterminate hidden Thing, and tumbled for the second Time into the Dirt. As I fell, my Shin grazed against whatever it was that had brought me down: some metal Implement, perhaps a broken Scythe, or a Plough-tip, rusty with Age, but sharp enough nonetheless to part the soft Flesh from the Bone. I cried out in Shock and Alarm, and acting automatically, covered mine injured Leg with both mine Hands. At once I understood the Wound to be exceeding unpleasant; mine Hands became wet with my Blood; and as I explored the Scrape with my Fingertips I felt the unmistakable Texture of living Bone exposed beneath them. I had sliced off the outer Skin of my Shinbone from below the Knee to the Ankle.

Mine Head reeled for an Instant at this Realisation; then mine other Instinct, the Surgeon's, waked suddenly into Life. With my right Hand I untangled my silk Cravat from my Neck, and crouching in the Darkness, I bound up my Shin as well as I could, and then sate back on mine Haunches as the Wave of Pain crashed in upon me.

Pain. I could not comprehend wherefore it was so strong. I held my Leg against my Chest and cried aloud, as mine agonised Tears scalded the bone-Line of my Jaw. For some Reason, I know not what, I found My Self thinking of Captain Simmins.

Even as I do not know how long I walked, neither do I know how long I sate, keening, Blood from my mutilated Leg slowly seeping thro' my Bandage like a River thro' wet Silt. But after some while the initial Shock began to subside, and I opened mine Eyes, which I had shut against the Tears that had overwhelmed them, and peered once again into the Darkness.

It was no longer Uniform. The Clouds had shifted. Thro' them, to the East, I could discern a faint silvery Halo in the Sky. The Moon had risen. Moreover, some far Distance behind me, flickering like a marsh-Light, was the Glow of a small Lanthorn; and by the excited Drumming of mine Heart I realised that it was not the Light of any ordinary Traveller.

"Nathaniel!" I shouted out. "Nathaniel Ravenscroft!"

My Voice disappeared into the Night. I turned My Self about, and attempted to rise.

"What dost want with Nathaniel Ravenscroft?" The Voice came, suddenly, seeming in front of me. It was a fluting, pretty Voice, innocent as a little Child's; and yet something besides: a thin, wheezing Hiss; that of a Creature antient in its Dayes.

"What?" I whirled mine Head around, but I could see nothing.

"I asked, what do you want?"

"I want—" I broke off in a sudden Confusion. "I do not know," I confesst. "Who are you? Shew yourself."

"I am My Self," the Voice replied. "My Mother gave me one Name, I am called by another. But I am, still, My Own Self."

I began to feel a Clenching in my Gut, as I had done that Night when I had met the old Crone in Mary Fielding's Kitchen. 'Tis one of Viviane's Creatures, I thought. I could not help but ask, tho' I dreaded the Answer. "By what Name," I said, trembling, "are you called?"

There was a faint Shift in the Pattern of the Night, a quick, flitting Movement, the which I felt, rather than saw. The Creature was direct in front of me. I put out my bloodied Hands, groping midst the pitch Grasses. If it be a Goblin, I thought, I will strangle it.

"Bat," replied the little Voice. "I am called Bat."

Mine Heart stoppt. "Bat!" I cried. "What? Bat? My Bat?"

"No," came the sorrowful Answer. "Not your Bat, Tristan Hart."

"You know me?"

"I do, for your Name was spoke so often in mine Hearing that I never might forget it; and by that I do know you, and might find you anywhere. But I would never use't against you, for you should have been my Father; and you were kind to me, and would have raised me as your own. Now I have come to help you, ere by your mouse Squeak you call down my Queen-Mother on your foolish Head. She hunts tonight. Dost seek Nathaniel Ravenscroft?"

"I do," I answered. "But I have been a long while seeking you, besides; I would have you come home with me, Bat, as my Daughter, whether we be blood-Kin or no."

My Words met only with the swift Rush of oncoming Rain. The Storm had broken.

The Water drummed upon my Forehead, like a new Baptism. I put mine Hand up to mine Eyes to shield them, for even tho' I could not see an Inch in the Darkness, I could not bear the Thought of being blind. "Bat?" I said. "Art there?"

"Poor Tristan Hart," Bat said. "You do not see a thing."

I reached out again in front of me, towards the Space from which emanated her Voice. "No," I admitted. "I cannot see anything, Bat. Stand close, that I might know you by my Touch."

It seemed to me an Eternity that I knelt there, muddy, drenched, and still bleeding, mine Hand outstretched, a pagan Adam, prayerless in the Dark. Then all on a Sudden I felt her small Fingers taking strong hold, sharp, wicked little Claws piercing like Scalpels into the Skin of mine unprotected Palm. I yelped aloud, and as a Reflex tried to pull mine Hand away; but she dug her tiny Talons deep into my Wrist, and pulled mine Hand up to explore her Face. Her infant Skin stretched like living Velvet beneath my Fingertips.

"I have lost my Mother," Bat said. "If I fetch Nathaniel Ravenscroft to you, you will take me home, to her."

The Darkness parted before mine Eyes, like a Veil. But before me, as clear as if upon a Stage, I saw not Bat, but only the Vision of My Self, standing in full Light on Mary Fielding's Doorstep, reading Katherine's Letter:

The Tale of Raw Head and the Willow Tree

"Katherine!" I shouted. My Voice was louder than the rattling Rain. "Katherine Montague!"

"Now you see," Bat said. "And I go." The Aire fluttered once; then there was Emptiness.

CHAPTER FOUR-AND-THIRTY

I perceived everything. I watched how I had stood upon the
Fieldings' Step and read the Epistle Katherine had sent; and how
the World had unravelled about me, and re-woven itself into a
Nightmare. I remembered every damning Character, every cursed
Word of the Tale of Raw Head, which I had tried to make My Self
believe a Fiction; which my Mind had for so many Months kept,
under an obscuring Cloud of Unbelief, from Memory's clear Sight.
I cannot go on, she had explained, excepting thro' Leonora. Black
Words, in Katherine's spiderweb Handwriting, spun themselves
anew across the white Page of mine Imagination, laying open to
my Conscience the Chapter Book of Revelation.

Bat was not, and she never could have been, my natural Daughter. The Rain poured on over mine Head. I did not mind it.

The Tale of Raw Head and the Willow Tree

Once upon a Time, before Bloody Bones the Lover of Leonora hath saved her from the Vicious Goblins, she had a strange and evil Dream. And every Body said 'twas Nothing but a Dream, and she must Forget Everything about it; but Leonora knows it was a True Dream, not one of the Kind that mean Nothing, and are meere Passing Fantoms of the Night.

In the Garden of the House, there groweth a Willow Tree, and it is as Fair and Slender as a Girl, with leaves like Tresses and Bark like the softest whitest Skin; and when it rustleth in the Wind it sounds as if it is Whispering. And Leonora Dreamed she was this Willow Tree, come all to Life, and that the Willow Tree was Leonora.

The Willow Tree was sade because she had no one to Love, and she wished Daye and Night that she might have a Lover. Then one Summer's Evening a tender Youth appeared beneath her Trailing Branches, and he was Dark and Beautifull as the Night Sky; and the Willow Tree fell Utterly in Love with him. But tho' she Quivered and Shook, he noticed her not, and she was very sade.

But Willow was Patient, and she knew that if she waited Long enow, her Love would look up and see her, and so she bided her Time and Watched. And for Foure Yeares she waited, and he did not Look.

Then one Daye a Wicked Magician, who was really Raw Head, came along, and he saw how it was that the Willow was in Love, and he said to her: "I will Make you into a Woman, so that you may Shew yourself to him you Weep over, who is my Brother."

So the Magician hath cast a spell upon the Willow Tree to change her shape; and now she Walks and Talks as if she is Really a Girl, and not a Tree. And she goes a-walking in Search of her Love, but she hath only gone a Little Waye along the Road when the Sunne beginneth to Drop toward the Horizon, and soon it will be Dusk. And she is Frightened because it is Christmas Eve, and very Cold. So she turns about and tries to run Home, but she is Lost. Then she sees an olde House in the Middle of the Wood, which looks exactly like her Home, and so thinking she is safe she Knocks upon the Door, and asks if they will let her in.

But she doth not Know that the House is an House of Goblins; and the Master of that House is Raw Head.

There was a sudden Flash of Light against mine Eyelids.

"Well," said a Voice, breaking in upon me. "If it isn't Tom O' Bedlam."

I opened up mine Eyes, which I had not realised that I had shut up. A featureless Form, thick set and broad as a Bear, a rattling Lanthorn held aloft in one great Paw, loomed up between My Self and the thinning Blanket of Sky. I started violently back, and toppled again onto the Grass, mine Hand missing by a Fraction that broken Edge that previously had felled and wounded me.

What Monster is this? I thought. Is it one of Viviane's Hunters?

The titanic Brute leaned close in over me, thrusting his Lanthorn quite into my Face. I turned mine Head aside, and coughed. Even thro' the Rain, I could not help but breathe the rank Miasma of Beer and Sweat that hung about the Stranger, like a Cloud of thunder Flies. Is it a Man? I thought. Surely, it cannot be! Yet verily it hath the Stink of one.

"Do not do that," I said. "Stand away. You stink like a Pig."

The Man, if indeed he was a Man, laughed, and in Reply shook his Lanthorn violently direct in front of my Nose. Wax spattered the Glass like a crushed Insect.

"Fool," I said. "You will put out your own Light if you do that."

"Ha! Dont 'ee like 'un?"

"I do not. Neither like I you. Remove your ridiculous Lanthorn and your disgusting Self from my Presence immediately."

"Squeal on, Coney, caught in Snare. Not so brave now, be 'ee, wi'out yer high Horse and yer Stick? I doesn't 'ave to do nothin', I do reckon." The Words were slurred; either the Speaker was extreamly drunk, or something else was amiss. Is it, really, a Man? I wondered.

Thunder pealed about mine Ears like an Alarum. The Rain fell faster. Then came a second Lightning Flash, closer, brighter than the first must have been, tho' I had not properly seen it; and as it snaked across the eastern Heaven I saw, for a split Second illuminated by the Storm, the devilish Visage of mine Adversary.

It was the pig-Man.

I scuttled backward like a Crab.

Now the Willow Tree, thinking no Harm, doth not Recognise Raw Head, for he hath disguised his Appearance. But that Night she hears Someone a-Knocking at the Door of her Bedd-Room, and she goes to Open it, feeling no Feare.

Joseph Cox spat, deliberately, into the Grass, then steppt after me. "Filthy Jew-bred Whelp," he said. "I 'opes they Gypsies do get 'ee. Idn' no one going get no Answers off o' them, I do reckon, if'n 'ee do have a Accident in th'Dark."

And she hath opened up the Door and it is Raw Head, Raw Head in the Dark, while all the Family lies asleep. And he is Come Bursting into her Chamber with Wine and Laughter on his Lips, and he wishes her a Merry Christmas and Kisses her upon the Mouth, and she thinks that he will Leave. "O," she says, "'Tis the Middle of the Night." And he says: "The Middle of the Night, that is the Best Time for Mischief." Then he hath seized Willow and he hath gone and Stoode beside the Bedd, and he hath a great Unkindeness in his Eyes.

"Tidn' right," the Monster said, "that a Tom O'Bedlam like you should ever ha' laid down with a fine Beauty like she. What did she ever see in 'ee? If'n 'ee 'adn't a bin yon Squire's Pup she'd never even ha' looked at 'ee. But she'm always been a Money grubbin' little Bitch—"

And Raw Head he hath Torn the Curtain down, and he hath Ravished the Willow Tree. It is all his Pleasure. And then Afterwards he says: "Kitty, you are a Woman. But you must not tell a Soule, or my delightful and compassionate Father will Throw us Both out in the Snow and we will Freeze to Death."

Suddenly I was aware that the Rain had stoppt. Yet its Drumming still continued, deafening loud atop mine Head. "Beware your vile Tongue, Goblin," I said, scrambling slowly, carefully, to my Feet. "I will not permit that you speak thus of any Woman. Let alone her."

"I sh'l say whatever I do want," Joe Cox said. "No bastard Jew tells me what to do."

No, I thought. You work for James Barnaby! You are ripping out the Withy Wood. You are ravishing an intire Grove of Willow Girls.

"Raw Head," I said, as Comprehension dawned. "You are Raw Head."

Raw Head, Raw Head in the Dark. Raw Head come hither not at Viviane's Command, but at his own Desire. Raw Head come to murder me and grub up my dear Katherine from her Bed, and steal her for his own. Raw Head come to make a final End of our Enmity, to duel with me unto the Death.

Did Barnaby not know that he had hired a Demon?

A Demon, not a Man, no, not a Man; not Joseph Cox. A Changeling, who could steal any Form; a Goblin Sorcerer, Knight and Prince, who had upon one horrible Night assumed the Shape of my beloved Friend and ruined the Life of the Woman I loved best in all the World: Leonora's other Self: Katherine Montague.

Not a Man, not a Man; so what was he? A Cartesian Horrour; a Demon clad in possesst Flesh, Flesh that did not truly live, unless it was as an Automaton; Bone and Blood and Entrails all unsouled and conscienceless, yet all, mechanically, functioning. Matter animated by Evil, not by any Principle inherent within. Soule-less Flesh that endured no Pain, that felt neither Cold nor Wet upon its Skin. Clockwork, Clockwork.

And I had thought La Mettrie's Proposition so different; yet all in that Moment I perceived that his Theory was not so far distant from Descartes', for it tried to deal with the Difficulty surrounding Communication betwixt Soule and Body by denying the Existence of the one, but not the other. It was Nonsense, Nonsense; and I had been right, right all along.

As Erasmus, Curette in Hand, had indicated, as Dr Hunter had pronounced, Man is more, so much more than a soule-less Mechanical.

But this Raw Head was not a Man.

A yellow-brown Revulsion, deeper seated and more potent than any mere Disgust or Hate, uncoiled within me, like a wound Spring unexpectedly freed from the Catch that had held it in check for a Lifetime. It felt as if I had sustained a Blow to my Stomach. Winded, I struggled for my Breath.

"The only Way out," I gasped, "is to smash the Clock."

The Drumming filled mine Ears. With Effort, I caught my Breath again and looked up. The Clouds shifted above mine Head, and the Stars pricked the Dark. I saw the Goblin Raw Head raise up its Lanthorn, and its Physiognomy was twisted by Hatred and by Contempt into a Devil's Mask, a Parody of an Human Face. It steppt forward, its Lip curled, and raised up its other Fist, preparing to strike.

So, it begins, I thought. I am no unsouled Machine. I am Man; Spirit and Matter unified, Body and Soule mixt together into one Being. I am, I am, and I am.

As Raw Head strode forward, I sprang full forcibly towards it, Head down like a Stag in Battle. A wild, deep Roar vibrated in my Chest, echoing in mine Ears louder than Thunder. My Forehead caught the vile Brute square upon the Chest, bowling it over with a Speed and Power that astonished me. It fell with a wet Crunch upon its Back. The Candle at once winked out; there was a small tinkling Crash as the Lanthorn flew from the Goblin's Hand and landed some Way off amidst the Tussocks.

Rage overtook me. I leapt upon Raw Head's Chest and pinned it fast to the Ground with my Knee. "Goblin Knight," I cried. "Raw Head! Thou shalt neither murder me, nor bring Shame and Sorrow upon my Willow, whom I love more than my very Life! Thou art a Cancer on my Soule! Begone!" I balled up both my Fists, and with mine whole Strength I battered the fallen Monster over and again upon the Cheekbones and the Chin until the small facial Bones of the Skull creaked and slid away beneath my Blows, and my Hands were both too sore and bloody for me to continue the Beating any longer.

Eventually I sate up. The Drumming in mine Head had stoppt, compleatly stoppt, and all about me and inside me was Silence. The shattered Body of the Goblin Raw Head lay quite still beneath me, its animating Force seeming fled; and I, the living, ensouled Man; I, Tristan Hart; I, Bloody Bones— for was I not all of these?— was victorious. Katherine was safe.

The Sky was now comparatively bright, the Storm having passed over. I remained for several Minutes unmoving in the Stillness. Then, when I had caught my Breath, I looked again, in the fresh Light, at the felled Thing, which still wore the Appearance of Joseph Cox, altho' it was perhaps hard to be certain in the Darkness; and I began, out of long established Habit, to examine the Body.

I discovered almost immediately that it was not yet dead. Moreover, neither was it intirely senseless; although it did not move, as I crawled about it, mine Hands passing swift over its Form, its Eyes opened surprizing wide in its battered Skull, and seemed as if to follow me, and its ruptured Lips opened as if in a vain Attempt at Speech.

As if it had an Injury beneath the Cranium, I thought.

My Pulse quickened.

There seemed to be a significant Amount of Blood; more, I thought, than could have resulted from my Phrenzy, and also emanating from the wrong Place. I felt around the Creature to discover its Cause, and found that it was lying upon that same Implement over which I My Self had tripped. I had been lucky, I thought; Raw Head's Fall, or perhaps its senseless Weight, had flattened the vicious Object so that it had posed no farther Danger to me as I had carried forward mine Attack. I rolled the Body off the Implement, and carefully, with stiff Hands, I felt around it. I desired to ascertain for My Self exactly what it was, this Lump of broken Metal that had cost me, and also mine Enemy, Blood and Pain.

Still the Creature retained the Appearance of Joseph Cox. This puzzled me. Raw Head had been defeated; why therefore had it not given up his false Countenance, and revealed its own?

Unless Raw Head and Joseph Cox had always been one; unless the Evil that I had long ago sensed in Cox had been Raw Head's own, and this smashed Body no temporary Flesh, but the Machine in which the Goblin Knight had hidden, undiscovered till tonight, these many, many Yeares.

Perhaps there was no Joseph Cox.

Perhaps there had only ever been the Goblin Knight.

With a little Effort, I wrested the metal Shard from the Soil's grip, and wiped it upon my sodden Breeches. In the watery Moonlight I perceived that it was part of the Blade of a Scythe, its Tang still buried within a Fragment of wooden Handle. The Length of the Blade was missing, but the Fraction that remained was still as solid and sharp as a Broadsword, and almost as long. It was old and rusty, but, as had already been proved to me, it could be a formidable Weapon.

Or an Anatomist's Knife, I thought.

I looked again at Raw Head.

I had remembered what was in my saddle Bag.

If it is a Simulacrum of a Man, I thought, a Man of any Kind, then it ought to possess the vital Organs of a Man; and it might require some of the Viscera necessary for the Processes of Life. It might require a Stomach and Intestinal Tract. It certainly hath both Skeleton and Muscle. But hath it a Brain, and an Heart?

Curiosity truly now had succeeded to the Crown which previously had been worn by Rage. I could not resist; the Imperative was as pressing and incontrovertible as a Caligulan Decree: I had to know whether Raw Head possesst an Heart. If it possess both Brain and Heart, I thought, Excitement growing in my Bowels, it might at Least shew me what Appearance hath an Injury to the Brain, even if 'tis not the spontaneous Injury associated with Stroake. I can learn something useful from this Creature, this defeated Enemy, this Raw Head.

Putting the broken scythe Blade to one Side, I rolled the Creature back into an useful Position and laid its Arms flat beside it upon the Turf. For a long Time then I did nothing, whilst considering carefully the Steps by which it was best to proceed. Then I opened up the Creature's Coat. Its Chest quivered. I put mine Hand upon the Sternum, and felt the Life hopping like a Toad beneath my Touch.

I had made my Decision.

With a great Effort, for the Creature was not light, I hefted it upon my Back, and with my saddle Bag clenched between my Teeth, and the Lanthorn, which I had recovered, in mine Hand, I began the long Tread towards the River Coller and those Ruins belonging to my Father that stood there; waiting, I knew now, for the time when I might make some practical Use of them.

Those Ruins were my Theatre.

As I staggered, slowly, thro' the Night, I considered the Case of Joseph Cox. Cox had supposedly originated, I knew, somewhere in the West Country, and in his own Way he had been much more the Foreigner than I, for all my Jewishness. The whole Neighbourhood knew the Story of my Mother. But what could anybody truly know of a strange Man who turned up, as Margaret Haynes had told me Cox had done, as if from nowhere, without Name or Kin, and not even a proper Trade to place him. He had worked here as a hired Labourer, but who knew what had been his Trade before he had arrived in the Valley of the Horse?

He hath no Trade, I thought, nor Name, nor Kin, because in Truth he hath no Humanity. I remembered the Dream I had experienced upon my wedding Night, and it seemed to me that it had been a Warning. Pig-Man, I thought. Monster, Goblin, Fiend. You did not expect that I would have recognised you for what you were.

Finally, out of the grey Dark loomed the river Cottages, like a Ring of blue Stones. I stumbled thro' the empty Gateway and made my way across the overgrown Soil to the first Doorway, and seeing the Door to be half off its Hinges, dealt it an hearty Kick, at which it fell inwards. Dust and Dampe rose up like Ghosts within, and then settled back into the Gloom. I coughed.

Quickly I carried Raw Head within, and lowering the Goblin with much Care upon the earthen Floor, for I did not wish him presently to expire, I set the Lanthorn upon the rotting Table and reset the Candle. I had no Means of lighting it upon me, but I guessed that a country Man like Cox had seemed to be would have about his Person Flint and Steel, and so it proved. After a good many failed Attempts I had it lit, and the obscure Interior of the Cottage began slowly to make Appearance as the yellow Light advanced, and then drew back, and then advanced again, thro' all its Shaddowes.

The Creature made a low, inchoate Sound and its Eyes rolled in its Head. I knelt beside it upon the cold Earth and, laying my leather saddle Bag beside me for Convenience, spread open its Body for mine Attention. Deciding, with little ado, where to cut, I withdrew my largest Scalpel from mine Etui and sliced quickly thro' its outer Garments, removing Coat and Shirt, and baring the Goblin's Chest to my Knife.

"You will be of some Use, Monster," I said. "You will do some Good in this World, despite your Inclinations. By your foul Sorcery you have taken the Form of a Man; I shall therefore, in you, discover that Form, and you shall thereby aid me in advancing the Cause of Medicine, which is a noble and an human thing. Out of your Darkness, Raw Head, there shall spring forth Light."

I supposed that the Creature could hear me, and understand me too, for it gave another Moan at these Words, and its rolling Eyes fixt staringly upon my Countenance. Spittle rolled out of the Corner of its open Mouth.

It is terrified, I thought. So it should be. It hath lost the Battle; Bloody Bones will tear it into Pieces.

I had decided firstly to remove the Heart, if there was one; and thence to progress upon a more general Dissection of the Corpse before arriving finally at the Brain, which I had realised would be better examined for Injury in Dayelight than by that of one mere Candle. Having removed all Obstructions, I took the Knife once again in mine Hand, and depresst it slowly and carefully into the open Space between the lowest Ribs. Blood spurted upwards, spattering my Face. I wiped it away and padded the Area around the Incision with the Creature's own Shirt, to soak up the rest of the Blood, which was spilling faster than I could contain it. I should cauterise the Arteries, I remembered; but 'tis too late now, and anyway there is no Need; I do not intend that this Patient should survive. I waited awhile until the Flow began to cease, and then continued the Procedure. The Blade I held was not as thick or as strong as the Tools commonly employed in an Autopsy, and the Process was far from easy in the Dark, but with Patience and Determination I achieved an Entry into the Body's Cavity.

The Specimen was naturally in far better Condition than the one I had dissected under Dr Hunter's Tuition. For the one thing, it was not yet dead; for another, Cox, or Raw Head, had lived a country Life, and the body's Tissues were taut and tough. Feeling mine Actions to have more in common with those of a Butcher than an Anatomist, I broke thro' the Ribs and wrenched the Chest apart. I slid mine Hand inside the slippery Opening I had created.

My groping Fingers encountered the Membrane of the Pericardium. The Creature's Chest gave a great Heave, and I felt the left Lung swell against my Fist. Reflexively, I withdrew mine Hand, and then tentatively re-inserted it. Again my Fingertips disclosed to me the Presence of that smooth imperforate inner Skin, bloody and warm, and weakly pulsating still. My large Scalpel was too unwieldy to be introduced into the pericardial Cavity, especially in the Dark. Tho' it was mine Intention afterwards to dissect the Membrane, I pushed mine Hand forward against it, not in any Hope of tearing, but instead to feel, if I could, whether any Organ lay within it.

Raw Head possesst an Heart.

I cried out. I know not to whom. The Muscle was unmistakable, its weakly fluttering Presence beyond Doubt.

Then it stoppt.

I withdrew mine Hand and reached for my smaller Scalpel.

But then, as I sate poised over the Body, in the dim Light, my Gaze wandered across the Face of Cox, its Features slack, its still open Eyes, sightless now, widened in an Horrour beyond any I had ever beheld in my Life; and the Understanding came to me, all of a sudden, in a vivid Flash that set mine Head a-spinning. Faeries have no Hearts.

This was not Raw Head.

I had murdered a Man.

CHAPTER FIVE-AND-THIRTY

I do not remember what it was that I did directly. The next Memory
of which I am aware is that of perceiving a fragile Brightening in
the Sky over the eastern Horizon, and of hearing the Rushing of
fast Water at my Feet. I had left the Cottage and I was standing at
the very Edge of the River Coller. There was an heavy Weight
upon my Shoulder. I let it fall.

To mine Horrour, I saw that I had carried upon my Back the
dissected Corpse of Joseph Cox; and in the dawning Light it seemed
inconceivable to me that I had ever thought it anything but the
real Body of a real Man.

Joe Cox it was, or had been; the stinking, drunken pig-Man Cox;

and tho' I was certain in my Bones that he had been neither a good Man, nor an innocent one, I knew too that he had never been the Goblin Knight. What he had been, to the eventual Cost of his Life, was a brutish, bullying Tosspot. He should not have sought to attack me; he should not have sworn so hard against my Mother's Race; he certainly should not have spoken with such Insolence about my Wife.

Or had it been Margaret Haynes he had been speaking of?

"Tristan," said a Voice behind me. "What in all the nine Hells do you think you are about?"

I whirled round upon the Spot.

Outlined against the dark green of the Ridge Way, shaking her Head and stamping in Protestation at her Rider's requiring her to stand, was a white Mare.

I caught my Breath. The Animal was immense. Its pale Body shone against the looming Hill as bright as if it had been the very Moon in the nightly Heavens. Its unshod Feet were feathered to the Knee, and as I watched, it raised one and brought it crashing down upon the Sward with the Force of an Hammer upon a mighty Anvil. Its Mane was braided and beribboned in every Colour of the dawn Sky, and its Tail, which was as long as that of any wild Horse, flicked like a Scourge across its broad Quarters. It wore a Bridle of bright scarlet Leather, threaded about and buckled with what looked to mine astonished Eyes like pure Silver; beneath the Saddle, which was similar, lay a saddle Cloth embroidered in a Design so intricate I could scarce make out what it contained. I thought I saw Flowers, Butterflies, Bees, and the Leaves and Branches of more Trees than I could name. But I was not certain.

I stared at the Mare and it appeared to me that I was staring thro' Time itself, at a Creature that could have borne upon its Back one of the antient Kings of Britannia.

Then I looked up at the Rider.

It was Nathaniel Ravenscroft.

For an whole Minute, I was too amazed to speak. Nathaniel dismounted and landed right before me, as agile upon his Feet as a pine Marten. He was dresst exact as I had seen him in my Dream, in brilliant green hunting Coat and Breeches, but this Time, upon his lily white Brow he sported a Diadem of brightest Mistletoe, green berried for the Spring, and as intricate a Crown as if it had been of finest Silver-work. He smiled at me, and handed the heavy Reins to a small, hooded Figure whom I had not previously noticed, who was crouching on all fours hard by one of the Mare's great Hooves. The tiny black Shape came barely up to the Animal's Knee, but it took the Reins from Nathaniel without apparent Fear, and remained silent.

'Tis Bat, I thought; and a Surge of the electric Fluid jolted my Spine.

"Oh, Nat!" I cried, finding my Tongue. "I have committed Murder! I have butchered a Man!"

Nathaniel laughed. "Oh, come off, Tris," he said. He wandered lazily to where the Body lay, still oozing scarlet over the green Grass, and stirred it lightly with his Boot. "You can not regret the Death of this shit-Sack? You know full well what he was; I cannot credit that you believe the World is not a better Place without him. Murder, mine Arse! He hath beaten his Wife till she hath fair lost her Wits—and her Child, too, that is mine, tho' I have never owned it. He hath insulted you, and would have tried for sheer Spite to have snappt your Neck; and moreover he hath half destroyed the beautifull willow Wood, that is beloved to us both. He was a Churl, a Braggart and a Rogue, and he hath done more Harm by his own Design and that of his mortal Masters than you ever will. "

"But he was not Raw Head," I said.

"No," said Nathaniel, with a strange Smile. "He was not."

So the Willow Tree hath Fled that Place, and she hath Run back Home in Great Feare and Anguish; and Leonora's Mother hath taken her in and kept her Secret and Hidden until her Time shall Come. And the Willow Tree was brought to Bedd of a lovely Girl, who hath Grey Eyes and Skin like a Sweet Peach, and because she is a Faerie Child, she hath huge soft Wings, that some Daye she might Fly.

I let my Gaze drop to the small black cloaked Figure that squatted, quiet, at Nathaniel's Side; and I wondered whether I had loved the winged Baby so much because she looked like him, and Katherine Montague because she looked like her.

And the Willow Tree loves her Daughter dearly, despite the Shame she hath brought, and she talks to her Often about the Beautifull Youth whom Willow Loves right well, who should have been her Father, if Anyone was to have been, and would have but for Wicked Chance and Raw Head. But Leonora's Mother can not abide it, and one Evening she gives the Babe away to an Old Gypsy Woman who hath come to the Door a-selling Cloathes Pins.

Then the Willow Tree Despaired, and wept and wept until she wept herself into a Tree again, and was nothing but Wood; and they buried her in the Garden, the weeping Willow Tree.

Katherine's Eyes, large and grey, and slightly prominent, set in a smaller, finer Copy of Nathaniel's Face.

But Raw Head when he hath discovered about the Babe, he hath—

"So," Nathaniel interrupted. "Finally using your Sight in Conjunction with your Wits, Tris! What mean you to do? Kill me, as you killed the ill-met and unlucky Joseph Cox? I think not."

"You are Raw Head," I said. "You are Raw Head."

" I am not; but I have been called thus."

"You have no Heart," I said.

"That is true. Now tell me, if you can, why 'tis so?"

"You traded it, to Viviane," I said, Tears springing to mine Eyes. "For a skin Drum."

"Yes," said Nathaniel. "Yes."

My Knees gave Way. I fell upon the river Bank. "I made a Mistake," I cried. "I thought that Evil could not lie beneath a beautifull Face. I would not let My Self believe that the Monster who had ruined Katherine Montague was really you."

"Ruined? But she is not!" Nathaniel exclaimed, in plain Astonishment. "She is respectably married, to you, who love her far more than she ever hath deserved. She hath her Name, her Honour and her Happiness intact. She hath not even Cause to suffer the Shame of raising a bastard Child, for I did her the great Favour of removing it. How, by all the heathen Gods, is Katherine Montague ruined?"

"You stole her Honour!" I shouted.

"If I did, then you restored it. Now you would cast it away again.

I have done no Harm to anybody. You, by your own Admission, not to mention the Evidence, are a Murderer."

"But I should rather be a Murderer, Nat," I stammered, thro' the Tears that coursed, fast as grey Hares, over my Cheeks. "Than be a Monster of the same Kindred as you; a Monster who could force himself upon a Maiden of twelve Yeares, and think no Harm."

"You were not there, Tristan," Nathaniel said, sharply. "And if you had been, who knows what had been the Outcome? You may not sit in Judgement upon me. Dost think that I know nothing of your wild Adventures in the City? I know what you did to Annie Moon, and to Lady B.——; I know it all. Do not dare to presume that you are any better than I am. Open up your Eyes. I do only as my Nature inclines me."

"Nature!" I cried. "What of free Will?"

Nathaniel laughed again, and his Eyes glinted like Emeralds in the silvery dawn Light. "By my Free Will," he said, "I act according to my Nature; and so doth the Ploughman in the Field and the Magpie in the Wood and the Leaf upon the hawthorn Tree; and so do you."

"I am a Man of Reason!" I shouted. "And I act accordingly!"

"Do you?"

That Question brought me up short. I had no Answer, none; excepting to shout again mine Assertion that I was in Fact a rational Man. But 'twould have been a Lie; in that Moment I verily perceived that I had no more Faith in mine own Reason, or in its Goodness, than I had in the Almighty. A chilling Shudder ran thro' my Body. My Stomach clenched. I realised what was happening, and in sudden Desperation, dragged My Self away from the Remains of Joseph Cox and crawled across the Greensward. Whatever Insults I had inflicted upon the Person of Cox, I had greater Respect for the Dead than to vomit on him.

When the Seizure was over, I sate up, shivering and cold. The dawn Aire slapped me like a Glove. I put mine Hand to my Forehead and found it hot and sweaty.

"What is happening?" I cried.

Nathaniel crouched down beside me. His Coat, I realised, must be the exact same Shade and Colour as the Grass, for where it fell among the Tussocks there appeared no Difference 'twixt the one and the other. Celandine and periwinkle Stems began to creep across the Fabric of the Cloth, as if it had been new turned Earth. He put his Arm affectionately around me, as he had done so many Times during our Friendship; and despite mine Horrour at the Reality of what he was, and everything that he had done, I did not attempt to shake him off. "Virtue," he said. "Virtue and Vice, Good and Evil, Reason and Madness, Life and Death. We are taught, those of us who go, as damnable Society says we must, to Church, to School, to marriage Bed and waiting Grave, to think these things Opposites. What would you think, Tristan Hart, if I were to tell you that there is another Truth?"

A Shaddowe swooped across the Grass.

"What?"

"Do you not recall my telling you about the Gnomes, who cannot perceive how easily they could climb up, up and out of the Chimney?"

I caught his Arm. "What art telling me, Nat?"

"Alas!" shrieked Bat's shrill, small Voice. "My Queen-Mother approaches! She is come!"

The White Owl droppt out of the many coloured Sky, and landed with a gentle feathery Thud upon the rain soaked Grass. It opened up its Beak, soundlessly, just once, as if it were catching its Breath, and then before mine Eyes began its Transformation: its domed Head, no longer owlish, but springing forth long, black, Tresses, rising quick toward Heaven on a white and slender Neck that was graceful and womanly; on perfect Shoulders no longer winged, but clad in a Gown of sheerest Tiffany, which even as I watched appeared to grow by teazing Turns first translucent, then opaque, as if it were a Veil thro' which my poor Sight could but partly penetrate. But her Face—ah, that I could plainly see, for it was the Face that had tormented me ever since that Morning underneath the Thorns; an high cheeked, ivory skinned Vision more beautifull than Joy, than Wonder itself; yet more dreadful to my Sight than black Despair—for as it was the Countenance of Viviane, so too was it that of Annie Moon, of Lady B.——, of Polly and of Mrs Haywood and of Margaret Haynes; of my Mother, and Katherine Montague. And then it was Viviane's once more, Viviane's and none other's, glorious in the dawning Rays of the uplifting Sunne. My Forehead was burning. My raked Shin roared.

How is this possible? I thought. How is this real? I began to quake.

Nathaniel instantly got up from my Side, and stepping forward apace, fell upon one Knee at the Faerie Queen's Feet. Meadow Flowers tumbled from his Pockets. "My Lady Viviane," he said.

Viviane lowered her magnificent Gaze, and smiled. Her Expression was tender. But her Teeth still are sharp, I thought.

"Ah," she said. The pure Note of her Voice was brighter than the singing Wren. "My Goblin Knight. How doth your Hunting, my Lord? Hast brought down thy Hart?"

"No, My Lady."

"So," Viviane said.

Do not give her your Name, Nathaniel had told me. I remained silent.

Viviane steppt toward me. As she walked, a pure Sliver of Brilliance crept over the Horizon to the East, and the Sky at her Back became the Daye's Cradle, radiating into fragile Bands of burnished Saffron and palest Blue. Yet for all this, the Grass beneath her Feet could have out-shone the brightest Sunne, for where she trod it sparkled and winked incandescent, like the white Heart of a blacksmith's Fire.

"Caligula," Viviane said.

"Viviane." I bowed mine Head.

"You owe me a Debt, Caligula. Art ready to pay it?"

"I did not ravish you, Viviane," I said, getting unsteadily to my Feet. She seemed to grow even taller as I rose, so that when I finally stood upright before her it was as if I faced a Goddess, or a Titaness of antient Greece, or, perhaps, an hawthorn Tree. "I know that I did not. My Guilt was wrongly placed. It was not mine, and it was not for thee."

"No," said Viviane. She shook her Head, and her many Earrings chimed and sparkled with the Motion. "You did not. And that is well for you, for to have done so must surely have meant your Death. But you thought to force your Will on me, regardless of mine; you, a mere Man, and a mortal Man, besides. 'Tis not so unlike a Matter, in my Mind."

"I am not that Kind of Monster!" I shouted.

"What Kind, then, are you?" Viviane said. "Wilt pay? For I require Reparation of you for the Insult you did me, and I shall have it. If you will not pay willingly, then for seven Generations my Curse shall fall upon every male Heir of your House. Misery shall be your Lot; your Wives shall die, your Children wither in the Womb. Answer."

I knew that it was Truth, as readily as I knew my right Hand. "What wouldst have of me?" I whispered. "I am not ready to die!"

Viviane raised her dark Head and looked down upon me. My Knees began to shiver. "Thinkst," she said, "that this Fool who lies at our Feet was ready? He was not; Death came, you came, regardless. Now he is released from all his Duties. I have no Interest in your Release, Caligula. I want your Service."

"My Service?"

"Seven Generations shalt endure, in my Service, Caligula."

For the second Time my trembling Knees gave Way. I fell before her, on the silver Grass. "No!" I cried. "No! Oh, I beg you, Viviane, if you have any Mercy in your Heart. I cannot pay you thus! I cannot! I have a Wife, and she is with Child! I cannot leave her!"

"Cursed, then, be."

In my Mind's Eye I saw Katherine, beautifull and lost and very much in need; and I knew that if I were to be gone, she would be on her own, exiled within her crystal Shell, the which I had penetrated with so little Effort that I had forgotten it was there. Oft had I pondered whether I would live without her—but would she live, I thought, without me? Who would tell her what to do? Then I remembered again my poor innocent unborn Child, and the Apprehension woke within my Breast that it was indeed a male, upon whom Viviane's Curse would fall, and fall the heavier for its Lack of Desert; and I wondered how I could consider letting such an Event come to pass.

Nathaniel now rose up from his Knee, and came once again to my Side. He bent over me, and putting both his Hands upon my Shoulders, stared into mine Eyes. "Come with us," he said. "Come with us, and we shall hunt together, Brother with Brother, Yeare by Yeare, until the Sunne grow cold and the Stars revolve no longer in the Firmament. There is naught to fear. My Lady's Service is neither arduous nor displeasing. What a great Jest it shall be! What Mischief we shall make! What Wonders we shall see! What Joys! What Marvells! What untold, incalculable Delights!"

If I had been an Hero, if I had been an Hercules or a Theseus; or if I had been sung about in any of Nathaniel's Ballads; if I had been bold Jack the Giant Killer, or the Brother of Bluebeard's darling Wife, I should have in that Instant stolen me Nathaniel's own silver hilted Dagger from his Belt and plunged it right thro' his traitorous Breast, and thus avenged us all, my Katherine, My Self; but even as I thought it thus I knew I had no Power left in me to slay my dearest Friend. I could not do it. I could not. I loved him.

And I wanted to say Yes. And I understood, tho' I would have torn my Tongue out sooner than admit it, that I wanted to say Yes not only because I wanted to save my Son, but because I wanted to leave with Nathaniel, to join his Gypsies—or his Faeries, for such they really were—for My Self; that I need never again think about Viviane, or Joe Cox, or Annie, or Lady B.——; or my poor Father, or Erasmus, or little Simmins; or my Sister and her dying Marriage and her Mother-in-law and Barnaby and the half ruined willow Wood. I remembered those bucolic Dayes spent a-walking with Nathaniel in the Country about Collerton and Shirelands Hall, and I wished, more than ever I had wished anything, for their Return. I had been vice-less, then; vice-less and free of this great and present Grief that rolled over and over mine Heart like a Millstone. I looked into the verdant Glitter of Nathaniel's Eyes and I wanted to forget that he, Nathaniel Ravenscroft, who had been to me closer than a Brother, was Raw Head. He was Raw Head, and he had ravished Katherine, my Katherine. He was Bat's Father. But – and I heard, rather than I thought it—but—there had been

Wine and Laughter on his Lips, and mayhap he had intended no Harm. Mayhap, being Nathaniel Ravenscroft, he had intended nothing at all, and had merely acted, rashly, capriciously, without Reflection, without Reason, without Thought.

I had been rash also. I contemplated my too-soon Marriage, and my coming Boy, and how unready I was to raise him; and all at once it seemed to me that both he and my Katherine would be far better off if I was gone. My Son had a Murderer for a Father. What would happen if the Matter came to Court? I had slain an innocent Man; innocent, at least, of the Crime for which I had contemned him. Perhaps, I would not hang, since I could perhaps plead Benefit of Clergy and Defense of Self besides; but it would be a terrible thing for Katherine, that I should stand Trial; and the Shame of it would kill my Father.

Mayhap Nathaniel had made Katherine's Child a better Father than I would.

"But I do love Katherine," I said. "And she me."

"Then so much the Better," Nathaniel said, "that you come away with us now, and spare her the Ordeal of your facing the Assizes for the killing of this verminous Lout."

His hand moved to his Dagger's Hilt.

The white Mare stamped her Foot impatiently, and the Bridle rang out sharp against the violet Dawn. Bat ran her clawed Hand tenderly down the Creature's nearside Leg, bidding her softly to be still and patient just a little while longer. Then she turned her Attention, like a steel Lance, upon me, and for the first time, her grey Eyes met with mine from beneath the black Hood of her Cloak. The Force of her Look shattered my Phantasy, as if 'twere Glass.

They have Laws, Katherine had said. Laws that cannot be broken. I had promised Bat that I would take her home if she fetched

Nathaniel to me, and because she had fulfilled her Part of that Bargain, the Conclusion that I would fulfil mine was as inevitable as the End of Sunnerise. I must take Bat home. Not thro' any Dictate of Honour, or even of Love, but because if I did not, then it would never have been possible that she had done her Part. Time had reversed itself; the Consequence had been prior to the Cause— and yet impossible as this ought to have been, it was not only possible, but Fact. What other Things, I wondered, might happen thus?

I shook My Self. "I must go home, Nat," I said. "I must go home, and take my Wife's Daughter with me. I have given her my Word."

The white Sunne froze upon the far Horizon. There was Silence. Then, Viviane said: "What?" The Aire shook. "What?" she repeated. "Bat! Come forth!"

The little Bat scuttled tentatively forward over the wet Ground. For the first Time, now, since she had been a Baby in Mary Fielding's Kitchen and in mine Arms, I perceived clearly her Visage and Shape; and even as mine Heart skippt for Love of her, my Stomach lurched.

Katherine's Eyes, Nathaniel's Face; yet the knotted Hair that spilled rough around her sharp Cheekbones was dirty yellow in Colour, and her long, pointed Ears violently twitched at every tiny Rustle in the Grass or in the Aire. Not an Human Child; no, no; despite all that I had said to Mary, despite everything I had believed. Her Hands were nut-brown, as were her bare Feet, and from the Tip of every Digit projected a sharp, black Claw of astonishing Length. But most disturbing of all was the Method of her Locomotion, for she did not walk, or even crawl as an Infant might, but crept upon her four Paws as if she were verily a Bat upon the ridge-Pole of a Roof, and her black Cloak folded and dragged beside her like the membranous Wings I knew lay underneath it. As she approached Viviane, I saw her Mouth fall open and her Lips draw back in a fearful Gesture of Appeasement, and I perceived her Teeth as needle sharp and multitudinous as they had been in her Babyhood. She eats Insects, I thought.

An obscene Horrour ran thro' me. Could I take her home? Verily, how could I do it? How could I return this rape-born Freak to Katherine, who without her—Nathaniel had been right—was not shamed, let alone ruined, but respectable and happy—and expect that she should mother it? The Bat was horrible, monstrous, an Hag in Infant Shape, a Grotesque, a Parody of Maidenhood; of Humankind itself.

Viviane stared hard at the Bat. A Mask of violet Fury spread itself slow and thick over her beautifull Countenance. Her black Eyes glittered like Star-spun Jet. "Ungrateful Brat," she said. "Three Times now you have tried to leave me. You will not try again." She raised her Hand.

And it seemed that it was not the little Bat who cowered shivering before her on the Blood-smeared Green, but my Katherine; Leonora weeping herself into a Tree. Brat and Bat, I thought, separated by an R.

A yellow Anger ignited in my Gut, and my Thoughts began to swirl and ream like Smoake.

How dare he! Ravenscroft, Raw Head, whoever he be! How dare he! I care not if he is my dearest Friend! What he hath done—what he doth now—is beyond Contempt. What Goblins have I left to slay, what Monsters? I prised my left Knee from the Earth, forced the Sole of my Foot to lie flat where it had lately been. My Leg trembled.

You were wrong, Nat. I thought. You were more than wrong, when you said that you knew not what would have happened had

I been with you upon Christmas Eve; you were wicked—for Monster that I am, I would not have harmed a Maiden of her Yeares, and tender Virtue. Had I been with you, Katherine would have been safe, and Bat, my little Bat, would not ever have come to be. But I was not, and she is Katherine's Child, Katherine's; and that makes her mine. If Bat be Monster, I am Monster too, and if I make a poor Father, better be that than a Father whose only Claim is Force. You feel nothing for Bat. You traded your Heart to Viviane for a Drum, and now the only Beat you hear is heartless Musick. You did not take Bat away from Katherine out of Duty, or even Kinship, tho' you would pretend it so, for you did not take Rebecca Clifton's Child. No, you took her because Viviane, your Faerie Queen, wanted her, like a Toy; and Viviane hath no Intent to let her go. But she hath no Power to prevent it. The Thief owns not his stolen Bounty. Goblin Knight and Faerie Queen both, be damned.

I stood up.

"Strike her not, Viviane!" I said. "She is not yours to harm. You stole her from her Mother, and that Mother loves her, and misses her, and would have her returned. You shall not strike her."

Viviane had not sent Bat to torture me. She had not sent Bat to me at all. It had been at Viviane's Order that she had been stolen back; but the Infant Bat had come, by herself, by her own free Will and fay Enchantments seeking the mortal Man whose Name she had never forgot; the Bloody Bones her Mother loved, who should have been her Father: Tristan Hart.

Why ever had I thought it otherwise? The Bat was not an Human Child; in her Spirit and Mind she was as antient a Being as the Changeling who had never seen Water boiled in an Egg-shell; but in her Body she was still a Babe, and she needed Love. Love of a

Species, I thought, that was as alien and incomprehensible to Nathaniel and Viviane as their own was to me.

Viviane turned again upon me, and her Face was as white as that of the Chalk Horse itself, or of the Owl she had so very lately been.

They have Laws, Katherine had said.

"You have not her real Name," I said, hoping, as I said it, that 'twas true. "You have it not, even as you have not mine. You cannot curse me, Viviane! You have no Power over either of us! Bat is not yours. You must surrender her. You must let us go."

"What!" cried Viviane. "Ha!"

For an Instant it appeared, and verily I thought, that she should wrap her Gown up into Feathers and fly away again, in Rage. Her black Eyes seemed as if they would burst from her Head, so wide and furious were they, and her Lips became as thin as silver Wires.

Nathaniel held up an Hand. He glanced in a questioning Manner at the Countenance of his Queen, and then, seeing perhaps therein some Assent: "Wait," he said. "Have Care, Sir. 'Tis true that my Lady's Curse cannot touch you. But consider what it must mean to you and yours, to the very Land of which you shall be Lord, if you incur upon your Family seven generations' Enmity with my People. Also, consider that the Bat is not, and hath neither the Behaviours, nor the Appearance of an Human Child. If you take her into your House, your Servants will panick and your Neighbours will shun you."

"Egad," I said. "They do that already. I do not mind it."

Nathaniel shook his Head, in a wondering Fashion. "What a fascinating Being you are," he said. "An Houre ago you tore open a Man's Chest because you thought, mistakenly, that he had fathered a Bastard upon your Wife; yet you would take that same Bastard into your Family, and raise it as if it were your own."

I glared at him.

"So," Viviane said. "So. You will not come, and we will be Enemies. Is that your Decision? Consider your Reply, Caligula, for I have asked three Times and I shall never ask again."

But my Mind was tired, and I could not perceive how I might answer otherwise. I was certain that Viviane's Ignorance of my real Name would somehow protect my Family from her direct Wrath. But Nathaniel was right. If I did not hang, then when my Father died, I would be Squire of Shirelands. I saw it plain: Viviane's People, and her Followers amidst the Bees and Creatures of the Field and Hill, would no longer buzz and flutter amid the Crops and Trees. Every creeping, crawling, slithering thing, every Snail and gnawing Worm that cankered the Heart or strippt bare the Leaf, would turn against us. Shirelands Estate would starve, and its Tenancy fall victim to as much Disease and Misery as the Inhabitants of St Giles in the Field; whilst I, the Cause of it, would dwell untouched within the four Walls of my Study, studying Medicine to cure Humanity of its Ills whilst Men died for me in Droves; and all the Time being afraid, horribly afraid lest Viviane or any of her Ilk should come a-creeping in, and by some Sorcery learn, at last, my Name. And after seven Generations of such terrible Decay, what Estate, what Humanity, would be left?

I remembered how I had taken the Blame for Nathaniel in his Father's apple Orchard.

"Tristan," said Nathaniel's Voice, distant in Memory. "It is possible. It is real. Look thro'."

CHAPTER SIX-AND-THIRTY

Look thro'. Virtue and Vice, Right and Wrong, Life and Death. Verily, it doth seem to us that these things stand opposed, each facing the other across a trackless Void, like Images reflected in a window Pane; but the Truth is that this Seeming is dependent upon the Place in which we, the Watchers, stand. One small Movement upon our Part, one Step to the right or the left, and the Illusion is dispelled. Take but another Step, and then another, and what seemed before in Opposition stands conjoined. One last, and both have ceased to be.

And at last I remembered my Mother; and she was, this Time, neither a Voice in a Poem, nor an Image in the flickering dream-Vision of Infantile Memory, but my real Mother, clear and present and profound as if she had been that Instant in my physical Sight. I remembered her as she had looked, when she had sate before the changing Window, thinly drawn, no longer laughing at the Shaddowes, trying one last Time to capture with her Brush the faint Impression of the fading Light.

"Come here," she said. "Come here, Tristan. Look. Do you see? Do you see this Flower? 'Tis a Primrose, Tristan, the earliest little Flower. Dost perceive how delicate are its Petals, how tender its Perfume?"

"I see a Flower, Mama," I said, with a Shrug.

"Whence came the Flower?"

"Our Lord made it."

My Mother put her Arm around me. "Listen," she said. "Listen well, but tell no one; especially not the Rector Ravenscroft; but do not ever forget. When I was a Girl in Amsterdam, my Uncle Jacob told me of a Man whom he had known in his own Youth. A Man of great Courage, Tristan, who made Lenses, so that People might see thro'; who dared to say, even to write, unspeakable things. And he told my Uncle a great Secret; which is great because it is true; and my Uncle told it me, and I am telling you. This Flower was not made by God, Tristan, because it is Part of God. It is the living Body of our Lord, the very Form of his Name. All things are One."

For th' Atomies of which we grow,
Are soules, whom no change can invade.

And then I perceived that betwixt Matter and Spirit there is, truly, no Difference; that the Difficulty we identify regarding Mind and Body, the Impossibility of their Interaction, which seemeth an Interaction betwixt two independent Substances, is a Fallacy arising from our Use of Words: for what we call Matter, and what we call Mind are really two different Properties of the same Substance, which lies at the very Fundament of all Reality. And some even call it God, and some the World, and some Faerieland; and it matters not, for all these, anyway, are Human Terms, mere Words, Names; falsely boundaried and constrained by Human Rationality and Human Conceit, and as such none of them can hope to comprehend the Nature of the thing.

Matter and Spirit, One; God and Aether, One; Sky and Heaven, One; Heaven and Earth, One; Mind and Body, One; Dream and Conscience, One; Love and Pain, One; Life and Death, seeming opposing Faces in a Mirrour, that one small Step will reveal as merely two Points upon one continuous Line.

I looked up at the stoppt Sunne in the East, and I knew that to Viviane and her Kind, seven Generations was as the Blinking of an Eye, and the Differences betwixt Life and Death, Presence and Absence, as meaningless as Human Words. And this was so because of what they were, which was not Mortal, not Human, but Entities timeless and unboundaried as the whole, intelligent, World; like Sylphs, or Ideas, or Dreams.

"I shall not die," my Mother said. "I shall become the Soil and the Aire, the Barley and the Green, the brown Wren and the Nightingale. I shall be Part of Ha-Shem, still, even as I am Part of Him now. I shall not die."

Whatever happens, I shall not die.

Leave my Katherine? No. Abandon my Son? No. Betray my Bat? No. Allow Ruin to descend upon my Land, that compasst within it the Body and Soule of my beloved Mother?

I am the Red Kite. I traverse the high Heavens, and the Whole of my green Valley is in mine Eye. Mine House, my Family, my Meadows, my Woods, my Fields, my Chaffinches, my Chalk, my People; all mine to protect or to destroy, but never to forswear.

But even as I formed the Image in mine Imagination, some other, half submerged Part of my Mind cried: No! Death might be meaningless, to a dying Woman in search of Comfort, or to a Faerie, or to the Earth itself; but 'tis not so to me!

I want my mortal Life! I want to see my Son grow up. I want to become a Surgeon, to battle against Death, and control Disease and Pain. I want Katherine, Katherine, Katherine.

They may hang me, I thought, but—

"My Lady Viviane," I said. "Help me, I beg you. I would repay you, if you would allow me Time. You have no Power over me. You can neither Curse nor Compel me. But I mislike much the Idea that mine Heirs and mine Estate must suffer for a Mistake that was mine only. If you will but stay your Hand against my Fields, as I have stayed mine against your Goblin Knight, and permit me to choose the Service I shall render you, then I swear that you shall have it."

Viviane looked upon me, and her Countenance was harder than Stone. "And what," she said. "would you choose?"

"Let me live," I said. "Let me return home, to my Wife, and care for her, and steward this Valley, until the Daye on which I should naturally die, upon which I shall come to you, and you should have full seven Generations' Reparation from me, and it shall be gladly rendered."

"That Daye," she answered, "may be closer than you think, Caligula."

"Indeed," I said. My Breath felt raw upon my Lips. "I know it;

still I pray you, Viviane, grant me this! Grant me this, and let all War be ended between us. I will no longer call your People Gypsy, but give them fair Treatment in my Lands. Ye shall not be harried; never shall ye be hanged. Your antient Rights and Ways shall be protected; your Woods and Waterways and Chalklands kept open, never inclosed."

Viviane stared at me, and tho' there was no Time, it seemed to me she looked upon me for a Century. "You jabber like a Monkey," she said, at last. "But it is enow. The Bargain you would offer me is fair and seemly. No more will there be bad Blood between us. You shall steward my Valley. But if you think ever to betray me, if you think to depart it; to break your Word, to abandon your Wife, neglect your People, forget your Promise, my Anger shall fall swift and deadly as the White Owl. The Bat may go to her Mother. She will come back to me of her own Choice when the Seasons change. None of my Kind can endure long amongst yours."

The white Horse tossed her Head, and the Bits jingled; the Sunne moved again.

Viviane steppt back into the slanting Light. I squinted up mine Eyes to see her, for it seemed the Rays shone thro' the faint Gossamer of her Dress so bright that she was become the very Dawn. Then she was changing, transforming once again into her other Form; and I wondered whether Viviane was truly the White Owl, or the White Owl was Viviane; or whether both Shapes were never more than Signs.

As soon as the Owl was gone from my Sight, Bat jumped up from her Place and ran to leap into mine Arms. Startled, I caught her.

The Bat's Body was light and dry, brittle seeming as a small Twig that hath been left near to a roaring Fire. Yet she had an Heartbeat, and I felt it it rattle furious and strong against mine Hand. So, she is not as inhuman, I thought, as Nathaniel and Viviane would have had me believe.

"So, Tris," Nathaniel said, rising to his Feet and stretching lazily, his Hands linked behind his Head, as if he were a Fencer cooling his Muscles after a Match. "All's well that ends well, as the Play hath it. Now all that remains is for us to toss this useless Lump of Flesh in the River, and you shall have carried the Daye."

"Dost care not," I said, "that this Flesh, which lately was a Man, died not for his own Fault, but for yours?"

"That," answered Nathaniel, "may be true; or it may not. What you feared in Joseph Cox was not my monstrous Nature, Tristan, but your own; who shall say whether he died not for that? Anyway, I care not; he was a brutal Swine who did not deserve to go on living, even if he had not earned the Death he got. Better for all he died by your Hand. What matter? Now pick up the Corpse and shov't as far out as you can into the Current. It is strong."

"Will it not float?" I said.

Nathaniel laughed. "Nay, Tris, not in these Waters," he said. "Swollen as they are, they are as treacherous as the Avon. 'Twill be many Weeks before the thing is found, and you know full well what Condition it may attain in that Time."

I did not move.

"Tristan," said Nathaniel impatiently. "I am trying to assist you. Be discovered with the Body if you will; there will surely be an Inquest, if not a Trial, and as Joe Cox hath a gaping Hole in his Chest several Inches wide, it cannot go well for you. In vain may you plead Defense of Self when the Look of the Business is that you insanely murdered the Man for Anatomy."

I knew Nathaniel was right. How I wished that he was not.

"If they do not hang you," Nathaniel said, "they will lock you away in the Hospital."

I lowered my Bat, gently, to the Ground. "Stand forth, sweet Heart," I told her. "I must rid me of this Cadaver, ere it betray me."

I did not intirely trust Nathaniel's Assertion regarding the River, so to be more certain of my desired Result I scrabbled around in the dirt Bank until I had unearthed sufficient Quantity of large Stones to have filled Joe Cox's Coat, and fastened about his Neck a farther two of such Weight that I could scarce lift them together. It was mine Hope that the combined Drag of all these would anchor the Cadaver in Place against the gassy Pressure that would build up within it as it began its Decay, and safeguard against its Rise before the river Eels had done their Work upon it.

With an almighty Effort, I dragged the whole Load across the Grass and droppt it at the River's Edge.

The swollen Waters roiled before me, black and endless in the long Shaddowe of the Bank, and I recalled how I had sate upon the daye of my Collapse staring into the Thames; and in mine imagined Memory the Thames rose up above the Rooftops of the City, rearing like a black water-Snake, seeking me out, wrapping me up in its Coils and drowning the Life from me. The little River Coller was not the Thames, was not a Fraction of that great River's Span and seething Depth, but yet it seemed to me in that Moment that it had become't, and my Balance reeled.

But as I began to tip forward, I felt Nathaniel's Hand upon mine Arm, strong as a Blacksmith's Vice, and abruptly my Senses returned to me, like the sharp Clang of an Hammer upon Steel. "Do it," said Nathaniel.

With one final, Herculean Shove, I pushed the weighted Corpse of the pig-Man, that I had mistaken for Raw Head, into the hurling Waters. It sank immediately, and vanished.

"Come," said Nathaniel at once. "You shall not be found here. Get up on my Mare, and we shall carry you back to the Highway, where you first fell. There I shall depart you, and you shall never see me more; at least, with mortal Eyes."

I did not argue, neither did I resist. Both would have been futile, and neither intirely justified. I did not want Assistance from Nathaniel, and I had not asked it; but it appeared he wanted nothing in Return, and I had not the Strength left after mine Efforts with the Cadaver to repel him.

One doth not, unless one is inordinately stupid, blame the Magpie for being what he is. He is not culpable for his Cruelty, tho' it may be savage; he doth only what his Nature inclines him to do. So it was with Nathaniel Ravenscroft, Goblin Knight, Changeling, Raw Head. Those Gnomes, of which he had upon that distant Afternoon laughingly told me, could not perceive up; 'twas not in their Nature. Nathaniel, Faerie too that he was, could not perceive when he had caused Harm, or done wrong, because to him neither Term had any Meaning. I might have beaten him, and not his Scapegoat Cox, to Death, but never would he have evinced even the slightest Understanding wherefore I had done so. To imagine, then, that he might have comprehended my Sentiments at being asked to ride with him was as fantastic a Design as to think that mine own Chestnut might be taught to read the Greek. I kept my Peace.

Nathaniel mounted before me, and Bat, at mine Insistence, also, and we rode in steady Quietude thro' the awakening Valley. After a good while, we reached the Crossroads 'pon which stood the Bull, and Way-stone, and here Nathaniel reined in his gleaming Mare and explained that I should dismount. "Right here is where you fell," he said. "Your Family are all out a-seeking you, in a rare old Panick, the Lot of them. Is't not remarkable, Tris, that you should be so loved?"

"What of Bat?" I demanded, dismounting clumsily and tumbling once again upon mine Arse on the Greensward.

"You shall have her home; but not upon this Morning. You have need to recover your Health and your Wits; there was Poison on that Scythe, and even now it spreads. If you are still alive on All Soules' Daye, when the Gate lieth full open betwixt our Kingdoms, look for her then, and you will not be disappointed; tho' mayhap you'll come to wish that you had been. Farewell, Bloody Bones, my Brother, mine other Face. I have hugely enjoyed your Company. I shall see you again on your dying Daye. Till then, Tristan Hart."

He tippt his Hat, as if we had been but fellow Travellers upon one Road, and with a glittering Smile jabbed his Spurs into the Mare's snowy Flanks. The great Creature half reared, then leapt forward into a Gallop, sinuous and swift against the distant Chalk Hill like white Water all a-flow. I heard her Hooves, loud as Heartbeats, long after she had vanished from my Sight; but I knew not whether I heard them with mine Ears or in mine Imagination.

Perhaps Nathaniel had spoken true about the Scythe, perhaps not; he was, after all, no Surgeon. But the Wound upon my Shin was raw and hot, and mine Head was aching and spinning as if a Devil had got quite inside it. In this debilitated and bloody State I was found some short Minutes later by Erasmus Glass and my Sister; and while Jane wept, Erasmus got me up into the Chaise, wrappt me in a thick Blanket, and drove me back to Shirelands. I remember little of the Journey except that upon mine Arrival at the Hall I was not permitted to see Katherine—which Denial I vehemently contested, but to no Avail—and put to Bed, where I remained, I later learned, for the succeeding three Weeks.

My Family feared, naturally, that I had again gone mad; but of course I reassured—and in two Cases, disappointed—them by waking from my Month long Fever apparently sane, and untroubled in my Mind by that Dread of Viviane and the Goblin Knight that previously had maintained such a cruel and unrelenting Influence over my daily Existence.

Erasmus, who was with me when I woke, sent at once for Mrs H. to tell the Household of my Restoration, and described to me in affectionate and touching Terms the Effect my sudden and dramatick Sicknesse had had upon them. Jane, faced with the Possibility of my Death, had gone intirely against her Husband's expresst Wishes and moved herself back into her old Chamber, opposite to mine own, in order to assist Katherine, and Erasmus, with my Care. She was not now on any better a Footing with the one Barnaby than our Father was with the other, and Erasmus doubted that she would ever return, sans Force, to Withy Grange. Somewhat to my Surprize, he did not seem at all displeased by this unexpected Turn of Events, and very much the Opposite; but I had neither Strength nor present Inclination to interrogate him on his Change of Heart. This Return of his favourite Child had proved a veritable Tonic to our worthy Father, who, despite an evident and real Distress at my Sickness, had begun himself to recover at an even faster Rate than heretofore, and had regained some Rudiments of civilised Speech; tho' only, Erasmus cautioned, in my Sister's Presence.

These Newes pleased me much, but now that I had regained my Senses the only Person I wanted of course to see was my Katherine, and I waited impatiently for her Appearance.

Profound indeed were the Newes I had for her concerning the Restoration of her stolen Child; tho' I was not certain of the Words I should use to impart them, my Resolve was steady, and mine Excitement great. I was not without some Apprehension of her Reaction. I knew that Katherine had loved her Baby; but whether she would love her now she would be made to raise her seemed a different thing, and one that I could not easily fore-guess. But whatever my Wife's Sentiments, I knew too that on All Soules' Morn my dear Bat would fly home to me, and remain with me as my Daughter until she decided of her own Will to return to her natural Kin: as the Changeling Nathaniel had done before her.

I will have that in common with the Rector, I thought. We will both have raised, and lost, a Goblin. The Notion amused me for a Moment, and I laughed aloud; then to my immense Surprize I found that I was weeping, and I did not know for why.

I rubbed at mine Eyes in a vain Effort to forestall these unex-pected Tears, but to no Avail; and as I touched mine Eyelids for the third Time I seemed, all on a sudden, to see right thro' them, as if they had been glass Lenses; and verily the willow Tree appeared in Katherine's Shape before me, as clear as if she had been living Wood an Arm's Length from my Face; and before I was able even to cry out in Surprize, she had begun, silently, inexorably to trans-form into a tall, smooth trunked Ash, and I was peering upwards, thro' the Foliage, seeing—

Mistletoe.

But Raw Head when he hath discovered about the Babe—

Mine Heart lurched. 'Tis the End of the Tale, I thought. *The Tale of Raw Head and the Willow Tree*, that Nathaniel interrupted, and would not let me hear out.

"No!" I cried in sudden Dread, for I apprehended already, without in Conscience knowing—what a Marvell is the Mind—what the utter End of the Story was to be—or more truly, what already it had been; and I did not want it; nay, no Part of it, neither to hear it nor to know it nor to understand; but only to misplace it, as far away from me as possible, to lock it away in a sealed Room deep in mine Head, and never think on it again.

Sometimes, Memory whispered, that is how Grief works.

But even as I voiced forth this my Denial, there stole upon me the Understanding, gentle and unexpected as my Mother's Hand upon the Crown of mine Head, that altho' during mine Illness my Conscience had done everything in its Power to prevent me from remembering anything of Katherine's Story, now that I was well, it could—indeed, it must—continue to do so no longer. If I truly wanted to stay sane, I must permit my Memory to unclose the Whole of the Tale, and face up to whatever Truth I had exiled within.

Time to wake up, Tristan Hart.

Slowly, I let my Skull sink upon my Pillow, and the final Words of Katherine's History washed over me, like white salt Water.

But Raw Head when he hath discovered about the Babe, he hath gone upon the first Morning of May, all by himself under an Ash Tree; and for Shame he hath Hanged himself upon it, high among the Mistletoe, and hath Taken his own Life. This is the worst thing of all, the Secret Never to be Told. But O Bloody Bones, it happened. It was Real.

Now Katherine Montague looks into her Mirrour; and she cannot tell verily if she dreamed Leonora was the Willow Tree, or if the Willow Tree dreamed she was Leonora. And she Prayes beyond all Expectation that Tristan Hart will Forgive her all these Sins, that are too Many, and too Terrible, and too Painfull for one little Heart to Comprehend.

When my Katherine finally found me, sobbing, I had no Words at all with which to tell her anything. Instead, I let her hush my weeping with a Kiss, and hold me – for in all Honesty I was too weak for it to have been the other Way about; and all those things, both wicked and virtuous, that I had heard and seen and felt in mine Illness melted away from me like Ice before the Stove, and I was no longer sure whether what was real had become Dream, or Dream real. And verily it mattered not.

"We shall never see Nathaniel Ravenscroft again," I said at last to her. It was the only thing I knew for Truth.

"Oh, Tristan," she said, pressing my wet Cheek against her Breast. "Tristan, Darling, I know. I know. I know."

She presst Mary's Sketch into mine Hand, and we lay still together, in Silence.

CHAPTER SEVEN-AND-THIRTY

Despite all Katherine's Efforts to chear me, for the next few Weeks after mine Awakening, I drooped like a sick Cat, seeking mine own Company and burying my Thoughts in Silence. I could not go near to my Study, for the Aire within conjured such Associations of Simmins, and of Joseph Cox, that I could not breathe it. Erasmus said that I must take my Time, and expect a slow and incremental Progress in my Recovery; I had been exceeding ill, and would not get well in short Order.

I had been all one Afternoon languishing in my Bedchamber with the Window ajar, reading my Mother's Copy of Spinoza's *Tractatus theologico-politicus*, when there came thro' it another

Sound, more piercing than Nathaniel's hunting Horn, more compelling than the Drumming: a Scream.

The Daye had been quiet; I had been listening idly, as I read, to the Wind rustling the Ivy. Then, on a sudden so sharp it cut mine Attention all in two, the Scream resounded: an high, agonised, blue-white Shriek, Lightning tearing thro' the Sunne; a Scream of Pain more vivid, more intense even than the terrible Howl Lady B.— had given at the first Incision of Dr Hunter's Knife. It rose before me, vibrating, a naked Rainbow of exclusive Agony, imprinting itself upon the Arc of Heaven. My Lungs quickened; Aire and Blood mixt in my pulmonary Vein, spread like liquid Electricity round my Body, jarring my Spine. The Cry hung on the Aire, a thin curving Line, humming slightly; still pure, still perfect despite that. An Human Sound, closer to Perfection than a Musician's finest Note: Pain distilled into Sound, Sound into Beauty, Beauty.

Katherine.

I threw down the *Tractatus*, and I ran.

The Aire in the Ha-ha, whence echoed the Cry, was as cold as a Grave, for no Ray of Sunne had penetrated the Whole of that dampe Summer to dry the sodden Earth. The mossy Path between the Thorns was slippery. I clambered down into the Ditch and looked for her, but there was no Sign. A white Panick leapt up in my Bones, setting my Marrow afire. Surely, I thought, the Babe comes, and before its Time! My Knees shook, and I staggered. "Katherine!" I shouted. "Katherine!"

Where was she?

A blinding Pain crosst my Brow.

Was this Pain Katherine's Answer? Was it Katherine's Pain? Or was it the Echo of mine own, returning, many Times increased, from between the high thorn Hedges?

"Tristan?" Her Voice was brittle, a thin, piping Sob, a broken-winged Bird. I took one slow Step toward it, and, at last, I saw her: crumpled in the wet Dirt on the far Side of the Stile that led into the High Field. Her Skin was the whitish grey of old Parchment, drawn tight around the Bones of her Face. Her Lips were almost blue in their Bloodlessness, and her Breath was shallow. Her grey Eyes stared into mine. She seemed antient of Dayes.

Thinking nothing of it, I leapt over the Stile into open Country, and knelt beside her. And then I perceived it; not *partus praetemporaneus*, but a bodily Dislocation, monstrous in its Degree: the right Humerus displaced from the Scapula, and lying where a Bone had no Purpose to lie; a brutal Disjuncture, ugly and agonising perhaps beyond even my Comprehension. Katherine had slippt upon the Stile, and, in falling, had reached out to try to save herself.

Directly mine Eyes settled upon the Injury I could discern exactly what I needed do in order to remedy it. Every Ligament, every Bone appeared before my Gaze as clear as if I had had her living Body opened up in front of me; and imposed upon them, as if they were writ upon a Pane of Glass, appeared the devilish Sequence of Pulls and Twists I must inflict upon her Limb to restore it to its proper Station.

A raw Breath escaped me. My Loins leapt. The Beauty of her Scream, my Knowledge that I could put everything aright, combined within me into a sudden alchemic Lust: Lead into Gold, Gold into Extasie. By harming, heal; thro' Torture, love. And how I love you, my Katherine; how I love you.

Hippocrates would have had me put mine Heel in her Axilla; but instead, following my Vision, I grippt her Arm tight in mine Hands and began a slow counter-clockwise Rotation of the Humerus against the shoulder Socket, seeking out the one magical Location, and one Instant, when the balled End of the Bone would slot easily and quickly into place. Katherine began to shake, and a new Scream burst from her. I drew in Breath, and I was breathing in the Sound, a Cry most piercing; mixing Pain with the Aire and Blood that pumped into mine Heart.

My Vision began to cloud. Katherine's Scream was everything; mine Universe, my sensitive World, my rational Mind, my Conscience. By it, I knew the very Depth of our Connexion; the Vastness of my Love; knew too the aweful, irrational Reality of my Terrour that I might fail; that our Child also might have been injured in her fall; that it might not survive. And thro' it, thro' it all, undilute, continued the maddening Importuning of mine incomprehensible Lust, that seemed to achieve a greater Potency with every Increase of mine own Distress.

Potency, I thought suddenly, madly. Is that what Lust is? Hope vivified by Dread, the animal Instinct rising to do Battle against the Fear, the imminent Presence of Death? Not Cruelty at all, not Vice, but the erotick Force turned Weapon against black Despair? These Thoughts had no sooner passed thro' my Conscience than all on a Sudden, her arm-Bone shifted, gliding underneath the Pressure of mine Hands towards its Socket. Hope whirled within me; I was fascinated by the Movement's Fluidity; and my Surgeon's Curiosity flared back into Life.

The Bone moved as if thro' Water.

One short, sharp Shriek, then Stillness. In the Silence, a Magpie chattered loudly from the high Hedge, and took Flight.

I took hold of Katherine's Hand and watched her Eyes, as the Texture of her Features changed from Parchment to Vellum, and thence to her, more than Human, Skin. She was shedding Yeares before me: sixty, thirty, sixteen; growing vibrantly alive beneath mine Eyes.

Mine other Hand was upon her Leg, positioned high against her Belly; and as I sate with her I felt, against my Fingers, a vigorous, wriggling Twitch. The Child lives! Mine Heart skippt a Beat, then slowly eased.

Sometimes the World is mercifull.

Carefully, I lifted her delicate Form in mine Arms; so close that I could taste upon my Breath the Sweat of her Forehead. I will never let her fall, I thought. She is my Work; my darling Girl, my Brat, my Leonora.

My Recovery from this Daye on was amazing swift, and utterly confounded even the most optimistic Expectations of Erasmus Glass.

Perhaps a Sennight after this Experience I received a Letter from Captain Simmins in London, regarding which, I must confess, I had great Reluctance to break open the Seal. After a short while, however, I got up my Mettle and prepared to discover its Contents, whether they be fair or foul, and with Katherine by my Side I sate in the Garden, and we read it thro'.

The Letter was short, but not unfriendly, and, despite the Fact that as I perused it I seemed to hear the good Captain's perpetual Stammer, which unfortunately deprived it of some of its Force, compleatly to the Point:

My Deare Sir,

I have been Offered a desk Posting in the North, which it suits me well to take. I have to leave this Daye, so by the Time this Letter reaches You I will be many unhappy Miles from Shirelands Hall. I have no Expectation of Returning South in the foreseeable Future. If by any Chance You ever make the Journey to Edinburgh I should be most Happy to see You. Pray commend me to Your good Wife and Your worthy Father.

I remain forever

Your humble Servant,

Captain Isaac Simmins

Once my Strength was fully restored, I took it upon My Self to discover the Widdowe of the unfortunate Joseph Cox, and to subtilely make a Provision for her and her Children, that they need not starve. Joseph's Corpse was never found; but after many, many Months his Coat appeared, wrappt around a willow Root that had grown far out into the river Channel. By this the local Coroner ascertained that Cox had stumbled into the swollen Coller whilst drunk, and had drowned himself by Misadventure, and so the Case was closed.

Cox's unexpected Disappearance meant that Barnaby was forced to abandon his Plan for an uninterrupted View from his drawing Room, as Matt Harris flatly refused to continue by himself, and Barnaby was quite unable to find any other Labourer within fifty Miles now prepared to take on the Task of grubbing up the Willows. I later learned that a Story had begun to circulate in the local Hostelries that Cox had thereby offended the Lords and Ladies of the Chalk, who had driven him, by various Enchantments, to his Death. Mr Barnaby, it was muttered, would be next.

There are a few small Details more to relate, and I must leap forward in Time to the Morning of All Soules' Daye, when Mrs H., returning with Molly Jakes from the Village, found deposited beside the iron Gates of Shirelands Hall a ragged beggar Brat with sharp Teeth and no Name; and being in all Truth too kind hearted a Woman, and also much too frightened of the Faeries to have left her where she might have come to harm, she picked her up and brought her inside with the Intent of somehow there concealing her from me, who she feared would not agree to her Residency.

Her Plan failed; the Girl, while playing innocently by the kitchen Fire, burnt the top of her Foot upon a tumbled Coal, and screamed, and almost brought down the Roof; and this being within Katherine's and mine Hearing, it brought us down instead to see what was the Matter.

"Eleanore!" Katherine cried out, at Sight of the Infant. "Eleanore!"

So that became—or perchance had always been—the Baby's name.

We adopted Eleanore, and raised her as our Ward. She was a clever, affectionate Child; we loved her well. I am certain that Viviane, or some kindly Faery, had placed a Glamour upon her Appearance, for tho' she had the blonde Locks and grey Eyes of the Bat-Changeling I had met upon the Road, her Shape looked intirely that of an Human Girl, and she walked upright. Sometimes, tho', I would seem to hear the Rustling of Wings, and perceive upon her Countenance the very Semblance of Nathaniel; and I would remember Viviane's Warning: "None of my Kind can endure long amongst yours."

Mayhap you think this really was a Dream, or some Misapprehension, or an Event that occurred upon some other Level of Reality.

If you do, I do not mind it. It signifies naught, which of these it was.

Viviane had told me that I might never again leave the Chalk; and in Obedience to the Bargain that I struck with her, never have I done so. Cut off in this harsh Manner from London, and those Pillars of the Scientific Community who lived and practised there, I was obliged to give up mine Heart-held Ambition of becoming the next Paracelsus, and to content My Self with lesser Achievements. This may not, I think now, have been altogether a bad thing, altho' in the Months and Yeares immediately after mine Arrest I suffered terribly and long upon Hearing Newes of any Advancements within my Sphere, particularly those to do with Aneurysm or Apoplexy, which I thought I should have made My Self. I did not, however, abandon my medical Studies compleatly, for I still had my Theatre; and in seventeen fifty-eight I began to offer my Services freely to any Poor of my Parish who were in Need of Surgery. This Practice, which I grew to enjoy beyond any Expectation, eventually led to my being appointed, after some while, Assistant to the Coroner; and after that I had easy Access to any Cadaver I required. The Intelligences I gained thereby, and the growing Body of Evidence I obtained from my continued Observation of my Wife, formed the Bases for several short Treatises upon Hyperflexibility of the Skeletal Joints and Diseases of the ligamentary Tissue, but altho' these may have been read by some among my Peers I gained little Fame by them, and I do not believe that they have ever had any Influence.

My Son—our only Child, as things fell out—was born easily, and he was an healthy Infant with his Mother's Flexibility and my dark Complexion. We named him John, after my Father, and Erasmus, for my Friend; but I did not suffer him to be christened, despite the strong Horrour this occasioned on the Part of the Rector Ravenscroft. Mankind, however, being what it is, and young John having inherited my wilful Nature along with my Skin, he ultimately decided by himself that he would be baptised a Christian; so, in Deference to the passionate Conviction with which he stated his Belief, I reluctantly permitted him to wet his Forehead. Mine own religious Practice, or more correctly, my Lack of it, remained quite unchanged. Like my Father, like mine immortal Mother, I knew for sure and certain that there was no God, unless that be a God of material Extension, immanent within this common World of Mind and Matter.

My Father's medical Condition did not shew any Improvement, but his Temper did, and after the Birth of his Grandson in that September of seventeen fifty-three he finally put away his Black and began occasionally to leave the House, altho' always in Company and never without Mrs H., who remained his devoted Nurse. The Chasm that had opened betwixt himself and his Sister never fully closed, altho' after several Yeares they resumed speaking, and remained on civil, if chilly Terms thereafter. The Jewish Naturalisation Bill, that he had cared about so deeply, was finally passed only to be met with such continued Opposition from the James Barnabys of this World that the Government was forced to repeal it. Nevertheless, I understand that he continued after this to be associated with Mr Pelham's Party, tho' we did not ever discuss Politicks.

My Father's good Friend, Mr Henry Fielding, resigned as Magistrate of Westminster in seventeen fifty-four, and headed on Doctor's Orders for Lisbon, where, in October, he died. His Brother John took up his Mission, and his Wigg. Dr Hunter became Physician to Queen Charlotte, and a Surgeon-Anatomist of great

Fame. His Engravings for the *Anatomia uteri humani gravidi*, the Sketches for which had so disturbed my Mind while Katherine was with Child, were published to great Acclaim twenty Yeares later.

In the Spring of fifty-five, Erasmus unexpectedly announced that he was returning to London to take up a Post with Dr Oliver at St Luke's Hospital. Within the Fortnight he had decamped. Shortly after Easter, my Sister ran off to join him. The Scandal occasioned by this Elopement, and the subsequent Divorce, gave Barnaby a severe Shock, and he was never the same Man afterwards. I would assert that he was greatly improved, but that may have been merely my—arguably, unobstructed—View of him.

I never found out what became of Annie Moon. I can only hope that she succeeded in buying her Freedom of Mrs Haywood, acquired honest Employment somewhere else in the City, and did not fall Victim to some Monster more murderous than My Self; but in Truth, I have scanty Confidence of that.

I often wonder at Nathaniel, and whether he could be truly dead; and if dead, at the Thoughts that must have passed thro' his Head as he had stood beneath the ash Tree, in the May dawn Light.

"I am going home." Indeed, indeed. Had it really been for Shame? Had it even been for Love of Leonora, or Katherine, whom he had so briefly possesst, and yet could not have? Had it merely been for Boredom with this Human World, and its relentless ticking Time? Or had he perhaps formed some Apprehension that there was a Monstrosity in him that he could not defeat: a black Shaddowe, a Cancer, a Goblin; and he had perceived that the only thing to do to excise it from his Conscience was to strike that Conscience intirely from the World?

Sometimes, I ask My Self: what would have happened had I gone with him? It is a futile Thought, and Heart-breaking; I do not permit my Mind to linger upon it. I do not know, and I never shall.

I do know that there is terrible Monstrosity in me; that I, if I were to permit My Self, would happily and at one Moment's Provocation, transform into a Bloody Bones of chilling worldly Ambition and ruthless Curiosity, who would drag to my grisly Den and do real harm to Friend and Foe alike with little Care for anything except the Fulfilment of mine own Desire for Knowledge. I know too that this intellectual Evil, which is of a Species peculiar to me and other Men of Science, will remain within me, spreading its bloody Filaments thro' my Tissues until the Daye I die; but I will never seek its Excoriation. I control it. I am that Kind of Monster.

If God is a Balladeer, then we are no mere Characters, our Roles and Choices fixt for us providentially within a Song. The World, this World, my Mother's Lord, mine intellectual *Deus*, is a Deity of living Thought, cloathed in Atomies; star-Fire and earthly conscious Flesh. He—nay, It—may not merely be worshippt in a Church; it must be known, perceived, interpreted; seen thro' the bright Lens of a May Morning's Mist; heard in the Whispering of the Wind above the High Chalk. God is this World, and this World only, which is the one World of all things. It hath no Plan, It doth not judge; simply It is, and all are of It; and thus It is within the free willed Man, who may choose, or not choose, to recognise It.

Good and Evil, Right and Wrong: Human Terms, misguided and sorry; for, in Truth, there is but one Choice, and that is whether to act or to refrain from Action. A Man, an Human Man, Angel and Beast incarnate, may choose to inflict Pain and Harm, or not to do so, but the Authority to make that Choice lies with him and with him alone, and there is neither Hell nor Heaven presumptive upon it.

And even as there is great Sorrow in the World, even as there is Tragedy as dark and ignoble as any dreamed up by Aeschylus, so too is there Mercy, even if there be no mercifull Father to dispense it. And verily, this is good, for Mercy is not therefore dependent upon Conduct, hath not to be earned, as if it were a Wage; receiving it dependeth not upon a Christian Life or on a virtuous one, but only upon one's Capability to perceive that this Mercy freely exists, and flows; and it is beautifull. And there is Mercy in shared Pain, and in Lust, and in Human Love; in the Crying of a newborn Babe and the Sighing of the Dead. It is present in the Rain, and in Heaven's bluest Bowl, and in the sudden Death of a Mouse; and the Screaming of a Woman, and the Incision into her Breast of the surgical Blade that aims to save her Life. It is in that visionary Madness of the Mind that permits a Madman to perceive Truth *in extremis*, when all else had seemed lost. Mercifull, indeed, is this worldly Existence, and cruel; and beautifull; and vile, and filled with Pain; and greater in its Scale, and in its Depth, and its Complexity than mere Men can ever hope to understand; and profound wonderfull in its Capacity.

Acknowledgements

I would like to thank Tracy Brain at Bath Spa University for her unwavering support during the early stages of this novel, Will Francis for seeing it thro' to the end, and everybody else along the way who read bits of it and persuaded me to get rid of the ones that weren't working. Special thanks to Becky Hardie for her clear thinking and perceptive criticism in the final stages.

My thanks also to various Druids, Artists, Musicians and other Spirits for introducing me to the beauty and mystery of the Land around the Uffington White Horse.